WHISPERING PINES

BLUE FEATHER BOOKS, LTD.

As always, this is for Heather

WHISPERING PINES

A BLUE FEATHER BOOK

BY

MAVIS APPLEWATER

This is a work of fiction. All characters, locales and events are either products of the author's imagination or are used fictitiously.

WHISPERING PINES

Cover design by Ann Phillips

A Blue Feather Book
Published by Blue Feather Books, Ltd.

www.bluefeatherbooks.com

ISBN: 978-0-9794120-6-6

First edition: October, 2008

Printed in the United States of America and in the United Kingdom.

Acknowledgements

Bringing a story to life takes a lot of hard work. Admittedly, I have the easy job. There are so many people to thank. If I forget anyone I do apologize. First, Caitlin and Emily, who for some reason continue to endure my shenanigans. Mary Phillips and Nann Dunne who were forced to endure editing my ramblings. I am amazed that they haven't taken to drinking heavily. I'd like to thank my mother in-law, Lillian Bardsley, for her unwavering support. I need to thank my mother, Barbara Kessler, for not only giving birth to me but loving me no matter what. And my Aunt Sunny and my Nana for inspiring us even after they left us. Most important, I'd like to thank my wife Heather MacMaster, who not only inspires me, but puts up with my endless quirks.

Chapter 1

Stewart, Massachusetts
Halloween Night, 2002

"Doctor Williams!" an overly perky voice called out.

"Oh, brother, here we go," Shawn muttered, watching the bubbling blonde race towards her. The cool autumn air had assaulted her as soon as she stepped out of the rental car, and she pulled her navy blue parka closer around her. She brushed an errant strand of dirty blonde hair out of her hazel eyes and tried to sound friendly. "Ms. Larsen." *Lanie Larsen can't be her real name. Of course, I doubt those breasts are real, either.*

"Hey, call me Lanie."

"Sure, and I'm Shawn."

"This is going to be terrific." Overly exuberant, Lanie blabbered on while Shawn retrieved her equipment from the back of the car. "A real ratings grabber."

Shawn simply smiled at Larsen, who ranted wildly as they trudged up the hill. Shawn noticed that the woman with big hair, whose ego seemed to match the size of her breasts, failed to offer her assistance with her heavy equipment.

Shawn glanced around the environment where she would be spending the night. She could see that the brick, Whispering Pines Mansion, covered with ivy and overgrown bushes, must have been quite spectacular in its day. Now it was run down, giving it an ominous look. The grounds were almost barren due to the change in season. The cemetery lay off in the distance; the layer of fog covering it added to the creep factor. All in all, the place looked like a typical assignment for the young paranormal investigator.

The stairs leading up to the weathered entry porch creaked beneath Shawn, and she chuckled. "I can see why the locals think this place is haunted."

Lanie snorted. "It better be, or we're just wasting film. And the other teams are going to try to show us up. No way am I letting Phil Rogers get over on me with his Winchester Mansion schtick. If half the stuff people claim to have seen in and around this mansion actually happened, we should kick some serious butt."

"What kind of stuff?" Shawn asked.

"The usual. Lights going on even though the electricity is off, seeing some old guy walking towards the woodshed, the figure of a woman standing in the window."

Shawn simply shrugged, since the events that Lanie had just described were pretty common in her line of work.

"Shawn!" a familiar voice called.

She smiled when she saw the slender ebony woman exiting the house. "Hi, Althea," Shawn said as her friend and current employer approached her. Althea instantly relieved Shawn of some of her burden while Lanie brushed past them without a second glance.

"I take it 'Wonder Woman' didn't offer to help." Althea grunted, lifting the heavy equipment.

"Of course not," Shawn replied with a smirk.

As they stepped inside and set Shawn's belongings down, Shawn shivered slightly and the hair on the back of her neck prickled. Her eyes brightened slightly and then fluttered shut. She relaxed into the feeling. *Oh yeah, this is good.*

"Do you feel something already?" Althea asked enthusiastically. "Oh, this is going to be good," she echoed Shawn's thoughts.

"So what's the setup this time?" Shawn asked, being a last-minute replacement for another psychic.

"You get to spend Halloween night in a house that may, or may not, be haunted. We'll be airing the special at midnight. We have teams set up in suspected haunted houses across the country," Althea explained. "Anything extra we get after midnight, we're using for a second special that will air later. I think *The Travel Channel* wants to pick that up. But we'll be offering it around to all the syndicated markets."

"Midnight on Halloween sounds perfect." Shawn felt as if there were something Althea wasn't telling her. "What are some of the other sites?"

"We're here at Whispering Pines. Then there's the Winchester Mansion in California, the New London Light House in Connecticut, that farmhouse in Alton, Iowa, and the Myrtles Plantation in St.

Francisville, where a slave murdered the wife and kids. We tried to get the Amityville house, but the owners refused."

"There's nothing going on at Amityville," Shawn said. She had visited the famed house and was disappointed to discover it was all an elaborate hoax.

"We've already wired the place with cameras and sound equipment. You just need to set up your own equipment. Lanie, Jasper, Kyle, and I will be outside in the van keeping an eye on you." Althea rubbed her hands together, practically frothing at the mouth. Still, Shawn sensed that there was more she should know, and Althea wasn't forthcoming with the details.

"I'll be by myself?" Shawn asked, thinking it was odd.

"Well, not all alone." Althea's zeal suddenly abated.

"Other paranormal investigators?" Shawn tried to shake off the strange vibes she was feeling. "A film crew?" She still didn't get a response from Althea. "A debunker?"

"Yes," Althea finally said.

"So it's just me and some blowhard who will swear up and down that it was the wind and creaking floorboards," Shawn said with a smile. "Nothing unusual about that. Makes the show more interesting."

"I hoped you'd see it that way," Althea said with a sigh. "After Milo pulled out, I was in a panic that my unit would be cut from the program."

"Who's the professional naysayer I get to spend the night with?" Shawn asked. No sooner had the words left her mouth than she sensed her. "Faith Charles." Her body warmed, and she turned to see the dark-haired woman approaching her from the staircase.

"Well, if it isn't little Shawn," Faith Charles said in a condescending tone. Shawn shook off the remark. She knew Faith had only said it to get some kind of reaction out of her. "What happened to Milo?"

"You happened, Ms. Charles," Althea responded curtly. "Dr. Williams was kind enough to join the team at the last moment. So play nice."

"I'm always nice," Faith Charles said and walked away.

"Relax," Shawn told Althea. "She's not that bad, once you get past the condescending attitude and that stick she has wedged up her ass."

"I heard that," Faith yelled from the other room.

"Of course you did, with those big ears," Shawn replied. It was a familiar game between them. They took turns taunting each other, to see who would blow a gasket first.

Althea laughed lightly. "Just between us, what kind of vibes do you get off of her?"

"None," Shawn responded with a frown. At times she tried to see whether she could get any signals from the stuffy, albeit attractive, Faith Charles. She received nothing. It happened that way occasionally; some people were easy to read and others offered nothing.

"Nothing?" Althea pouted. "Come on, you always get a little something."

"Not always," Shawn said dryly while she began unpacking her equipment. "Some people are very good at shutting me out, or I simply can't tap into them. I kind of enjoy being around people like that."

"Why?" Althea inquired as she assisted Shawn. "I'd love to know what's going on in people's heads."

"No, you wouldn't." Shawn sighed heavily. "It can be quite disturbing having all that inside information. Like knowing that someone's husband is cheating on her," Shawn added, causing Althea to wince.

"You did me a favor," Althea said. "If you hadn't shaken my now ex-husband's hand, I would have never known about that bimbo he had on the side."

Shawn wished she could explain the alienation she felt at times, and the way people shied away from her once they learned about her gift. She had to give Faith Charles credit; she simply blocked her out, although Shawn doubted that Faith was even aware of what she was doing. Faith was a professional debunker who scoffed at the paranormal. But then again, it was her job to do just that.

Faith was there to cast doubt upon anything Shawn discovered. That's how this type of show worked. Shawn was a psychic by birth and had chosen to make it her profession. Faith was a reporter who specialized in debunking psychic phenomenon. They would both go to places that were thought to be haunted and take part in a documentary or television special. They debated for the camera, and afterwards, both wrote books about it.

Much to the crew's disappointment, at times Shawn would agree with Faith when she could find nothing but overactive imaginations. Faith, on the other hand, never agreed with Shawn. On camera, at least. On a few occasions when it was just the two of them, Faith admitted that she had no explanation for what she had seen or experienced.

Normally, on camera, they would fight tooth and nail, giving the viewers some entertainment. Off camera, they took great pleasure in exchanging barbs, and Shawn enjoyed their banter. That, and she couldn't help but notice Faith's physical attributes.

"What happened with Milo?" Shawn continued to set up her equipment. She had decided to use the large parlor as her center of operation.

"I don't know," Althea said. "He was about to start setting up and checking the place when he and superbitch got into a row. He just packed up and drove off."

"Any coffee around?" Faith grumbled as she strode into the room like she owned the place.

"Kyle set up some supplies in the kitchen," Althea said. "There should be a couple of thermoses of coffee."

"No power?" Shawn looked down at the cable for her camera equipment.

"No," Althea confirmed. "We'll run your cables out to the van."

"Having fun with your toys?" Faith asked. Shawn smiled at the double entendre.

"Yes," she teased in return. "Didn't you bring any?"

Faith released a hearty laugh as Shawn flashed her a saucy smirk. "You're the psychic," Faith said in a husky tone. "You tell me," she added with a purr.

"Cute." Shawn was enjoying their teasing.

Faith's sexuality wasn't a secret, and truth be told, anyone with a pulse would be attracted to her. Shawn brushed her hand across Faith's forearm.

"Naughty," she said. "But I hope you brought some extra batteries for that. I don't think the van's generator can handle it." Shawn was shocked when Faith blushed and pulled her arm away.

"I was just teasing," Shawn said. "I thought you didn't believe in any of this."

"No comment," Faith muttered. "Between us, I'm glad Milo pulled out. That guy drives me nuts with all that clutching objects and humming."

"That's his specialty," Shawn said. "He can touch objects and get a sense or image of the past or future."

"And you do people," Faith said.

"That's because I seem to be able to see things or feel things about people, living or dead."

"Whatever."

"Yeah, well, sometimes it's like being caught in between stations on the AM dial." Shawn ignored Faith's brush-off. "And growing up, it sucked the life out of Christmas."

"Bummer," Faith noted dryly. "I guess you don't get thrown too many surprise birthday parties either?"

"What's the point?" Shawn said.

"Shawn," Althea said, "We need to get some shots of you outside and down at the cemetery before you finish setting up. Jasper's waiting for you."

"I'm on my way." Shawn left her equipment behind and stepped out into the crisp autumn air.

Once outside of the run-down mansion, Shawn sensed a strange unease. As Jasper followed her around with a camera, she walked the grounds, giving a short spiel for the intended audience.

When they reached the cemetery, Shawn's pulse started beating rapidly. Her having this sort of reaction in a graveyard wasn't unusual. Too many souls could reach out to her. She understood that they reached out to everyone, but she was one of the few gifted with the ability to hear them. "They're missing," she said absently.

"What?" Jasper asked.

"They should be here, but their graves are empty," she said in a distant tone, her mind wandering. Jasper looked pale as he peered out from behind his heavy camera.

Towards the center of the cemetery stood a large, dilapidated crypt, obviously built to house generations of the same family. Yet Shawn sensed that only one person had been laid to rest in it. She felt anger emanating from the cold marble.

Off in the distance, on a small hill, she spied a second crypt that cast a warm feeling over her. It was filled with a loving family. Yet something was telling her that two people were absent from it. She could sense bitterness passing between the two marble structures. She shook her head as the different feelings passed through her.

"What is it?" Jasper squeaked.

Shawn smiled at him. He worked on many of these films with her, but he still seemed edgy about the subject matter.

"Well..." When she motioned that they were done, Jasper seemed relieved to be exiting the cemetery.

"It's just that it always amazes me that families can carry their dysfunctions into the afterlife," Shawn explained in a wry tone.

"Great," Jasper grumbled. "You mean I might end up spending eternity listening to my parents bitch at one another while they remind me that my older brother was captain of the football team?"

"It can happen," Shawn said. They walked back up towards the crumbling mansion. "Usually it takes more than that." She turned again towards the cemetery and pointed. "See the crypt in the center?"

"Yeah."

"It was obviously built to house several generations of the same family," she continued. "But I got the feeling that there's only one person buried inside. See the second crypt up on the hill? It was built so that it would literally look down on the first. Someone buried on the hill feels that two members of his family are missing from his crypt, and he blames whoever is buried in the first crypt for their absence."

"You got all of that just by walking around?" Jasper sounded amazed.

"Yes," Shawn said with a smile. "That, and someone named Greta blames her sister Beatrice for stealing the only man she ever loved. Beatrice thinks Greta should shut up about it, since Boyd was lousy in bed. I think I have to agree with Beatrice on that one."

"You made that last part up," Jasper teased her as they stepped up onto the entry porch of the old brick mansion.

"No," Shawn answered. "Greta and Beatrice are buried closer to the edge of the cemetery, and they probably passed on only about sixty years ago or so."

"Do you think they have something to do with whatever's going on in the house?"

"No," Shawn said flatly as she felt a chill pass through her. "I think it has to do with whoever's buried in the first crypt."

"How was the family cemetery?" Althea inquired as they reentered the mansion.

"Ooh. Can I tell her?" Jasper asked.

"Go ahead. I need to finish setting up." Shawn laughed at the young man's excitement as he began to fill Althea in on what Shawn had said in the cemetery.

As Shawn continued to set up her equipment, she didn't miss that Faith followed her around, watching her every movement. The house was devoid of furniture and filled with dust and cobwebs. Shawn couldn't help the uneasy feeling that was surrounding her.

"Something very bad happened here," she whispered.

"What about me?" Faith suddenly asked. "Do you get any impressions from me?"

"I can't get any feeling from you. Happens sometimes. I think you're very good at blocking me out." Shawn and Jasper set about connecting her cables. "Jasper here, he reads like a cheap novel."

Jasper snorted. "I think I should be insulted. Maybe I'm just a lot more interesting than some people," he said with a slight wheeze.

Shawn ignored Faith's scowl and Jasper's sad attempt to flirt with both of them and went about setting up the rest of her equipment as Kyle, the second cameraman, entered the room.

"Hey there, Kyle," Shawn greeted the young Asian man. "I'll be ready for the preliminary shoot around the inside of the house in a few." Kyle and Jasper were sweet boys who were damn good at their jobs. However, whenever a pair of breasts was within a twenty-mile radius, they both acted like a couple of high schoolers. When she and Faith worked with them, they would practically do handstands to get their attention. Basically, the boys needed to get out of their editing bay a little more often.

Shawn bent over to pick up her bags. "Stop staring at my ass," she said to Kyle, who was standing behind her.

"Sorry," Kyle muttered. "I keep forgetting about that psychic thing."

"Yeah, I'd have to be psychic to know that you were ogling my ass." Shawn rolled her hazel eyes in amusement.

"Shawn," Althea said, "we need to film your intro. Just the usual: background on yourself, what you do and why you do it kind of thing. Lanie will interview you while Kyle films. You can do it while you finish setting up your gadgets, and then you can explain how they work. We've already shot Faith, so that's out of the way. Then I want a shot of Lanie's intro in front of the fireplace, which Jasper is going to light a fire in." Jasper grumbled before stomping off in search of wood. "After that, it will be just the two of you until midnight. If nothing interesting is happening, we can pack up after the airing. If we get lucky and something does happen, the two of you can sleep here and we'll get you in the morning."

"Cozy," Faith said.

"We've all done this before. Nothing new, except that neither of you has been told the history of this place," Althea ignored Faith's comment and continued. Truth be told, Shawn preferred not knowing the history; it made her job much easier when she didn't have preconceived notions.

"We'll fill you in on all of that when we shoot Lanie's narration," Althea said. "Hopefully, we'll have something that the network and viewers will like. Our equipment is set up. We've already gotten the shots of the cemetery and the house. All we need now is Shawn to do her thing."

Everyone stood there once Althea had finished her explanation. "Come on people, we're losing our light. I want this to be a Halloween special, not a Thanksgiving spectacular."

Upon hearing Althea's warning, they sprang into action. "Why don't I have a hair and makeup person?" Lanie whined while the small crew gathered up the equipment.

"You're as beautiful as ever, Ms. Larsen," Althea said. "Now why don't you give our little psychic friend a hand and film the usual Q and A about her gizmos and gadgets?"

Shawn bent over to gather up the last of her equipment while Lanie continued to complain. She felt Kyle's eyes on her once again, not to mention some very lustful thoughts the pimple-faced young man was thinking.

"Stop staring at my ass," she repeated with a fierce growl.

"Sorry," both Kyle and Faith apologized.

Shawn spun around quickly to find Kyle looking apologetic while he lifted his camera up onto his shoulder. Faith, on the other hand, was blushing as she stared at her feet. Shawn laughed heartily at Faith's sudden shyness before she returned to the task of setting up her equipment.

"Could you explain what you're doing?" Lanie asked in a bored tone while Kyle filmed Shawn.

Shawn chatted happily as they went from room to room. Faith trailed along behind them as they continued to set up Shawn's equipment. Of course, they had performed this routine many times before.

"Now these things I love," she explained, holding up a small tape recorder. "These are voice-activated tape recorders. I'm setting one up in each room. Sometimes, when it's played back you can hear voices that weren't picked up when I was in a room. Sometimes they pick up voices in rooms that are empty. This is known as Electronic Voice Phenomena, or EVP. I'll also be using electromagnetic field, or EMF, radiation meters and infrared non-contact thermometers. Many times when a spirit's around, the temperature will drop. When an entity is present, the room temperature can drop a full thirty or forty degrees. I also like to use a digital camera. Quite often you can pick up orbs. Orbs are floating balls of light that appear when a spirit is lurking about."

Shawn made a note on the appearance of the interior of the house. Like the outside, it was run down and had seen better days. She didn't know the history of the place; Althea had instructed her not to investigate it. She would be told the history later.

She felt energy throughout the rooms. It was very strong in the first-floor foyer, a larger room on the second floor, plus one small room on the third floor. The latter two of these rooms were also the only ones in the house devoid of dust or cobwebs. Also, in both of these rooms, Shawn felt a warm and gentle presence. The only room she hadn't seen yet was the kitchen.

"Do you like what you do?" Lanie asked when they began to descend the staircase.

"You mean making a living from the dead?" Shawn gave that a little thought. "Yes. I'll let you in on a little secret: some of this stuff spooks me, too." She winked at Faith, who was still following them. "You want my interview now?" Shawn asked, eager to get on with things.

"Yeah, but in front of the fireplace," Lanie instructed her when they entered the downstairs parlor. "Althea thinks it will add flavor."

From all appearances, the room had been quite grand at one time. Shawn removed her coat and took her place in front of the now blazing fireplace.

"Ready?" she asked, straightening her clothing.

"Almost." Kyle checked the room with a small hand-held light meter. "Okay." He lifted the heavy camera up onto his shoulder.

"Just a sec." Faith interrupted them. "You have a…" She waved her hand, indicating that Shawn should brush back her bangs.

Shawn smiled slightly before she tucked her long, curly hair behind her ears. "How's that?" she asked, smiling warmly at Faith, who was shifting nervously.

Faith shook her head and crossed in front of the camera. Shawn reeled from her closeness. She could feel the heat emanating from Faith's body as her shaky hand brushed a strand of blonde hair off of Shawn's brow.

The brief touch of Faith's fingers sent a jolt through Shawn. Her mind captured a slight image that made her smile brightly. For the first time, Faith hadn't blocked her out. Shawn saw Faith watching her earlier that day as she stepped out of her car. Then the image shifted to Faith racing through what appeared to be a war zone. That image vanished and was replaced by another image of Faith's naked body arching in the throes of ecstasy.

As the last image remained, Shawn was all too aware of Faith's lingering touch. Reaching up, she captured Faith's hand in her own. She looked up, knowing that her eyes betrayed her true emotions. Her thighs trembled as she watched Faith's lips parting slightly.

She could hear the faint murmur of the other woman's thoughts. It was always like this for her; knowing what another person wanted or was thinking and feeling. "Yes," she answered in response to Faith's unspoken thoughts. Faith pulled away suddenly and retreated behind Lanie and Kyle.

Shawn felt the walls go up around Faith instantly. She had overstepped and entered without permission. It happened sometimes. The result was always the same; people just didn't like it when you could see inside them.

"I think we're ready now," Faith said coldly. She turned away from Shawn's pleading look, as if to shield herself from Shawn's intrusion.

Shawn simply went on with the interview, knowing that an apology wouldn't be welcomed. *I learned a long time ago that most people would rather ignore it. What do you say to someone? Oops, sorry, I peeked into your inner thoughts. Damn if I didn't like what I saw there.* She recalled the sense of warmth the stoic woman kept carefully hidden. *This assignment gets more interesting by the minute.*

"Tell us about yourself, Dr. Williams," Lanie cued her.

Shawn worked up a smile before beginning her spiel. "I'm a licensed paranormal investigator and a member of the International Society of Paranormal Investigators. What I do is nothing like the *Ghostbusters* movies. I use scientific methods when researching a paranormal occurrence. Unlike what you see on television, there isn't a gadget that will point to a specter. I use tape recorders, cameras, and EMF meters to research and document my findings."

"That's not all you use," Lanie cued her once again.

"No," Shawn responded. "I'm a psychic. My gifts can give me a sense or a feel for people. Not only the living, but for those who have died. I can see things, some very clearly, almost like a movie playing in my head. Others are just quick flashes or blurbs that are sometimes difficult to decipher."

"And how long have you been able to do this?" Lanie continued in a dry, professional tone.

"All my life." It had started when Shawn was very young. She would catch a glimpse of some long-dead relative, or see shadows of people skulking about. She could touch someone's hand and hear his or her thoughts. For the longest time, Shawn assumed that the words she heard had been spoken out loud. The occurrence was a constant source of trouble until she finally realized that she was hearing unspoken thoughts.

Then, there was her pesky, imaginary friend. Her parents assumed that Catalina was imaginary. Shawn would argue up and down that Catalina was real. The Williams family just laughed it off until the day Shawn led them to a startling discovery. She was all of seven years old when she finally convinced her father to look in the abandoned well that sat on the edge of the property. Her father never quite recovered from the shock of finding the skeleton.

For Shawn, it was a relief. Catalina finally disappeared for good. Catalina could be nasty at times, always pinching and teasing Shawn. She was glad to be rid of her. What Shawn failed to realize at the time was that Catalina had targeted her simply because Shawn could hear her. After that great discovery, Shawn's family had a hard time accepting her gift. Nothing could shake up a quiet little family like discovering their little girl communed with the dead. From that moment on, Shawn was treated differently, an experience that plagued her throughout her life. Now, standing in the abandoned mansion, watching Faith avoiding eye contact with her, she felt that alienation once again.

"How did you get involved with this?" Lanie prompted her.

"I wanted to use my gift, not hide it," Shawn said, growing weary. She just wanted to be alone with Faith and apologize for peeking into her thoughts.

Thankfully, the interview ended. Althea returned and they began to set up for Lanie's blurb on the history of the place. One camera would be on Lanie and the other on Faith and Shawn, to record their reactions. The setup was taking a while, and Shawn was tired of standing next to Faith, who was trying to ignore her.

"I didn't," Faith finally said quietly.

"Didn't what?" Shawn asked in confusion.

"I didn't drive Milo off," Faith said in a hushed tone. "Sure, I gave him a hard time like I always do. But that wasn't what made him run. He was by himself, searching the house. When I came downstairs, he was shaking, sweating more than usual, which is hard to believe, since he's constantly perspiring. Then he grabbed his stuff and bolted out the door. Not that I'm complaining, I'd rather be locked up with you all night than that sweaty old windbag."

"I wonder what happened."

"I have no idea," Faith said. "So, did you see anything interesting?"

"When?" Shawn hedged, trying to turn her attention towards Althea and Lanie, who were arguing over how tight the hostess's close up should be. The two may have been an annoying sight, but it was more enjoyable than facing Faith's questions.

"You know what I'm talking about," Faith said.

"Nothing much."

"Maybe there's nothing to see." Faith sounded sad.

"True," Shawn said in a bored tone, knowing that she was taunting Faith, who snarled at her comment.

"Why did you give up being a real reporter and start doing this kind of stuff?" Shawn asked. Granted, Shawn didn't view what she did as frivolous, but she was well aware that the news industry did. In all honesty, even she viewed the tragedies that encompassed the world to be far more important than crawling around a dusty old mansion, looking for long-forgotten souls who couldn't figure out that they were dead.

"Long story." Faith paused for a moment. "I was working for CNN. Real news stories: war, human tragedy, that kind of stuff. I was a good reporter, and I loved working the hot spots. One day I was sent off on a fluff piece. A punishment from a producer who objected to something I did. That guy had no sense of humor. The story was one of those spooky creepy things for Halloween. Kind of like this gig. The whole thing was a hoax, and I proved it. It got a lot of attention, so I wrote a book about it, and suddenly, I had a whole new focus. It was a hell of a lot safer than Bosnia, and by that time, I had seen too much violence. This stuff is more interesting and more profitable."

"It must be nice not getting shot at anymore," Shawn said in an effort to keep the friendly conversation going.

"Yeah, now I just worry about being bored to death," Faith teased. Shawn was about to spit out a clever retort when the hairs on the back of her neck stood on end.

"Grab the camera, Kyle," she urged him, frantically waving him away from the bickering Althea and would-be actress Lanie. He immediately complied.

"Want to come?" she asked Faith, who was looking on with interest.

Chapter 2

Stewart, Massachusetts
December 15, 1947

They stood on the porch looking at the house that had fallen into disrepair. It was no longer the grand home that either of them remembered.

"Are you sure about this?" the sheriff asked tersely, watching the car chug up the long driveway.

"We've tried everything else." Richard Stratton rubbed his weary eyes.

A plump man extricated himself from the car. He huffed and puffed while trying to hurry.

"Let's hope he doesn't have a heart attack." The sheriff snorted, his eyes narrowing at the man who finally greeted them.

"Gentlemen." Panting, the rotund man offered his sweaty hand.

"Mr. Comstock." Richard shook his hand. "Thank you for coming."

"My pleasure." Comstock beamed.

"Sheriff," Richard said, "this is Virgil Comstock." The two men shook hands.

"So, what is it that you do?" the sheriff questioned in a surly tone.

"I, sir, am a medium," Comstock proclaimed with obvious pride.

"Uh-huh." The sheriff grunted and slipped a toothpick between his teeth.

"Shall we begin?" Comstock asked.

"Yes." Richard cleared his throat and waved his hand towards the front doorway.

"I'll go alone," Comstock said. "If I need you, I'll call out."

"Very well." Richard silently prayed for the answers he had been seeking for such a very long time.

Comstock strode confidently into Whispering Pines and closed the door, leaving the other two men standing on the grand porch.

"A medium?" The sheriff snickered and sucked on the wooden toothpick, "I would have guessed an extra large."

"We need answers," Richard said, not feeling very confident that Virgil Comstock would be competent in finding them.

"I know." The sheriff's eyes dimmed. "But I don't hold a lot of trust in Mr. Hocus-Pocus."

Richard silently agreed with the sheriff. Still, he had tried everything else.

"Maybe I should just tear it down," Richard muttered under his breath. "Perhaps then I'll find them."

"Anything has got to be better than this charlatan," the sheriff huffed with disdain.

Richard could think of nothing to say. He suspected that the sheriff's assessment of Mr. Comstock's character was accurate. *So this is what it's come to. Seeking the advice of a flimflam man. When will this nightmare end?* The silence loomed over them. The only sounds came from the wildlife lurking about and the stomping of the men's feet in an effort to ward off the cold. Suddenly, the silence was shattered by a high-pitched wail. Before they could react, Virgil Comstock bolted out the door and rushed past them.

"Mr. Comstock?" Richard called, rushing after the large man who was suddenly moving with lightning speed.

"I'm sorry," Comstock sputtered, backing his way towards his car. Richard couldn't help but notice the way Comstock's robust complexion had turned a sickening gray. "I'll refund your money. Send you a check in the morning." Comstock shrank away from Richard, and his beady eyes glimmered with fear.

"What happened?" Richard demanded, stunned when the large man had managed to dart past him. Not only had Comstock slipped away, but he was halfway in his car before Richard could reach him.

"I can't stay," Comstock whimpered like a frightened child.

"Can you tell me anything?" Richard asked.

"Stay out of the kitchen," Comstock blurted out before speeding off.

"Tell us something we don't know!" the sheriff screamed at the speeding car.

Chapter 3

Stewart, Massachusetts
Halloween Night, 2002

The entity was dark and sinister. It challenged Shawn to follow it and eerily promised a surprise. Shawn shivered, not liking this entity one bit. Still, she felt helpless to refuse the challenge. "I have to check this out," she said to her companions. "Who wants to come with me?"

Shawn saw Faith's eyes twinkle with excitement. "Follow me guys," Shawn encouraged her grinning cohorts. Kyle and Faith followed her eagerly out of the parlor and down a long hallway. Shawn sensed, though, that they were more interested in getting away from Lanie's bitching than in following her.

Suddenly, in front of them, a door slammed shut. It slowly opened once again. "Hello?" Shawn said tentatively. The door opened fully in a violent movement. "Are you getting this?" Shawn asked Kyle softly as she inched next to Faith.

"Uh-huh," Kyle squeaked.

"It wants us to go in there." Shawn trembled from the sudden coldness.

"It?" Faith asked.

Shawn nudged her. "Let's go, before it leaves."

"Again with the *it*," Faith said, and gave Shawn a hard shove. "You first."

"You know, I find it very interesting that you had no problem going into a war zone, but a little bump in the night has you hiding behind me," she teased Faith, who was trying desperately to hide her larger body behind Shawn's.

Shawn braced herself before taking a careful step through the doorway. Faith clung to the back of her shirt, and Kyle trailed behind them. They entered another, smaller hallway that was dark and dusty. Shawn jumped slightly when a light appeared behind her. She steadied her breathing when she realized that it was Kyle's camera.

They followed the narrow hall until they approached a door. Before Shawn could reach for the tarnished doorknob, the door swung open.

"Okay," she muttered, pausing, unable to shake the disturbing feeling that pulsated through her.

Shawn stepped into the room and immediately began to shiver. It felt as though she had walked into an ice storm. The barren kitchen was covered with dust. As she explored the room further, she noticed Faith and Kyle had lingered in the doorway. An icy hand gripped her shoulder. *"I know what you are,"* a low voice muttered in her ear. She spun around wildly to find that Faith had moved closer, but was still standing too far away from her to have spoken those words.

"Did you hear that?" she asked.

"What?" Kyle continued to film the brightly-lit kitchen.

"Why is it so cold in here?" Faith stepped a little closer to Shawn. "What did you hear?"

Shawn fought the desire to run and opened her senses. The room smelled like death. Another icy hand touched the back of her neck and gripped it tightly. *"You will suffer for your sins."*

A shiver ran down her spine, and her eyes widened in fear. This was bad, very bad. Going against her normal curiosity, she threw in the towel.

"Let's go!" She grabbed Faith by the arm. Quickly, she led her and Kyle towards the main doorway. There was no way she was going back through the dark passageway. "I'm serious. If anything starts to happen just run," she said as Faith slipped behind her.

The loud sound of a slap from behind her made her spin around. Faith cried out and pulled away from her. Her face was red. "What the fu—" Faith squawked, furiously rubbing her cheek.

"We need to get out of here. Now! Let's go," Shawn repeated forcefully.

The three of them raced out of the kitchen and returned to the sitting room. Althea and Lanie looked over at them with concern. Kyle sat on the floor and tried to calm himself. "That was really weird," he said. Faith just stood by Shawn's side and rubbed her cheek. Shawn reached up and touched the reddened spot.

"Are you all right?" she asked tenderly.

"What the hell was that?" Shawn could hear the fear in Faith's voice.

"Where did the three of you go?" Althea asked.

"I'm so glad I'm staying in the van tonight," Kyle blurted out with obvious relief. "Not staying here." He rocked back and forth like a frightened child.

"Someone slapped me," Faith told the others.

"Did they say anything?" Shawn asked, moving closer to Faith.

"'Sinner,'" Faith said with a grunt.

"Does someone want to tell me what's going on?" Althea asked.

Shawn chuckled slightly, more out of fear than humor. "It appears that our entity is hostile," she said. "Probably a poltergeist. They tend to be more physical than your ordinary ghost."

"Hostile?" Faith groused. "Excuse me, but this sucker is more than hostile, it's violent. I don't get it. The guys went in there earlier and nothing happened," she said. "Did it?"

"Nothing like what I just saw," Kyle answered. "It was just an empty kitchen."

"Maybe it doesn't like women," Shawn said. "And the kitchen is where the murders took place," she added in a low voice.

"Excuse me?" Faith looked startled. "Murder? Wait, you said murders, as in more than one?"

"I think so." Shawn still trembled from what had happened in the kitchen. "I get a sense of something." She shook her head, frustrated. "I can't quite grasp the image. Are you all right?"

"I... um," Faith stammered.

The normally controlled woman seemed flustered and more than a little frightened. "Faith, whatever we encountered is simply energy trapped in this plane of existence," Shawn said, hoping to calm the ashen-faced Faith.

"Oh, really? Well, it isn't very comforting when a professional ghost hunter and psychic tells you to run," Faith pointed out. "I've filmed about a dozen of these things with you, and not once did you say 'let's get out of here.' Usually it's all earthy-crunchy 'I feel a presence' kind of crap. 'Let's get out of here, now' is the type of thing I usually hear when people are shooting at each other or bombs are going off."

"Will someone please tell me what happened?" Althea looked from one to the other.

"I got the whole thing on tape," Kyle said.

"Let me see." She rushed over eagerly.

Althea watched the playback. "This is thrilling!"

* * *

As it grew dark, candles were lit and the crew set about preparing to film. "We need more light in here," Althea said.

"You said candles," Jasper said.

"Look, I want spooky but we still need to see the house and the talent. Bring in some lights from the van and run the cables out."

"Hey, if it's spooky you want, just try getting a bagel from the kitchen," Faith said. "That was a really eerie encounter."

"This is going great." Althea beamed while Kyle and Jasper scurried about to fill her demands.

"Great?" Faith asked.

"Yeah, with what Shawn said at the cemetery and then with the whole thing in the kitchen. We even picked up a voice calling you a sinner on the tape. It's very faint and could have been a gust of wind, but if you listen real closely, you can hear it."

"The batteries are dead again," Kyle grumbled, interrupting the conversation.

Everyone groaned in exasperation. It wasn't an uncommon occurrence on these assignments. Entities drew energy from whatever source they could find. The crew's equipment was a favorite source of power. "What happened at the cemetery?" Faith asked Shawn while Kyle went in search of new batteries for the cameras.

"I just sensed something," Shawn said, and Faith glared at her. "Okay, I sensed that two people who should be there aren't," she tried to explain.

"I'm not liking this gig," Faith said. She looked towards Althea. "I know you wanted us to be surprised, but this is ridiculous."

"I think it's safe to say that Whispering Pines is haunted," Shawn concluded.

"No kidding," Faith shot back sarcastically. "I think that was confirmed when something slapped me."

"I can see you're troubled by that," Shawn said.

"Well, yeah." Faith waved her arms frantically. "Other than the nuns back in school and one ex-girlfriend, someone slapping me across the face isn't something I'm accustomed to."

"Maybe if you hadn't cheated on her, the girlfriend, not the nuns, she wouldn't have slapped you," Shawn said, not really comfortable with the idea of someone reacting violently.

Faith pulled Shawn off to the side. "How much did you see when you took that tour around my head?" she asked in a low voice.

"That, my dear, was just an educated guess." Shawn laughed in response. "All I saw was you caught in a war zone and you watching me get out of my car earlier today."

"I don't believe you."

"Okay, one little blurb of you having sex, but that's it," Shawn said.

"That's it?"

"That was more than enough, thank you very much." Shawn was growing weary of the conversation. "Don't you find this place interesting?"

"No. I find this place scary," Faith said. Shawn rejoined the others, and Faith followed.

Lanie primped while reviewing her script. Althea set everything up for Kyle and Jasper to start filming. Once everything was in place, they began. Althea gave Lanie her cue as the camera began to film in front of the fireplace.

"Welcome to Whispering Pines," Lanie said. "This mansion was built in 1907 by sea captain Horatio Stratton. Captain Stratton had amassed a small fortune, though no one knows where the money came from. He settled here with his young bride, Anna, just outside of the small seacoast town of Stewart, Massachusetts. He built Whispering Pines deep in the woods.

"By all accounts, Captain Stratton was a cold, distant man who rarely ventured into town. Anna, on the other hand, was well liked by the townspeople. The couple lived alone. Their servants weren't allowed to stay on the premises after nightfall, even when the captain was away at sea. Somewhere around 1912, Captain Stratton's spinster sister, Catherine, came to live with them."

Both Faith and Shawn rolled their eyes at the term "spinster." Lanie continued her monologue for the camera. "The two women were often seen together in and around town and seemed to be very close. No one could have predicted what happened on the morning of October 31, 1916. The servants arrived early that morning and discovered Captain Stratton alone in the house, sitting calmly in this very room, smoking his pipe. What the maid found in the kitchen sent her screaming from the house. The kitchen was covered with blood. Captain Stratton never offered an explanation, he simply instructed the staff who were brave enough to remain behind to clean up the mess in the kitchen.

"His wife and sister were never seen again. Despite rumors and inquiries by the local authorities, no one ever learned what happened in this house eighty-six years ago this very night. Not even Captain Stratton's young son, Richard, who had been away at boarding school at the time, ever discovered the truth. Captain Stratton simply lived out his life in solitude until his death at the age of eighty-nine, quite possibly taking a dark secret with him to the grave. The son, Richard Stratton, built his home on the very edge of this property, and when his father died, Richard left Whispering Pines and its dark secrets behind.

"Over the years, several of Captain Stratton's descendants have tried living in this once-elegant mansion. No one has managed to stay for an entire night. Dr. Shawn Williams and reporter Faith Charles have agreed to spend Halloween night here. Dr. Williams wants to learn the secrets hidden here at Whispering Pines. Ms. Charles wants to prove that the local legends are nothing but a myth."

"Cut," Althea called out.

"Nice guy." Faith scowled. "Anyone else think he killed them?"

"That would explain what I felt at the cemetery," Shawn said. "Anna and Catherine are the ones who aren't buried with the family, and Stratton is the reason why. He killed them and hid the bodies, denying them a decent burial."

"Maybe we should do another shot in the kitchen before we leave the two of you alone," Althea suggested.

"No." Faith and Shawn flatly refused.

"I'd rather walk through broken glass," Faith said with vehemence.

"What has gotten into the two of you? The last shoot I did with you guys, you willingly crawled into a rat-infested dungeon," Althea said.

"We also did tequila shooters with the crew before we went in there," Faith said.

"You what?"

"She's kidding," Shawn reassured her. It was a lie, but Althea didn't need to know that they had decided to celebrate Shawn's birthday a little early. It was a boring shoot in England where nothing remotely interesting was happening, except the constant rain.

"Look," Faith said, "a few rodents is one thing, but being bitch-slapped by some unseen entity that probably hacked his family up just for kicks is not my idea of a good time."

"We'll all go in together," Althea offered.

"All of us?" Lanie squeaked.

"More camera time." Althea tried to bribe the self-centered blonde.

"Normally, I'd be all over that," Lanie said, "but when Faith comes running in looking like she just wet her pants, I don't think so."

"Jasper, you and Lanie go first and take shots of the kitchen." Althea ignored their protests. "Kyle, Faith, Shawn, and I will bring up the rear. Come on, people," she urged the nervous-looking group. "Shawn, how can you pass this up? You have the great Faith Charles willing to admit on camera that there's something here."

Not totally convinced, the crew nevertheless gathered their equipment and Lanie and Jasper went off to the kitchen. Shawn and Faith listened carefully to the radio contact they shared with Althea. They were nervous, but after a few moments, it was more than apparent that nothing was happening.

Reluctantly, Shawn followed Kyle and Althea back to the kitchen while Faith trailed behind them, once again clutching at Shawn's shirt. As they stepped into the kitchen, Shawn was shocked that it was now warm and absolutely nothing was happening.

"Maybe it's gone," Faith said as they stepped farther into the room.

Just as the words escaped her mouth, Shawn felt uneasy. The temperature suddenly plummeted. "Why is it cold all of a sudden?" Althea asked as everyone looked around nervously.

Shawn's heart pounded against her chest. She could feel something closing in around her. "*Sinner,*" the same low voice from earlier hissed into her ear while a cold hand gripped her throat and began to choke her. She struggled to breathe and was aware that Faith was trying to pull her away from whatever had a hold on her. Suddenly, Faith went flying across the room as if someone had shoved her.

Faith struggled to her feet. Shawn fought to free herself from the icy hand that gripped her throat. The others managed to free her before rushing both her and Faith out of the room. Once they were safely back in the sitting room, Faith wrapped her arms around the trembling Shawn.

"Wow, whatever that is, it doesn't like either of you," Althea said, visibly shaken by the events.

"Kyle, shut the camera off!" Faith barked while she rubbed Shawn's back. "What are you saying?"

Shawn felt the fear rolling off of Faith's body. She also sensed that Faith felt a need to protect her. The thoughts that she sensed from Faith muddled the images of what was in the house that were filling her mind. Reluctantly, she pulled herself away from Faith's tender embrace.

"It went after us," Shawn said in a weary tone. "It didn't bother anyone else except us."

"Why?" Faith asked, keeping her voice level. Shawn could see that Faith was desperately trying to make sense out of what was happening. "Maybe it's what you said earlier about it not liking women."

"It didn't do a thing to Althea or Lanie." Shawn dismissed the theory. "Just the two of us."

"And maybe Milo," Faith added.

"I thought you drove Milo off?" Lanie piped in.

"No. Why does everyone think that I'm some kind of bully?"

"Did he say anything?" Shawn asked.

"No. He just took off like a scared rabbit." Faith folded her arms across her chest in a defiant manner.

"Can we call him?" Jasper suggested as he put his camera down.

Instantly everyone reached for his or her cell phone. One by one, they each found the battery dead. "Every time we come to one of these spook houses, anything with a battery just dies," Faith complained.

"They need the energy." Shawn began to pace nervously.

"I'll go out to the van and plug mine in," Althea offered. "Why don't you boys come along and bring your cameras? I'll take the film and we can put fresh batteries in."

Left alone, the three women paced nervously as every creak and gust of wind made them jump. After what seemed like an eternity, Althea returned alone. "Well?" Shawn asked hopefully.

"He touched the kitchen counter and saw blood everywhere," Althea said in a shaky tone.

"Did it touch him?" Shawn asked.

"No. And the room temperature never changed. He said there was so much blood the walls looked like they were bleeding and there was a woman screaming in agony. He did add that he had never seen anything quite so graphic or horrific, and that there was no way he was spending the night in this house. Speaking of which, it's getting late and I need to know if the two of you are going to bolt. Honestly, I wouldn't blame you."

"I'm staying." Shawn bent over and picked up her sleeping bag.

"Me, too," Faith said, "but I'm staying out of the kitchen."

"I'll have one of the boys move the food out here." Althea waved to Lanie. "Come on, Lanie, we're camping out in the van."

Lanie was out the front door before Althea finished talking. Faith grunted. "Well, that gave me a sense of comfort." She grabbed her sleeping bag and looked at Shawn. "Do you want to bunk down here?"

"There's a room on the second floor I got a very warm feeling from. I think we'll be happier up there," Shawn answered.

"Now you tell me," Faith said.

After Althea gave them a set of handheld radios and Kyle moved the food out into the sitting room, they were left on their own. The lights the crew had installed for filming purposes began to dim. "Peachy," Faith grumbled as they retrieved their flashlights. "So show me this room that gave you the warm fuzzies."

Shawn led Faith up to the second floor, feeling a strange sense of comfort as they passed by the cameras that had been installed in the empty house. The doorknob to the room felt warm when Shawn turned it. They both stood in the doorway, staring at the sight of a fire burning in the fireplace.

"Althea?" Shawn said into her radio. "Did you have one of the guys light a fire in one of the upstairs rooms?"

"Um, no," Althea responded hesitantly. "Are you getting the fire in the shot?" she heard Althea say to her crew.

"Can you see us?" Shawn asked.

"Yes. We got the fire, too."

"I'm thrilled," Shawn said.

"I guess we're expected," Faith said as they stepped into the room.

Shawn found the room warm and inviting. She looked around, smiling at the welcoming feeling that encompassed her. Shawn and Faith shared a warm glance before they placed their sleeping bags onto the floor. "Do you notice anything about the room?" Shawn asked.

"Besides the warm, cozy fire that apparently started all by itself?" Faith nudged her sleeping bag closer to Shawn's with her foot.

"No dust," Shawn said.

"You're right," Faith replied thoughtfully as she looked around. "Strange, since the rest of the house is covered with it."

Shawn stifled a laugh when Faith once again nudged her sleeping bag closer to hers. "You know, if you keep doing that, we might as well zip them together," Shawn teased her.

"Okay," Faith agreed.

"Knock it off, you two. This is network television," Althea said over the radio.

"Killjoy," Faith grumbled. "I like this room. It feels safe and warm."

"According to the floor plans, it was Anna's bedroom," Althea said.

"No wonder it's so big," Shawn said. "As the lady of the house, she would have had to entertain her guests up here whenever her husband was away at sea."

"Excuse me?" Faith asked, her curiosity seemingly piqued.

"It was a custom to close off the formal sitting rooms and entertain lady guests for sewing or tea in her bedroom whenever her husband was at sea," Shawn explained. "Also, she wouldn't throw any formal dinners or parties."

"Not a bad deal." Faith chuckled. "The hubby is away for months or years, and your girlfriends hang out in your bedroom."

Shawn felt herself blush. Faith relaxed, and Shawn caught a glimpse of what she was thinking. "I doubt it was the naughty slumber party you're fantasizing about," Shawn told her as she watched the mini-orgy that Faith had conjured up. Her eyes widened as something occurred to her. "Or maybe it was."

"Guys, the video and sound are cutting in and out," Althea's voice crackled over the radio. "Could you move to another room?"

"No!" they both said adamantly into the small radio.

"What's going on in that pretty little head of yours?" Faith asked Shawn, who was finally putting all of the pieces together.

"Why us?" Shawn asked. Faith returned her inquiry with a blank stare. "Why did the entity attack us and ignore everyone else in that room?"

"Don't know. It's not because we're women, since Mr. Spooky ignored Althea and Lanie."

"No, but we do have something else in common."

"Like what?" Faith scoffed. "You're a crystal-wearing, sprout-eating psychic, and I'm a normal person."

"Think about it," Shawn insisted, but Faith continued to stare at her blankly. "Okay, we'll try something else. Why does a man kill his wife?"

"He's an evil bastard."

"Why else?"

"Money," Faith said. "Of course, that doesn't fit since we know Captain Stratton was loaded. So that leaves everyone's favorite, infidelity. It would have to be her who was unfaithful, since back then he could have been sleeping with farm animals and she wouldn't be able to say spit about it. I still don't get it."

"What's the common thread?" Shawn asked her.

"Mrs. Stratton cheating on her husband and something you think we both have in common? The only thing you and I have in common is that we're—" Faith's eyes widened with sudden understanding. "We're both gay," she finally said.

"I think Anna and Catherine were very close," Shawn said with a knowing smirk. "That would explain why this room feels so warm. It's probably where they spent their intimate moments. The only other room that felt this warm was upstairs, on the third floor. A very small room that would have been reserved for a spinster sister."

The light sound of a woman's laugh echoed through the room. "They're here," Shawn said with a bright smile. "This was their favorite place." Fleeting images flew through her mind. "They would sit here." She moved to a spot where she could see a table clearly. "Drink tea and steal soft touches, always careful, so the servants couldn't observe them. And at night they would share Anna's bed whenever Horatio was away. There were times they risked everything by sleeping together when he was around." Shawn moved to the spot where she pictured the canopy bed. Their sleeping bags rested upon that same spot. "This is the room where they made love for the first and last time."

"How did Horatio find out?" Faith asked eagerly.

"I don't know," Shawn said. "This room is like a haven to them. They blocked him, and what happened, out of here."

They turned suddenly at the sound of heavy footsteps racing up the staircase and down the hallway. They stared at the open doorway as the door slammed shut and the footsteps vanished. Shawn was filled with a sense of love and serenity. Faith's smile told her that she could feel it as well.

"Um, guys?" Althea's voice crackling over the radio disrupted their bliss. "Not to worry you or anything, but all of the downstairs lights just went on."

"I thought the power wasn't on," Faith said.

"It isn't."

The women took a deep breath before picking up their flashlights. "Ready to have more fun?" Faith asked. The way her voice was squeaking alerted Shawn that Faith felt anything but calm.

Shawn waved to her as she opened the bedroom door. "After you."

"No way."

"Chicken," Shawn scoffed before she led Faith out into the empty hallway.

"Normally, I'd be real upset at a comment like that," Faith said. She followed closely behind Shawn. "But after everything that's happened today, I can live with it. Just remember to let me know when it's time to run."

"You got a deal." Shawn peered over the banister to the brightly-lit lower level. "He came back early." The images of a long-ago night consumed her. She jumped as a stout man with a white beard ran up the staircase. "He always did that."

"Did what?" Faith gently clasped Shawn's shoulder.

"Horatio would barge into the house when he returned and race up the stairs to his wife's bedroom. It didn't matter if he was returning from a voyage or a trip into town. Whenever he entered the house, he would storm up the staircase and barge into Anna's bedroom. He always feared that someday she would take a lover. He never suspected his sister."

"This pinhead gets more and more charming. Did he figure it out that night?"

"No," Shawn responded absently, lost in the images. "Horatio returned from a journey in the middle of the night. At first they thought it was an intruder. They rushed to put on their bed clothing and descended the staircase. Catherine was holding a rifle."

As Shawn and Faith crept down the staircase, Shawn could see the scene unfolding before her. The foyer was brightly lit, and the home was now elegantly furnished.

The image changed, and night faded into early morning. Shawn saw a tall, slender woman dressed in a simple gray dress, with long blonde hair bundled high upon her head. "It's Catherine," she said as Catherine's image descended the staircase. Shawn watched as Catherine passed them and smiled down at a younger, redheaded woman who was standing in the foyer. They exchanged a long, loving gaze before they both donned a solemn expression. "They were very good at hiding how deeply in love they were with one another."

Shawn was captivated by the sights and sounds that now became very real to her. Catherine entered the dining room behind her lover, who continued into the kitchen. Catherine took her place at the table, away from her brother who was seated at the head of the table. "Brother," she greeted him, her face and voice devoid of all emotion as she folded her napkin on her lap. Horatio ignored her greeting.

"They ate breakfast," Shawn continued. "It's so real, I can smell the food. Anna served the meal, and no one spoke except Horatio, and that was only when he wanted one of them to serve him."

"You can see all that?" Faith asked.

"Everything." Shawn watched the family eat their morning meal in silence. Occasionally, she caught the shy glances the two women exchanged. "I can see the polished pine table, the lace curtains. I can see, hear, and smell everything."

"Shawn," Faith warned when they stepped deeper into the room.

Ignoring Faith's words, Shawn watched the two women begin to clear away the dirty dishes. They made their way down the same hallway Shawn had been drawn to earlier that day. Horatio remained behind, reading some papers as he puffed on his pipe. She heard him move to the sitting room, just off of the dining room. She almost choked on the pungent aroma from his pipe.

Shawn reached for the door that led into the kitchen.

Faith sounded panicky. "Shawn."

"Where's she going?" Althea asked over the radio.

"Shawn," Faith repeated in a fearful tone.

Shawn stepped into the bright and sunny kitchen. The two women moved about the room confidently. "He never goes into the kitchen. They know that they're safe. They touch one another lightly as they brush past each other while they clean up after the morning meal. They're finished, and Catherine stands behind Anna. She caresses her neck and shoulders. They stop when they think they hear something. They listen and hear nothing more.

"Catherine wraps her arms around Anna's waist from behind and begins to kiss her lover's neck." Shawn cried out as she saw the shadowy figure enter the room from the back door.

"I know what you are," Horatio said as he raised the axe. "Sinner." He struck his sister down with one blow. He wrapped his hand around his wife's throat. "Sinner," he hissed again.

"Oh, my God, oh, my God," Shawn chanted as the bloody scene unfolded before her. Even when she closed her eyes, she could still see the scene playing out. She was only dimly aware that Faith had pulled her from the room and dragged her back upstairs to Anna's bedroom.

Shawn slowly relaxed as she felt her body wrapped in a warm embrace. She shook her head when she realized that she was upstairs, sitting on her sleeping bag, nestled in Faith's arms.

"It was awful," she choked out.

"Do you want to talk about it?" Faith asked gently.

"I should do a recap for Althea." Shawn sniffed as she looked up at Faith.

"Too late," Faith said. "After you started screaming 'Oh, my God,' they lost all contact with us."

"What do you mean? Are the video and sound completely down?" Shawn tried to process what she had just heard.

"Everything," Faith said. "First the feed from the cameras, and after you really started to freak, I lost radio contact with them. The last thing Althea said was they saw a figure heading towards the woodshed. Oh, and I can't get the door or windows to open. They slammed shut, and the cable feeds were disconnected. So we're stuck in here."

"How long was I out of it?"

"Quite a while. You really freaked out."

"We should be safe if we stay in here." Shawn clung tightly to Faith.

"Really?" Faith asked her in a hopeful tone.

"I think so," Shawn tried to reassure her. "At least the fire's still going."

"It won't be so bad," Faith said softly. "You and me curled up in a sleeping bag next to a cozy fire."

Shawn released a light chuckle into Faith's chest. She pulled away and took a deep breath. "What he did to them was horrible," she said, trying to detach herself from what she had witnessed. "They were in the kitchen and felt safe since Horatio never went in there. Why would he?

"They were simply holding hands and touching each other. He saw them from the doorway. They never knew. Horatio left the house through the front door, went out to the woodshed, and got an axe. Then he came back into the house through the kitchen door. They were embracing and never heard him coming. You can figure out what happened next."

"What a sick bastard," Faith said. She began to caress Shawn's shoulders.

"No kidding," Shawn agreed, leaning into Faith's touch. It was then she noticed something that made her smile. "You zipped the sleeping bags together?"

"It's not what you think," Faith said defensively as Shawn flashed her a suspicious smirk. "Come on, you know what I'm thinking."

"No, I don't. True, a few times I did get a glimpse, but it only happened three times, when your defenses were down. The first time was when you brushed my hair out of my eyes. The second time was when you got angry with Kyle for filming us while you were trying to comfort me. The last time was when that filthy mind of yours was picturing just how the lady of the house would entertain her female guests while her husband was at sea."

"Did you like that one?" Faith wrapped her arms around Shawn's waist.

"You're very creative." Shawn sighed. "So if you aren't making a pass, Ms. Charles, then why did you zip our sleeping bags together?"

"I don't know about you, but I'm not planning on closing my eyes in this house," Faith said in a serious tone. "I just feel a need to be close to you since, well, you're the only other person running around here who's actually breathing."

"Oh," Shawn responded with a hint of regret. She tried to pretend that she wasn't disappointed that Faith wasn't interested in her. She glanced at her wristwatch. "It's just after ten thirty. Wow, I really did lose a big chunk of time. We have another hour and a half, that is if we can get out of here at midnight."

"We'll be fine as long as we stay in this room." Faith pulled Shawn closer. "It's so warm, it's almost like I feel the love they shared."

"I know. I feel it, too," Shawn said. "I can also feel the passion," she added shyly, nestling closer to Faith.

The strangest sensations were enveloping Shawn. She could feel the warmth of Faith's body behind her. She could even feel the steady beating of Faith's heart. Yet there was something or someone else she was feeling as well.

Then she saw the lace-covered canopy bed emerge. Anna and Catherine stood next to the bed. Shawn felt the nervous tension that surrounded them when Anna reached up and cupped Catherine's face.

As Anna touched Catherine's face, Shawn leaned back in Faith's tender embrace and touched her face in the same fashion. Shawn was lying across Faith's lap as she watched Catherine capture Anna's hand. Faith's strong gentle hand seemed to mirror Catherine's actions.

"Sister?" Catherine whispered nervously.

"Don't call me that. For what I feel for you is anything but sisterly," Anna said in a breathy tone as she pulled Catherine's face closer to her own.

Without realizing what she was doing, Shawn gently drew Faith's face to her own. The feel of Faith's warm breath caressing her face was mixed with the passionate feelings emanating from Catherine and Anna. As the faint image of the two women kissed, Shawn felt Faith's soft lips brushing against hers. Shawn gave herself over to the feeling of Faith's mouth exploring her own. She parted her lips, and Faith's tongue traced her bottom lip.

In her mind's eye, she watched Catherine lower Anna down onto the bed. Faith mirrored Catherine's actions, lowering Shawn onto the sleeping bags. Shawn's eyes drifted shut as Faith's warm body melted against her own. She kissed Faith deeply, yet could still see the images of Catherine and Anna.

Catherine kissed Anna deeply and began to slowly remove Anna's cumbersome clothing, while Faith did the same to Shawn. Shawn tingled with excitement as Faith caressed her. Her body was pulsing with desire. Faith began to kiss down Shawn's neck while Catherine lovingly did the same to Anna.

Shawn clutched at Faith's clothing, her body demanding more, while Anna mirrored her. "They're making love," Shawn managed to choke out as she felt Faith's mouth worshipping the swell of her exposed breasts. She saw Catherine doing the same to Anna. "Everything we're doing, they're doing." She didn't want to break the spell, but she feared that she and Faith were caught up in something that had nothing to do with them.

"Do you want me to stop?" Faith whispered against her skin while Catherine echoed the words.

"No," Shawn and Anna responded in unison.

Faith's body lifted slightly off of her own. "Open your eyes, Shawn," Faith said. Shawn blinked her hazel eyes open. Her breathing hitched as Faith captured her in a fiery gaze. "Look at me," Faith said softly. "I can feel them. I can feel their intense passion. This has nothing to do with them." Faith's eyes smoldered with raw desire as she reassured Shawn.

The look in Faith's eyes conveyed the sincerity of her words. A fleeting image flashed through Shawn's mind, showing her Faith's true feelings. Shawn reached up, gently guided Faith down, and reclaimed her lips. The fire that burned in her came solely from her lover, and not from the passion that filled the room from the energy of Catherine and Anna's love.

"I need to see you," Shawn and Anna pleaded.

Both Catherine and Faith lifted their bodies and stood before their lovers. Each of them undressed under the lustful gaze of their lovers. Then both lowered themselves into the arms of the naked woman lying before them. Shawn moaned deeply when she felt Faith's body nestling into hers.

Shawn ran her hands down Faith's body and murmured softly when once again Faith began to kiss along her neck. With each kiss, Shawn's body burned with need. She cried out when Faith's tongue circled her nipple. Once again, she was aware that they were mirroring Anna and Catherine's actions.

Instinctively, Shawn's body arched. Faith captured Shawn's nipple in her mouth, and Shawn's thigh slipped between Faith's legs. Shawn's heart was beating rapidly from the feel of her lover's desire painting her skin. Shawn's hands drifted down Faith's body; Anna mirrored her movements. Each clasped her lover's hips, gently guiding their bodies to grind against welcoming thighs. Shawn's need raged through her as Faith worshipped her breasts with her mouth and rocked gently against her body.

Shawn trembled as Faith kissed her way down her body while Catherine did the same to Anna. Shawn was no longer able to speak or think as Faith's warm breath caressed the inside of her trembling thighs. The only thing she was aware of beyond Faith's touch was the fiery image of Catherine and Anna lost in the throes of passion.

Shawn tried to erase that image. Looking down her trembling body, she watched Faith feasting upon her wetness and gave herself over to Faith's touch. She clutched at the nylon sleeping bags as her body erupted and then quickly pulled Faith up in her arms and wrapped herself around her. Her body ignited again when she tasted herself on Faith's warm, inviting lips. Their hands caressed and pleasured each other. The images of Anna and Catherine faded. Shawn and Faith continued to explore one another until they collapsed into a loving embrace.

The sensation of Faith spooning her naked body invoked a contented sigh. Shawn's gaze drifted to the bedroom window. "The sun is coming up," she said softly.

"Hmm," Faith murmured in response just as the bedroom door slowly opened.

Both women sat up and reached for each other. The morning light began to fill the room. Shawn looked around, relaxing into Faith's embrace. "The fire's gone." She stared at the fireplace. There was no wood, not even ashes; it was barren. Her attention quickly turned to the camera mounted just above the doorway. Thankfully, the telltale red light that blinked brightly whenever the camera was on was still dim.

"We should get dressed," Faith whispered in her ear. "I have a feeling that the film and sound equipment is going to be back on line soon."

They moved quickly and gathered themselves together. Just as they made their way downstairs, Althea and the rest of the crew burst through the front door. "Thank God!" Althea blurted. Shawn just smiled and began to collect and check her equipment. "We've been trying to get in here all night," Althea said, looking frantic.

"How did the airing go?" Shawn asked, casting a shy smile over at Faith.

"Great," Lanie said. "The stuff from the kitchen blew everyone's socks off."

Everyone started to babble on and on about how well the segment had been received. Shawn continued to pack up her equipment while she and Faith exchanged warm glances. She roamed the house, collecting her belongings. They had one more filming to endure, and then they were free to go and leave Whispering Pines behind them. Shawn checked her readings and played the tapes from the recorders. Her blood turned cold when she played back the one she had left in the small bedroom on the top floor. Shivering uncontrollably, she played it over and over again. Each playback confirmed what she had heard the first time.

"Help us!"

The words were garbled, and the sound was terrible. Each time Shawn played it, hoping beyond hope to hear something different, it was still the same. "I can't," she said with a hard swallow. For the first time in her life, she refused to help a spirit find peace. At that moment, Shawn was convinced there was nothing she could do.

"What was that?" Althea was positively frothing at the mouth when she heard the recording. Dutifully, Shawn replayed it. Althea's dark brown eyes lit up with excitement. "I can't wait to get that on film. What does it mean?"

"Don't know," Shawn lied. "Honestly, Althea, when are you going to learn that these things don't come with an instruction manual?"

"Now there's an idea," Faith said. "A playbook would have been real handy last night when all that funky-ass shit was going down."

"Last night was fabulous." Althea sounded proud.

"Easy for you to say," Faith growled. "You were hiding in the van. Those of us who had a ringside seat for Spook Central were not amused."

"Save it for the camera," Althea said with a cackle.

As if on cue, the crew set up and Faith took her mark. While Faith began her story, Shawn couldn't help but wonder what would happen between her and Faith once they left the old mansion. She had to bite back a snide comment when Faith admitted on camera that Whispering Pines was indeed haunted.

Shawn filmed her commentary quickly, eager to leave the mansion as she felt Captain Stratton's presence lingering around them.

Once they had wrapped up everything, she and Faith stared at one another. Each seemed to be searching for something to say to the other. When no words were forthcoming, Shawn simply gathered up her heavy equipment. Without a word, Faith relieved her of some her belongings. They strode out to Shawn's rental car and loaded the equipment.

"I guess I won't be getting a book out of this one," Faith said in a light tone once the equipment had been packed away.

"You could co-author one with me," Shawn said as they both leaned against her car. Faith seemed to be lost in thought. "What is it?"

"I just wish we could do something for them. Anna and Catherine. I wish there were some way to release them from this. It seems that they're forced to relive everything. Some of it's nice, but they still have to face losing one another again and again. And in a horrible way."

"They're caught up in a vicious cycle. They're asking for help, and I have no idea what to do," Shawn said grimly. "A cleansing might help."

"Oh, please. Some idiot waving incense and telling them that they're free to go. Do you honestly believe that no one has told them to get out before now?"

"You're probably right," Shawn said. "It's probably been tried already. I don't know what we can do, other than finding their bodies and finally giving them a decent burial. Without that, they're probably destined to remain trapped here. Personally, I don't have the courage to go up against Captain Stratton again."

"Neither do I," Faith agreed. "This has been the strangest twenty-four hours of my life."

"Mine, too."

"So where are you off to now?" Faith asked.

"I have a room booked at a hotel a couple of towns over. It won't take us long to get there. After we get cleaned up, you're taking me to breakfast."

"Pretty sure of yourself," Faith said with a brilliant smile.

Shawn wondered if what had happened last night was just a fling for Faith. Her fears vanished the moment she felt Faith's arms encircling her waist. Shawn turned to face her.

"I'll follow you," Faith said with a smile before placing a promising kiss on Shawn's soft lips.

"Yes, you will," Shawn responded confidently.

Chapter 4

Stewart, Massachusetts
September 1912

Anna wiped the tears from her son's eyes. "I don't want to go away," Richard pleaded, the teardrops rolling down his chubby cheeks.

"I know." Anna's voice trembled as she spoke. "I don't want you to leave, but Father says it's for the best."

"Why?" he pleaded once again.

Why indeed? What kind of monster sends a five-year-old child off to boarding school? Anna gathered up her son's belongings while her husband shouted for her to "bring the boy down!" *The boy, not our son.* Anna fumed. *Of course, he isn't a son to you, is he? Just another possession, like myself.* Anna wearily escorted her only child down the staircase.

She had long ago accepted her fate that had begun on that rainy night when her father woke her and her sisters and lined them up in the family room for the great Horatio Stratton. "That one," the old man had grunted as he pointed to the small, redheaded sister, the helpless Anna. He had selected her to be his wife with no more interest than he would exhibit in selecting a pair of socks.

Before she had a chance to realize the gravity of the situation, Anna was a married woman. In less than two days, she had been sold off, wed, and taken away from the only home she had ever known. Her wedding night wasn't the magical event she had read about. It was a horrendous nightmare with Horatio lying on top of her, puffing and grunting like a hog that needed to be fed.

The only bright spot in her dreary existence was her son. Thankfully, her husband ignored Richard. But he insisted on sending him away for his education, as though fearful that somehow Anna would spoil him. *How can I spoil him when I'm barely allowed to speak to my own son?* Before her blessed son's birth, the only things Anna looked forward to were her trips into town and an early death.

Anna ushered her still whimpering child down the staircase and handed him over to her husband.

"Stop that sniveling!" Horatio barked as he backhanded him. Anna flinched in horror as she watched her son's head snap back. "I will be returning after I deposit the boy," Horatio said with a scowl. "The spinster's coming to stay with us. Another mouth to feed," he added in a bitter tone.

Anna was confused until she realized her husband was referring to his younger sister. She possessed very little knowledge of the woman, only that she was unmarried. Anna wondered if Miss Stratton would provide at least companionship for her lonely days, or would she prove to be bitter and cold like Horatio?

"Yes, Husband," she responded dutifully as she patted her son's head.

While her husband took Richard to the train station, Anna busied herself preparing the small room on the third floor for her sister-in-law. The top floor of the manor had remained vacant since Horatio strictly forbade that servants or guests spend the night.

"I don't even know her name," Anna said softly as she placed a small vase filled with asters from her flower garden. The small flower garden was one of the few joys, besides her son, that Anna was allowed to indulge in.

"Catherine," a sultry voice said from behind her.

Anna almost knocked over the vase when she spun around. Her breath caught when she spotted the tall, elegant blonde standing in the doorway. "My name is Catherine," the woman said, her warm brown eyes crinkling as she smiled.

Anna trembled as she fought to control her breathing. "Mine is Anna," she said and tore her gaze away, unable to understand why she had been staring or why her body was quivering. She took several quick breaths in an effort to calm herself. "Welcome to Whispering Pines," she finally managed to say, forcing her gaze to remain on the tiny vase.

"Thank you for welcoming me into your home," Catherine said in a soft tone. Her gentle demeanor surprised Anna. Her gaze snapped up, and once again she shivered.

"Where are my manners?" Anna babbled as she approached Catherine. "Please, allow me to assist you with your belongings."

"Thank you." Catherine accepted in the same gentle tone as they carried her meager belongings into the small bedroom.

"Wife!" Horatio bellowed from the main floor.

Anna cringed. The only saving grace was that when Horatio shouted she was mildly safer than when he explained things in a measured, chill tone of voice. When his eyes darkened and his voice calmed, Anna knew all too well that meant trouble.

"If you will excuse me?" Anna turned away, not missing that her sister-in-law's lips curled into a sneer.

Perhaps we shall become friends after all. Anna hurried off to answer her husband's summons.

"Husband?" She greeted Horatio respectfully, keeping her head lowered and her gaze locked on the floor. Over the years, she had spent so many hours looking down that she was now fully acquainted with every scuff mark, nail, and board in the flooring of the house.

"I'm going into town," he said curtly. "While I'm gone, try to find something for her to do."

Anna glanced up and followed his icy gaze to the staircase. Her breathing caught when she spied Catherine standing at the top landing with a defiant gaze. "Yes, Husband," Anna meekly agreed, her attention never straying from the tall blonde. Horatio grunted in response.

Anna didn't move as the slamming of the door echoed through the house. She saw Catherine flinch at the loud banging and open her mouth to speak. Anna pressed her fingers to her lips, cautioning Catherine to remain silent. Anna listened carefully; she didn't need to look out on the front porch to know that her husband was lurking around.

Catherine watched quietly as Anna listened until she heard his heavy footsteps pounding down the gravel walkway. She released a tense breath as Miranda, the downstairs maid, passed by. "Miranda?" Anna called. "Once Miss Stratton is settled, bring her to the parlor for afternoon tea," she instructed the girl without ever looking at her. Anna's focus remained on Catherine.

"Certainly, Mrs. Stratton," Miranda dutifully responded.

Anna nodded to her sister-in-law and went about her morning chores. Horatio expected her to tend to her duties regardless if he was away at sea or right under her feet. She had no relief since she was well aware that he paid the servants a little extra to keep a watchful eye on her. The only respite she would receive was when he was away and she was alone for the evening. After the servants left for the day, she would retire to her bedchambers and enjoy the quiet time with Richard.

Every morning, Anna awoke and said a silent prayer that she would find her husband's travel bag sitting in the foyer. That was the only way she knew when he planned a trip. Of course, many times he only pretended to travel so he could sneak back and catch her doing something she shouldn't. Anna often wondered whether her husband was disappointed by her obedience and fidelity. *If you wish to strike me, you evil sod, then just do it. I will not add kindling to the fire.*

By early afternoon, Anna sat in the parlor working on her needlepoint while she waited for her guest to join her. Catherine breezed into the room like a breath of fresh air. "Do sit, Sister," Anna greeted her with a smile.

"Thank you, Sister." Catherine took a place on the small settee.

Just as Catherine took her seat, Miranda entered with the silver tea service. "Miranda, I believe the captain would prefer we use the everyday china," Anna told the maid. She knew that Horatio would be displeased if they entertained his sister with the good service. Miranda turned slightly pale, then nodded and returned to the kitchen. "Please, do not be offended, Sister." Anna continued to neatly stitch the pattern she had been working on. "The captain is very particular when it comes to running the household."

"I can see that," Catherine dryly responded. "The maid came so quickly it was almost as if she knew we were waiting."

"She did," Anna said as their eyes met. Anna shivered once again as she gazed into Catherine's soft brown eyes. She had the same eyes as her brother, but Anna could see and feel warmth that was absent from her husband's gaze. There was something else lingering in Catherine's eyes that Anna couldn't place.

"They watch you?" Catherine asked.

"Yes." Anna gave her sister-in-law a warning glance. "Perhaps after tea you will join me in the garden?" she suggested just as Miranda reentered the room with the proper tea service. "Thank you, Miranda," Anna said as the tea was placed on the table.

Miranda nodded and quickly left the room. Anna served the tea and offered a cup to Catherine. "I understand I have a nephew," Catherine said with a smile as she accepted her tea.

"Yes, Richard." Anna carefully prepared her own cup of tea.

"Where is he?" Catherine asked with enthusiasm.

"He's at school."

"Oh? I look forward to meeting him later today."

"He is away at school." Anna was unable to keep the sadness she felt from slipping through.

"Isn't he much too young for that?"

"The garden really is lovely this time of year," Anna said, as if nothing were amiss. "I look forward to showing it to you." She said a silent prayer that Catherine would understand it was the only place that would allow them the privacy to speak freely.

Catherine set her cup down. "The tea was lovely. I truly wish to see the garden as quickly as possible."

Anna finished her tea with a smile, realizing that Catherine understood. She led Catherine out the front door, linked arms with her as they walked towards the back of the house, and began pointing out each flower she had painstakingly planted.

"Anna, it's beautiful," Catherine said as they stepped past the woodshed and stable.

The garden, Anna's pride and joy, was spread out before them, just a short walk away from the main house. Once they were in the garden, Anna looked around to ensure that no one had followed them. She inhaled the soft fragrance of the autumn blooms and relaxed into the feel of her arm resting in Catherine's.

A strange, delightful warmth spread through Anna as she felt Catherine's thumb absently brushing against her arm. "I finally understand what my mother tried to tell me," Catherine said as they ambled through the garden.

"What's that?" Anna asked.

"The only thing worse than being an unmarried Stratton woman is being a married Stratton woman," Catherine said bitterly. "You're a prisoner here."

"Yes," Anna said without emotion. She had long ago accepted her fate. "My garden and my son are my solace."

"Richard can't be more than a child."

"He'll be six next spring. Thankfully, God gave him to me early in my marriage."

Catherine scowled. "He's far too young to be sent to boarding school."

"I know. We should head back. The captain will be returning soon, and I must prepare the evening meal."

"I'll be happy to help you. Our other brother paid Horatio to take me in," Catherine said as they walked towards the house. "So it seems I'll be joining you in captivity. Perhaps I can add to your solace?"

"I'd like that." Anna smiled, then she saw her husband rush into the house.

"Where's he going?" Catherine asked.

"My bedchambers," Anna answered dryly, as she guided Catherine towards the kitchen entrance.

"And what does he think he'll find there?"

"A man."

"Have you ever given him cause to suspect there might be a man hiding in your bedroom?" Catherine asked.

"Never." They entered the kitchen and immediately began to prepare the evening meal.

"How often does he search for your phantom lover?"

"Every time he returns to the house, since the day we were married," Anna said coldly.

Chapter 5

Faith was shocked by what she had just heard. "You want to run that by me again?" She wasn't at all pleased by the way Althea avoided making eye contact with her.

"I'm sorry," Althea said, her voice just above a whisper. "I don't have anything for you."

"Althea, I know I'm a pain in the ass." Faith wasn't enjoying the fact that she was about to grovel. "I've been working for you for years now. All of a sudden you don't have an assignment for me? What gives?"

"Whispering Pines," Althea said wearily.

"Whispering Pines?" Faith didn't grasp the situation. "As I recall, that was one hell of a shoot. In fact, it moved you up the food chain. I also recall the way you impressed the big boys was because I got smacked around and scared out of my wits. Not to mention what it did to Shawn."

"You're also writing a book with Shawn," Althea said. "And you went on camera confirming that Whispering Pines is haunted."

"If you hadn't noticed, that place was Spook Central," Faith snapped. "There isn't a skeptic on the planet who could have gone on camera and denied that the place is haunted."

"A professional skeptic can't admit it." Althea had the grace to wince as Faith glared at her. "Not ever. In doing so, you ended your career as a skeptic. I'm really sorry, Faith. It was the best gig any of us have ever worked."

Faith mulled over Althea's words. What could she say? Althea had a really good point. "I get it," she said. "I've made my living by claiming there's no such thing as ghosts. I can't very well expect to be taken seriously after Whispering Pines. I guess it's time for another career change."

"I'm truly sorry." Althea sighed. "I wish there were someway I could send you on assignment."

"Don't be." Faith chuckled. "Losing the job pales in comparison to what I've gained. Speaking of which, I'm going to be late. Shawn and I are having dinner at this new restaurant in the Village."

"I can't believe the two of you are still together," Althea said.

"Why not?" Faith gasped with mock indignation. "I'm quite the catch."

Althea laughed. "So is she."

"I know that." Faith grabbed her coat. "Like I said, being unemployed isn't that much of a hardship. Knowing that she's in my life means everything. The only downside is it gets a little creepy at times."

"How so?"

"Dead people." Faith shivered. "They follow her everywhere. Even her apartment's haunted. I have to go. Traffic's going to be a bitch."

*　*　*

When Faith arrived at the restaurant, she apologized for being late and then proceeded to recount the details of her meeting with Althea.

"They fired you?" Shawn gaped at her.

"Technically, no, since, like you, I'm contracted gig to gig," Faith said. "They just aren't going to hire me again."

"And the difference is?"

"Look at it from their standpoint. I'm a skeptic who isn't skeptical. You know Althea is making the right call. If we weren't talking about me, you'd agree with this."

"But we are talking about you." Shawn took her lover's hand.

"I'm going to be fine. We have a book to write, which should keep me out of trouble until I find a new career. Do you mind if I keep tagging along on your gigs?"

"Are you kidding? I love it. Especially since you dream about sex almost every night. Makes my sleep time really enjoyable."

"I do?" Faith choked, and her cheeks turned red.

"Yes." Shawn smirked.

"Glad to know that I'm so entertaining." Faith chuckled. "Shawn, I've enjoyed traveling with you. I'd like to keep doing it.

Well, until I get a job. Where are you off to next? Someplace warm and tropical, I hope."

"You can always hope." Shawn couldn't stop smiling. It amazed her that she and Faith were still going strong. She had half expected the passion to fizzle quickly, given the way the two of them constantly bickered. Funny thing about her gift. She knew other people's deepest, darkest secrets, and yet the inner workings of her own life remained elusive. "Vermont is our next destination."

"Skiing!" Faith clapped her hands. "Maybe some snowboarding?"

"Oh, sure, go hit the slopes while I'm locked up with things that go bump in the night." Shawn feigned jealousy.

"I meant that we can hit the slopes," Faith said with a dazzling smile. "We could head up early or stay on after you wrap up. Early is probably best. You get some mighty nasty headaches chatting with dead people."

"Occupational hazard." Shawn grimaced. "Sometimes what I see and feel is so painful. I feel that pain."

"I've noticed," Faith said quietly. "After Whispering Pines, I thought you'd never bounce back."

"That place was a trip," Shawn admitted with a hard swallow.

"No kidding." Faith shivered. "I read your first book. You were just a kid when you found that body. How did you deal with it?"

"Finding her was an affirmation. I finally understood why my imaginary friend poked and pinched me constantly. She wasn't imaginary. She was real. And when her remains were finally placed in a proper grave, she left. Knowing that I helped make that possible made my gift bearable. Totally freaked out my parents. In time they came to understand that I was given a gift that should be used, not hidden."

"I can kind of understand their apprehension," Faith said. "Can you imagine your little baby girl dragging you to an abandoned well and finding a body?"

"If I'm ever blessed with a child," Shawn said reluctantly, "there's a better chance of something just like that happening than not. This sort of thing tends to be genetic."

Faith raised her eyebrows. "Then why were your parents so surprised about you?"

Shawn snickered. "Did you read my book or just skim through it?"

"I read it," Faith said. "Well, most of it."

"My writing style has improved greatly since my first book."
Shawn sighed. "I'm adopted."

"Oh?" Faith looked surprised and opened her mouth to speak.

"Yes, yes, no, no, and because I no longer want to," Shawn said,
already knowing what her overly-inquisitive lover was going to ask.

"Huh?" Faith gaped at her. "Did you just tap into my head?"

"No, but I've heard the questions before," Shawn said. "Yes,
I've wondered about my birth parents. Yes, I've tried to find them.
No, I didn't find them. No, I'm not still looking for them. Because
I'm no longer interested in knowing. My parents are the people who
raised me."

"Fair enough."

"Faith, I'm serious." Shawn could see the wheels spinning in
Faith's mind. "I know that look. The reporter in you is just itching to
find the truth. If they were interested, either of my biological parents
could have found me. After all, at least one of them must be gifted.
Ergo, finding the child they gave up shouldn't be that difficult. As far
as I'm concerned, my parents are Daria and Albert Williams. They
raised me and loved me unconditionally. End of story. Speaking of
parents, how are yours?"

"Good." Faith shrugged with a bored look on her face.

For the life of her, Shawn couldn't grasp just what was amiss
between Faith and her parents. They seemed to be a very warm and
loving family. Still, there was something lingering just beneath the
surface. Something that kept Faith away and distant from her parents.
Since she had just lectured Faith about not prying into her family
matters, she thought it would be for the best if she, too, respected
Faith's privacy.

"Ready to order?" she said casually, looking forward to a nice
dinner before relaxing at home. Based on the look Faith gave in
response, she understood her lover was seeking the same.

Chapter 6

In the few weeks since she had arrived at Whispering Pines, Catherine came to realize that her mother had indeed been correct. It truly was far worse being a married Stratton woman than an unmarried Stratton woman. Growing up in frigid surroundings with only the joy of boarding school keeping her away from the family home, she had failed to understand that staying behind in the home was a horrible fate.

After reaching a proper age and managing to avoid the institution of marriage, Catherine led a fanciful life. She had completed finishing school, which had relentlessly drilled her into becoming a proper young lady. When she had concluded her so-called studies, she bolted for Europe where she proceeded to lead her life in a highly improper manner. She returned to the United States on only two occasions. Both times were for the funeral of one of her parents. Each time, she paid the proper respects, collected her inheritance, and, much to her boorish brothers' joy, instantly disappeared. She held no doubt that she received her inheritance very quickly because the family was glad to be rid of her. Unmarried and outspoken, Catherine Stratton was an embarrassment.

Catherine was more than happy to hightail it out of the country; she found life abroad far more interesting and freeing. In the end, however, she had learned some very harsh lessons. The money wasn't never-ending, and love wasn't always the everlasting bliss she had mistakenly believed it was.

Her purse was quickly emptied by a charming, silver-tongued viper with smoldering eyes. Catherine had foolishly believed that the love she felt was reciprocated. She returned home penniless, much wiser, and determined not to turn to her family for help. She was flailing in dark waters when her brother Sebastian found her. He dragged her kicking and screaming back into the fold.

It had been one thing when they could hide her on another continent, but for her to have the bad manners to return without a penny to her name was unthinkable. Sebastian had mistakenly assumed that she would do her duty and marry the first suitor he brought home. When it became painfully clear that she would not yield, he paid Horatio to take her off his hands.

She thought life under Sebastian's roof had been insufferable. It was a paradise compared to the internment she was enduring at Whispering Pines. If not for Anna, dear sweet Anna, Catherine would have fled that first night, but if there was to be a prison break, she refused to leave poor Anna behind, alone with Horatio.

Now, she was spending her evening sitting on the front porch with Mr. Riley Van de Meer. When Horatio brought poor Mr. Van de Meer home for dinner, Catherine almost burst into laughter. Apparently, Horatio was unaware of the fact that Sebastian had already tried to wed her to the quiet man. Riley wasn't as insufferable as many of the others. Still, he wasn't what she was seeking, a fact that he readily accepted. Catherine suspected she was far too outspoken for his tastes.

Apparently Riley considered himself to be progressive simply because he agreed that when it came to marriage a woman knows her heart. "Two people should only be wed if they truly love one another," he had said. Other than that, though, he was as narrow-minded as most men she knew. He truly subscribed to the school of thought that a woman's place should be limited to the kitchen and nursery, since that was what all women desired from life. *Silly twit*, she silently snarled while pretending to listen to his boring commentary.

"I'm boring you," he echoed her thoughts.

"Not at all." She made a slight effort to look interested.

"Miss Stratton," he said with a light laugh, "I'm fully aware that you and I view the world differently. Pity that your brothers don't communicate very well. I tried to explain to the captain that I had already paid you a visit, and that you and I aren't suited for one another."

"Both my brothers seem to be hard of hearing." She wearily sighed. *If we absconded with the buggy, I wonder how far away Anna and I would be before Horatio realized we had fled?* She pondered yet another scheme. She contemplated the possibilities of escaping almost every moment of the day. "Don't misunderstand me, Mr. Van de Meer. I find you quite pleasant company. Yet as you've said, we aren't compatible."

"Trust me, I do understand, Miss Stratton." He smiled politely. "I wish to marry a woman who loves me just as deeply as I love her, and who respects the role God had placed her in. Not a woman who is off fighting for the frivolous right to vote or some other useless cause."

"Useless?" Catherine slowly repeated, then pursed her lips. "I do agree that marrying for love is vital. You may have noticed that in our social standing in the world, that is often the last consideration. Women are not given a voice. If you doubt me, take a good look at my dear sister-in-law."

"My heart aches at the sight of such a young woman being trapped in an obviously loveless marriage," Riley agreed.

"Young is right," Catherine sneered, her anger getting the best of her. "She's young enough to be his daughter. The way he treats her is positively shameful."

Riley expelled a sigh as he stood and brushed out his suit jacket. "I must concur," he whispered solemnly, "although I'm not shocked. I learned a long time ago that the captain fails to hold the sanctity of marriage in high regard. Seeing the sadness in Mrs. Stratton's eyes gives me pause. I'll take my leave and not force you to endure this charade any longer. I just need to bid the captain a good evening and thank him."

"Thank you, Mr. Van de Meer." She smiled up at him.

"Have a pleasant evening, and good luck," he added with a wink before entering the house.

After Mr. Van de Meer departed, Catherine suffered a lengthy lecture from her brother. "Dear Brother," she finally interrupted, exhausted from the evening's events. "I'm not what Mr. Van de Meer is seeking in a bride. He has courted me before, and neither of us holds a spark for the other."

"A spark?" Horatio sneered maliciously. "Rubbish."

"Be that as it may," she curtly said, "he won't be asking for my hand. I'm certain he has already conveyed that sentiment to you. There will be no need to invite him to supper in the future."

"You will do as I say," Horatio spat out.

"Brother." She fought to keep her emotions in check. "I can't stop you from inviting gentlemen callers to your home. That doesn't mean your feeble attempts will succeed."

"Are you forgetting whose roof you sleep under?" Horatio growled. Catherine flinched when he raised his hand to strike her. She reached deep inside herself, bolstering her courage. Her eyes darkened, and with a sneer, she challenged him to hit her.

"Do it. Give me solid ground to thoroughly shame you. A nice welt on my face will certainly be fodder for the good people of Stewart. Better still, turn me out. I shall gladly take my leave."

"Conniving bitch," he hissed, lowering his hand.

"Probably," she responded dryly and donned a bored expression. "Dear Brother, you are not master of all you survey. Push me hard enough, and I'll prove that you aren't a god. Now, if you'll excuse me, I wish to retire. Unless you prefer that I pack my bags now?"

"You'll not win," Horatio said. "I'll have my dowry. I just need to find the perfect fool who will take in a loathsome wretch such as yourself."

"Good evening." Catherine rolled her eyes, not missing the way her brother's fist clenched. She hiked up the hem of her skirt and made her exit before she pushed him too far. She was playing a very dangerous game, and she knew it. If not for Anna, she would take very drastic measures and flee. *I can't leave her behind. Some way, somehow, I will free us.*

Chapter 7

New York City
June 2003

Not for the first time, Shawn realized that just being a psychic didn't mean she understood her own life. She certainly hadn't seen this one coming. She had seen Faith's growing despair, the walls going up as Faith grew increasingly displeased with her new role in life. Shawn didn't need the gift of ESP to see that Faith was tired of following her around. A blind man could see her restlessness.

Shawn had done everything she could to make Faith feel a part of things. In the beginning, when they were working on the book, Faith seemed content. Now that the book was heading to print, there wasn't anything left for her to do.

Shawn was unable to fathom what had happened. Faith had left to run a quick errand and returned a few hours later, happily announcing that she was leaving the country for an indefinite period of time. "What?" Shawn finally blurted out, overcome with fear.

"I said that I got a job," Faith slowly repeated, "with CNN."

"In Afghanistan or Iraq? Correct me if I'm wrong," Shawn said slowly, fighting the urge to freak out, "but aren't we in the middle of war in those areas?"

"That would be why they're sending me." Faith shook her head, as though failing to see the problem.

"I don't begrudge you the opportunity." Shawn chose her words carefully. Internally, she was on the verge of screaming. "When were you going to tell me?"

"Right now."

"Sweetie, weren't you going to discuss this with me? I discuss my assignments with you." Shawn hoped that by pointing out that she valued Faith's input, she would somehow enlighten her. *That's what couples do*, she silently added.

"Why?" Faith asked.

Faith's question made it painfully obvious that she didn't view their relationship in the same light Shawn did. The conversation quickly turned into a full-fledged blowout. Shawn reached the breaking point when Faith made it clear that Shawn's feelings were not a consideration.

Furious, Shawn stormed out of the little café. She knew that she had gone from being concerned to being completely unreasonable in the blink of an eye. She couldn't help it. Faith had managed to break her heart in record time.

She failed to calm down when she returned to her apartment. Seeing Faith's belongings strewn about just opened another wound. "I can't deal with this." She sniffed, knowing that Faith would be arriving soon to either talk or collect her things. For one of the few times in her life, Shawn opted to take the coward's way out. If Faith was leaving, she knew that watching her leave was something she couldn't handle. She left before Faith arrived.

Shawn headed towards the first car rental agency she could find. She rented a sedan and headed upstate. "Running home. Could I be a bigger crybaby?" she berated herself when she was about halfway home. By the time she pulled up the gravel driveway, she felt completely despondent. Her parents were pleased by her impromptu visit, until they realized that something was wrong. They gave her three days before they cornered her.

"Shawn," her father greeted her on the front porch.

"Dad." She furrowed her brow as she looked up at him. Once again, she didn't need to be gifted to know that something was up. She sipped her coffee and turned her gaze towards the vineyard her parents owned.

"Shawn?" He sat down next to her. "Not that we're unhappy to see you, but do you mind telling me why you're here?"

"I missed you."

"You lie like a rug," he said. "Must be a biggie if you're fibbing to your old man."

She sat in silence for a moment, contemplating whether or not she was ready to talk about her troubles. The determined look in her father's dark brown eyes gave her the answer. "Faith and I broke up," she muttered. Saying it out loud drove another dagger into her fragile heart.

"What? I don't believe it. I would have bet that the two of you were in it for the long haul."

"Well, believe it. We split, or at least I think we did."

"Whoa, back up," he said. "Either you did or you didn't. If there's a chance of working it out, hiding up here isn't the answer. Why don't you just tell your dear old dad what happened? Maybe I can help."

"She got a job," Shawn said reluctantly.

"Normally that's good news. Especially these days."

"With CNN," Shawn said with a hard swallow.

"Again, good news."

"Overseas, as a war correspondent." Shawn felt the bile rising in her throat.

"Oh, my." He turned pale and patted her shoulder. "Faith knows her stuff. I'm sure she'll be fine. I'm guessing that your fear took over, and instead of saying you were afraid for her, you got angry."

"Absolutely." Shawn placed her coffee mug down and snuggled against her father. He wrapped his arms around her. "It wasn't just being terrified that she might be killed, although that's a big part of it. She didn't even tell me she had an interview. She said she had an errand to run. I got a call a few hours later to meet her for lunch. We met up, and that's when she told me everything. Not only did she accept a job halfway across the world that's putting her life in danger, she didn't even want to know how I felt about it. That's when I took a nutty all over her sorry butt. I'm terrified that she isn't coming home, and finding out that she wasn't serious about us really hurt."

"Hold on," her father said. "I know I haven't spent a lot of time with Faith, but from what I've seen, she's just as committed as you are."

"Then why would she just take this job?" Shawn yelled. "I'm not thrilled, but if it's what she wants, I would have given her my blessing. I just think that if you're serious about your relationship, your partner's feelings should be taken into consideration."

"True. You do know that I'm not the one you should be saying this to, don't you? Call her."

"Dad?"

"At the very least, wish her well," he said. "Speaking of which, she's going to be okay, isn't she?"

"I don't know." Shawn clung a little tighter to her father. "Trying to read Faith is like trying to see through a brick wall. And I try not to read her. I really don't want to invade her privacy."

"Call her," he insisted. "Tell her how you feel. Without screaming and shouting this time. You know I'm right."

"Fine, you big meanie." She sniffed and extracted herself from his embrace. Knowing that her father was right was no comfort. She went inside the house and made her way up to her childhood bedroom. She fought to calm her rapidly beating heart as she dug her cell phone out of her travel bag. She roamed around her bedroom, searching for a signal. When the bars finally appeared and she could make her call, she hit speed dial. Shawn knew that Faith had already left even before she heard the recording informing her that the number was no longer in service. "Damn it," she snarled, when a clear image of Faith boarding an airplane locked in her mind.

"Shawn?" Her mother peeked into the room. "I just talked to your dad. Have you reached Faith yet?"

"No. Her service has been disabled. I could call her parents, but she's left already."

"Are you sure?"

"Mom." Shawn cleared her throat. "This is me we're talking about. She hopped a plane this morning."

"So e-mail her. Mrs. Ruggeri's son is over there. She gets e-mail from him all the time."

"I will," Shawn said wearily. "Not today. I need to chill out first. If I don't, I'll say things that I shouldn't."

Four days later, Shawn was back in her apartment, finally writing the e-mail. She apologized for the things she had said and wished Faith all the best. She went on to explain why she had reacted so badly. She told Faith everything about her fears and why she was hurt. She ended by saying that she loved her, wished her nothing but the best, and if Faith was serious about the two of them, she'd be waiting. Holding her breath, she hit the send button. Her heart was still pounding in her chest when the e-mail bounced back. Apparently, Faith's phone service wasn't the only thing disconnected.

"You don't make things easy!" Shawn screamed.

A couple of weeks later, Shawn received the one and only letter Faith would send to her while overseas. It was nothing if not short and to the point.

I arrived safely. Can't tell you where I am. I hope you're well. I'm sorry things ended the way they did.

"Well, doesn't that just suck," Shawn snarled, ready to tear the letter to shreds. Instead, she slipped it back in the envelope and stored it in the top drawer of her bureau. She was tempted to write back saying everything she had expressed in the e-mail she had written, but she never worked up the nerve to do it. Granted, Faith had never been great at expressing herself, but her intentions had come through loud and clear.

Instead of wallowing in self-pity, Shawn packed a bag and headed off to her next assignment.

* * *

Shawn looked around, shivering slightly in an effort to fight off the early morning chill. She felt a sudden craving for coffee. She was confused about whether she was craving caffeine or her absent companion. She approached the crew gathered under a tarp in the middle of a field. She had dropped off and set up her equipment, and now that the rush to get ready was over, it hit her. This was the first time in over a year that she would be on her own. *This is going to be harder than I thought.*

Only a few weeks had passed since Faith had returned from running errands and announced that she was leaving the country. Shawn knew she overreacted when Faith dropped the bomb, and she had said things that could never be taken back. She was hurt, and she lashed out. Now, she was alone. "Williams," Sue Simpson, one of her colleagues, greeted her. "Ooh. You're looking rather glum. Where's that gorgeous groupie of yours?"

"Faith is on assignment," Shawn said absently.

"Wow." Sue shook her head. "I thought her days as a professional skeptic were over."

"Um..." Shawn hesitated. "Not a haunt. She's working for the network again. Doing coverage on the war."

"Overseas?" Sue inhaled sharply. "God, you must be worried."

"Yes," Shawn responded quietly, not wanting to elaborate that she was actually terrified. It wasn't simply Faith's well-being that concerned her. It was the thought that they had truly said good-bye.

"Pity that after Whispering Pines she wasn't hirable anymore," Sue said. "I have to confess, I miss working with her. Nothing like having Charles accusing me of being full of crap on camera to make things interesting."

"Not much work for a skeptic who has admitted on camera and in a book that she believes in ghosts," Shawn said, thinking that Whispering Pines had been the beginning and the end of their relationship. "It wasn't a friendly parting. I hate that I'm incapable of turning my keen insight on myself."

"I hear that." Sue smiled. "Would have saved me from my first husband."

"So, why are we here? Not that I'm not enjoying standing in the middle of a muddy field at the butt-crack of dawn," Shawn said, feeling completely miserable.

"Oxford Farms." Sue yawned. "Some spectacular pitting: three of us against three professional skeptics. Should be interesting."

"Who?" Shawn asked, sensing tension brewing. There was someone among the living that was troubling Sue. "Ah, Rose." She shook her head. Rose Schumacher, like herself and Sue, was a professional psychic. And like Sue, Shawn didn't enjoy working with her. Everyone had some degree of intuition. Some, like Rose, claimed to be much more gifted than they were. It made working with her a very trying experience. "Do I even want to know who the naysayers are?"

"Rossi, McKenna, and York."

"What is this, a battle of ghosts or the battle of the sexes?" Shawn found herself laughing. "The boys are always a lot of fun during the downtime."

"Yeah. Pity Rose is such a pain in the butt."

"Okay." Ronald Sinclair, the director, drew everyone's attention. "Welcome to Oxford Farm," he said, "unoccupied at the moment, and possibly haunted. The new owners have given us three days to run amok. We'll be divided into three teams. Tape, photograph, and film everything that happens or doesn't happen.

"Even though this is a big place with the fields, the barn, and the old house, there's a chance you'll be running into one another. Team one has priority, team two is second, and team three is last in the pecking order. Each team will have one sensitive, one skeptic, one cameraperson, one sound person, one assistant director, and so on. Play nice, and for the love of my career, get something the brass will wet themselves over.

"First team: Williams, York, Briscoe, Fox, Lennox, Myers, and Silver." He read off the rest of the teams and allowed everyone to meet before insisting that they get started. Shawn noticed the way Rose seemed to be slighted by being selected for the last team.

"Shawn, your team is the lead. Where do you want to start?" Ronald asked.

"The house." Shawn yawned and poured herself a cup of coffee. "Might as well be warm. I'd like to go back there tonight if I feel anything interesting."

"I love being on your team," Len York said eagerly.

Shawn and her crew went about setting up in the main house. It was a two-story structure dating back to the 1600s. Attempts to preserve the crumbling building had come too late. *I suppose you don't care one way or the other, so long as people stay away,* she mentally addressed the dark figure lurking by the fireplace.

"Get out!" the dark figure whispered.

How original. Shawn scowled and rolled her eyes.

"Get out," it repeated.

And redundant, to boot. Shawn glared at the figure dressed in a long black coat and a three-corner hat.

"They're trying to fix this place up," York commented absently just as the camera began to film them.

"Losing battle, I'm afraid." Shawn sighed wearily.

"I agree, it's going to take more than a coat of paint to restore this heap," York muttered while he looked around.

"He doesn't care for your assessment." Shawn snickered, catching the dark figure hissing once again.

"Who?" York laughed.

"Gideon," the specter snarled.

"Gideon," Shawn repeated. "He's lurking next to the hearth. He doesn't like strangers. This is his home, always will be."

"Right." York moved towards the fireplace and waved his arms about. "Nothing." He spun about, gloating as he faced Shawn.

Her eyes widened slightly as she watched Gideon raising a gnarled walking stick. "No need to do that," she cautioned Gideon aloud.

"Do what?" York sighed dramatically. "Dr. Williams, I do believe that you're toying with me." He gave a sharp yelp when Gideon struck him soundly on the shoulder.

"I know I shouldn't laugh, but that just tickles me every time," Shawn said.

"I'm beginning to think people should collect combat pay for working with you." York rubbed his shoulder.

Shawn scrubbed at her eyes. York's off-the-cuff comment had hit a little too close to home. "I'm going upstairs." She stomped off and York followed. She ignored his questions as she went about opening her senses and trying to get a feel for the area.

"Anything going to hit me?" he asked.

"No," Shawn replied curtly as she felt her way around the upstairs. "Lots of residual energy, but no ghosts. Gideon doesn't like to share his home. Big bully that he is, he has a nasty habit of chasing off anything that tries to linger. Still, even he can't stop residual energy."

"What exactly is residual energy?" Rory Fox, one of the assistant directors, cued her.

"The remnants of an event, or emotions that linger long after the event or feelings have passed on," Shawn said. "It's like watching film that's playing in a loop. It starts, plays itself out, then starts all over again."

"What's playing here?" Fox once again prompted her. He had asked her the very same question on at least a dozen shoots.

"There's a little girl," Shawn related what she was seeing. "She's right there by the window, sewing. She's rocking back and forth, humming the same tune over and over again. I think she's challenged, possibly autistic. I can't be certain. I don't feel what she feels. I do get a sense that this is all she knows. Sewing the same pattern over and over while humming the same nursery rhyme."

York scoffed at Shawn's assessment, but Shawn ignored his snotty attitude. They each took turns searching about and offering commentary on what they discovered. Shawn tried to relax. Faith's absence was wearing on her. They were preparing to move to the field when Rory's walkie-talkie chimed. Apparently, there was a problem back at the barn. Something to do with Sue wanting to smack Rose around.

"This should be fun," Shawn groaned as they headed towards the barn.

"Hey," York said, "once we wrap for the night, a bunch of us are heading to this little tavern in town. Interested in joining the party?"

"Yeah." Shawn nodded.

She stumbled when she entered the barn and discovered what the problem was. "Are you a fucking idiot?" she screeched, stunning everyone with her harsh tone and unusual vocabulary.

"Um, Dr. Williams," Ron said, "I'd really like your input, but please remember we aren't airing this on Showtime."

"Sorry." Shawn rolled her shoulders in an effort to wash away the tension. "Rose, you do know that you're playing with something dangerous, don't you?"

"I find the Ouija an invaluable tool," Rose said, waving her hand over the board.

"Don't you folks use these things?" York was clearly confused.

"Not all of us," Sue said. "A good old-fashioned séance, if done correctly, isn't a problem. Those things, on the other hand, aren't true séances."

"There are two schools of thought when it comes to the Ouija," Shawn said. "Some mediums, like Rose, believe it's a valuable tool in reaching the other side. Others, such as Sue and I, think it's an invitation for trouble. The Ouija opens a vortex, inviting all comers. You never know who's going to show up, and it's realistic to say that most of the spirits who enter that vortex aren't who they claim to be.

"Case in point, many years ago a bunch of college students decided it would be fun to take a Ouija board to the oldest graveyard in town. It was late, and they thought it was nothing but a lark. They clowned around with the board for a while before heading back to their quiet apartment. From that night on, nothing was quiet in their home. Chairs turned over, the telephone dialed itself, and no matter how many times they locked them away, there was always a deck of cards spread out on the kitchen table, the ace of spades always turned over. Those were just a few of the things they endured for over two years."

"They stayed?" York's eyes were wide.

"They were students, and the rent was cheap." Shawn shrugged. "Using a Ouija is similar to going to a maximum security prison, having all the cell doors opened, then parading in front of them naked, inviting all comers. You never know what you'll get, and chances are you'll never get rid of it. Sometimes even moving doesn't stop whatever is chasing you.

"Personally, I feel that the best place for a Ouija board is in a fire pit. The bummer is, if you burn it after you use it, you're leaving the vortex wide open. So if we're voting on this, I cast a resounding no."

"I don't think you're being reasonable," Rose huffed.

"Hey, my life sucks enough right now," Shawn snarled. "I'm really not in the mood to have something dark and dangerous following me back to the city."

* * *

The shoot at Oxford Farms turned into an exercise in patience for everyone involved. The cast and crew failed to visit the tavern until they wrapped the project. "Doubles for everyone," Fox offered when they entered the barroom that evening.

"Thank you, kind sir," York eagerly accepted. Once everyone had settled in, he raised his glass in a toast. "Pity Rose couldn't join us. Honestly, that girl is a problem. I don't mind going around about with Shawn or Sue. They will at least admit when there's nothing amiss."

"Wish I could say the same about you." Shawn laughed and downed her glass of wine while waving for another round.

"I think we've all learned a valuable lesson from Ms. Charles," Sal Rossi said. "Saying that you've seen something that can't be explained by science is career suicide. Where is she, by the way?"

"Shh." Sue tried to caution him.

"Ah, is that what has your knickers in a twist?" York sighed. "I'm sorry, Shawn. I thought the two of you were still in the happy, sappy stage."

"She got a job overseas." Shawn tried to sound casual. "Come on, guys, next round is on me." More drinks arrived, followed quickly by another round. "Don't peek," Shawn said to Sue, who was giving her a thoughtful look. "Professional courtesy."

"I'm sorry. It's just that—"

"Don't," Shawn warned, half-tempted to just let Sue have her say.

"Fine," Sue said. "Nice bracelet by the way."

Shawn curled her lips while tucking the silver bracelet back under her sleeve. "I said, don't." Shawn narrowed her gaze. "Or I'll be forced to return the favor."

Rory laughed. "I love it when psychics get drunk. The last time, you scared the piss out of the bartender."

"That's right." Sue chuckled. "After he found out we were in town, Shawn shook his hand and screamed 'Oh, my God!' I almost peed myself laughing at his reaction. By the way, Shawn, I'll gladly give you a peek if you just let me say what I need to say. You know how it is. You get a message, and no matter how hard you try not to, you need to pass it on."

"She's—" Shawn blanched.

"No, she's not on the other side," Sue quickly reassured her. "Faith is fine. She'll be back a little shell-shocked, but in one piece, I swear. What I need to tell you is, she didn't know it was wrong."

"What was wrong?" Shawn sighed and waved her glass for another drink. Normally, she didn't drink that much. But tonight she was desperate to self-medicate.

"The way she handled things," Sue said. "She didn't know it was wrong. I know, little comfort and doesn't make sense. That's the message."

"From whom?" Shawn tried to get a bead on things. A slightly difficult task, since she was already loaded.

"Your mother," Sue said, after apparently giving it some thought.

"My mother is alive," Shawn groaned while the three skeptics snickered. "Sorry, Sue, but she is."

"Not this mother," Sue tried to clarify. "Why do you have two mothers?"

"Are your parents gay as well?" York asked.

"No." Shawn rolled her eyes. "Does no one read my books?"

"Wait, I've read your books," Larry Briscoe chimed in. "You briefly mentioned in your first book that you're adopted. So, in a way, you do have two mothers."

"Brilliant." York beamed. "Do me next."

"I love you skeptics," Shawn groused. "You deny and deny that what we do is possible until you want to know something. I'm doing Sue first."

"Even better." Rossi grinned.

"Pig." Shawn reached out for Sue. "Okay, SueBee, you know the drill. Give me your hand." She took a calming breath once she clasped Sue's hand and then closed her eyes. "Geez, you're so boring," she said after receiving only quick flashes. A soft heartbeat was echoing in her mind. The only image she could see clearly was Sue playing with her drink.

"Hate to disappoint." Sue laughed.

"Hold it." Shawn shivered slightly. Flashes whizzed through her mind along with the faint sounds of mingled voices. The image of the drink worried Shawn as the sound of the tiny heartbeat suddenly became louder. "Stop drinking." She snapped her eyes open.

"Okay." Sue put down her glass. "I've been sticking to ginger ale, if that's important."

"It is." Shawn's face lit up. "Congratulations. You were right, that test you took was defective. I suggest you pay a visit to your doctor, because you, my dear, are pregnant."

"Are you sure?" Sue asked eagerly.

"Yes. Do you want to know the sex?"

"Yes. No! I have to call Ted." She ducked out of the tavern.

"Happy news indeed." York offered his hand to Shawn.

"I think you just want to hold my hand," Shawn teased him. Her smile quickly vanished. "Oh." She frowned and released his hand. The image she had received hit her like a tidal wave. There was no mixing or scattered imagery. The vision was crystal clear, and it spelled bad news for York. "Your wife knows, and she's going to rake you over the coals in court."

"Whatever do you mean?" he asked in a squeaky voice.

"Vanessa," she spelled out for him, watching his face turn ashen. "She knows about Vanessa, your assistant. And you'll be lucky to walk away from the divorce with your jockey shorts."

"Good Lord, I hope you're yanking my chain."

"Sorry, but it's your own fault." She wagged her finger at him. "Well, after that happy little tidbit, does anyone else want a reading?"

"I do." Rossi offered his hand.

"No need, I can read you from here." Shawn smiled. "Call your parents."

"Why?"

"Just call them. It's important."

The rest of the group were all clamoring for some insight. Shawn was happy to oblige. Dealing with other people's lives was a lot easier than dealing with her own. Doing so many readings at once, plus her intoxicated condition, left Shawn completely spent.

Chapter 8

Evansville, Indiana
November 2004

"Welcome to the Midwest, Williams," the droll voice greeted Shawn when she entered the cozy, albeit small, hotel room that had been assigned to her.

"You're way too chipper, Wu." Shawn returned the greeting with a slight scowl. She hadn't meant to sound so harsh. She just found it increasingly harder to smile. For some reason, performing her job for the past year seemed far more arduous than it had ever been.

"Shawn?" Farrah Wu gaped at her. Shawn always found the tiny Asian woman's first name amusing. Apparently, Farrah's father had been a huge *Charlie's Angels* fan. Farrah was still looking at her with concern as she stepped over and helped Shawn with her luggage. "You've got some heavy vibes coming off you," Farrah said with concern.

"Sorry," Shawn quickly apologized. "I don't know what's with me lately. Except some personal stuff."

"Ah, woman trouble. Affairs of the heart can suck the life out of you. I always thought you gals would have an easier time of it."

"Trust me," Shawn said. "Women are just as difficult to understand as men. In case you were thinking of hopping the fence."

"Me?" Farrah giggled. "Sorry, I have a thing for hairy chests."

"Thanks for the image."

"My pleasure," Farrah said with a grin. "No, that's not it. Not all of it."

Shawn didn't need to ask. She understood that Farrah had picked up on something other than Shawn's troubled love life. "I hate bunking with my own kind."

"I know. Two sensitives in the same room." Farrah sighed in agreement. "I don't think Jerry's got a roomie."

"Steiner's back on board?" Shawn was pleased. Jerry was one of the few skeptics she really enjoyed working with.

"I love working with him, too," Farrah responded to Shawn's unspoken thoughts. "Jerry and I started out together. Problem is, over the years, he's not as skeptical as he used to be. The suits don't like that."

"I've noticed," Shawn grunted while she unpacked.

"Right. The brass gave your favorite naysayer the boot a few months back, didn't they? Charles could always be a bit brisk, but off camera, she was a whole lot of fun." Instead of answering, Shawn blushed. "So, the rumors are true." Farrah squealed like a schoolgirl. "My, my, my, you are a naughty girl."

"Not anymore," Shawn said. "She's overseas. New subject, please."

"Spoilsport." Farrah pouted. "Fine, we can talk about those dark circles under your eyes, which aren't only from Faith's impromptu departure. You're feeling more. Aren't you?"

"For just over a year now." Shawn turned to her. "My gift was always strong. Lately, it's been overpowering. Physically, it's become unbearable."

"Happened to me a few years ago," Farrah said. "Back-to-back gigs in very hyperactive places. You've opened another door. Makes your gift stronger. It will take time before your body catches up."

"But it does catch up?" Shawn asked hopefully.

"Mine did."

"Good to know." Shawn felt a mild sense of relief. "Ever since that shoot on Halloween last year, I've been a mess. Talk about overactive spots."

"And since then, you've bounced from one hot spot to the next," Farrah said. "The dead just won't shut up will they?"

"Not just the dead. The living are coming in loud and clear. Used to be, I'd get a blurb here or there. Now, almost everyone is readable to me. Is that what happened to you?"

"Pretty much," Farrah said. "The good news is, this shoot should be a cakewalk. The library is supposed to be active but not malevolent."

"Good. I've about had my fill of bitter spirits. Living or dead. A nice, mildly haunted library is just what I need right now."

* * *

The talent and crew gathered at the Willard Library. Shawn felt at ease while the crew went about laying cables and setting up the required lighting. "What a beautiful building," she said.

"It is," Jerry agreed. "Have you met Claire yet?"

"Your partner in crime?" Shawn glanced over at the demure woman lingering in the background. "Althea told me she's the next Faith Charles."

"Bet you had an interesting comment about that," Farrah said with a light laugh.

"I just told her there was nothing wrong with the old Faith Charles," Shawn said wryly. "Have either of you worked with her before?"

"No," Jerry replied. "She's new to the dog and pony show."

"I've read her books," Farrah said with a slight grimace. "She's one of those who think that all sensitives are a bunch of greedy fakers."

Shawn cringed. "Oh, this is going to be fun."

"If I could have the talent over here," Althea commanded. "Dr. Williams, Dr. Steiner, Dr. Wu, and Dr. Marin, this is Randy Hiller. He'll be your tour guide."

"Welcome, ladies and Dr. Steiner," Randy greeted the ensemble once the cameras began rolling. The group responded in kind. "The Willard Library was built in 1885 from a grant by the eccentric philanthropist Willard Carpenter. It's the oldest public library in the state. Mr. Carpenter insisted that, and I quote, 'the library was to be a public library for the use of the people of all classes, races, and sexes free of charge forever.'"

"Why his first name?" Shawn asked softly.

"I'm getting that, too," Farrah said. "I think 'eccentric' was putting it lightly."

Claire grunted loudly, and the other two women grimaced.

"The building is Victorian Gothic, designed by James and Merritt Reid," Randy continued, appearing unflustered by the obvious tension growing between the women.

"Impressive," Jerry said. "I understand that beyond the large collections of books and architecture, there's another." Shawn watched carefully as Jerry prompted the tour guide. Suddenly she understood the need for a second skeptic. This time around, Jerry's role was to be more of a host rather than to be the resident naysayer.

"Over the years, there have been many reports from the staff and visitors of strange happenings," Randy said. "Most of the sightings have centered around the Lady in Grey."

"When did they start?" Shawn asked, her curiosity piqued. Like most shoots, neither she nor Farrah had researched the location.

"The first sighting was in 1937," Randy said, while guiding the group farther into the library. "On a cold, snowy night, at about three in the morning, the janitor came to shovel coal into the furnace, which is located in the basement. Wary of uninvited visitors, he was armed with a gun and a flashlight. He made his way down to the unlit basement.

"When he neared the furnace, he dropped the flashlight, frozen with fear. Standing before him was a veiled lady dressed in a glowing grey dress. When he could finally move, he bent down to pick up the flashlight. That's when he noticed that even her shoes were gray. Then, just as suddenly as she appeared, she vanished. Since that night, the Lady in Grey has been seen numerous times. Each time, she appears suddenly before vanishing into thin air.

"Also, here on the second floor in this washroom, the water faucet mysteriously turned on once while an employee was in the room. Others have reported a strong scent of perfume. In the children's room there have been reports of books flying off the shelves."

"She's angry," Shawn said, shaking off an uneasy feeling. "She's convinced that she was denied what was hers."

"Who?" Jerry asked while Claire released an audible tsk.

"Lori, Lois." Shawn fumbled for the name of the presence she felt looming around her. "Louise," she said.

"Her father was unbalanced," Farrah added.

"Oh, yeah," Shawn agreed. "She's got issues with Daddy, all right. Mostly financial issues."

"That's correct," Randy confirmed, earning more grunts from Claire. "Louise Carpenter, the daughter of Willard Carpenter, the library's founder, went so far as to sue the Board of Trustees. She claimed that her father wasn't in his right mind and was unduly influenced into funding the library. She lost her lawsuit. It was after her death that the sightings of the Lady in Grey began."

"And these appearances haven't hurt business," Claire interjected snidely.

"It's a public library," Shawn said. "That wouldn't be Louise, would it?" She pointed to a black-and-white photo of a portly older woman that was hanging on the wall.

"She looks like the life of the party," Jerry said.

"Cut," Althea called out.

"Sorry," Jerry said.

"Don't worry," Althea said. "We'll fix it in editing. We have a lot of territory to cover. We need to split you guys up. Dr. Wu and Dr. Steiner will be one team. Dr. Williams and Dr. Marin will be the other. Farrah, upstairs or down?"

"I want to start in the basement," Farrah answered. "That's where the first sighting was."

"That means you can start at the top," Althea told Shawn.

"My favorite position," Shawn quipped, surprised when Claire actually cracked a smile.

Shawn gathered up her equipment and followed the crew. "I love this staircase," Shawn noted with appreciation. "So, Claire, are you enjoying working for the camera?"

"Definitely different. Normally, it's just me and my computer. I do go on location, but again, it's usually just me."

"I get it," Shawn said. "You travel to haunted places and use scientific means to explain what's happening. I can respect that. Out of curiosity, haven't you ever come across anything you couldn't explain?"

"Never."

"Never?"

"No, never." Claire's voice was dry and unwavering. "Take this Lady in Grey. Honestly, it's so simple. People see the picture after hearing the stories. Then they see her."

"Really?" The hair on the back of Shawn's neck prickled, and she smirked. "This should be interesting. Carl, can we set up in this room?"

The room was small, elegant, and filled with books. The smell of vintage books greeted Shawn as she entered after Carl and the crew had set up. "Very warm." Shawn noticed a shadow passing by the rows of books.

"What was that?" Jasper asked from behind his camera. "Shawn, was that a—"

"Lights from passing cars," Claire quickly said, waving towards the window.

"Shawn?" Jasper seemed to be pouting. The poor boy had been extremely eager to find specters after his experience at Whispering Pines.

"Claire's right," Shawn said. "Nothing but traffic. Of course, you might want to turn the camera over there. Just left of the window." She couldn't help gloating as the crew gasped at the mist swirling away from the outside lights. "Claire, if I'm not mistaken, the mist seems to be taking the shape of a person."

"Nonsense," Claire said. "It's just dust or steam from the heating system."

"Then why is it so cold in here?" Shawn said.

All eyes turned to Claire, who suddenly appeared to be very uncomfortable. "I'll get back to you on that," she finally said. Shawn just smiled while taking pictures with her digital camera.

The following night, Farrah and Shawn were splitting a bottle of Bailey's while reviewing their separate experiences. "You were right. This is a nice, relaxing gig," Shawn said. "Claire's okay. Won't budge an inch, but okay just the same."

"What about when that book flew off the shelf in the children's room?" Farrah asked.

"According to the eminent Dr. Marin, it fell." Shawn chuckled while reaching for the ice bucket. "Damn, we need more ice."

"I'll go."

"No, you went last time. My turn." Shawn snatched up the ice bucket. She hummed as she made her way to the ice machine. She was still humming when she scooped out the ice. Suddenly, a searing pain blinded her. The bucket crashed to the floor, and its contents spilled noisily. Shawn reached out in an effort to steady herself. When her knees slammed against the floor, she knew she had failed.

Horrific images kept bombarding her until she realized that she was back in her room. "Shawn?" She heard Farrah's voice.

"Did you see it?" Shawn cleared her throat and rubbed her throbbing temple. She groaned when she spied Claire and Jerry looming over her.

"Yes," Farrah said. "When I found you. The desk clerk said it happened about five years ago. They caught the guy."

"I know," Shawn whimpered, the pain still pulsating. "It was her husband. She came here after running away. He found her. This gets better, right?" she asked Farrah in a pleading tone.

"It does." Farrah patted her gently on her shoulder.

Chapter 9

Faith stormed into the tent, almost ripping the flap off, and stomped past her cameraman. Her temper was worsening, along with the desert heat. "I'm telling you, Todd, if that knucklehead walks in here and asks me if it's hot enough," she barked, "I'm gonna bitch-slap that little wiener. We're in the middle of a freaking desert. What's he expecting, a sudden snow squall?"

"Always the charmer, Charlie," Todd said. "Maybe if you'd calm down and get out of that crappy mood, you wouldn't feel so overheated."

"Am I wrong?" Faith snapped. "Why, for fuck's sake, did they stick all of us together?"

"Can't argue with that," Todd said. "Corralling the press in a bunch of tents and not letting them wander around had disaster written all over it."

"I blame Geraldo," Faith said, flopping down on her cot. "What was he thinking? Now the military won't let us out of their sight."

"Hot enough for you?" Wyatt merrily asked as he sauntered in.

"That's it," Faith growled. "You're a dead man."

"Charlie," Todd cautioned.

"Yes?" She glared over at him.

"Hells bells, woman." Wyatt waved at her. "You were always wound a little tight. A little crude, not to mention crass, at times. But you're a newsman, it's expected. However, during our internment you've made me miss my mother. I had her committed after she started strolling around Safeway wearing nothing but a pair of flip-flops and a smile."

"Someone give me a gun," Faith said coldly.

"Damn it, Charlie!" Todd slapped his fist on his thigh. "You're starting to scare me. Can you explain to me why you opted for more time here? You don't have the same passion for this that you once had. I thought you had a girl waiting for you back home. That's what you keep saying."

"I'm the one waiting," Faith muttered. "She's... Hell, I don't know what she's doing. We were kind of at odds when I left."

"So," Todd said carefully, "in your infinite wisdom, you decided to hide here? I can think of better places to hide. Hawaii comes to mind. Hell, sitting on my grandma's porch back in Indiana sounds better than this."

"Yo, Todd," Faith snarled. "Did you come all this way to take pictures or hand out love advice? 'Dear Abby' you ain't. It's bad enough my hands are tied here. Now, I've got you and knucklehead here telling me I'm cranky."

As the words spewed out, Faith felt the venom behind them. The boys were right. She had been a bitch on wheels since she arrived. True, it wasn't out of character for her, but this time was a lot worse. In the past it had been born out of frustration, from the situation, or the limitations put on her by the still ever-present old boys network.

Breaking up with some girl had never affected her this way. Then again, she wasn't entirely certain she and Shawn had broken up. And Shawn wasn't just some girl. For the first time in her adult life, Faith had fallen hard. She still didn't understand why Shawn had reacted the way she had.

The most frustrating part was that for at least a few more months, she could do absolutely nothing about it. She was stuck in the middle of a war, becoming close to young men and women who might be dead before the sun set. Again, not a new experience for a seasoned reporter. Yet, this time around, it tore at her. She no longer possessed the steely reserve she needed to do her job.

"I don't belong here anymore," she ruefully confessed.

"No, you don't, Charlie," Todd said sadly.

"And I'm stuck here for at least another seven months. Time to pull my head out of my ass." She was determined to get her edge back. Her life of crawling around creaky old houses with Shawn was over.

"Have you talked to this girl since you've been here?" Wyatt asked.

"No," Faith said reluctantly. "What would I say? I still don't understand why she flipped out."

"Ask her." Todd stated the obvious.

"Sure thing." Faith scowled. "I'll just drop an e-mail asking why she freaked out about this job. Very romantic."

"Wait," Todd said. "She got pissed at you because you took a job? That doesn't sound right."

"I don't get it either." Faith shrugged, not realizing that was part of the problem. She just didn't understand. Each time she thought of writing Shawn, she was at a loss as to what to say. Should she apologize? And if she did, just what was she was supposed to apologize for?

She spent many nights sitting in front of a computer, trying to work up the right words, before she had an inkling of what had upset Shawn. By then, Faith had been gone for over two years and felt there was nothing she could say.

When, finally, she was about to go home, she felt she needed to get Shawn back. She was completely clueless as to how she could make that happen.

Chapter 10

Stewart, Massachusetts
1912

In many ways, my sister-in-law seems to be a kindred spirit, Anna thought happily as she brushed out her hair before preparing to retire. Catherine seemed just as disgusted and distrusting of the captain as Anna was. Each time Horatio spoke during the evening meal, Catherine seemed to restrain herself from speaking her mind.

When the two women had retreated to the kitchen to clean up the dinner dishes, Anna's suspicions were confirmed. Catherine admitted that she was fighting an internal battle to refrain from informing her older brother that he was nothing more than a pompous, bullying, blowhard.

The only regret Anna possessed regarding her newfound friend was that Catherine would probably grow weary of the captain's bullying and simply leave. Anna sighed heavily, already regretting the day Catherine would leave her. Neither Catherine nor the captain were in good spirits after Mr. Van de Meer left. Anna feared the worst.

She placed her brush down on the bed and went to the door. She was careful when she opened it, hoping not to awaken the captain. The last thing she wanted was one of his late-night visits. She listened carefully to ensure that he wasn't wandering about. When she heard nothing except the wind, she stepped softly out of her room and closed the door quietly behind her.

She crept along the hallway and up the staircase to the third floor. Her heart fluttered as she timidly raised her hand and tapped on the door. She trembled slightly when the door opened a crack. Her heart leapt when Catherine's warm smile captured her.

"Good evening, Sister," she said shyly and lowered her gaze as Catherine continued to smile at her.

"Good evening, Sister," Catherine responded warmly, her voice caressing the nervous Anna's fragile heart.

"I just wanted to see if you were settled in for the evening," Anna said, feeling suddenly silly for her late-hour visit. "Is there anything you need?"

Anna timidly looked up at her sister-in-law when she failed to respond. She could have sworn that Catherine was blushing. Anna brushed aside the foolish notion, rationalizing that it must have been the dim lighting playing tricks on her.

"I'm fine, thank you," Catherine responded softly.

"Well then, I bid you a good night and sleep well." Anna felt oddly reluctant to leave.

"Sleep well." Catherine leaned down and lightly brushed her lips against Anna's cheek.

Anna released a small gasp when Catherine's body brushed against her own. She felt flushed, and her skin burned where Catherine's lips had touched her. "Good night," Anna said before fleeing from Catherine's gaze. A wash of confusion and heat coursed through her body as she quickly retreated back towards her own bedroom.

"What are you doing out of your room?" Horatio blocked her bedroom door. She trembled beneath his cold, glaring look. "Well?"

"I was just checking on Sister," she said, her gaze downcast.

"Leave her be," he said in a nasty tone. "I wish to be rid of her as soon as possible." He grabbed Anna roughly by her arm. "I have need of you tonight." He closed her bedroom door behind them.

Anna felt sick as she removed her nightgown and climbed into her bed. She reclined and waited for him with her eyes closed. She waited to hear the bed creak as he joined her. She said a silent prayer that he would be quick about his duties and leave. She never understood why he still demanded her services, since he seemed extremely displeased with her.

Catherine seemed distant the following morning as they prepared the morning meal. "The servants leave every day at dusk and don't return until after the morning meal?" Catherine finally inquired while Anna went about preparing her husband's breakfast.

"Yes." Anna smiled, happy to finally hear her sister-in-law's voice.

"Always?" Catherine asked, still not looking at Anna. "Even when he's away?"

"Yes," Anna answered, not understanding why Catherine refused to look at her. All Anna could think about last night was the chaste kiss Catherine had placed on her cheek. There had been something in Catherine's touch that held her captive even as the captain was making his feeble attempt in her bed.

Silence reigned once again as they continued preparing the meal. "Have I done something to offend you, Sister?" Anna finally asked, weary of the silence that was strangling her.

"No," Cathcrine said flatly, her gaze meeting Anna's for a brief moment.

Anna cringed when she caught the accusing look in Catherine's eyes before she looked away. "He's my husband." Anna felt suddenly betrayed.

"I understand," Catherine muttered in a weak voice.

"Do you?" Anna asked harshly.

"Yes." Catherine sighed and looked deeply into Anna eyes with a gaze that seemed filled with sadness and regret.

"Don't pity me," Anna said coldly and then turned away, her arms filled with plates of food.

"I don't." She heard Catherine's weak sob from behind her.

Later that day, Anna still felt the anger linger as she tried to distract herself by working in her garden. She felt her skin prickle when a shadow was cast over her. She didn't need to turn or look up to know that Catherine was standing above her.

"I'm sorry, Sister," Catherine said tenderly.

Anna ignored her and focused on her precious flowers.

"I forget my place. It was wrong of me to say or imply anything," Catherine said. Anna could feel the anger and tension slipping away as she was lulled by the soothing sound of Catherine's voice. "I just cannot abide the way he treats you."

"Nor can I, but I have no choice." Anna finally lifted her gaze to look up at Catherine, who was peering nervously down at her. She shielded her eyes so she could see Catherine more clearly. "I can't even vote."

"There are places where you could," Catherine said in a conspiratorial whisper as she knelt down beside Anna. Anna smiled at Catherine's sudden playful attitude.

"So you wish to whisk me away to California?" Anna played along.

"If I could," Catherine said in a suddenly serious tone.

Anna was taken aback by the strange sense of warmth that spread through her body from Catherine's simple jest. Catherine looked around nervously, and Anna wondered if she was teasing her.

"You could divorce," Catherine suggested in a hushed tone.

Anna clutched her bosom when a wave of panic rushed through her. "And then what?" she asked fearfully as she looked around to ensure that there was no one nearby who would hear their conversation and go running to her husband. "Lose my son? My home? I'm without an education or a penny to my name. My family won't take me in, since it was my father who sold me to your brother."

"But you've thought about it?"

"Yes, I've considered fleeing with my child," Anna confessed. "Taking Richard and running off one night while the captain's away at sea. Never to look back, and to be truly free for the first time in my life. Yes, dear Sister, I've thought about it every day since the moment the captain placed this cursed band on my finger." Anna was almost shouting as she held up her hand and showed Catherine the simple gold wedding band that to her signified her enslavement. She calmed herself before she continued. "As I've said, I would have nowhere to go. And do you think that the captain would simply allow me to leave?"

"No. My brother's very careful when it comes to his possessions," Catherine said bitterly. "He would never allow you to leave or free his heir from his grasp."

"No, he wouldn't," Anna said in a defeated tone. "I doubt that he cares for either of us, but it would wound his pride. He would never allow us to be free."

Anna felt a warm tingling when Catherine brushed her fingers across her cheek. "I wish I could bring light to your eyes," Catherine said sadly. Her fingers lingered on Anna's face.

"And I to yours," Anna replied softly, covering Catherine's hand with her own. They sat there, each unwilling to move as they stared deeply into one another's eyes. Anna was experiencing the strangest sensation of excitement as she leaned into Catherine's touch.

Chapter 11

New York City
Spring 2005

Every inch of Faith Charles's body ached. *It's good to be home,* she thought as she looked down the bustling New York City sidewalk. *Now I just need to find out if I'm still welcome.* She sighed as the last conversation she had with Shawn replayed in her mind. *What was I supposed to do?* Faith shouldered her bag and headed towards the hotel she would be staying in while she tried to track down the quirky little ghost hunter.

"Salvation," she said with smile as she neared the hotel. Visions of a hot bath and a comfortable bed filled her weary mind.

"Ms. Charles?" a voice called out to her just as the doorman was opening the door for her.

Faith turned and saw a dark-haired woman approaching. "Yes."

"Faith Charles?" the brunette asked her eagerly.

"Are you with the network?" Faith asked.

"No."

"You don't have a summons, do you?"

"No." The woman smiled. "I'm not a process server."

"Stalker?"

"No, Ms. Charles." The woman chuckled. "As charming as you probably think you are, you aren't my type."

"Well, what do you want?" Faith was eager to end the conversation and check into the hotel.

"My name is Delia St. James."

"And?"

"I'm one of the owners of Whispering Pines, and I'd like to talk to you," Delia said. Faith trembled with fear.

Chapter 12

Stewart, Massachusetts
1912

"What a glorious day," Catherine sighed happily, linking her arm in Anna's.

"Hard to believe we'll soon have snow," Anna said. "And with the snow, my son will be returning. Richard will be home soon. I'm counting the days."

"We could—" Catherine began to say when they entered the small shop.

"Hush," Anna cut her off. "Husband owns most of the town. Many will do anything to be in his good graces," she said in a quiet voice.

"My dear brother," Catherine sneered, looking like the words tasted foul.

"I know what you were suggesting," Anna said while she perused the bolts of fabric. "As I said before, he won't allow us to go quietly. The risk of his wrath is far too dangerous."

"There must be a way." Catherine appeared desperate to find the solution.

"If there is, I'm unaware of what it could be." Anna's shoulders slumped in defeat.

Chapter 13

New York City
May 2005

"Just how does one acquire a white elephant like Whispering Pines?" Faith yawned as she stirred her coffee. They had been sitting for almost half an hour in the small coffee shop she had allowed Delia to drag her to, and the woman still hadn't explained what it was she wanted.

"The old-fashioned way. I inherited it," Delia said with a sad smile.

"Lucky you."

"White elephant is an apt description," Delia continued. "Ownership of Whispering Pines is a huge responsibility that sucks you in. You can't tear it down or sell it. Despite the trust my grandfather set up, renovating it has proven to be impossible over the years."

"Hard to find good help?" Faith quipped.

"To say the least." Delia sighed. "The noises, the apparitions, the garden in the back blooming overnight, and one out of every ten workmen running from the kitchen in a blind panic, aren't helpful."

"So you know?"

"Yes. We've always known about the kitchen," Delia said. "It can be unpleasant for anyone, but if you're batting for the wrong team it can be dangerous. My poor Uncle George was never the same after his one and only visit to Whispering Pines."

"Uncle George a bit light in the loafers, is he?" Faith teased with a knowing smirk. "So hire a straight crew."

"First of all, my grandfather was very big on gay rights even before homosexuals called themselves gay. Tolerance and working for change is a lesson he passed on to his children, and they passed it on to us," Delia said. "Second, how do you know if someone is in the closet, or in denial? That kitchen is the best gaydar on the planet."

"Oh, so Grandpa was light in the loafers as well." Faith yawned.

"No, his mother."

"Your grandfather was Richard Stratton? That poor man. Wait, you know about Anna and Catherine?"

"Yes," Delia replied. "It wasn't a secret. I don't know how my grandfather found out, but he knew that his mother and aunt died because of the love their shared. At least, that's the way it's always been explained to us. How did you know?"

"I was there," Faith said. "Shawn, I mean, Dr. Williams, saw them together. And I could feel how they cared for one another."

"And that's why I've been looking for you," Delia said. "In the history of Whispering Pines, only six people have ever spent the night in that house. The captain, Anna, Catherine, my grandfather, and after the captain's death, you and Dr. Williams are the only others who have been able to sleep there."

"Trust me, I didn't sleep much." The memory of her visit played out in Faith's head. She felt the blush rising to her cheeks as she recalled how she and Shawn made love together for the first time.

"Ms. Charles, I'm straight and I've never lasted more than an hour in that house," Delia said. "Whispering Pines has a secret that you and Dr. Williams finally revealed. Despite what my grandfather knew, he was never completely certain that the captain murdered them."

"Oh, yes, he did. Dr. Williams saw the whole thing." Faith blanched. "So, what do you want from me?"

"As I said, ownership of Whispering Pines is a huge responsibility. And part of that responsibility includes finding and putting Anna and Catherine to rest. What I want, what I'm asking for, is that you and Dr. Williams return to Whispering Pines.

"Not a chance in hell," Faith said flatly.

"Please, hear me out."

"No. You don't need me. I'll be honest. I'd love to bring peace to Anna and Catherine. Their fate has troubled me since the day I left that house. But I'm not in any hurry to go back. Dr. Williams is the one who connected with them, and let me tell you, she isn't in any hurry to walk back into that house, either."

"Yeah, she pretty much said the same thing," Delia reluctantly admitted. "Only she added not for a million dollars and Julia Roberts strapped naked to her bed."

"That sounds like Shawn." Faith laughed as she stood and picked up her bag. "I wish you luck, Ms. St. James, but as I said, I wouldn't be any help. Dr. Williams is the gal you need, and knowing her the way I do, I suggest you try finding yourself another psychic."

"I'm sorry to have wasted your time, Ms. Charles. I just thought if the two of you worked together again, it might point us in the right direction. Or at least get her to talk about what really happened that night. The book you wrote together was a little vague."

"Well, there's the other problem with your idea," Faith said sadly. "At the moment, Dr. Williams and I aren't on speaking terms."

"I'm sorry to hear that."

"Me, too," Faith muttered as she lifted her bag strap onto her shoulder.

"If you don't mind my asking, what happened?"

"Basically, I'm a jackass," Faith said in a flippant tone. Delia gave her a strange look. Faith shrugged and left her sitting in the coffee shop.

Chapter 14

Adams County, Pennsylvania
May 2005

Shawn tightened her suede barn jacket in an effort to fight off the chill. It was a rainy day in Pennsylvania, and the house they were shooting at was full of bad energy. She tried to shrug off the nagging feeling that a telephone was ringing. It took her a moment to realize that the telephone wasn't ringing in the house she had just exited. No, this phone was miles away. "Please, I need to find her," she distinctly heard Faith say. She shook her head and tried to focus on the sounds, but they grew quiet and vanished.

"Faith?" she whispered, wondering why her ex-lover's voice was echoing in her head.

"What was that?"

"Sorry, Milo." She blinked as the strange feeling left her. "What were you saying?"

"I was saying that you've been in high demand since Whispering Pines," he said. "I wish I had stayed."

"No, you don't." Shawn shivered. The memory of what had happened over two years ago had never fully left her. "I've never experienced anything like that place, and I hope I never will again."

"Still, spending the night with Faith Charles might have been worth it." He snickered, thoroughly amused by his comment.

"Back off, Milo," Shawn said, not caring for his lecherous tone.

"Whatever happened to her?" He apparently missed Shawn's hostile glare. "She just seemed to drop out of sight."

"She got back with CNN a couple of years ago," Shawn said with a hint of sadness in her voice. "Last I heard, she was in Afghanistan. Probably in Iraq by now. Hard to say."

Shawn didn't have a clue where Faith was. Since her unceremonious departure, all Shawn had was one letter and sporadic mystical messages. Getting your mail via ESP quite often proved to be exasperating, not to mention unreliable.

"Hmm. Probably for the best. Couldn't be much work for her doing this since it's her job to prove that we're nothing but frauds. Whispering Pines ruined her."

"I suppose," Shawn muttered as she tried to distract herself. A terrifying and amazing experience brought her and Faith together and later drove them apart. Mentally, she understood that Faith was unhappy in her newfound role as Shawn's tagalong. Emotionally, she was still hurt by Faith's sudden decision to run off. As much as she understood that Faith had to move on, Shawn never accepted the way Faith had handled things.

"Shawn?" Milo asked, reaching out to her and accidentally grasping the sterling silver bracelet. The bracelet never left her wrist. Shawn had put it on the day Faith dropped the bomb, and she refused to take it off. Milo's eyes fluttered shut as he began to hum in the most disturbing manner.

"Bastard," Shawn spat out, jerking her arm away. It was a hazard of traveling with the people she did. Occasionally, quite by accident, she would experience what she did to other people and someone would get a glimpse inside of her. It happened. There was no way around it. Still, it was considered to be poor etiquette to comment on what you've seen. Even worse was to try to dig farther.

"I'm sorry," he said as his eyes snapped open. "It was an accident! You and Faith Charles? She's so arrogant and bitchy. Of course, she is hot. I'm confused. The woman I saw when I touched your bracelet was shy and nervous."

"Milo," Shawn fumed. "Drop it. Wait. What do you mean she was shy and nervous? That doesn't sound like Faith."

"Certainly not the woman I've met," Milo said, sounding surprised. "But when she was picking out that bracelet, she was very nervous."

"You mean my parting gift?" Shawn sneered, holding up her wrist and showing off the silver band.

"That isn't what she meant it to be. She wanted it to be a promise."

"Right," Shawn scoffed as she recalled the last time she saw her former lover. Faith had looked exhausted. She pleaded with Shawn to listen to her and accept the bracelet. Shawn had been too angry to listen to what Faith was trying to tell her.

In the end, Shawn had stormed off after Faith practically shoved the bracelet at her. Shawn felt weak when she placed it on her wrist. Now, each time she looked at it, she had to remind herself that Faith was gone and their romance was over.

"Dr. Williams?" the director called out to her, snapping her out of her thoughts. "We need for you to do your walk-through."

"This place sucks," Shawn muttered in a dismal tone. "I hate places where there's been a suicide. There's so much pain."

Later that night, Shawn returned to her hotel room and called Deb, the woman she had been seeing. She enjoyed Deb's company, but there was something missing. As Shawn took a soothing hot shower, she wondered how long she was going to keep lying to herself about her new relationship. Once again, she was forced to accept that being a psychic didn't mean she knew anything when it came to her own life.

She dried off her aching body and threw on a pair of tattered old sweats before reclining on her bed. She stared up at the motel's drab ceiling and tried to convince herself that she just needed to forget about Faith and give Deb a chance.

Her body erupted in a rash of goose bumps as a familiar sensation invaded her. She sat up quickly and stared at the door, knowing that she would hear a knock at any moment. She also knew whom she would find on the other side. The knock came and she climbed off of the bed. Her palms were perspiring as she reached for the handle. She hesitated and placed her hand on the door, trying to balance herself.

Finally feeling prepared to face her visitor, she opened the door. She knew who was waiting on the other side; she just wasn't expecting to find the woman looking so haggard. She spoke in a cold tone despite the rapid beating of her heart. "Hello, Faith."

Chapter 15

Stewart, Massachusetts
1912

The morning brought a smile to Anna's face as she finished descending the staircase and spied her husband's travel bag sitting in the foyer. The hair on the back of her neck prickled with excitement when she felt another presence approaching from behind her.

"Good morning, Sister," she greeted Catherine without turning around. "I pray that you slept well," she said brightly.

"How did you know it was me?" Catherine asked as they made their way towards the kitchen.

Anna gave Catherine a shy smile. "I always know when you're about." Anna herself didn't fully understand how she could simply feel Catherine's presence when they had only become acquainted such a short time ago. "We should begin preparing the captain's meal." She brushed something from her white lace dress and reached up nervously to ensure that her long auburn hair was still neatly tucked into a bun.

Anna felt relieved when Catherine simply smiled and nodded in response. The mood was light in the kitchen that morning as they went about preparing breakfast. Anna felt a sense of peace working alongside Catherine and knowing that the captain would soon be departing for what she hoped was an extended voyage. She found herself humming a simple tune.

"You are in fine spirits this morning, Sister," Catherine whispered playfully in Anna's ear as she leaned in from behind her.

Anna swayed slightly. Her skin tingled from the feel of Catherine's breath caressing her neck. Catherine's hands came to rest on her shoulders in an effort to steady her. Anna quivered when she felt Catherine's body brushing against her back. She blinked her eyes in confusion as she leaned into Catherine's touch.

Anna stumbled slightly and reluctantly stepped out of Catherine's embrace. "He's leaving," she said in a hushed tone, unable to look at Catherine. "At least, I think he is."

"Wouldn't you know?"

"There are times when he only pretends to be leaving." Anna gathered up the food. Her heart was pounding in the most disturbing manner. She fought valiantly against the desire to look at Catherine. "Yet he hasn't traveled in a long time. I pray that he's really departing on a voyage."

Anna's movements were halted when Catherine patted her lightly on the arm. "The more I learn about my brother, the less I understand," Catherine said in a weary voice. Anna's arm trembled, and she felt her skin warming from Catherine's simple touch. She was unable to speak as she stared at her sister-in-law's hand that was still resting upon her arm.

"Wife!" the captain bellowed from the dining room.

Anna's eyes fluttered shut when Catherine's fingers left her arm. She felt cold, as though she missed her touch. "Please be going," she pleaded softly. Slowly she opened her eyes and steeled herself to serve her husband.

After the morning meal had been served and the remnants cleared away, the captain announced his departure. He didn't explain where he was going or how long he would be at sea. He just said he was leaving on a voyage and walked out of the manor. Anna smiled brightly as she listened to his fading footsteps.

That evening, Anna was relaxing by the fire in her bedchamber, neatly stitching a piece of embroidery she had been working on. She felt at peace, knowing that she and Catherine were alone in the house. She was humming softly as she focused on the tiny stitches when there was a soft knock on the door.

"Enter, Sister," she called out eagerly, setting her embroidery down onto the table. She couldn't stop the smile that emerged when Catherine stepped into her room. "Please, sit with me," Anna said, watching Catherine make her way into her room.

Anna's throat felt suddenly parched when she noticed that the light of the fire illuminated Catherine's nightgown in such a manner that Anna was treated to a glimpse of her well-sculpted body. Anna tore her gaze away and adjusted the collar of her own dressing gown as Catherine approached her and took a seat at the mahogany table.

"Here," Catherine said, holding out a tiny crystal glass filled with a dark liquid.

"Sherry?" Anna asked, puzzled, as she accepted the glass. She shuddered when their fingers touched lightly. "I've never tasted spirits before."

"Then it's high time you did, dear Sister." Catherine raised her glass. "You cook for him, clean for him, raise his child when he allows it, at the very least you deserve a drink every now and then."

"If you insist." Anna prepared herself for her first taste of alcohol. She took a tiny sip and was surprised by the warmth that invaded her mouth. "Interesting."

"If you enjoy this, you should really try rum," Catherine said with a hearty laugh.

"Sister?" Anna squeaked in surprise. "You are shameless."

"You have no idea," Catherine said in a deep, rich tone that made Anna blush. "It's good to be able to simply sit and chat without worrying about who might be listening."

"It is." Anna took another careful sip of her sherry. "I enjoy the nights when the captain has been called away."

"I can understand why."

"This is nice," Anna said softly. Warmth spread through her as she fingered the fringe on the white shawl that was draped over Catherine's shoulders. The long fringe felt so light. The shawl was embroidered with large blue flowers and hung down past Catherine's waist. "It's so soft."

"Silk." Catherine leaned back in her chair and sipped her sherry.

Anna continued to sip her drink, her fingers absently playing with the silk fringe. She felt slightly light-headed as she placed her empty glass on the table. Her fingers continued moving through the fringe until they drifted to the light blue embroidery. She watched the steady rise and fall of Catherine's chest, her fingers all the while lightly tracing the delicate pattern.

Anna was mesmerized by the way her fingers tingled as she continued to trace the blue flowers. Her focus remained on Catherine's breasts. She licked her lips without understanding why, as she noticed Catherine's nipples pressing against the sheer material of her nightgown. Anna's lungs fought for air, and she felt her face flush. She wondered if the sherry was causing the unusual stirring she felt in her stomach and lower anatomy.

Anna's eyes drifted up to Catherine's full lips, which were parted slightly. The sight sent another rush of warmth through her small body. She leaned slightly closer as she noticed Catherine leaning forward to place her empty glass on the table. Anna had no sense of reason. Absently, her hands drifted along the shawl until her fingers were caressing the opening, which was dangerously close to Catherine's breasts.

Shyly Anna looked up to find Catherine watching her. She was mesmerized by the way Catherine's breathing grew steadily heavier. There was something electrifying in Catherine's flushed features. Catherine's smoky gaze encouraged Anna's fingers to continue until she felt the swell of Catherine's breasts beneath her touch. Anna's eyes once again drifted to Catherine's inviting lips as her fingers slowly traced the supple curve of Catherine's breasts.

Anna's heart pounded in a demanding rhythm that was mirrored by the strange throb emanating from her lower body. Her lips began to quiver uncontrollably. Catherine brushed Anna's hair back from her cheek. Anna's entire body was shaking as Catherine's fingers glided down along her neck.

Suddenly, Anna felt cold as Catherine jerked her hand away. Catherine jumped up and looked down at Anna with a stunned expression. Anna was terrified, realizing what had just transpired between them. "Good night," Catherine blurted out before dashing out of the room. Anna looked down at her trembling hands as if the appendages were foreign to her.

"Sweet Jesus," she said, a horrific feeling filling her. "What have I done?"

Chapter 16

Adams County, Pennsylvania
2005

"Can I come in?" Faith finally asked in a weary tone as she ran her fingers through her long, dark hair. They had been staring at one another uncomfortably for a long time. Shawn chewed on her bottom lip, wondering if she should just refuse and send Faith away.

But the sight of Faith looking so tired and pale tugged at her heart. She stepped aside and motioned for Faith to enter. She was careful not to touch her as Faith stumbled into the motel room.

Shawn could feel her heart racing. In an effort to calm herself, she turned away from Faith and closed the door slowly, taking deep breaths. Her body failed to obey as she turned back to Faith, who was standing with her back to her, her shoulders slumped. She had never seen Faith looking so frail or so vulnerable. "When did you get back?" she asked, in an effort to calm both of them.

Faith rolled her neck before turning around. Her face was gaunt; her blue eyes were tired. She looked down at her watch.

"Today?" Shawn asked, surprised.

Faith dropped her bag onto the floor. "Shawn, I need to talk to you," she said in an uncharacteristically shy tone.

"No." Shawn folded her arms across her chest. "You need a shower and a good night's sleep. Then we can talk."

"Shawn, I—"

"I'm seeing someone." Shawn hadn't meant to be so blunt or cold, but she felt it was best to get it out in the open before there were any misunderstandings. Internally, she knew that she had blurted it out more for her own benefit than for Faith's.

"That was quick," Faith snapped.

"No, it wasn't," Shawn said. "Faith, you've been gone for a very long time. I honestly didn't know if I was ever going to see you again."

"Some psychic." Faith sneered as she bent over to pick up her bag. "I'll just get out of your way then."

"Stop," Shawn said in a calm tone. "I can't let you just wander off in the condition you're in. You may be a jerk, and things between us may be a complete and utter mess, but it's the middle of the night and you look as if you haven't slept in days." Shawn held up her hands, still careful not to touch Faith as she implored her to accept her offer.

"You're afraid to touch me?" Faith asked.

"No, I just don't want to see where you've been." *Or who you've been with.* "Normally you can shut me out, but not when your defenses are down. And with the state you're in, I don't need to see you being shot at, or worse."

"I'm so tired," Faith muttered. "I can stay?"

"For tonight." Shawn fought the urge to wrap Faith in her arms. "Go take a shower, and then we can go to bed."

Shawn's eyes widened in disbelief when Faith flashed her a cocky smirk. "No way," she said. "I can't believe you."

"What?" Faith asked innocently.

"You can barely stand, and we haven't seen one another in years. Not to mention we didn't part on very good terms. And you think you're going to get lucky?"

"Who, me?" Faith protested with mock indignation.

"Yes, you." Shawn wasn't pleased by the overly cocky smirk plastered on Faith's lips. "Go take a shower, and I suggest you make it a cold one."

Faith stumbled off towards the bathroom. She left the door wide open as she shed clothing and stepped into the shower.

"She's incorrigible," Shawn muttered under her breath while resisting the urge to peek into the bathroom. "And still sexy as all hell," she added with a heavy sigh and a tiny whimper.

Shawn's nerves were on edge, to say the least. Finally, she pried herself away from the foggy view of her former lover's naked form peeking out from behind the flimsy shower curtain. She crawled up onto the bed and reminded herself that she was dating someone. She frowned when she realized that her current lover's name had momentarily slipped from her mind.

"Deb," she muttered in an effort to remind herself that Faith was in the past. It didn't help when the leggy brunette emerged from the bathroom, clad only in a skimpy towel. "Get dressed," Shawn demanded, her body shaking.

"I don't like to wear anything to bed," Faith said with an inviting smile. She added more fuel to the fire by raking her fingers through her long, dark tresses. "You know that," she added with a sultry purr.

"I'm not playing this game with you." Shawn quickly averted her gaze. "Now get dressed, and for once, try to act like an adult."

"I'm all for acting like an adult," Faith replied in a husky tone. She snickered playfully as she planted her body down next to Shawn's. Shawn's skin erupted in a rash of goose bumps. She could literally feel the heat flowing from Faith's body.

"Besides, what does it matter? You're the one with the girlfriend," Faith said in a breathy tone, her lips lingering dangerously close to Shawn's ear.

Shawn's eyes drifted shut. Her body quivered with a surge of desire. She bit down on her bottom lip and shivered from the feel of Faith's warm breath teasing her neck. She snapped her eyes open in a panic.

"What's her name?" Faith taunted Shawn. Her lips brushed lightly across Shawn's sensitive earlobe.

Shawn jerked away in an effort to distance herself from Faith and her inviting advances. "Deb," Shawn said, glaring at Faith. "Her name's Deb, and she's very important to me. Now, put something on and behave."

"Fine," Faith answered in a dejected tone. She stood and tore the towel from her body and threw it on the floor. Shawn's eyes darkened with desire. She couldn't help it; she watched the naked woman bend over and start to rummage through her bag. Shawn's eyes remained fixated on Faith's attributes until Faith stood up and turned back to face her. "Having trouble breathing, Sparky?"

"I'm having a really bad day," Shawn grumbled, her eyes still riveted on Faith. Faith chuckled snidely again and then pulled on a well-worn T-shirt that was emblazoned with an image of the robot from *Lost in Space*, with the words "Danger, Will Robinson," sprawled across the front.

"Understatement of the year. Underwear for you, pervert," Shawn muttered.

Faith rolled her eyes before slipping on a pair of boxer shorts and climbing into the opposite side of the bed. "Spoilsport." She pulled the bed covers up.

"Hold on," Shawn said suddenly. "Isn't that my shirt?"

Faith rolled over. "Good night."

"Jerk," Shawn muttered before she climbed under the blankets. She was once again careful not to touch Faith, which led her to hang off the edge of the full-sized mattress.

"I'm in hell," she muttered, unable to keep her gaze from drifting over to Faith, who had fallen fast asleep. Shawn studied her profile. Faith always looked deceptively at peace when she slept. Shawn fought against the tears that had begun to fill her eyes. "I missed you," she whispered, before rolling onto her side and away from Faith.

Chapter 17

Stewart, Massachusetts
1912

Anna was still sitting in the same spot, staring at a point on the wall, when chirping birds announced the new day. She had failed to find sleep or comfort. She had been unable or unwilling to move from the place she was sitting in when the mix of firelight and alcohol clouded her mind and she crossed a line that she never knew existed.

She finally turned her head to gaze out her window. The morning sky looked gray and cold, much like her heart. The fire had died out hours ago. Now it was a cold morning, and she was forced to face the day, and Catherine. She felt numb as she rose from her chair. Her body was stiff from sitting up all night long. She shook off the stiffness and began her morning cleansing.

She dressed in a simple gray dress and wrapped her hair up in a bun, as was her usual manner. She performed her routine out of habit. Finally, she descended the staircase. She felt a sense of loneliness when she entered the empty kitchen. She pumped water into the sink and filled the teakettle.

The hair on the back of her neck prickled with anticipation. Without looking, she knew that Catherine had entered the room. She was filled with a sense of fear, and thought it was for the best to continue her chores. She lit the stove and settled the teakettle down to boil. Anna never turned to face Catherine as she went about her morning duties. Neither of them spoke nor acknowledged the other while they prepared a simple fare of tea and biscuits.

Anna sat silently at the dining room table, stirring her tea and staring blankly at the lace tablecloth. She never looked at Catherine, and she sensed that Catherine never lifted her gaze in her direction, either. They cleared away the cold tea and untouched biscuits and went about their daily routine as the servants arrived for the day.

The day proceeded sluggishly, each woman avoiding the other, never daring a glance. When dusk arrived, the servants departed, and neither woman attempted to prepare anything for supper. The moon was rising, and Catherine was nowhere to be seen. Anna stood in the kitchen, feeling the emptiness that filled the grand manor. She could hear Catherine's footsteps in the foyer. Anna felt like a coward when she slipped up to her bedchamber, using the servants' passage that only she knew existed.

A hidden door by the pantry opened onto a narrow stairwell. The winding staircase led up to the second and third floors. One of the hidden exits was located in Anna's bedroom. The staircase also led to hidden panels in the hallway of the second floor near Richard's room, and the linen closet. Another panel was nestled in the corner of the small room Catherine now occupied.

Anna had been thrilled when she first discovered the passageway that had obviously been designed so the servants could pass from their quarters to the kitchen or the Lady's bedchamber without using the main stairway. Since the captain had never intended for outsiders to live in the house, Anna doubted that he knew of its existence. She used the hidden passageway on more than one occasion to avoid him.

Now she was using it to avoid her husband's sister and the strange stirrings that Catherine had unwittingly planted in Anna's fragile heart. She washed, dressed in a nightgown, and sat once again in her chair. Her embroidery lay untouched in her lap as she spent a second evening staring at the walls of her bedchamber.

The following morning was colder and damper. In the early hours, a nasty rainstorm cracked open the dark skies. The day proved to be a repeat of the day before. Anna grew despondent when dusk grew closer and the servants departed. It was Saturday, and they would not be returning until Monday. The heavy rain looked as if it would make the carriage ride into town for Sunday services impossible. She was trapped in the manor alone with Catherine until Monday morning. And now, thanks to the weather, she would be unable to escape into town or to her beloved garden.

She pressed the panel next to the pantry and slipped once again up to the hidden stairwell to her bedchambers. It was far too early to retire, yet she was exhausted. She was standing by her bed, pondering her fate, when her skin prickled with a sense of excitement and the room filled with the delicate scent of lilac.

"Good evening, Sister," Anna muttered in a weary tone, without turning to face the woman.

She felt Catherine approaching her until she was standing directly behind her. Anna's body trembled, silently yearning for Catherine to close the distance between them.

"In retrospect, perhaps I should have offered you rum?" Catherine said in a halfhearted tone.

"I don't understand," Anna muttered, pretending to study the pattern of the comforter that was covering her bed.

"Well, rum is a lot more fun."

"What other secrets do you have tucked away in your room, dear Sister?" A small smile finally creased Anna's lips.

"You wish to know my secrets?" Catherine's voice cracked as she whispered her question, and Anna felt Catherine's hands hovering just above her shoulders.

"I'm just discovering my own," Anna confessed tearfully.

"If I had any sense of decency, I would leave Whispering Pines," Catherine said in a hushed tone, her breath caressing the nape of Anna's neck. "Leave you and this place, and run from the pain I've inflicted upon you."

"I'd die without you," Anna exclaimed, finally spinning around to face her fears and desires.

"Don't," Catherine said. "You don't know what you're saying."

"No, I don't know what I'm saying." The constant pounding of her heart reminded Anna that she knew nothing at all. "I have no understanding of anything, anymore."

"Leave it at that," Catherine said tenderly, her eyes filling with tears. "It would be for the best."

"No!" Anna protested. "I would perish without you! I shan't let you leave me. I'm sorry for this. I don't know what I was doing, and I promise it shan't happen again."

"Dear Sister, you fail to understand," Catherine said in a sorrowful tone as her eyes drifted shut and she shook her head. "I wanted it to happen. I want it to happen again. Yet you're a good woman who is married to my brother. I shall not make your burden heavier than it already is. I'll go."

"No." Anna pleaded with Catherine to understand what she couldn't put into words. Anna clenched her hands tightly, unable to release the tension, even after her hands became numb.

They stood there, the only sounds in the room those of the rain beating against the windowpanes and their labored breathing. Anna used the stilted silence to drink in every curve of Catherine's inviting body. She released a timid squeak when Catherine's eyes drifted open.

"It's quite chilly this evening," Catherine muttered absently, as if nothing had transpired between them. "Shall I light a fire?"

Anna felt helpless as she watched Catherine move away to tend to the kindling and spark a fire in the fireplace. She trembled, missing the warmth of Catherine standing close to her.

Catherine looked over her shoulder and cast a small smile at the confused Anna, who was still standing in the same spot, her eyes never wavering from Catherine's body. Catherine stood slowly, and brushed the soot from her hands just as the fire began to burn brightly. Anna felt warmth spreading through her, and she knew in her heart it was not from the flames of the fire.

Anna's breathing hitched when their gazes met. Catherine slowly moved across the room until she was standing before Anna. Catherine's nearness clouded her mind with lurid thoughts. She took a small step back until her legs brushed against the large canopy bed. The room was filled with nervous tension as Catherine took a small step closer.

Anna could hear her heart beating wildly, the sound filling her head as her palms began to sweat. She reached up and cupped Catherine's face. Catherine captured Anna's hand with her own shaking one.

"Sister?" Catherine whispered.

"Don't call me that," Anna choked out, her heart beating rapidly as each word passed her lips. "What I feel for you is anything but sisterly," she confessed in a breathy tone. She pulled Catherine's face closer to her own.

Catherine's breath burned as it caressed Anna's face. Anna's stomach clenched, and her eyes drifted shut. She guided Catherine closer to her until their lips met in a soft, inviting kiss. Anna's heart swelled as she allowed her lips to linger against Catherine's. Anna had never really been kissed until that moment, and she was certain that she was about to melt into Catherine's embrace.

She clutched Catherine tighter. Their lips moved softly against each other. Anna gave in to the feel of Catherine's mouth exploring her own. She parted her lips when Catherine's tongue traced her bottom lip. Anna's lower body was humming, her nipples inexplicably hardening. She released a deep moan when Catherine lowered her onto the bed.

Anna gave herself over to Catherine's touch. The kiss deepened, and Anna returned it with fervor. Catherine's hands roamed Anna's body and began to remove Anna's burdensome clothing. Anna tingled from the sensation of Catherine caressing her. Her body pulsated with desire as Catherine lovingly began to kiss her neck.

Anna was surprised when her body arched in response to Catherine's mouth upon her neck. She filled her small hands with the material of Catherine's dress.

"Please," she gasped, "I need more." She cried out as Catherine's tongue worshipped the swell of her exposed breasts. Anna couldn't quell the violent tremor that overtook her body.

"Do you want me to stop?" Catherine whispered tenderly against her skin.

"No," Anna moaned as she undid the ribbon that was holding Catherine's beautiful hair in place. She needed to feel the silken tresses on her skin. Anna ran her fingers through Catherine's long, blonde hair. She could feel the fire inside her growing as Catherine's hair tickled her naked skin. Never before had she exposed her body in such a manner, and yet she felt complete freedom as she lay before Catherine. Her only regret was not being able to see the treasures that surely lay beneath her clothing.

"I need to see you," Anna said.

Catherine lifted her body and stood before her. She slowly removed her clothing as Anna watched her every movement with a lustful gaze. Anna swallowed hard as the last of Catherine's clothing fell to the floor. Her eyes drank in every inch of Catherine's body.

Catherine lowered herself into Anna's arms. Anna moaned deeply as her body melted into Catherine's. She ran her hands over Catherine's long body as Catherine began to kiss her way down Anna's neck. With each kiss, Anna burned with a needy desire. She cried out as Catherine's tongue circled her nipple.

Anna's body arched when Catherine captured her nipple in her mouth. As Catherine teased her breast, Anna's leg slipped between Catherine's legs. Anna's heart was beating rapidly as she felt her lover's desire on her skin. Her hands drifted down Catherine's body until she was clasping her hips, gently guiding their bodies to grind against welcoming thighs.

Anna was amazed at how her body simply took control and how truly wonderful it felt to touch and be touched by Catherine. Her need raged through her as Catherine worshipped her breasts with her mouth and rocked gently against her body.

Catherine kissed her way down Anna's body, her warm breath caressing the inside of her thighs. Anna trembled. She had no concept of what Catherine's intentions were, but she was willing to give anything to her. She whimpered when Catherine parted her.

Anna cried out when Catherine's tongue dipped inside of her passion. Her body arched. She pressed herself against Catherine's mouth. She was mesmerized as she looked down her naked body and watched Catherine feasting upon her. Anna's world spun out of control as Catherine's fingers teased her nub and her tongue slipped in and out of her.

Catherine's hands held her steady as Anna thrust urgently against her. She cried out and clutched at the bedding. Her heart exploded with love. She fell into an abyss and collapsed against her lover.

Anna was unable to focus; she felt complete for the first time in her life. Her thirst had been quenched, and yet the fire was still blazing inside of her. Anna pulled her lover up in her arms and wrapped her body around her. Anna had no idea of what she should be doing; she simply allowed her body and heart to guide her as she pulled Catherine in for a lingering kiss. Her body ignited as she tasted herself on Catherine's warm lips. Their hands caressed and pleasured one another until they collapsed in a loving embrace.

Anna felt at peace as she rested her head on Catherine's chest. She ran her hands along Catherine's body, listening to Catherine's heart beating in a steady rhythm.

"I thought the first time I held my son in my arms I finally found a reason to be happy," Anna murmured against Catherine's skin as her lover caressed her back. "Yet tonight you have shown me another form of bliss."

Anna felt a wave of panic when Catherine remained silent. She jerked her head up and found herself locked in Catherine's smoky gaze. "I love you, Anna," Catherine choked out in a fearful tone.

"And I love you, Catherine," Anna responded, needing to calm Catherine's fears. Catherine's smile made Anna's heart leap. Anna snuggled up against Catherine, and they held one another as they drifted off to sleep.

Chapter 18

Adams County, Pennsylvania
2005

"I can't believe this!" Shawn shouted as Faith stared back at her. "You said you had an errand to run. How did a simple errand turn into 'I'm leaving the country for an indefinite period of time'?"

"It's just a job, Shawn," Faith said. "I need to be doing something besides following you around."

"A job in the middle of a war zone," Shawn said. "Something you said you were tired of."

"I said that when I had other options. I'm a reporter who specializes in debunking haunted houses. I can't do that anymore. Not since Whispering Pines. I wasn't expecting this offer, but I won't be foolish enough to pass on it."

"Fine." Shawn wasn't really listening to what Faith was trying to tell her. "Go, then. It isn't like we're living together or anything."

Faith reached out for her and Shawn jerked away.

Shawn felt Faith's pain for just a moment, and then the scene changed. Faith was standing aboard an aircraft carrier talking with a gorgeous woman in a naval uniform.

"Trust me, Lieutenant, I understand perfectly what you're offering," Faith said in a dry tone. "As I said before, I have someone waiting for me back home."

Shawn could feel the rush of sadness Faith was trying to hide, and again the scene changed. Now Faith was dressed in a khaki vest, standing by a tank and looking at a crumpled newspaper photo with Shawn's picture. A sudden blast jerked Faith out of her thoughts.

"That was close." She stuffed the picture back into one of her vest pockets. "Get the camera ready."

"No," Faith said into the small video telephone. "I'll pass on Iraq. I need to go home."

The image shifted once again.

"This is Faith Charles reporting live from—" Faith addressed the camera and then the image blurred and Faith was gripping the receiver of a payphone.

"Althea, I know you know where she is," Faith said. "I just want to talk to her." The sounds of city traffic drowned out Faith's voice. "Fine. I'll do it!" Faith barked. "Now please, tell me where Shawn is."

The scene shifted, and Shawn saw Faith talking to a young woman. Delia St. James.

"What I want, what I'm asking for, is that you and Dr. Williams return to Whispering Pines," Delia pleaded.

"Not a chance in hell," Faith said.

Shawn's eyes flew open as the garbled images continued to assault her. She could see Faith with soldiers, Faith staring at a crumpled picture of Shawn, and then a confusing array of images that slowly slipped away. Shawn looked around in confusion until she realized that she was lying in Faith's arms.

She carefully removed herself from Faith's embrace and slipped out of bed. "Sometimes being a psychic sucks," she grumbled, trying to understand what she had seen as she slept in Faith's arms.

"She couldn't just dream about sex like she always does," Shawn muttered in a bitter tone, shaking her head and stumbling into the bathroom.

Once Shawn had showered and dressed, she quietly slipped from the hotel room and made her way to the coffee shop, knowing that Faith would be craving caffeine when she woke up. Shawn bought two large cups of coffee and a bag of doughnuts and then headed back towards her room. She was pleased when Faith emerged from the bathroom dressed in appropriate attire.

"Here." She thrust the large cup of coffee at Faith. She felt a jolt as their fingers brushed and then a disturbing image filled her mind.

"You jerk!" she suddenly shouted.

"What?" Faith asked.

"You weren't even going to tell me." Shawn shoved the bag of doughnuts into Faith's body. "Why did you answer the telephone?" she ranted on. Faith grimaced while Shawn rushed over to the telephone and began to dial.

"It rang and woke me up," Faith said. "I answered it out of reflex. I was half asleep. Believe me, talking to your new girlfriend wasn't my idea of a fun way to wake up. You know, she wasn't very pleasant."

"I wonder why." Shawn listened to the phone ringing. "She must have been thrilled when she called my hotel room this morning and another woman answered."

Shawn was about to go off on a tirade when Deb's voice greeted her. "Hi, honey. You called?" Shawn asked in an innocent tone.

"Shawn, what's going on?" Deb asked. "I called you first thing this morning, and a woman answered the phone and said you had just stepped out."

"One of my colleagues crashed here last night," Shawn said in an effort to placate her lover. She reasoned that it wasn't really a lie. Still, she felt a pang of guilt stabbing at her as she listened to Deb wishing her a good morning.

"I miss you, too," Shawn said.

Faith grunted. "I'm going to be sick."

Shawn hurled a pillow at her as she tried to listen to Deb.

"Ouch!" Faith shouted when the pillow struck her in the head. Faith raised the pillow, preparing to throw it back at Shawn, but Shawn's icy glare halted her movements.

Shawn continued to chat with Deb as Faith rummaged through the bag of doughnuts.

"What, no chocolate frosted?" Faith asked loudly.

"Deb, sweetie, can you hold for just a moment?" Shawn said in a sweet tone before she covered the receiver. "Stop it! Check the bottom of the bag and stop pouting. I need to finish this call, and then I have a shoot to finish. Just eat something, drink your coffee, and if you behave, you can go with me. But I don't want to hear one peep out of you until I hang up. Understood?"

"Fine, Miss Bossy," Faith said with a pout. "Hey, are those my socks?"

Shawn looked down at her feet and realized that Faith was right. "Damn it," she muttered bitterly.

She returned her attention to the call while frantically removing her shoes and socks. She tossed the socks in question at Faith, smacking her in the head. Faith looked at her with narrowed eyes. Knowing she was in for a squabble, Shawn wrapped up her telephone call.

"We really need to clean out our wardrobe." Shawn dug out a clean pair of socks. "Seems like our stuff got mixed together."

"We spent almost every waking moment together," Faith said, taking a sip of her coffee. "Most of my stuff is in storage back in Massachusetts."

"Why are you thinking of going back?" Shawn asked.

"To Massachusetts? For starters, my stuff is there."

"Whispering Pines." Shawn yanked on a clean pair of socks.

"I'm not," Faith said. "I did meet the owner, and I told her no. Wait, did you sneak a peek inside my head while I was sleeping?"

"It was an accident," Shawn said. "And yes, you are thinking about it."

"Well, it doesn't matter." Faith shrugged. "I've already accepted another assignment. Althea talked me into being the lead on her next project. It was the only way I could get her to tell me where you were."

"Hammond Castle?" Shawn stared at her.

"Yeah, how did you..." Faith's words drifted off and a bright smile formed on her lips. "You're on the team? This is great!"

"No, it isn't," Shawn said weakly. "This is a freaking disaster."

"You say tomato," Faith quipped.

"Please, stop," Shawn pleaded helplessly.

Chapter 19

Stewart, Massachusetts
1912

Catherine shifted her body and felt a weight pressing against her. Her eyes fluttered open. She looked down and found her naked breast covered in a blanket of soft auburn hair. She traced Anna's creamy white shoulders with the tips of her fingers. *Now I've really done it, haven't I? In all the years I've pursued my perversion, sleeping with one of my brother's wives was never among my transgressions,* she berated herself. *Of course, the other wives were pasty prigs, like their husbands. Anna is a breath of fresh air. She's the light in this dark world, and now I've ruined everything between us.*

"Troubling thoughts," Anna's sweet voice interrupted her inner turmoil. "Please don't tell me you regret the love we shared?"

"Never," Catherine honestly answered the pleading look in her young lover's eyes. "The only regret I possess at this moment is that you belong to another," she added, in hopes that Anna would understand her fears.

"I never belonged to him," Anna said. "I was sold to him for a handful of coins. He may rule my life, but my heart has never been his. It's yours, and yours alone."

"Do you understand what you're saying?" Catherine asked in a slow, careful tone.

"Yes." Anna snuggled closer to Catherine. "I'm yours, if you want me."

"Of course I want you," Catherine said quickly.

"There were others before me?" Anna asked shyly, as she rested her chin on Catherine's chest.

"Yes, my love." Catherine frowned. She took a moment to collect her thoughts while running her fingers through Anna's long, auburn hair. "In my travels, I was granted the luxury of exploring my true self. I stayed away from what my family considered to be my home for as long as I could. I thought I had discovered my heart and my true home in Paris. I stayed there until my money ran out, and I limped my way back here with an empty purse and a broken heart."

"Ah." Anna sighed heavily, tracing Catherine's face with her fingers. "The depth of her love was equal to the depth of your purse."

"Hmm." Catherine filled her hands with Anna's hair. "I was a fool."

"No," Anna said. "She was the fool. You, my love, are a treasure that should be worshiped."

"Worshiped?" Catherine laughed. Her body tingled where Anna's naked body brushed against her. "Surely you jest?"

"Never." Anna poked Catherine playfully. She lifted her body slightly above Catherine's. "You have freed me. Unlocked my heart with a simple smile." Anna emphasized her point by placing Catherine's hand against her rapidly beating heart. "I was drawn to you the first time I heard your voice. From the very beginning, my heart knew that I belonged in your arms. It just took my head time to catch up."

Catherine could feel her own weary heart soaring as her fingers caressed Anna's soft skin. "This is far too dangerous," she whispered, her touch drifting to the swell of Anna's breasts. "We shouldn't even speak of such things."

"Hush." Anna cupped Catherine's face with her hand. "I know, and yes, I understand the danger. For today we have each other, and tomorrow he could return. We will tread carefully, as though we're crossing a pond during the winter thaw."

"If we fall, we fall together," Catherine vowed.

Her gaze drifted to Anna's breasts that were swaying dangerously close to her lips. "Now, how shall we spend this rainy day, my dear Anna?" She flicked her tongue across one of Anna's nipples. She was pleased by Anna's sharp intake of breath. "Shall I show you how much I love you?"

"Yes," Anna whimpered.

Their days passed merrily, both of them being careful around others. Catherine had never experienced such joy. Eagerly they prepared for Richard's return for the coming holiday. The only cloud lingering over them was that with the changing seasons, Horatio's return was nearing.

"I wish we knew when Horatio would arrive," Catherine said one evening as she held Anna in her arms.

"God forgive me, I wish he would never return," Anna whispered against Catherine's flesh. "If only his beloved sea would claim him. I'm a horrible person."

"No, you aren't," Catherine said. "He's not worthy of you. I fear his return will bring out my ire."

"I need to show you something." Anna slipped from Catherine's embrace. She put on her robe before continuing the conversation. "He often returns when it's dark. He must not find us together."

"I almost wish he would. That would certainly wipe his smug look off of his face," Catherine said with disdain.

She climbed off of the bed and donned her dressing gown. "Yet, I understand that we must be careful for the sake of your child. Now what is it you wish to share with me, other than your heart, my love?"

Catherine was filled with curiosity as Anna crossed the room and placed her palm on the wall, pressing against it. A small section of the wall opened. "What is that?" Catherine crossed the room to join Anna.

"No one but me is aware of this," Anna said. With a smile, she opened the panel and revealed a dark entryway. "It must have been constructed with the servants in mind. If you follow the stairs all the way up, it opens into your room. If you descend to the bottom, it opens in the back of the kitchen near the pantry."

"A servants' entrance?" Catherine was astonished. "But why does no one else know of its existence?"

"I think it was constructed in error," Anna said. "I can't really be certain. If the captain were aware of it, he would force the servants to use it so he wouldn't need to see them. There's another exit just down the hall that opens by the linen closet. I discovered it not long after we arrived and the captain had set off on a voyage."

"If he knew, he would most certainly use it to spy on you," Catherine readily agreed. She couldn't help thinking it was truly a wondrous discovery. Anna closed the door, and Catherine looked at the wall, amazed that, even knowing the doorway was there, she couldn't see the seams.

"It's a true stroke of luck that I'm housed in what was probably meant to be the maid's chamber. We need to keep our clothing nearby so we can dress quickly."

"When he returns, flee," Anna said. "Don't look back, no matter what you hear."

"I can't promise you that. I won't endure him mistreating you."

"You must." She took Catherine by the hand and guided her back to the bed. "Now take me to bed, my love."

Almost a week later, in the middle of the night, they heard him. Catherine did as Anna had pleaded with her to do. She fled up the back stairwell. She felt like a lowly coward as she listened to her brother berating Anna.

The next morning she felt sick. All it took was one look into Anna's tired eyes to set her off. Anna cut off the tirade she was about to release by holding up her hand and giving Catherine a pleading look. Since the captain's return, the only thing that kept Catherine from striking her brother down was the secret passageway that Anna would use whenever she could. They stole a few hours together in the safety of Catherine's tiny room, losing themselves in one another's embrace.

Chapter 20

New York City
2005

"Oh yes, baby!" Deb cried out as Shawn pleasured her. Their bodies rocked wildly; Shawn straddled her lover, riding her urgently until Deb cried out one last time before collapsing against the mattress.

"I missed you," Deb whispered happily. Shawn felt sick, fighting against the pangs of guilt that were tearing at her heart.

"I missed you, too," she said, not understanding why she couldn't just relax and enjoy their reunion. "I'm sorry I won't be home long."

"Another job?" Deb sighed. "Why don't you take some time off?"

"I can't do that. I'm in demand now. That could change at any time, and the jobs won't be as good. I could end up reading cards for Miss Cleo. Or whoever has taken her place after the police shut her down."

"Right." Deb chuckled. "Come here, baby, let me make you feel as good as I do."

Shawn allowed Deb to lower her down onto the bed. One thing that had first sparked her interest in Deb was that she didn't believe in psychics. It was nice for Shawn not to have to deal with the constant do-you-know-what-I'm-thinking crap for a while.

Deb caressed her body while Shawn tried desperately to feel something from her ministrations. There had been a time, when their relationship was new, that Deb could make Shawn scream out with the slightest touch. But now Shawn was lost in guilty images as Faith clouded her mind and her mood.

The guilt was strangling her. Finally, she did what every woman did at least once in her life: faked it. She cried out and arched her body, wailing to the heavens like it was the second coming. She hated

106

pretending that she had climaxed, but she knew if she didn't, Deb would keep trying to pleasure her. Deb was a perfectionist. She would finish the job whether Shawn wanted her to or not.

Deb had more than her share of foibles. Topping the list was that she didn't take Shawn seriously. Many times, when she spoke of Shawn's work, Deb made it sound like Shawn didn't work for a living. Deb was often very controlling. Shawn hadn't taken stock of her relationship before that moment. Still, listing Deb's numerous faults did nothing to abate the guilt Shawn felt. The problems in their relationship didn't excuse her thinking about her ex while she was making love to Deb.

"I'm a jerk," Shawn muttered repeatedly under her breath as she made her way down to the baggage claim area at Boston's Logan International Airport.

Chapter 21

A young man named Myron met her at the hotel. He was an intern for the production company that was funding the shoot at Hammond Castle. He helped Shawn unload her luggage and took her equipment inside.

"I'm really looking forward to this," Myron said as they rode the elevator up to her room. "You'll be sharing your room."

"No problem." Shawn shrugged. "That happens all the time. Who's sharing with me?"

"Ms. Charles. She checked in yesterday."

"Son of a…" her biting comment trailed off as the elevator doors opened. "I can't believe it." She stumbled slightly. She collected herself and followed Myron down the hallway.

"Here's your keycard." He handed her the thin plastic card after he opened the door for her. He helped her load her things into the room. Shawn scanned the room nervously for Faith. Thankfully, she was nowhere to be seen.

"If you need anything, I'm on the floor below," he said. The hair on the back of Shawn's neck began to prickle.

"Thank you, Myron." She fought the butterflies that were fluttering about her stomach. She took a deep breath before turning around. She wasn't the least bit surprised to find Faith leaning in the doorway.

"Ms. Charles," she coldly greeted Faith, who had the nerve to smirk at her.

"Dr. Williams, always a pleasure," Faith said with a wink.

Shawn released a low growl and glared at her. Myron quickly excused himself. The tension in the hotel room grew steadily. Shawn's anger had almost boiled to the surface when she caught the puppy-dog look Myron gave Faith on his way out.

Great, now I'm jealous. Still seething, she watched Faith saunter into the room. "Why?" Shawn tossed her suitcase onto the bed.

"Why what?" Faith was acting very pleased with herself. She even went so far as to sprawl across the bed Shawn was using to unpack. Faith propped herself up onto her elbow, grinning like an idiot while she watched Shawn carefully. "Why do you always find a parking space in front of your house after you've parked twelve blocks away? Why does it always rain after you've washed your car?"

"Stop it, you big freak. Why am I rooming with you?"

"Because we're the only two members of the talent on this shoot that are women," Faith said bluntly. "As talent, we're entitled to nicer rooms than the crew."

"I'd rather sleep in a shoe box than next to you," Shawn hissed. She knew she was acting like a callous idiot, but she couldn't stop herself.

"Forget it." Faith sighed heavily. "I already asked Althea about changing the sleeping arrangements, and she said it wasn't possible."

"You asked for a room change?" Shawn asked her suspiciously.

"Yes, I did," Faith replied flatly.

"Oh." Shawn was suddenly feeling a little dejected.

"What?" Faith said. "I thought I was doing the right thing. I left and I lost you. It hurts, but I'm not a complete idiot."

"Sorry, it just surprised me."

"You sound a little disappointed, Sparky," Faith said with a smirk. "Don't tell me you've been missing me."

"Get off my bed, you arrogant jerk," Shawn yelled. She hadn't meant to lose control. Perhaps it was the gleam in Faith's eyes, or her confident tone, or maybe the way Faith's image popped into her head the last time she was making love to Deb. Perhaps it was simply that Faith was right, and she really hated it when that happened.

"You know, I was about to thank you for being so understanding and mature about the situation, and you just had to act like the big overgrown goober that you are."

Faith's lips curled into a sneer as she climbed off the bed. "Just for the record, Shawn, I was trying to be understanding," she said in a solemn tone. "So, in the spirit, no pun intended, why don't we just drop this and try to get some work done?"

Shawn blew out a frustrated sigh as she calmed herself. "You're right." She was feeling guilty at the way she had overreacted. "I didn't mean to go off. It's just that we have a history, you know? This isn't easy for me. So, why don't you tell me what exactly you're doing on this shoot. And I promise to stop being such a bitch."

"I'm the host," Faith said.

"My God! You're the new Lanie Larsen?" Shawn teased her, unable to control the smile that suddenly emerged.

"Only with smaller boobs and a brain."

Shawn could have smacked herself for allowing her eyes to drift down to Faith's chest.

"Anyway," Faith drew out the word, clearing her throat and redirecting Shawn's gaze to her eyes, "I'm really enjoying this. I get to research the whole thing and lead you guys around and ask probing questions. This is going to be a lot more fun, and safer, than my last assignment."

"I was thinking about that the other day." Shawn's smile faded. Faith looked back at her with a curious expression. "I was watching the news the other night; that reporter from Jordan was killed. I'm glad you passed on going to Baghdad."

"Me, too," Faith replied quietly. "I've done my time. I can't do it anymore. And if I do well on this gig, I won't have to. So, want to hear about Hammond Castle?"

"I'd love to." Shawn smiled. "No more trying to discredit me or my colleagues?"

"Nope. In fact, I can't take sides. I'm just along for the ride. Ready?" Shawn nodded as she sorted out her clothing. "Between the years 1926 and 1929, John Hays Hammond, Jr., built this medieval-style castle. He used the castle as his home and to house his collection of medieval and Renaissance artifacts. He also used it to house the Hammond Research Corporation.

"Mr. Hammond was an inventor, with over four hundred patents to his name. Only Edison had more. Guess what he's best known for?"

"Besides having more money than God and good taste in artwork?" Shawn's mood was becoming lighter the more playful Faith became.

"He invented the remote control."

"Wow." Shawn blinked. "If you think about it, that's probably the most popular invention of this century. I know you break out in a sweat whenever you can't find it."

"At least I don't surf constantly, like some people," Faith protested. "But getting back to the Castle: it has eight rooms, including the great hall. You're going to love that room. Then we have an indoor courtyard, Renaissance dining room, two guest bedrooms, the inventions exhibit room, the Natalie Hays Hammond exhibit room, the tower galleries, lots of passageways, and some smaller rooms."

"You've seen it already?"

"One of my cousins got married there."

"At a castle?"

"It really is beautiful. A lot of people get married there. They also do Renaissance Faires, and at Halloween, they do the best haunted house in the area. The only exception is the real thing, of course. If you get a chance, you should take a stroll around the grounds. They're amazing, and the view of the Atlantic is breathtaking."

"Okay, between looking for things that go bump in the night, I'll take time to stop and smell the roses," Shawn said. "Speaking of things that go bump in the night. It sounds like Mr. Hammond was a nice, normal guy, and the castle isn't that old. Do we have things that will go bump in the night?"

"You'll tell me. The place isn't really known for it, but several tour guides and staff members, over the years, have seen and heard some mighty strange things."

"Sounds like fun." Shawn was finally feeling better about her renewed working relationship with Faith.

* * *

Magnolia, Massachusetts
2005

"I can't believe you losers are drunk," Althea bellowed at the top of her lungs. The inebriated crew and talent were doing their best to hide under a tarp or duck under the tables in an effort to escape the director's wrath. The tarp had been put up when the skies opened up and doused the weary crew with an unrelenting rainstorm. Unlike the rest of their slovenly companions, Faith and Shawn had the bad manners to laugh at Althea's outburst.

Shawn started to slip from her perch on Faith's lap, and Faith tightened her hold. She tried to recall just how Shawn ended up curled in her lap. *Right, Shawn's birthday, crappy weather, and a shoot that's a little on the dull side, always equals tequila,* her foggy mind finally pieced together.

"Relax, Althea," Faith said. As a peace offering, she handed Althea one of Clyde's special blue shooters. "We can't shoot inside the castle because of the private party, and we can't shoot outside because of the rain. And it is our little Shawn's birthday."

"Do I want to know what's in this?" Althea asked, holding up the shot glass.

"Ask Clyde." Faith motioned towards the burly cameraman who was hiding beneath his well-worn Dodgers cap. "He calls them Baby Blue Ritas."

"Wait, I remember," Shawn said, shifting her position. Faith bit back a moan as Shawn squirmed in her lap.

"Liked that, did you?" Shawn's tone was husky. "Anyhow, these have tequila, tequila, pineapple juice, tequila, and blue whatcha called it?"

"Blue Curacao," Faith said with a slight hiccup.

"Right, blueberry and tequila," Shawn finished triumphantly. "Wasn't it nice of Clyde to do this for my birthday?"

Althea eyed the way Shawn and Faith were curled up together on the tiny folding chair. She looked over at Clyde. For his part, Clyde was scratching his thick gray beard as he watched the couple. "I think he was just hoping to get the two of you drunk enough so he can watch you make out," Althea said before she downed her shot.

"Well, duh." Shawn chuckled and snuggled closer to Faith.

Faith was having a hard time keeping her hands from wandering. Shawn's constant touching wasn't helping.

"Pervert," Faith mumbled when Shawn's hand slipped between her thighs.

Clyde smirked. "I'm only human."

"I wasn't talking to you," Faith told him in a dry tone, looking down at her former lover. "Although you're next on my list."

"It's my birthday." Shawn's gray eyes twinkled back at her in a defiant manner.

"Goodie, does this mean I get to give you spankies later?" Faith's off-color comment caused Althea to choke on her drink.

"If you're good," Shawn purred into her ear. Faith bit down on her bottom lip. Her body tingled when she felt Shawn's hand slipping farther between her thighs.

"I'm always good," Faith panted, unable to stop her body from trembling. "You're playing with fire," she said hotly in Shawn's ear. Shawn leaned closer, and her breath tickled Faith's sensitive earlobe.

"I know what you're thinking," she whispered softly. Faith's eyes fluttered shut as she enjoyed Shawn's caresses. She bit back a moan when she felt Shawn's tongue trace her earlobe. She opened her mouth to offer some form of protest. Her carefully chosen words were forgotten when Shawn's hand cupped her mound.

"What happened to Steve?" Althea asked.

"Passed out," Clyde said with a shrug.

Faith squirmed slightly, carefully extracting Shawn's hand from between her thighs.

"This day is a bust." Althea shook Steve harshly.

Faith squeaked when Shawn's hand slipped under her coat and cupped one of her breasts.

"Shawn!" she hissed, clenching her jaw. When Clyde suggested making the most of the rain and Shawn's birthday, Faith had forgotten one very important thing. Tequila in high doses made Shawn very frisky. Her libido was jumping for joy. If it weren't for that pesky part of her that was honorable, Faith would have dragged little Shawn back to the hotel over an hour ago. Alas, Shawn was drunk. Big no. Shawn had a girlfriend. Bigger no. *Life just isn't fair!* Faith silently howled.

"No one can see what I'm doing," Shawn whispered while her fingers searched for Faith's nipple.

Faith had no doubt that Shawn's actions couldn't be seen because of the heavy coats they were wearing. She also held very little doubt that everyone around was well-aware of what was going on. Faith was trapped, literally stewing in her juices. There seemed to be no escape. Except for the obvious course of action. Which, of course, entailed dropping Shawn on her lovely bottom before bolting to parts unknown. Faith quickly decided against that, feeling it would be rude. And she was really enjoying the way Shawn was torturing her.

"I haven't seen Steve this screwed up since the day we tried to do the shoot at Whispering Pines," Clyde said to Althea, who had given up on waking the reporter.

Shawn suddenly jerked away, causing Faith's overheated body to tense. "What?" Faith asked catching the terrified look in Shawn's eyes.

"Kitchen," Shawn said, tapping Faith's forehead.

"Sorry." Faith shivered when she realized that Shawn must have caught a glimpse of what had leaped into Faith's mind. She couldn't help thinking about what had happened in the kitchen of Whispering Pines.

"I didn't know there was a second shoot at Whispering Pines," Faith said, trying to clear the disturbing images from her mind.

"I said we *tried* to do a shoot," Clyde said. "We ended up folding before we really got started. How in the hell did the two of you spend the night there?"

"Not much of a choice after a certain point." Faith was assaulted with the memory of holding Shawn tightly as she tried putting her arm through one of the windows in a desperate attempt to get the two of them out of the house.

"When things got really wild, I couldn't open the doors or windows. We were trapped in there. Tell me about your experiences."

Faith had met Clyde when she was first starting out in the business. He had been her cameraman the first time she went into a hot spot. He never flinched as gunfire surrounded them. As he sat before her now, he was pale and shaking.

"When we first got there," he began to explain, "I thought the whole thing was a load of horse puckey. I went into the kitchen and nothing happened. I didn't understand what all the fuss was about. It was just an empty kitchen. Big whoop."

"I don't doubt that nothing would bother you in the kitchen." Faith chuckled. "You're straight. Captain Stratton saves his big show for us queers."

"Lucky you." Clyde stroked his beard. "With me, it started with the garden."

"What garden?" Shawn asked, suddenly lucid.

"In the back of the house," Clyde said. "I filmed around the house and there wasn't anything there, just a lot of dirt and trees. Later, I went outside to the canteen truck, and the place was filled with flowers in full bloom. After I stopped shaking, I filmed it. Steve was still boasting that the whole thing was a hoax, even after I told him what I had just seen. So I showed the arrogant bugger. He still wasn't buying it. Then we walked back to the house, and I felt like someone was watching me. He must have felt it, too, because we both looked up. Sure enough, plain as day, there was a woman standing in one of the windows, watching us."

Faith held her breath, waiting to hear just what drove Clyde out of the house.

"We ran back into the house," Clyde continued slowly. "I was filming the whole time. We reached the room on the third floor where we had seen her. Steve threw open the door, and there she was. My heart stopped when she stormed over and slammed the door in our faces. She screamed for us to get out before it was too late. I about peed my pants."

"Third floor?" Faith asked.

"Catherine," Shawn said. "Was she a really tall blonde?"

"From what I could see of her, yes," Clyde said. "She was misty, if that makes any sense."

"That's the way I saw her," Faith confirmed. "You got it on film, though?"

"The tape was blank when I played it back," Clyde said. "The most amazing thing I've ever shot, and it just vanished. But that isn't what sent us running. Later, the douser showed up. You know, they wander around with a couple of sticks looking for bodies."

"Oh yeah, those guys." Faith chuckled as Shawn swatted her playfully.

"We started to film this dude wandering around with his sticks, like he's looking for water," Clyde said. "No big deal, until we followed him into the house. Then it was like we were in an earthquake. No lie, everything was shaking, right down to the glass in the windows. The lens on my camera exploded. Then this voice booms, *'Get out!'*"

"What did you do?" Myron, who had been listening closely, asked nervously.

"I got the hell out of there. I wasn't alone. The whole team just took off once the floorboards started breaking apart. A team went back later, and the house looked just fine. It was like none of it had happened."

"They're in the house," Shawn mumbled. Faith could see the wheels in her mind turning.

"And that old bastard is making sure no one finds them," Faith muttered in disgust.

"Evil in life usually means evil in death," Shawn said grimly.

"Did you hear that the owners are trying to get a new team together?" Althea asked in a hopeful tone. "I heard they want both of you to go back."

"Not a chance," Shawn said

Faith thought about what Clyde had just told them. She wanted to flat out refuse, but something deep inside her couldn't let it go.

"Faith?" Althea asked

"Not without the good doctor," Faith finally answered, patting Shawn gently on her firm backside. "Speaking of which, Birthday Girl—"

"You never told me you saw the ghosts as well, Faith." Althea cut off the lewd comment that Faith was about to make.

"She didn't read our book," Faith gasped while Shawn giggled. "I'm hurt! It happened when I was trying to get Shawn out of the kitchen. My radio was dead, Shawn was freaking out, and I couldn't get any of the doors or windows open. Suddenly there she was, waving for me to follow her. I didn't stop to think about it, I just followed her out of the kitchen. It was easy, since she held the door open for us. Then she was gone, like she was never there."

"Enough," Shawn growled, snuggling closer to Faith. "It's my birthday."

Faith wrapped her arms tightly around Shawn, still fighting an internal battle between her overheated body and her overactive imagination. A small voice whined inside of her, a constant reminder that she and Shawn were no longer together.

"We'll be pulling a long day tomorrow," Althea said. "Start packing it in, guys, before someone decides to crash the wedding inside of the castle. And please tell me the drivers didn't join in the festivities."

"Nope, it was just us wayward idiots," Faith assured her. Shawn burrowed her face in Faith's neck. *Why are you doing this?* Faith's fingers slipped under Shawn's jacket and up under the dark gray sweater she was wearing.

"Which one of us are you thinking about?" Shawn murmured in her ear.

"Both," Faith confessed, feeling the muscles in Shawn's stomach respond to her touch. "Now stop peeking," she added with a playful smirk.

"Stop thinking so loudly, and I will." Shawn rested her head on Faith's shoulder. "It's my birthday, and I don't want to think."

"All right." Faith laughed. "No more thinking." She brushed back Shawn's long hair from her brow. Faith peeked around at the crew, who were busy packing up the tent. She placed a tender kiss on Shawn's cheek. Faith's heart was pounding, her lips tingling from lightly caressing Shawn's flesh.

"Happy birthday, Shawn," she whispered, smiling when Shawn began to caress her thigh. "We should get moving. The guys need to break down the tent."

Shawn murmured softly while Faith assisted her off of her lap and to her feet. Shawn swayed slightly as the alcohol hit her. Instinctively, Faith wrapped her arms around Shawn and held her steady. As they hurried through the rain to the van, their arms remained around each other's waists.

Faith helped Shawn up into the van and climbed in behind her. They nestled against one another. Faith's body warmed as she relaxed into Shawn's touch. During the ride back to Danvers, they continued to cuddle. Faith refused to give in to the fear that was calling out to her, that things were happening much too quickly, and that neither of them was sober enough to think clearly.

Instead of listening to her fears, Faith slipped her hand from Shawn's waist and began caressing Shawn's hip. Having Shawn back in her arms, even for one night, she reasoned, was worth the risk. She could feel Shawn's breath on her neck and Shawn's head resting comfortably on her shoulder. Faith inhaled the scent of Shawn's hair. She hummed softly as the sweet aroma of peaches filled her.

Faith managed to brush aside the pang of guilt and the troublesome thoughts that were creeping up, simply enjoying the feel and scent of her former lover. For the first time since she had arrived on the north shore, she was thrilled that they were sharing a room. Her hands continued to caress Shawn's body under the guise of warming her.

Shawn's fingers crept up along Faith's body until she was caressing Faith's neck. Faith smiled blissfully when she felt the cool metal of Shawn's silver bracelet touching her skin. She kissed the top of Shawn's head and once again drank in the soft scent of peaches. She couldn't help the way her heart swelled knowing that Shawn was still wearing the bracelet.

Each time she saw the silver band that was engraved with two swans on Shawn's wrist, she felt a small glimmer of hope. Perhaps someday they would be together again.

Before she had left the country and her lover behind, Faith had wanted to offer Shawn a token that would tell her how she really felt. Each time Faith had tried to verbalize her emotions, the words either failed to come or came out wrong. It amazed Faith that she could stand calmly in front of a news camera while mayhem surrounded her, but she couldn't tell one pesky little blonde that she was in love with her.

When she had found the bracelet in the dusty old antiques shop in Boston, she just felt right about it, and prayed that Shawn would see the deeper meaning. She found the bracelet not long after their visit to Whispering Pines. She'd bought it on the spot and then tucked it away, waiting for the right time to give it to Shawn. Little had she known that the right time would end up being a good-bye.

Despite the heavy clothing they were wearing, they managed to snuggle so closely that Faith could feel the rapid beating of Shawn's heart. She stifled a groan, feeling Shawn's fingers drifting back down the front of her body and slipping beneath her coat. Faith scanned the van in order to see if any of their fellow passengers were watching them. Clyde was seated up front with Seth, the driver. The two of them were engaged in a heated debate over baseball. Althea was busy working on her laptop, while Steve loudly snored next to her.

Feeling confident that their actions were hidden, Faith allowed her hands to continue exploring Shawn's body. She released a soft murmur when Shawn cupped her breast. Faith felt her nipples tighten as Shawn began to kiss her neck.

Faith was thankful for the cloudy, rainy day that cloaked them in darkness. She allowed her head to fall back, offering her neck up to Shawn's warm kisses. She filled her hands with Shawn's backside, quivering as Shawn's tongue teased her sensitive neck. Her skin tingled with excitement and her stomach clenched. Shawn's touch could always send her body into turmoil. After years of not being allowed to give herself to Shawn, Faith was ready to explode. She clenched her jaw tightly when Shawn began to suckle the pulse point on her neck.

Faith's heart was pounding as they instinctively shifted their bodies so that their legs became entwined. *As long as she doesn't kiss me, I'll be fine*, Faith reasoned, feeling confident that they could still stop what was happening between them. Despite her unrealistic rationalization, her body was already taking control as her hips thrust against Shawn's firm thigh. Their bodies became one. Faith continued to caress Shawn's body. Shawn's lips traced Faith's jaw. Faith dipped her head as Shawn inched closer. Their lips met in a searing kiss. Faith was lost in the taste of Shawn's mouth as they fondled one another. Her heart raced out of control, and she began to tease Shawn's nipples through the thin material of her bra.

"Ahem," Althea's voice disrupted their groping session. "We're at the hotel."

They stumbled out of the van and into the hotel lobby. Shawn took Faith by the hand and pulled her towards the elevators. Neither of them spoke; their hands remained linked while they rode the elevator to their floor. Faith could feel the electricity flowing between them. She was excited and terrified. Something about the way Shawn's thumb was rubbing across the back of her hand was driving Faith insane with desire.

Faith released a strangled breath as they lingered for a moment outside of the room they were sharing. She could feel the heat coming off Shawn's body. Faith swallowed hard, the nervous excitement taunting her. She was trapped by the dark pools of pure desire she could see in Shawn's eyes. Faith knew that she should protest, or simply put Shawn to bed and leave before she was led astray by her desires. Instead, her hand tightened around Shawn's as Shawn opened the door to their room.

Faith released Shawn's hand and assisted her in removing her wet coat. She turned her back to Shawn and removed her own coat. She could feel Shawn watching her. Slowly, Faith undid her damp shoelaces, in a valiant struggle not to look back at Shawn. She heard Shawn's shoes thumping across the carpeting. A jolt tore through her body when she heard the distinctive sound of a zipper being lowered.

Faith refused to turn around, knowing that seeing any glimpse of Shawn's body would be her undoing. She fumbled with her heavy, wet top. She jumped slightly when she heard Shawn softly sighing as the sound of wet jeans made contact with the floor. Faith's hands froze with her shirt halfway up her torso.

"Faith. If you don't want to, just say it," Shawn whispered.

"You know I do," Faith said, her resolve crumbling.

She bolstered her courage and turned around. Her heart nearly stopped when she looked down at Shawn reclining on the bed, dressed in nothing but her top. *Why did I walk away from this?* She crossed the short distance to the bed and knelt before her.

"I wish I knew," Shawn answered her unspoken question, brushing Faith's wet hair from her brow.

Faith chuckled. "I hate it when you do that." Her hands came to rest on Shawn's thighs.

"I told you, stop thinking so loudly," Shawn said playfully, sweeping the back of her fingers across Faith's cheek. "The first time we let Clyde ply us with tequila on my birthday, this is how I wanted the day to end."

"So did I," Faith confessed, clasping Shawn's wrist. Tenderly she ran her thumb across the bracelet she had given Shawn. She raised Shawn's wrist and placed a soft kiss on the cool metal. She could feel Shawn's pulse racing just beneath the silver band. Her lips moved to the palm of Shawn's outstretched hand, and she blew against her skin before brushing her lips against Shawn's palm.

Shawn cupped Faith's face and drew her closer.

"You're the birthday girl," Faith said in a hushed tone, falling into Shawn's embrace. "What do you want?"

"You did promise me a spanking," Shawn replied breathlessly.

The kiss was shy and gentle. It always amazed Faith how Shawn's kisses could be so soft and so electrifying at the same time. She was certain that her toes were curling from the intensity the tender kiss was invoking. Her body leaned into Shawn's as the kiss deepened. She felt Shawn teasing her lips.

Faith caressed the bare flesh of Shawn's thighs. Shawn's hands laced in her hair, and Faith's fingers dug deeper into Shawn's flesh. Faith released a moan from the back of her throat when she felt their bodies become one. She was stunned when Shawn suddenly broke away from the fiery embrace.

"Deb," Shawn gasped.

Faith's heart broke. She lifted her body, pulling slightly away from Shawn.

"I know it's been a long time," Faith growled, glaring down at Shawn, "but my name is Faith."

"No," Shawn said, her eyes filled with panic.

Quickly unwrapping her legs from Faith's body, Shawn pushed her away. Faith stumbled backward before standing.

"Yes it is." She narrowed her gaze, not caring that Shawn was clearly panicking. "Has been for some thirty-odd years now."

"Faith," Shawn growled, bouncing off the bed. "She's on her way up here."

"Who?" Faith felt suddenly sick.

"Deb!" Shawn was looking frantically around the room. "She's in the elevator."

Faith felt as though she had been hit by lightning. She watched Shawn struggling to climb back into her wet jeans. Faith clenched her jaw as her fear turned to anger. She folded her arms defiantly across her chest.

"Good, I can't wait to meet her."

Chapter 22

Stewart, Massachusetts
1912

Anna smiled as her son raced through the garden, squealing happily. His aunt was pursuing him as he darted about. That Richard was home added more to the light that Catherine had brought to Whispering Pines. Sadly, her husband had also returned. Anna's smile dimmed. She looked around to ensure that her husband wasn't watching. If he knew that any of them were enjoying themselves, he would certainly put an end to their merriment. *Why is he always so unhappy?* She watched Catherine scoop Richard up in her arms.

"I've got you now, you little scamp!" Catherine laughed, spinning around her precious cargo who was laughing loudly.

Anna's smile returned; she was caught up in her son's laughter and the way her lover's hair glimmered in the afternoon sun. Her smile dimmed once again when she felt a sudden chill. A dark shadow clouded the moment. Richard's laughter died on his lips, and his tiny body froze in fear. Catherine looked at both of them with confusion. Anna felt the chill running through her as she cast a cautioning gaze towards Catherine.

"Richard," Anna said with a tremor in her gentle tone. It broke her heart to see the panic filling his eyes.

"Boy, come here!"

Anna flinched, hearing her husband call her son with no more respect than he would offer to a stray dog.

"Richard, go to your father," Anna said. She had known her husband was behind her long before he spoke. A darkness always preceded him.

Richard squirmed out of Catherine's embrace. She seemed reluctant to release her hold on him. Anna gave her a pleading nod, silently requesting that she not interfere.

"Are you running the household now?" the captain demanded from behind her.

Anna's body tensed, knowing what was about to happen. She didn't offer any resistance. She simply stood there, allowing his fist to tighten around her neatly wrapped hair. She stifled her painful cry when he yanked her back.

"No, Husband," she squeaked out, looking up into his cold, dark eyes.

"Brother!" Catherine cried out.

"Don't, it will only make it worse," Anna heard Richard whisper to his aunt.

Anna braced herself, watching her husband raise his open hand. "You will not interfere with my family," the captain snarled at Catherine, who was now standing beside Anna and shielding Richard with her body.

"I wouldn't dream of it," Catherine responded coldly.

Horatio's grip remained firmly wrapped in Anna's hair. Helplessly, she watched the siblings square off, each standing their ground. Anna understood something at that moment; the captain wouldn't strike his sister. Anna and Richard were his property; his sister somehow fell out of his domain. Horatio's hand still hovered above Anna's face. She turned pitifully towards her lover.

"Husband," Anna choked out. "It's late, shouldn't I be preparing the evening meal and tending to the boy?"

"Yes." The captain scowled in agreement, finally releasing Anna from his grasp. "Get to the kitchen where you belong. You," he addressed Richard, who was clinging to Catherine's skirt. "Why are you wasting the day by following these women around?"

Anna chewed her lip nervously as tears welled up in her son's eyes. "Answer me," Horatio demanded in a ferocious tone.

"M-Mother insisted," Richard tearfully stammered out.

Catherine looked down at the boy with a horror-stricken expression. Anna simply nodded to her son, silently encouraging him to continue.

"She said that I needed to get outside, because if I stay inside all day, I'll grow to be lazy."

Anna allowed a thin smile to emerge on her lips as she listened to her son skillfully retell the lie she had taught him. The captain seemed stunned by the boy's words. "Quite right," the captain gruffly grunted before walking away from the three of them.

Anna released a heavy breath. She turned and listened to her husband's retreating footsteps.

"Come now, we have duties to tend," she instructed Richard and Catherine loudly, certain that her husband was still lingering about.

Later that evening, Anna sat at the table in her room with Catherine by her side. They both pretended to be enthralled with stitching.

"You taught him to lie?" Catherine whispered, keeping her eyes focused on the delicate needlework.

"Of course," Anna flatly responded, allowing her fingers to drift from her stitching. She listened to Catherine's breathing hitch ever so slightly as Anna ran the tip of her pinky along her thigh.

Anna was learning so many things since Catherine's arrival. One of them was how to handle her husband. Fabrications were quickly becoming second nature to her. When Horatio questioned her as to why she and Catherine sat up late chatting every evening, she looked up at him innocently like a good wife, and said, "Husband, surely the mindless chatter of females holds no interest to a man as well educated as yourself." She was proud at the way he nodded in agreement, puffing out his chest as he gave his silent consent.

Anna wanted to laugh at his bravado. Not once had he stopped to think about how she was better with the written word than he was. She had learned from Catherine that Horatio had been sent to the sea when he was younger than Richard. Her husband was a very wealthy man, probably from ill-gotten gains from smuggling or worse. But Richard was probably better at understanding the written word than his father was.

"He asked about our sewing sessions," Anna calmly said to Catherine.

"And what did you tell him?" Catherine asked nervously.

"That we are silly females." Anna smirked, her fingers massaging Catherine's thigh. "Such an arrogant man."

"If he only knew," Catherine said softly. "Richard is such a charming boy."

"Yes." Anna smiled at the statement. "I will die before I allow him to become his father's son. You bring out the best in him. As you do for his mother." Anna's tone dropped sensually as she captured Catherine's gaze.

"If only he could visit when his father was away," Catherine said in an almost pleading tone.

"The captain forbids it."

"We could—" Catherine began to say.

"Yes." Anna nodded, knowing what Catherine was about to suggest. If Horatio was away, then the three of them could run off. "And that, my dear, is probably why the captain forbids it. It's late. I must read to Richard and tuck him in."

Anna placed her stitching on the table, and Catherine followed her actions. "Later, come upstairs and tuck me in as well, my love," Catherine whispered hotly in Anna's ear.

"Of course," Anna purred.

Chapter 23

Danvers, Massachusetts
2005

"Faith, don't do this," Shawn pleaded. Her ire was growing as she struggled with her wet jeans that were now very snug against her body. "Whatever problems Deb and I have in our relationship, this would be a crappy thing to do."

"Oh, so it was okay when there wasn't any chance she could find out?" Faith sneered with disgust. "What happened to you, Shawn?"

"You happened to me," Shawn answered, a pathetic feeling washing over her. "Please? I'm begging you, don't do this. She may not be the person for me, but she doesn't deserve this. She doesn't seem to think there's anything wrong with our relationship, which, of course, is part of the problem. Hell, she even got me a present."

"Really? What did she get you?" Faith refused to budge.

"A first edition of *Ulysses*," Shawn said. *Damn. Twenty-eight-hundred bucks. What was she thinking? We haven't been together that long.* Shawn was still trying to slow the rapid beating of her heart.

"You don't like James Joyce."

"Faith, try to focus on the bigger picture here," Shawn pleaded.

"You don't," Faith said. "I seem to recall your exact words on the subject were, 'Young Catholic boy loses his virginity and throws up, yadda, yadda, yadda.' Why would she spend what I can only imagine is a huge chunk of change on something you wouldn't enjoy?"

Shawn's head was pounding as she realized that Deb was the one who liked James Joyce. She really hated that Deb was impaired when it came to listening to her.

"That isn't the point." Shawn glared at Faith.

"Sure it is," Faith said in a catty tone. "If she cared enough to buy you something nice, she should care enough to buy you something you'd enjoy. A first edition Hawthorne or Dickens would be much more appropriate."

"Fine, you've proven your point," Shawn said softly, tears welling in her eyes. "You know me better. Are you happy now? Or do you really need to stick around and win the pissing contest?"

"Trust me when I tell you that happy is not how to describe what I'm feeling at this moment," Faith said in a hollow tone. She finally began to adjust her clothing to a more appropriate state. They exchanged a cold stare before Faith stormed across the room and yanked the door open. Shawn looked on in horror as her present lover gaped at her glowering ex-lover. Faith released a throaty growl that made Shawn shiver fearfully.

"She hates James Joyce," Faith hissed, pushing her way past a stunned-looking Deb and almost toppling her as she marched out of the room.

"That woman is amazing," Deb said, watching Faith storm down the hallway.

"That's Faith Charles," Shawn said dryly.

Her senses were reeling from the utter absurdity of the situation. Deb looked completely embarrassed by her reaction to Faith. Finally, she turned her attention towards Shawn.

"That's the woman you work with?"

Faith heard the hint of jealousy in her tone. "Yes."

"You never said how stunning she is," Deb said in an accusing tone. When Shawn failed to take the bait, Deb held out the delicately wrapped package.

"Happy birthday." Deb froze for a moment. Her head spun around, and she looked towards the still open door and then back at Shawn. "How did—"

"I knew," Shawn interrupted in a miserable tone. "Deb, we have to talk."

And talk they did. During the conversation, Shawn learned some things about her girlfriend that she had obviously ignored in the past few months. Deb was manipulative, as evidenced by her gift for Shawn; Deb wanted the book, and giving it to Shawn was a way to justify buying it. Deb seemed to be under the impression that it would only be a short matter of time before Shawn moved into her apartment.

Another thing Shawn realized was that she was using Deb for a sense of stability. They argued bitterly. Shawn tried to convince Deb that they didn't belong together. Deb didn't agree with Shawn's assessment of their relationship. Finally, Shawn did the only thing she could think of.

"Faith is my ex-lover," she blurted out.

She hated slamming Deb, but she had run out of options. Deb just didn't seem to think that there was anything amiss in their relationship.

"Huh?" Deb's face turned a deep shade of scarlet as she gaped at Shawn.

"Faith is my ex-lover," Shawn repeated in a slow, careful tone, knowing that she was being cruel.

"Why was she in your hotel room?"

"This is her room as well," Shawn said.

"You're cheating on me?" Deb asked in an incredulous tone.

"I'm sorry." Shawn exhaled in relief, knowing that the accusation wasn't exactly the truth. Then again, it would have been if Deb's timing didn't completely suck.

"You bitch," Deb screamed.

"I'm sorry," Shawn repeated, truly feeling awful about what she had done to Deb. A wave of relief washed over her when Deb stormed out of the room, clutching her precious book to her chest.

"That was a shitty thing to do," Shawn admonished herself.

She scrubbed her face furiously with her hands. Then she stepped out of the room and locked the door. Allowing her instincts to guide her, she went searching for Faith. She found a very somber-looking Faith sitting at the hotel bar. Tracy, one of the very young production assistants, was hanging on Faith's shoulder. Shawn's chest tightened painfully, and she felt sick as she watched the couple stumble out of the bar arm in arm.

Chapter 24

Stewart, Massachusetts
1912

Anna's body was trembling. She clung tightly to the wall of Catherine's bedroom.

"You amaze me," she whispered. She still tingled as Catherine held her while the passion ebbed from her. Catherine's hand caressed her bottom, and Anna struggled to regain her breath.

The captain had gone into town, and Richard was playing in his room. Once the staff retreated for the day, Anna and Catherine had sneaked up to Catherine's room and stolen a few quiet moments. Catherine didn't waste a single second. She had pressed Anna against the wall, raised the hem of her dress up to her waist, and begun caressing her.

Noises drew Anna's gaze to the window, and her heart clenched when she spied the carriage careening up the path, followed by an automobile. "He's back," she said grimly. "He's brought a companion."

"Another would-be suitor," Catherine groaned with disgust. "Will he never stop trying to marry me off?"

"No." Anna sighed deeply, watching the vehicles approach. She adjusted her dress before turning in Catherine's embrace. "We need to hurry down to the kitchen."

"Wait," Catherine halted Anna's movements. "There's something I wish to give you."

"My dear, you give me so much," Anna replied with a sly look and a smoldering gaze that made Catherine shiver.

"Oh, what you do to me." Catherine trembled while fumbling to retrieve the box she had hidden in her dresser. She studied the contents for a moment before returning her gaze to Anna. She reached out and took Anna's hand. Anna looked up at her with curiosity. Catherine slipped a bracelet onto her slender wrist.

"I bought this the day I was leaving Paris. Spent the last of my money on it. At the time, I had no idea why I did it. Now I know. I was meant to bestow it upon the one who would capture my heart."

Anna smiled and studied the silver bracelet. She raised Catherine's hand to her lips and kissed it. "Thank you, my love," she said, holding her in a lingering gaze. "It will never leave my wrist. Now, we must hurry."

They used the hidden passageway and made their way to the kitchen before Horatio could enter the house.

"Why swans?" Anna asked as they set about preparing the evening meal. She listened carefully for the sounds of her husband hurrying up to her bedchambers. He did not disappoint. His thunderous footsteps echoed through the mansion. The sound of her bedroom door being slammed shut reverberated immediately afterward.

"Swans mate for life," Catherine whispered hotly in Anna's ear. She was so accustomed to her brother's boorish behavior that she simply ignored his stomping about.

"Wife!" he demanded with a fierce howl.

"Yes, Husband," Anna greeted him calmly as she stepped out of the kitchen. She was thankful that he expected her to gaze down at the floor. In doing so, she could hide the blush that she knew was covering her delicate features. The memories of Catherine's touch kept her balanced.

* * *

For Catherine, the evening meal was pure torture. Collin Ryan appeared to be a pompous blowhard who prattled on and on about himself. His main objective seemed to be to impress her brother. The only thing that she enjoyed about the meal was her nephew's constant eye-rolling. Apparently, Richard found Mr. Ryan about as entertaining as she did.

One thing about Mr. Ryan intrigued her, and she couldn't help but wonder whether it was true. Still, she amused herself by stealing silly smiles with Richard. "Boy!" the captain boomed just as the meal was coming to an end.

Richard's smile vanished, and his gaze darted down to his plate.

"He's restless," Anna said. Catherine cringed when Horatio glared over at his wife. Much to her surprise and pleasure, Anna didn't flinch from his hostile glare or from the way he curled his hand into a fist.

"I was much the same at that age," Collin said merrily, and that was when Catherine realized that, for the moment, Anna had nothing to fear. Horatio would never strike his wife in front of witnesses. Collin Ryan was seated just high enough in polite society to ruin Horatio's reputation.

"I bet you were a rascal," Catherine said in an effort to further irritate her brother. As Horatio glared at her, she wondered if he was aware of the way she and Anna played him.

"Perhaps you could share some of your tales with my sister?" Horatio trumped her. "A walk in the gardens would be nice."

Anna met her horrified gaze. Collin seemed to turn pale, his reaction further confirming Catherine's suspicions.

"Brother, I do have my chores to tend to," Catherine pointed out in a cocky manner.

"See, she'll make a fine bride," Horatio said.

Catherine's lips curled as Collin pulled out her chair for her. She shivered at the hateful look Anna cast upon the unfortunate man.

As they stepped outside, Catherine nodded towards the man standing by the motor car. "And who would that be?" she asked.

"My driver, Branford," Collin said as Catherine guided him towards the garden.

"He's very pretty." Catherine smirked.

"Pretty?" Collin's voice squeaked as Catherine turned towards the nervous young man.

"Just as I thought." She smiled as his jaw dropped. "Don't bother denying it, my friend."

He snorted out a soft laugh and rolled his eyes. "I had a feeling as well." He smirked. "Shall I manufacture the customary excuses?"

"Not just yet," Catherine said. "Lurk about every now and then. Hopefully that will keep my brother content."

"It would please my father as well," Collin said. "He's very eager to do business with your brother. Forgive me, but I can't say that I really care for your brother."

"Nor do I." Catherine linked her arm in his. "Now, while we're pretending to hit it off, tell me how you met Branford."

"It was glorious." He practically squealed like a schoolgirl.

* * *

Later that evening, as Catherine and Anna sat in Anna's room working on needlepoint, Anna was beside herself.

"Where's Horatio?" Catherine asked.

"In his study," Anna replied curtly. "He'll be drunk within the hour. If we're lucky, he'll pass out."

"I pray that he does." Catherine snorted. "Is something troubling you, Sister?"

"Nothing," Anna snapped, almost stabbing herself while working with her needle. "You and Mr. Ryan seemed cozy."

Catherine smirked at Anna's tone. "Yes." Catherine played along. "He's quite charming. It's no wonder Branford finds him so endearing."

"Branford?"

"Yes, his driver," Catherine said merrily. "Surely you saw the pretty man waiting by the motor car."

"Pretty?" Anna shook her head and then a brilliant smile graced her features. "Oh?"

"Yes," Catherine said. "A kindred spirit, dear. I hope you won't object to Mr. Ryan calling upon me again?"

"Now that I know he won't be touching you, I have no objections," Anna whispered hotly in her ear. Catherine shivered as her lover's words caressed her flesh.

"And would you like to touch me?" Catherine asked, clasping Anna by the wrist. Catherine guided Anna's tiny hand to her lap.

"Yes." Anna's eyes were burning with need as her hand slipped under Catherine's nightgown. Catherine licked her lips while parting her thighs. She inhaled sharply when she felt Anna's touch greeting her desire. They sat there, pretending to work on their sewing as Anna slowly stroked her.

The following afternoon, Catherine would reconfirm their love by pleasuring Anna in the safe confines of the garden. Later, she began to worry whether they were becoming careless. Still, no one seemed to notice what they were doing. Perhaps the heavens were finally smiling down upon them, granting them this small slice of paradise.

Chapter 25

Stewart, Massachusetts
1935

Richard Stratton watched as his elderly father, Horatio, huffed and puffed, once more trying to dig up the garden. It had bloomed overnight, again.

"She'll never let you have it!" Richard called out with malicious glee. "My mother will never give you her garden." He laughed as Horatio tossed the flowers about. "Give it to her," Richard taunted him. "How many times have you dug it up? Plowed it over? Salted the soil? And still she tends to it."

"Silence!" Horatio demanded as he barreled over towards his son.

"Or what, old man?" Richard stood his ground defiantly. He had stopped fearing his father long ago. Now, he wanted only one thing. He wanted to put his mother and beloved aunt to rest. He would never forget the smug look on his father's face the day Richard returned from school and went in search for them. Their rooms were empty, and all of their possessions gone. No sign remained of his mother or of Catherine. He would remember forever the cold look in his father's eyes as he told Richard, "The bitches are gone." The man cackled at the stunned boy. Richard knew in his heart that neither of them would abandon him.

When grown, he rarely returned to Whispering Pines. The only reason he went to his father's home at all was to get answers.

"Why are you here?" Horatio sneered. "I heard that you finally claimed your land just beyond the trees."

"Yes," Richard replied coldly. "I want to be near them."

"I also heard you married," Horatio said in an accusing tone. "Why wasn't I informed?"

"Why would I tell you anything?" Richard almost laughed at the suggestion. "Why would I invite a murderer to my wedding?"

"Why are you here?" the captain repeated.

"For the same reason I always come here," Richard said. "Where are they?"

The captain snorted, seemingly amused by the question.

"Let me put them to rest," Richard demanded as his father walked away. "What happened to my mother?"

The captain halted his movement and snickered before turning to his son. The cold, dark eyes made Richard flinch. "Your mother was a whore," Horatio said with an evil smile.

For the first and only time in his life, Richard Stratton gave into the anger and hatred he felt for this man. He crossed the distance between them, and before he realized what was happening, he struck his father down. It wasn't hard to knock the elderly man off of his feet. Richard felt ashamed for giving in to the violence his father had taught him.

Horatio was laughing like a madman when Richard turned, walked back to his car, and drove away. The captain's laughter was still ringing in his ears when he returned to his own home, just beyond the trees of Whispering Pines.

"Oh, Richard." Vera, his wife, sighed heavily when he entered the foyer. "I can always tell when you've been to see him."

"I hit him," Richard said in a miserable tone. "I finally sank to his level." He was unable to calm himself, even as he felt his wife's arms encircling his waist.

"You are not him," she said. She stood behind him, comforting him.

Richard clasped his hands over Vera's and allowed his eyes to flutter shut.

"I can still remember that last day I had with them," he said sadly, finally relaxing into Vera's tender embrace. "We had a picnic by the ocean and then walked around town. Then Aunt Catherine treated us to the photography studio at the far end of town. They gave me the picture of the three of us together. I took it with me when I went back to school. Mother said that if I kept it with me, then she and Catherine would always be watching over me.

"He didn't even let me say good-bye to either of them that last morning. When I came home for Christmas, they were gone. All of their belongings were missing. I learned later that he burned their beds and clothing. Then he sold off the rest of their possessions."

"How could someone as kind and gentle as you, my dear husband, come from that cold-hearted, forgive my language, bastard?" Vera leaned against her husband's back.

"Everything good in me came from Mother and Aunt Catherine," Richard said with tenderness. "They were the only two people who showed me what love was. Until I met you, of course."

"Happiest day of my life," Vera said. "He'll never tell you what you want to know," she told Richard, not for the first time. "He may be mean and old, but he isn't a fool. The sheriff has never stopped watching him. He knows he'll go to prison if anyone ever discovers the truth."

"I have to find them and put them to rest," Richard vowed in a weary tone.

Chapter 26

Danvers, Massachusetts
2005

Shawn's head was ready to explode even before the unnecessary wake-up call came. She had sat up all night crying and staring at the empty bed across from her own. She felt numb as she showered and dressed. When she met the crew down at the van, she noticed that Faith looked even worse than she did. She felt a pang of guilt until a certain production assistant slid up next to Faith. Shawn couldn't stop her scowl when she climbed into the opposite side of the van. She looked back at Faith, who had put on her sunglasses and leaned her head against the window.

Althea rushed around trying to wrap up the shoot. "Ten minutes," she finally called out, visibly frustrated by what was going on. "Someone do something about Charles's hangover," she shouted. Faith winced. "Dr. Williams, a moment of your time," she said, linking her arm in Shawn's and dragging her out back to the gardens.

Shawn rested on a bench and took a moment to inhale the sweet fragrance of flowers mixed with the ocean breeze.

"She was right." She sighed, recalling the promise she had made to take time out to enjoy the gardens.

Althea paced nervously. "I have a busy schedule this year," she said in a cold tone. "These shows are hot right now, and so are you. With any luck, we can wrap up Salem, Edinburgh, Fall River, and New York, and have everything packaged before the fall conferences."

"Should be a good year for Sunny Hill Productions," Shawn said absently, still drinking in her surroundings.

"The only question is, who will be going with me?" Althea said harshly.

"Are you asking me if I can play nice with others?" Shawn suddenly was upset.

"Normally, I'd be directing this question to Faith. I had gotten used to the banter and teasing the two of you shared before you teamed up. Heck! It made for some entertaining moments on and off film. Frankly, what I'm seeing today has me more than a little concerned. And more than a little surprised, since I would have sworn on my last Emmy that the two of you were about to get back together. What happened?"

"If you need to drop me from the projects, I understand," Shawn said, not wanting to reveal the events of the previous evening.

"Shawn, we can't drop you," Althea said in a softer tone. "You must know how much you're in demand at the moment. If I have to make a change, it won't be you."

"Wait." Shawn jumped to her feet. "You can't fire Faith. Not again."

"I won't fire her," Althea promised. "But if you can't work with her, then I'll have to reassign her."

"Right," Shawn grumbled. "Everyone knows that you head up the good shoots. She'll end up looking for aliens at a self-serve gas station in Roswell. I can work with her. I swear."

"I'm asking as your friend, not your boss, Shawn. What happened? You and Faith looked very cozy last night," she added in a sly tone.

"Deb happened." Shawn plopped back down onto the bench. "Damn good thing I felt her coming, or she would have gotten quite an eyeful."

"You're still with Deb?" Althea sat next to Shawn. "Girl, just when are you going to smarten up? She doesn't respect you. And what you have with her doesn't hold a candle to the sparks flying off of you and tall, dark, and moody."

"I know, and I sent Deb packing last night," Shawn said. "One day too late. By the time I caught up with Faith, she was otherwise engaged. Can't blame her. How many times can you hear, 'I have a girlfriend,' before you hit the bricks?"

"Okay, now I'm confused. You know, for a psychic, sometimes you're completely clueless..." Shawn stared at Althea as her voice trailed off.

Shawn shivered, and a strange feeling crept up on her. She looked off to the side and spied a familiar brunette approaching them.

"Ms. St. James, what brings you here?" Shawn asked cautiously. Something about this woman bothered her, and she knew what was causing her mistrust. Delia St. James wasn't being completely honest with her. Shawn couldn't get a reading on the woman, and it was driving her nuts. As much as she hated being privy to people's innermost thoughts, at times not knowing could prove to be far more frustrating.

"I got a very confusing telephone call late last evening," Delia said, twirling a large manila envelope between her fingers. "It was from Ms. Charles, and she sounded, well, she sounded drunk. She said she wanted to talk to me about Whispering Pines. I was visiting my family and promised to stop by for a chat."

"I'll get her," Althea said and hurried back inside the castle.

"I'm surprised to see you here, Dr. Williams." Delia hesitated slightly, seemingly in search of something to talk about. "When I met Ms. Charles, I got the impression that the two of you weren't getting along."

"Now there's an understatement." Shawn laughed as Delia took a seat next to her. "It's your work!" Shawn suddenly blurted out with surprise. "That's what you've been hiding. I don't understand. You're very good at what you do, and your work is important."

"That's really annoying." Delia looked over at her with a dumbfounded expression. "Yes, what I do is important. I build buildings that not only look good, but will continue to stand no matter what. But it's how I developed my technology that bothers me. My grandfather said that we must learn from the past, and he was right."

"Yes, he was," Shawn agreed as she felt the source of the young woman's anguish. "You learn from tragedy. You feel like you've earned your success by others' dying, instead of remembering that you're helping prevent more lives being lost."

"Now you're starting to sound like my mother," Delia said, still twirling the envelope.

"So the call from Faith must have made you happy," Shawn said. "Come to give us another sales pitch?"

"In a manner of speaking." Delia smiled. She handed Shawn the envelope just as Faith approached them.

Shawn's mind spun as she saw a flash; then she heard laughter and voices. *"You keep it, Richard. That way we'll always be there to watch over you,"* Anna's voice echoed.

Another flash hit her. A shimmer of light was catching something that was reflecting the light. She heard a man grumbling and a small boy giggling.

"Dr. Williams?" A voice called to her as her hands trembled and the envelope slipped from her fingers. Shawn ignored the voice as she buried her face in her hands and began to rock back and forth.

"What did you do to her?" A different voice demanded as Shawn felt comforting hands on her shoulder and face.

"Nothing, I swear," she heard Delia St. James say with a hint of fear.

Shawn blinked, opened her eyes, and saw Faith kneeling in front of her. It was Faith's hands that were offering her comfort. She could see the fear in Faith's eyes as she caressed Shawn's face.

"I'm fine," Shawn said weakly.

"That was a bad one." Faith's voice trembled, and her fingers drifted up to Shawn's furrowed brow.

"No, just strong," Shawn said, trying to stop the world from spinning.

"Hmm, those kind usually leave you with one hell of a headache." Faith picked up the envelope.

"No kidding." Shawn tried to smile. "Consider it payback for making you drink too much last night."

"Why are you here?" Faith asked Delia.

"You called me."

"I did?" Faith furrowed her brow and opened the envelope. "Wow, they look a lot better when you can't see through them." Shawn peered at the old photograph of two women seated with a small, dark-haired boy nestled happily between them.

"So, again, I have to ask what happened here, Ms. St. James?"

"Faith, you're scaring her." Shawn continued to study the photograph.

"I am not," Faith said. Delia nodded her head. "Sorry," Faith said with a frown. "So, the little boy would be your grandfather?"

"Yes." Delia backed slightly away from Faith. "That's the only picture ever taken of Anna, and the only one with the three of them together."

"No," Shawn mumbled as she slipped the large photograph from Faith's grasp. Her fingers tingled slightly as they brushed against Faith's. "They had to take the picture three times. Something kept reflecting the flash. Something metal, something to Richard's right," she said, studying the photo. "Holy shit!" Her eyes widened.

"Such language," Faith said with a playful smile as Shawn handed her the photo and pointed to Anna's wrist. Faith's eyes bugged out as she spotted the object Shawn was pointing to. Shawn drew back the sleeve of her jacket and held the bracelet up so they could all see. "How?"

"That's what I haven't been telling you, Dr. Williams," Delia said. "I noticed it immediately the first time we met. I thought maybe that was why they let you stay in the house. The captain either burned or sold off their possessions. I have to ask where you got that bracelet."

"It was a gift," Shawn said, feeling herself blush. Faith continued to stare at the photograph. "I didn't receive it until after my stay at Whispering Pines. This is just a coincidence, Ms. St. James." Faith's head jerked up with surprise. "As earth-crunchy as you think I am, Faith, I do know that coincidences do happen."

"But—" Faith began to say.

"I have to ask, do you know where the bracelet came from?" Delia said. "Perhaps another psychic could get something from it, and I can finally find out what happened."

"A small antiques shop in Boston, on Charles Street." Faith clasped Shawn's wrist and began to trace the bracelet with her long fingers. "The owner said it had been lost in the shuffle and sat in storage for years. He only found it a few weeks before I bought it. He didn't know the history, since it was probably purchased by one of the previous owners. He was certain that it was French, probably crafted around the turn of the century. The previous one," she amended.

"I asked my mother about it," Delia continued in a hopeful tone. "She said her father told her that his mother never took it off since it was a gift from Catherine."

"We don't know that it was Anna's," Shawn said as she caught the pleading looks coming from both women.

"I was drawn to it," Faith whispered as she continued to caress Shawn's wrist.

"You were drawn to the symbolism of it," Shawn said, finding it strange that she was the voice of reason in this conversation. "Milo saw that."

"Perhaps Milo should take another look?" Faith said as her caresses grew bolder.

"Are you sure the two of you don't get along?" Delia asked.

"Depends on what day you ask," Shawn teased as she felt a surge of warmth. Her mind spun as she caught the image of a bartender bringing one drink after another, then a flash to the toothy, young girl snuggling up beside Faith's body. The image faded as she heard the words, "Why not?" echoing. She snatched her hand away. Faith looked up at her with a confused expression.

"I'll have a colleague look at the bracelet, Ms. St. James, and I'll get back to you," Shawn said abruptly. She almost knocked Faith over when she moved around her. She marched back towards the castle, hearing Faith's frustrated grumble behind her.

She was fuming by the time she met up with Althea.

"A meeting with Delia St. James?" Althea gushed. "Should I be getting some contracts ready?"

"No," Shawn refused, even as she felt that all roads were leading her back to Whispering Pines.

"Oh, crap," Althea said. "Am I making staff changes to the upcoming schedule, instead?"

"No." Shawn was angry with Faith and herself, but she couldn't let Faith's career suffer because of it. "I told you I would play nice, and I will." She was about to walk away when she felt Althea's hand on her arm.

"Shawn, this is really none of my business," Althea said softly. "I don't know what you think happened last night, but Faith slept on the sofa in my suite. She showed up in the wee hours, really drunk and looking for a place to crash. I asked her what happened. All she said was, 'Bite me,' before she passed out." Shawn was dumbfounded as she tried to understand just what had happened last night.

Chapter 27

Faith was in a miserable mood that night. She didn't want to go back to the hotel room she was sharing with Shawn, but didn't have a choice. She needed a shower, clean clothing, and most of all, sleep. She felt sick knowing she could open the door and find Deb waiting inside.

Faith let out a sigh of relief when she discovered only Shawn in the room. Her relief was very short-lived. She caught Shawn's glare as she closed the door.

"Where did you sleep last night?" Shawn demanded in a hurt tone.

A flush of anger surged through Faith. "What do you care?" She tossed her card and wallet onto her nightstand. She had had enough of this game and was too exhausted to deal with Shawn's tirade. All she wanted was a long, hot shower and sleep.

"I care." Shawn folded her arms across her chest.

"I'm far too tired to deal with this," Faith said, kicking off her shoes and shrugging out of her jacket. "I'm not asking how your birthday celebration went with your girlfriend, am I?"

"I dumped her. Then I went looking for you, only to find you leaving the hotel bar with some youngster."

"Great," Faith grumbled. "Not that it's any of your business, but nothing happened. I kissed her, that's all. It wasn't right. I called St. James wanting to know more about Whispering Pines. Then I crashed in Althea's room. I may have thrown up at some point, although I'm not entirely certain about that."

Faith felt defeated. Unable to deal with the conversation, she began tugging her shirt out of her pants. "When are you going to believe me? When am I going to stop paying for one mistake? Tell me, Shawn, just when are you going to understand that it's you that I want?"

Faith's head was pounding, her body ached, and her heart was broken. To top off her miserable day, she had just exposed her heart to be hurt once again.

"Mmmf," was the muffled sound she made as Shawn knocked her down onto her bed and captured her lips. She was far too stunned to react at first. Once her mind caught up with her body, she eagerly returned Shawn's kiss. Her hands were gliding along Shawn's back as the kiss deepened. She became lost in Shawn's touch. Faith's hands drifted down to Shawn's firm, round bottom. She squeezed Shawn's cheeks through her jeans, and slipped her hand between Shawn's thighs.

"We can't," Shawn gasped, pulling away from Faith's touch.

Faith looked up at the woman straddling her body.

"Huh?" She was completely baffled by the situation. She hissed when she heard a knock on the door.

"It's Milo," Shawn said sheepishly. "I called him to come take a look at the bracelet."

"I hate my life," Faith whimpered as Shawn climbed off of her. Faith cooled instantly, missing the heat of Shawn's body pressed against her own.

"I'm going to take a shower." She climbed off of the bed and grabbed some clothing. As she entered the bathroom, she couldn't shake the nagging fear that the lip-lock she had just shared with Shawn hadn't changed anything.

Chapter 28

Stewart, Massachusetts
1914

"He won't be pleased." Anna almost snickered as she looked about her home, now decorated from top to bottom for the upcoming holiday.

"To hell with him," Catherine muttered under her breath as she glared over her shoulder at Miranda, who was skulking about as usual. "He's away on a voyage. You should be able to enjoy Christmas for once. Don't you agree, Miranda?"

Anna's hand flew up to her mouth in an effort to suppress her smile as she watched the maid jump with surprise.

"Whispering Pines is a beautiful manor, and it's only right that it be included in the joyous celebration," Catherine said triumphantly once Miranda proved that she was incapable of answering.

"Thank you, Sister," Anna graciously said as she gazed about the manor that finally looked like a home. "Richard will be beside himself," she added happily, knowing it would be well worth her husband's wrath. For now, she would simply enjoy the holiday with her son and her lover. For the first time in Anna's life, it would truly be a merry Christmas for her. In her heart, she knew that the joyous celebration wouldn't have been possible without Catherine's guiding hand. She felt the blush spread in her cheeks as the word *lover* echoed delightfully in her mind.

"Whatever you're thinking must be truly wicked for you to blush like that," Catherine whispered in Anna's ear. Anna trembled when Catherine's breath caressed her skin. She bit back a moan as she felt her body swooning.

"I don't know if I can wait for tonight," Catherine added, brushing her fingers lightly against Anna's bottom before stepping away.

Anna felt as though she were melting. She regretted that there was no way for the two of them to sate their needs until after the staff departed for the evening.

"This is going to be a very long day," she muttered.

As Anna went about her chores, she couldn't erase her blissful smile. Many times, knowing that they had to wait before they could be intimate only made her even more excited. She had never known that love could feel so good, and that making love could be so intense.

Later that evening, her long hair clinging to her brow, she collapsed against Catherine's body. She smiled when she heard her lover's contented sigh. Catherine's arms were wrapped around her waist, and Anna pressed her ear against Catherine's breast. It was her favorite time, when her body was sated, and she could just nestle against Catherine and listen to the steady beating of her heart.

Soon, Richard would be home and the three of them would enjoy a real Christmas as a family. She and Catherine would have to be careful around her son. Catherine had been hinting that perhaps they should flee once Richard returned. Anna knew it would be impossible to escape from Horatio's grasp. If the attempt failed, she would lose her son and her lover forever. She also suspected that the captain would be returning soon. He had never been absent whenever Richard was home.

"That Miranda is a pill," Catherine muttered softly. She stroked Anna's naked back. "Pity you can't dismiss her."

"You know I can't." Anna sighed deeply. She lifted her head and met her lover's gaze. "The staff is beholden to the captain. He pays them far too well for them to betray him, and he owns most of the town."

"I wouldn't mind her spying and sour demeanor so much if she were at least a decent maid," Catherine joked. Anna laughed softly. "We could leave the moment Richard returns."

"If I only knew how long the captain would be gone," Anna said in a pitiful tone. "If we could be certain that we could escape, I would agree in a heartbeat. But he could return at any moment. I won't risk losing either of you."

"Maybe his ship will sink," Catherine hissed.

"Catherine," Anna said, "I don't care for your brother, but wishing him ill isn't the answer. I know I've often uttered those very same words, but it isn't right. He is so much older than we are, and someday we'll be free. If you can't wait for me, I understand."

"I would endure an eternity in hell just to be with you," Catherine vowed. Capturing Anna's hand, she brought it to her lips. She kissed the bracelet that never left Anna's wrist, before she brushed her lips lightly against Anna's palm. The simple promising gesture awakened Anna's passion, and soon the two lovers became lost in a fiery embrace that would last until dawn.

Chapter 29

Danvers, Massachusetts
2005

Faith was lying on Shawn's bed, fully dressed, searching for the pack of gum she always kept in her travel bag. Days like this made her wish she had never quit smoking. She understood it was a filthy and disgusting habit, not to mention life-threatening, but all in all, she really enjoyed it.

"You don't need a cigarette," Shawn said, reminding Faith yet again that being near a psychic really sucked at times.

She glanced over at Milo, who was sitting on her bed. She smirked at the way he had combed his few strands of hair across his forehead in an effort to conceal the fact that he was balding. "Faith," Shawn scolded her once again.

Damn, I really must be on edge and vulnerable today. She isn't missing anything. Faith hoped Shawn had tuned into that thought and would back off.

"So, fat boy," she said. Milo looked up with an indignant expression on his pudgy face. "What can you tell us about the bauble?"

"Faith." Shawn handed Milo the bracelet. "You can be such a jerk at times."

Faith snickered at the comment and curled up behind Shawn. "You should know," she said, feeling mildly amused with herself. Her amusement faded when Milo began rocking and humming as he clutched the bracelet. "This guy drives me nuts," she muttered.

"Behave." Shawn swatted Faith in a playful manner.

"Don't want to," Faith grumbled.

"If you can't play nice, then you'll have to leave."

"Fine," Faith sneered. Milo began chanting in the most disturbing manner.

"'It needs to mean something,'" he said in a distant tone. "'I need to tell her that I'm in love with her,'" he rambled on. Faith felt the anger filling her.

"Son of a bitch," she hissed, noticing that Shawn's body had stiffened and she was averting her gaze. Faith was furious. It was the truth; she had wanted to give Shawn some token that would express the feelings she was unable to verbalize. It pissed her off that this was the way Shawn discovered the truth. She *was* hopelessly in love with Shawn; it just would have been nice if she had been the one to tell her.

Feeling the sudden distance that was emanating from Shawn's body made it clear to Faith that there really wasn't going to be a second chance for them. At that moment, all she wanted to do was flee from the room and find someplace private where she could wallow in her anguish.

"Stillness." Milo hummed, rocking. "'Toss it in the back with the other garbage he brought in. You'd think a rich man would have something better to sell us.'"

Faith was no longer listening to him. She stood up, with the full intention of leaving the room, and Shawn, behind.

"No!" Milo screamed, halting Faith's retreat. She watched him begin to shake violently. Suddenly, his eyes flew open, and he tossed the bracelet at Shawn.

"Why would you make me witness that?" he shrieked. "I never want to see that again. I'm going to be sick."

"I understand," Shawn said in a grave tone. "Did the bracelet belong to Anna Stratton?"

"Yes," Milo said, still trembling. "It was a gift from her sister-in-law. Catherine gave it to her as a promise." He directed his words towards Faith. "That's what you felt when you chose it."

Once again, Faith felt a rush of anger that her private feelings were being bandied about. Just as quickly, the anger slipped away when she felt Shawn's hand on her arm. She looked down at Shawn and spied a glimmer in her eyes that she hadn't seen in a very long time. It wasn't about the passion they once shared; it spoke of something deeper. Faith was filled with renewed hope that the bond between them might be returning.

"I should be going," Milo grunted. Faith and Shawn were ignoring him, staring at each other.

Milo made his departure, and Faith slumped down next to Shawn. Gently she covered Shawn's hand with her own. She caressed it tenderly.

"I can't believe that I've been wearing her bracelet," Shawn said.

"Like you said before, it's a coincidence."

"Oh, now you get all reasonable on me." Shawn snickered lightly. "You know, there's something else I can't believe." Faith held her breath while Shawn seemed to be collecting her thoughts. "I can't believe how badly I've been treating you."

"Why are you so angry with me?" Faith asked in a hushed tone.

"You left me," Shawn said, tears filling her eyes. Faith could handle anything except the sight of Shawn crying. Without hesitation, she cradled Shawn in her arms.

"When you just took that job, without discussing it with me, I thought I didn't matter to you." She sobbed as she clung to Faith.

Faith finally had the answers she had been seeking. She rocked Shawn in her arms. Finally, she understood why Shawn had lashed out at her. Shawn was afraid for her. Faith had placed her life in danger without thinking twice about how her lover felt about the choice she had made.

"I'm sorry," she said. "I never had to stop and think about how my actions affected someone else. I'm not good at being part of a couple. Before I met you, I never even wanted to try."

"No, this is my fault." Shawn sniffed and snuggled closer to Faith. "I got so damn angry. All I could focus on was that I wasn't important enough to you to be asked how I felt about the job. I might have supported it, but I didn't even get the chance to make that choice. To me, it said that we weren't really a couple."

"But we were." Faith's heart sank as she realized how far apart they really were. "We're not getting back together, are we?"

"Not tonight," Shawn said.

Shawn's eyes were swollen from crying, yet the fire in them still burned brightly. Faith was drawn in. She leaned closer, and her gaze drifted down to Shawn's lips. Shawn shivered in her arms. Just as she was about to capture Shawn in a kiss, Shawn pressed her fingers against Faith's lips.

"It will just confuse things," Shawn said.

"I hate it when you're right."

"I know." Shawn smiled. "Will you hold me tonight?"

"Now that's the best offer I've had in months." Faith guided them both down onto the mattress. She sighed contentedly as they snuggled together.

"You're going back, aren't you?" Shawn asked sleepily as she caressed Faith's stomach. "Whispering Pines. You're going back."

"Yes." Faith sighed. "If the next team asks me to go, I'm going to accept. I don't understand it, but I feel as if it's something that I have to do. Any chance you'll change your mind and join me?"

"I can't." Shawn trembled. "I saw it. I saw what he did to them. Every blow of the axe, every drop of blood, I witnessed the whole thing and felt their pain. I can't live through that again."

"I understand," Faith said, and she did. Over the years, she had witnessed things as a reporter that no one should ever have to see. That night she was just happy to be holding Shawn in her arms as they drifted off to sleep. In the morning, they would once again be heading off in different directions.

Chapter 30

Salem, Massachusetts
2005

Shawn shivered as the cool autumn air assaulted her. She had been watching the crew set up for hours. Glancing at her watch, she confirmed that she had more than enough time to slip away and enjoy a nice hot cup of coffee. She could also take the time to call Faith.

Faith had been pulled from the shoot at the Witch House and reassigned to a farmhouse in Kansas. Shawn was looking forward to spending more time with her after what had transpired between them during the shoot at Hammond Castle. At first, each of them feared that Althea had pulled Faith from the project because of their personal relationship. They were relieved when Althea informed them it was only because Faith wasn't needed this time. For the Salem shoot, they weren't using what Althea called a tour guide. Instead, some high-priced actor with a great voice would do the narration after the film was edited. Shawn reached in her pocket and extracted her car keys.

"I'll be back," she whispered to Althea before wandering over to the rental car. She drove a short distance until she reached the Dunkin Donuts located near the waterfront.

"I need coffee," she muttered. She parked the car across the street and went inside.

She ordered and looked around for a place to sit. A tall, dark-haired woman seated at one of the tables motioned for her to join her.

"You're with the film crew I take it," the woman, who was poring over a stack of musty old files, warmly greeted her.

"Shawn Williams, and yes I'm with the film crew," Shawn said as she took a seat. She couldn't shake the nagging feeling of familiarity that filled her when she looked into the woman's hazel eyes. "The locals cringe every time they see us coming. Can't really blame them."

"But, it's the stock-in-trade here," the brunette said, flashing Shawn a brilliant smile that sent another wave of familiarity through her. "Carey Jessup." The woman offered her hand.

Shawn accepted Carey's hand and shook it firmly. "You're a cop?" she said with a smile.

"Yes. How did you know that?"

"That's what I do."

"Oh, so you're one of those crystal-worshipping psychics?" Carey scoffed. "Was it the donuts that gave you the cop vibe, or did you just look down at the files on the table?" Carey challenged her with a friendly smile.

Shawn peeked at the files for the first time. "You must be here to meet with Althea," she said.

"Another psychic flash?"

"Nope, this time it was the files." Shawn laughed, thinking that Carey and Faith were going to work very well together. "I couldn't help noticing Anna Stratton's name."

"You're familiar with the Whispering Pines case?" Carey asked eagerly.

"You could say that."

"Wait, Shawn Williams, Dr. Shawn Williams?" Carey asked.

"Yes."

"Heck, I thought you were a man."

Shawn looked down at her breasts and frowned.

"I based my conclusions solely on your name," Carey said. "I'll be honest, I haven't read your books or heard a lot about your experiences. Frankly I don't believe in ghosts."

"No, you don't. I take it that Althea brought you on board to investigate the murders? Should make for an interesting sidepiece."

"We don't know that there was a murder," Carey said.

"I do."

"Sorry, I just can't take your word on it," Carey said, effectively dismissing Shawn's statement. "But I am looking forward to working with you."

"There isn't a chance in hell I would ever set foot in that house again," Shawn said, despite a niggling, troubling thought that whispered that she was going back.

"Interesting," Carey said. "Well, at least I'll get to see what one of these circuses is like. That's why I drove up here, so I could watch and learn how the filming process works."

"It's a lot of hurry up and wait." Shawn smiled, noticing again the sense of familiarity that surrounded this woman.

"So what's with the Witch House? Lots of scary old hags lurking about?" Carey asked.

"That's a very narrow-minded view of Wiccans," Shawn said abruptly. "The Witch House was where most of the interrogations took place during the witch trials. One of the judges lived there, and since there were no real courthouses in those days, they held the so-called trials in what we would nowadays consider the parlor. Some people have claimed to have experienced odd happenings."

"Oh, come on now," Carey scoffed.

"It's true."

"No offense, I but I think it's a boatload of crap." Carey stood.

"I'm not going to argue with you." Shawn shrugged. "I gave up on trying to convince people that I see what I see."

"Right, you see things," Carey said. "I think you sneaked a peek at my files, and that's how you knew I'm in law enforcement."

"That isn't how I knew." Shawn sighed. "Like I said, I'm not going to argue the point. I would only be wasting my time and yours. Oh, just one more thing. Can you tell me why you changed your name? I can't quite get a focus on that," Shawn said, flashing the stunned woman a cocky smirk.

"H-How did you know that?" Carey stammered.

"You and Faith Charles are going to get along just fine." Shawn chuckled as they headed towards the entrance.

"Wait!" Carey suddenly shouted. "Faith Charles?"

"Yes, she's working on the Whispering Pines project." Shawn eyed Carey suspiciously. "The two of you have very similar personalities. I think you'll really hit it off."

"I'm nothing like that bitch," Carey said. "I was told she wasn't working on the project. I asked before I ever agreed to come on board. I was assured that she wasn't even in the country."

Shawn was only mildly stunned by Carey's reaction; after all, Faith did have a reputation of rubbing people the wrong way.

"She only signed on to work on the project a couple of days ago," Shawn said.

"There's no way I'm working with that bitch." Carey stormed out of the coffee shop.

I wonder what Faith did this time? Shawn followed the angry policewoman.

Chapter 31

Stewart, Massachusetts
1914

Horatio returned to the manor around midday, just as Anna had predicted. Right in time to be home before Richard came back from school, he stormed into the house, startling Anna. He didn't look at the decorations; he just yanked his wife by her hair and dragged her off. Catherine had been in the kitchen when she heard the ruckus.

"What's happening?" she demanded from Miranda.

"The captain has returned, miss," the maid said in a grave tone.

"Where is Mrs. Stratton?" Catherine was in a frenzy.

"She's with the captain."

Catherine searched the house frantically and discovered Anna cowering in her room. "Go," Anna said, trying to hide her bruised body from Catherine.

"No." Catherine was furious.

"If you don't, it will only get worse." Anna's flat tone and vacant look shocked Catherine. "He'll take it out on Richard when he returns."

Catherine remained steadfast until Anna's pleas finally wore her down. She left Anna's bedchamber and listened to her wails for mercy all through the evening. She hated her brother and wished him dead. She hated herself even more for not rushing down and stopping Horatio any way that she could.

The next day, Catherine was livid as she listened to her brother berating her lover. She had to restrain herself from leaping across the dining room table and throttling him. Each time she was about to pounce, Anna would flash a warning look.

"I promise to remove the decorations before morning," Anna wearily said as her husband glared at her.

Catherine jumped in startlement when Horatio's fist slammed down onto the table.

"It's too late for that now," he bellowed. "Half the town complimented me on the festive state of the manor once I stepped off of the train. Leave them," he snarled. Catherine felt her skin crawling when she caught the hateful stare he cast upon poor Anna.

"I only thought—" Anna whimpered, her body shrinking in fear.

"You are not to think," Horatio yelled.

Catherine clutched the edges of the table, her knuckles turning white as she restrained herself from intervening. She had heard the horrible sounds last evening.

Now, as she watched the ire growing inside of her brother, she knew that this night was to be another evening of torture.

"Brother." She strained against the urge to lash out at him.

"You'll not interfere," he cautioned her with a wicked gleam in his cold, dark eyes.

"This is my doing," she said. She pressed on in a hurry, seeing that he was listening to her words. "I assumed that as the head of the community, you would insist on decorating the manor for the holiday. Sister protested," she lied. "I was the one who did this. You do, after all, have an image to uphold."

"What's this rubbish you're spouting?" he asked.

She gasped. "Brother, if the manor isn't glorified during this season, it might appear unchristian. The townspeople look to you for guidance. What will they think if you scoff at the holiest night of the year? Father always insisted that Collinsworth reflect the Stratton family's station in the community. I assumed that you would insist, no, demand the same of your family."

Catherine watched him consider her words. How easy it was to play him, and how sick she felt for not playing to his ego yesterday.

"See, Wife," he said, waving towards Catherine, who was still clutching the table. "Even this harlot understands the importance of family."

"Yes, Husband." Anna sneered at his words. He failed to notice her harsh tone and cold look.

Horatio laughed at them, pushed his chair back, and swaggered into his den. Anna winced painfully as she dutifully began to clear away the remnants of the evening meal.

"You're in no condition," Catherine said.

"I must," Anna muttered. Her eyes and voice were once again devoid of emotion. Knowing that any protests she offered would be refused, Catherine hastily gathered up the heavier items from the table and began cleaning the dishes before Anna could step in.

"Sit," she instructed Anna as she pulled out a chair. "He'll not come in here. The kitchen is no place for the man of the house. You're in no condition to be standing."

"Do you hate me?" Anna sniffled, clumsily lowering her battered body into the chair.

Catherine gasped in horror. "I could never hate you." Looking down upon the woman she had failed to protect, she said, "I hate him. And I hate myself."

"Why would you hate yourself?" Anna looked up at Catherine. The gaunt expression clouding Anna's normally bright features broke Catherine's heart.

"I let him do this to you. I sat back and let him beat you."

"There was nothing you could have done," Anna said flatly. "If you had tried to intervene, he would have beaten me more harshly, then Richard, before sending you away. He could have harmed you, as well. If any of those events had occurred, I most certainly would have perished. You saved me with your quick words. He won't beat me tonight, because of you. Tonight he'll sit in his den wallowing in delight that the town of Stewart thinks he's a great man. Then he'll drink himself to sleep. With him passed out in his sacred den, I'll be spared from his advances. For these things, and the light you've brought into my life, I'll be forever grateful."

"I'd be grateful if he were sleeping in a jail cell this evening," Catherine hissed with disgust.

"Jailed for what?" Anna scoffed. "I'm his wife, and he's the great Horatio Stratton. The sheriff would never take exception to his treatment of me. Rufus may be a good man, but I harbor little doubt that he owes his position to my husband. It wouldn't matter even if my husband weren't who he is. He could be Sam, the town drunk, and the authorities still wouldn't interfere in a family matter."

"A family matter?" Bile rose in Catherine's throat. "Beating your wife is a family matter?"

"Yes."

An uneasy silence encompassed them as Catherine went about the evening chores. "Did your father treat your mother in this manner?" Anna asked.

"I came quite late in their lives," Catherine said with a heavy sigh. "My brothers were already grown men. My father, for the most part, simply ignored my mother. He died when I was still young. Perhaps that's why I grew into such a free spirit."

"You were lucky." Anna smiled weakly.

"Perhaps Richard will be given the same stroke of luck," Catherine said, smiling wickedly.

"Catherine, it's wrong to wish him harm."

"Is it?" Catherine held out her hand to Anna. "Come now, it's time for bed. I'll help you."

"No," Anna whimpered in protest. She leaned her frail body into Catherine's. "I don't want you to see what he did to me."

"You need help," Catherine whispered as she wrapped her arms tenderly around Anna's bruised body. "I wish he would leave tonight, so I could hold you and bring you some sense of peace."

"Knowing that you're near brings me peace," Anna said as Catherine gently guided her up the main staircase.

Catherine was queasy as she assisted Anna into her dressing gown and helped her to bed. Rage churned through her when she spied her lover's normally milky white flesh marred with purple and black.

"I love you," she said softly. She placed a kiss on Anna's lips.

She stepped softly out of the bedroom and closed the door quietly. She vowed that she would sneak down the hidden corridor later and listen on the other side all night. No matter what happened to her, she could not allow her brother to go anywhere near her lover. She could smell the brandy long before she spied his presence lurking in the dark hallway.

"What are you doing down here?" he slurred. Catherine quirked her eyebrow in disgust at her brother's rumpled state.

"Seeing to Sister," she hissed. "Seems that she has injured herself. She took a nasty spill last evening." Her words were cold and her eyes narrowed. She was aware he understood fully that she knew what he had done.

"She's a clumsy wench." He shrugged in an uncaring manner. "I was th-thinking." He stumbled over his words, apparently lost in an alcoholic haze. "I might see fit to send you b-back to your beloved France. You'd be given an allowance, of course."

"Trying to get rid of me?" She chuckled, her angry gaze never straying from his cold dark eyes.

"I've been trying to rid myself of you since before you arrived," he groused.

"I think I'll stay on here at Whispering Pines for a little longer," she said. "Paris no longer possesses what I need. Tell me, dear Brother," she continued, boldly standing up to him. "Do you miss your beloved trips to the Orient and India? Is it true what I've heard about your other family?"

"Insolent bitch." Horatio scowled. "Those brats aren't mine."

"Of course they aren't." Catherine brushed past him. "A good Christian man such as yourself would never be a party to such degradation. Speaking of which," she said over her shoulder, "if Anna has another spill, it wouldn't do your reputation any good for that news to slip out, now would it? You may have the town in your pocket, but I know your business associates, and they include some that would frown upon your bride's clumsy nature."

"Are you threatening me?"

"Never, dear Brother," she said coldly. "But I'm very close to Mrs. Bonner, the wife of Jonathan Bonner. He's part owner of the wharf that harbors the family's ships, is he not? They're such a fine family, who find many things abhorrent, such as clumsiness, and respectable men weighing anchor in foreign ports."

"He's a very pious man," Horatio said bitterly.

"Yes, he is." Catherine beamed. "And so influential in the import-export trade. Best to let Anna get some rest tonight," she said, smiling when Horatio stormed down the staircase.

Never in her young life did Catherine Stratton ever think that she would be capable of blackmail. Now, she was berating herself for not doing it sooner. Horatio wavered only slightly, yet it was enough to spare Anna from any further abuse, physical at least. Catherine never revealed to her young lover just how low she had sunk in order to protect her. Instead, she reveled in the joyous holiday that she shared with the captivating woman and her adorable son.

Catherine vowed that she would indeed call upon Mrs. Bonner if Horatio ever struck Anna again. Of course, if the pious Mr. and Mrs. Bonner ever discovered just how close Catherine and their young daughter Lily had been in their youth, Catherine held no doubt that it would be she who would end up sitting in a jail cell. None of that mattered to her. What mattered was the light that had returned to Anna and Richard that Christmas. Soon after the holiday, Richard went back to school, and thankfully, Horatio returned to the sea.

What Catherine was unaware of was that at the same moment she was blackmailing her brutish brother, Miranda Wilkins was having a very intense conversation with Rufus Mulder, the town sheriff.

"It just isn't right." The maid wagged her finger at the stodgy man after she had badgered him in his office well into the night.

"Miranda," Rufus said, uneasy with the conversation, "you don't know that he's doing anything wrong."

"He beats that poor woman," Miranda said bitterly. "I swear, if you don't do anything, someday he'll kill her."

"What would you have me do?" Rufus said. The sick feeling in his stomach grew. He knew that Miranda was probably telling him the truth, but he was helpless. If it were any other man in town, he could pull him aside and threaten him. Employing the same tactic on Horatio Stratton would cost him his position and, more than likely, his home.

"She's his wife," he said.

"Don't make it right." Miranda scowled.

Emotionally, Rufus agreed with her, yet again he was helpless.

"It's because you're on his payroll, isn't it?"

"So are you," Rufus said. "Everyone in town knows how the staff up there does the old man's bidding for a few extra coins."

Miranda's shoulders slumped in defeat. "She's a nice lady," she said wearily. "I hate spying on her. She doesn't do anything wrong. Sets him off when you tell him that. I hate that he pays us so well so we'll treat her badly."

"He owns the whole damn town, and there isn't anything we can do," Rufus said. "I thought things were better after his sister arrived."

"Oh, she's a pistol that one." Miranda laughed. "She doesn't take any guff from the old man and can play him like a fiddle. At least she could, until last evening. I've never seen a man act like that just because they put up a tree and a few trimmings. The way he grabbed the poor missus by the throat, you'd think she was playing around with the butcher."

"Maybe she is," Rufus said. "I can't believe he started choking her for decorating the house."

"I swear to you, that's what got him going. She isn't stepping out on him. She spends all of her time with Miss Stratton. It's just the two of them up there in that big house. All they do is talk and work on their stitching. Half the men in this town would give their eyeteeth for such a devoted wife."

"Or Miss Stratton." Rufus leered. "Can't understand why a woman as pretty as that isn't married."

"That won't last with her looks and money," Miranda said. "Then poor Mrs. Stratton will be alone again, without any protection. Mark my words, after that happens, you'll be called up to the manor to cart Mrs. Stratton's body off to the morgue."

"Stop being so dramatic, woman," he scoffed at her. "You read too many of those damn detective novels."

Chapter 32

Rufus Mulder lived to regret dismissing Miranda Wilkins's warnings when the maid burst into his office, ranting frantically about blood pouring from the walls. It took him over an hour to calm the hysterical woman. During that hour, his one-and-only deputy, Thomas Sullivan, was dealing with other members of the manor's staff who had run from the house in a blind panic.

Rufus felt chilled to the bone as he listened to Miranda's wild ramblings. He spoke to the others who had gathered in the tiny building that housed the town jail and post office. When he journeyed to Whispering Pines, a few members of the household staff, all of whom looked frightened and pale, greeted his arrival.

Unlike his employees, the great Captain Stratton strutted out onto the front porch looking completely calm and at ease.

"Morning, Sheriff Mulder," he graciously greeted the man.

"Good morning, sir," Rufus said.

"What brings you by on such a fine day?" Horatio asked casually, as though he were strolling in the park.

"Seems there's been quite a stir up here," Rufus said carefully. "Some kind of Halloween prank, I'm certain. Captain Stratton, could I see your kitchen?"

"No." Horatio shrugged.

"Beg pardon?"

"I said no. There's nothing amiss here."

"I'm afraid I'll have to insist," Rufus said.

"And I'm afraid you don't have the authority to insist." Horatio snickered. "When you do, I'll gladly show you any part of the house you wish to see. In the meantime, good day."

Rufus was stunned into silence. The captain was right; he didn't have to show him any part of the house if he didn't wish to. Defeated, Rufus turned to leave, making one last inquiry before he left.

"Captain, may I ask how your wife and sister are this morning?"

"Very well, I suspect." Horatio snickered again. "They've been called out of town on a family matter."

And that was it. By the time Rufus had obtained legal permission to view the house, there was nothing to see, with the notable exception of deep gashes marring the kitchen cabinets, walls, counters, and floor.

Neither Anna nor Catherine Stratton were ever seen or heard from again. There were a few fanciful tales spun by the staff about seeing or hearing one or both women lurking about the house. Other than the wild stories of their ghosts lingering about the manor, the two women had simply vanished.

Rufus Mulder retired years later with one regret; he had never brought Horatio Stratton to justice. He knew the man had murdered the women, and even though he never stopped investigating the case, he could never prove what had happened to them.

On the day Horatio Stratton was laid to rest without any mourners, Rufus stood and watched, along with Richard Stratton and his former deputy, as the garden in the back of the manor was dug up with a backhoe.

Over the years, Captain Stratton had been seen digging up the garden while muttering to himself. Rufus felt certain that was where they would find the two missing women. He was so disappointed when nothing was found. He returned the next day for one last look around and was stunned. The plot of land that had been torn up the day before was filled with rows of flowers in full bloom. No one could explain it. Rufus never returned to Whispering Pines, yet even on his deathbed he still pondered the fate of the two women and blamed himself for their deaths.

Chapter 33

Atchison, Kansas
2005

The city of Atchison was nice enough, but Faith couldn't wait to get out of town. She was beyond pissed when she was pulled off of the Salem project. She had been looking forward to spending time with Shawn. Working together on the project might just have been the push Shawn needed to let Faith back into her heart.

After everything that happened in Danvers, it really looked as if Faith was about to get a second chance. She would have been working with the same team, and since the cities were so closely located, they wouldn't have had to move out of the hotel. As it turned out, the team didn't move out of the hotel; it was only Faith who had been reassigned to the Atchison team.

Adding grist to the mill was the little problem that everyone on the Kansas team had worked with Faith before, and they all had reasons for disliking her. First, there was Trudy Gorsy, the three-hundred-pound psychic with flaming red hair, whom Faith used to take great pleasure in annoying back when she was a naysayer. Then there was Dwayne, Trudy's ninety-pound balding wimp of a husband. He didn't like Faith because Trudy didn't like her. Of course, that didn't stop the weasel from staring at Faith's breasts every chance he got.

Next on the list was Billy Mariner, a scientist and professional naysayer, who viewed Faith as a sellout and didn't believe that her experiences at Whispering Pines were anything more than a publicity hoax. And finally there was the director, Ronan Summers. Faith had gotten the smarmy twit fired from the last project they worked on together after she caught him doing lines of cocaine in her trailer. Apparently, the production company decided to give him a second chance. The rest of the crew didn't like her, because at one time or another, she had been gruff or unpleasant with each and every one of them.

"Ms. Charles, if it isn't too much trouble, we need you on camera," Ronan snarled at her.

"Yes, Your Highness," she growled, taking her place on her mark in front of the nondescript house. For the first time, the crew actually chuckled at one of Faith's little barbs. "Ready when you are, Majesty," she said curtly to Ronan, who was doing his best to stare her down. Faith simply scoffed at his feeble attempt to intimidate her.

Ronan curled his lip. "Action," he shouted before she was properly prepared. Faith simply shrugged and began her spiel.

"This is just an ordinary house in the heart of Atchison, or is it?" Faith spoke in a cool and professional manner. "Not according to two former residents who claim to have been attacked by some unseen force."

As Faith continued her narration, she spied a familiar figure lurking in the shadows. Faith concluded her narration with a triumphant smile. She knew that she was dead-on, and that Ronan would probably complain and make her do several more takes just to annoy her.

"Let's try it again," Ronan sneered. "And try to get it right this time."

"I thought it was perfect." The commanding voice came from the man who had been lurking in the shadows.

Faith smiled brilliantly as all eyes turned towards Dave Sandusky. The tall, thin, dark-haired man folded his arms across his narrow chest, his demeanor daring anyone to challenge him.

"We need to set up inside," Ronan said and quickly ushered the crew away.

Dave was the man who decided which projects received funding and which projects were shut down. His role at Sunny Hill Productions was a close second to being God. His sudden appearance on a shoot was never a good sign, since it usually meant the suits weren't happy and someone was about to be fired. Everyone with the exception of Faith made a hasty retreat into the two-story home.

"You do know how to clear a room," Faith said as he approached her. "Am I being fired?" she asked in a flat tone.

"You?" Dave chuckled as he pushed his wire-rimmed glasses up. "Not this time. The powers that be are very unhappy with all of the grumbling they're hearing from this project. I've been sent here to make certain that everyone's getting along. I'm also here to see how well you and Trudy get along."

"We don't." Faith snorted. "Nothing against ghost hunters, but all I've ever seen Trudy do is convince people that they see things that aren't there. Why do you care if I get along with her? I've never been known for my ability to play well with others."

"She's on the short list for Whispering Pines," Dave said.

"No." Faith shook her head. "She wouldn't be able to deliver the way that Shawn did."

"Dr. Williams is everyone's first choice, but she's declined."

"So, you picked the bottom of the barrel? Trudy is all wrong. What about Wu or Sue Simpson?" Faith knew that going back to Stewart was going to be hard enough. If she had to endure the nightmare that was waiting for her there with Trudy Gorsy, she might just be forced to kill herself.

"Farrah passed. She feels that the shoot would be too intense even for her. And Sue's having another baby," Dave said. "The short list consists of Trudy, Schumacher, and Rupp."

"Schumacher? Another pain in the ass," Faith sneered. "And Andy Rupp couldn't find his way out of a wet paper sack, much less find a ghost. None of them compare to Shawn."

"Any chance you could change her mind?"

"I've tried." Faith sighed.

"We have a lot to talk about," Dave said in an uneasy tone that made Faith a little nervous. "How much more do you have to do tonight?"

"We have this place and a shoot in the cemetery," Faith answered. She studied him carefully. "I'm not looking forward to running around a cold, dark cemetery with Trudy and a bunch of screaming yokels."

"After you wrap up tonight, why don't we get a drink and talk?" Dave asked, and she nodded in agreement. "Good. Now I have to put the fear of God or unemployment in the rest of the staff."

"Go to it." Faith smiled, wondering why good old Dave was really there.

Later that night, Faith's head was pounding. The sounds of hooting and hollering assaulted her eardrums.

"When you suggested a drink, I assumed there would be alcohol," Faith shouted above the din.

"Can't have booze and full nudity together in these parts. I hate the Bible Belt," Dave shouted as he waved a couple of bills at one of the dancers. "What's wrong? It isn't like you not to enjoy a good tittie bar or a lap dance."

"Maybe my tastes have matured," Faith said as a dancer waved her obviously fake breasts at her.

"Maybe you're whipped." Dave laughed.

"Yeah, you want to make something out of it?"

"Not a chance." The smile slipped from his face. "Hammond Castle wasn't what we were hoping for."

"Why not?" Faith bellowed as Dave tried to coax a buxom blonde to entertain her.

"Nothing spectacular happened," he said. "Just a bunch of staff members telling stories, nothing great on film. We're going to re-edit with some reenactment actors and toss it in with other shoots for one project."

This wasn't good news for Faith, since all of her hard work had been reduced to a ten-minute segment. "Whispering Pines, that was a payoff. We only had about twenty minutes of film but it was a gold mine. We need Shawn," Dave shouted as he slipped a large bill in the stripper's G-string and waved towards Faith. "You need Shawn, and not just to save your career."

"Tell me something I don't know." Faith became exasperated as a blonde straddled her lap. She clasped the woman's hips in an effort to keep the dancer from falling as she gyrated in her lap.

"Yes," the woman whispered hotly in her ear. "I've been eyeing you since you came in."

"Whatever." Faith shrugged and slipped money in the woman's G-string. A strange vibration erupted in her pants pocket.

"What the hell?" She sputtered when the woman's enormous breasts were thrust in her face. The vibration continued, alerting her that her cell phone was ringing.

"Excuse me." Faith extracted her face from the dancer's bosom. "I need to take this," she said, retrieving her phone. "Faith Charles," she answered as the dancer nuzzled her neck.

"Faith?" a distant voice said.

"Who is this?" Faith asked, straining to hear the caller.

"I know you want me. Let's get out of here so I can give you a private lap dance," the dancer said, just loud enough for Faith's mystery caller to hear her.

Faith jumped back as the mysterious caller shouted, "Bitch," and hung up. Faith scowled as she wrestled away from the dancer so she could check her caller ID.

"Oh, fuck," she shouted and shoved the dancer off of her lap.

"What's wrong?" Dave asked when Faith sprang from her chair.

"That was Shawn." Faith dashed frantically towards the exit.

Chapter 34

Salem, Massachusetts
2005

"I'm an ass," Shawn muttered as she thought about throwing her cell phone into oncoming traffic. "Faith, get a cell so we can at least talk to one another," she mimicked herself.

"Yeah, so I can hear some bimbo offering to get your rocks off." She glared at the tiny cell phone she was still clutching in her hand as it chirped.

"Dr. Williams, we're just about ready for you to go in," Ronnie, the assistant director, said. The scrawny man recoiled when she released a threatening growl.

"Sorry," she said, once she realized what she was doing.

"Everything all right?" Carey asked.

"Peachy," Shawn barked, and the policewoman recoiled. "Sorry," she apologized for the second time.

"Shouldn't you answer that?" Carey asked, nodding towards the still ringing phone.

"I'm not certain that I should. If I do, you might end up having to arrest me," Shawn tried to tease.

"Oh." Carey nodded, seemingly understanding that it was a personal call.

They were standing outside in the cold. The cell phone kept ringing. The caller kept hitting redial each time the voice mail kicked in. Shawn's ire was growing with each ring. Finally, she couldn't stand it any longer, and she snapped the phone open.

"I can't talk to you right now," she said, already knowing who was on the other end. It was one of those times when she didn't need her special gift to know what was going on.

"I can explain," Faith said.

"Of course you can." Shawn was furious. "You always do. Go back to your bimbo."

"Shawn, it isn't what you think."

"Of course not," Shawn sneered. "I'm certain that you have a perfectly reasonable explanation for my calling in the middle of the night only to hear a party going on and some chick offering to give you a lap dance. I'm just not ready to listen to whatever load of horse manure you're planning to throw at me."

"Please? I—"

Shawn snapped the phone shut in the middle of Faith's words.

"Dr. Williams, we're ready for you to do your setup," Ronnie called out.

"We already did a walk-through and filmed the staff," Althea said. "Got some good stories. Mostly the usual stuff: lights flickering, things going bump in the night when no one else is around."

"Not surprising, given the history of the place," Shawn muttered as she entered the unique-looking house that had been converted into a tourist attraction. She went to shut her cell phone off when she noticed the battery was dead.

"Check the camera batteries," she called out to the crew. She listened to a collective grumbling as the cameramen scurried to replace them.

"I don't understand," Carey whispered from behind her. "I saw them putting new batteries in the cameras before we came in here."

"It happens." Shawn shrugged. "Entities love draining power sources. They need the energy. When we hit a really active spot, we tend to lose power."

The hair on the back of her neck prickled. The dead also loved talking to her, but then again, unlike most people, she could hear them.

"Are we ready?" she called out, stepping into one of the main rooms. She could feel the tension surrounding her. She was eager to do her job and leave as soon as possible.

"You're on," Althea cued her as Shawn walked about the room.

"So many voices, all pleading their innocence and devotion to God," Shawn said, listening carefully to each one. She could feel their pain as she wandered about the room. This was where most of the so-called trials happened.

"I can hear them, but not their accusers. I feel fear and outrage. There's a woman over here." She pointed to a long table that spanned the side of the room.

"She's confident that she'll be found innocent. She's disgusted that the people she thought were her friends have stood before her, accusing her of unspeakable acts. She's afraid now; they're taking her away to be interrogated by the sheriff. She's saying, 'I doubt I shall ever see my children again.'"

Shawn caught a look of disbelief in Carey's eyes when she repeated the words that had come to her as nothing more than a frightened whisper. The lights flickered, and Carey was the only one surprised by the way they turned on and off. Shawn ignored Carey's dismay. She headed up the narrow staircase that led to the second floor. She was well aware of the camera crew that followed closely behind her.

"None of the furniture belongs here," she said when she stepped into the room to her right.

"This isn't Corwin's furniture." Suddenly her lungs seized, filling her with a sense of panic. The musky aroma was stifling, but the years of dust weren't what were stealing her breath. She stood perfectly still. The floorboards creaked beneath her. She broke out in a cold sweat as she struggled to fill her lungs with air.

"Can't breathe," she choked, stumbling from the room. The moment she crossed the threshold, her mind cleared and the air returned to her lungs.

"What happened, Dr. Williams?" Althea prodded her as Shawn took a deep breath.

"Fear," she said with a hard swallow. "I felt the kind of fear that steals your breath. Let's check out the rest of the place," she said, feeling better and eager to end her work for the night.

The rest of the tour was uneventful. The cameras followed Shawn as she explained each passing image. With no more excitement, Althea called it a night.

"Where's our lady cop?" Shawn asked, noticing for the first time that Carey was missing.

"She bolted," Althea said, looking deep in thought. "When we were on the second floor in the room that really freaked you out, she turned pale and took off. So, what was up with the children's bedroom?" she asked as Shawn collected her equipment.

"That was the children's room?" Shawn squeaked in horror as they stepped back outside. She turned and spied Carey sitting on the lawn looking as if she had seen a ghost.

"That's what the staff said this morning," Althea said. She helped Shawn load her equipment into her rental car. "Why? What did you see?"

"I didn't see anything," Shawn said, nervously raking her fingers through her long, curly locks. "I was just filled with terror. If that's where the children slept, I really don't want to know what happened."

"Amen to that." Althea shuddered. "I'm worried about her." She nodded towards Carey. "If she can't handle this place, there's no way she'll be able to work at Whispering Pines. Then again, for her part, she really doesn't need to set foot in the place."

"She's going," Shawn said dryly. "She needs to."

"Really?" Althea perked up. "Tell me? I just love your little insights."

"Except when they're about you." Shawn snickered. "She has unfinished business."

"The murders."

"No, it's personal. I just can't get a read on what it is. I'll talk to her."

Before she said goodnight, Althea reminded Shawn to be at the dock at Willows Amusement Park by six in the morning.

"Hey," Shawn greeted Carey, who was now standing and kicking leaves about as she chain-smoked. "I've booked a room at the Hawthorne, want to join me for a drink?"

* * *

"Want to talk about it?" Shawn finally asked as they sat by the fireplace in the hotel bar.

"Talk about what?" Carey was staring blankly into the fire.

"What happened at the Witch House."

"I can't," Carey said. "I just..." She blew out heavily. "It must have been the house settling."

"Tell me?" Shawn urged.

"I was standing perfectly still, and the floor was moving," Carey said. "Then you started gasping, and suddenly I was afraid. I don't understand it. I've haven't been that afraid since..." her voice trailed off and her lips tightened.

"The gun jammed." Shawn finished Carey's sentence. "You got the all clear, stepped into the bathroom, and found yourself staring into the barrel of a gun."

"That's really annoying." Carey smiled for the first time in hours. "Yeah, I was still a patrolwoman, and thank goodness that weasel's gun jammed. Otherwise, I wouldn't be sitting here all embarrassed because I ran off into the night, just because of a creaking floorboard. How much do you see?"

"Oh, now you believe me." Shawn laughed. "Not much. You're a little difficult to read. I do know that you think you're going to back out of Whispering Pines, but you're going."

"I can't work with her." Carey snarled. "Do you know why?"

"No," Shawn said. She felt her cell phone vibrating. "Power's back on," she said, extracting the phone from her coat pocket. "Speak of the devil." She shook her head as she answered the phone. "I'm not speaking to you."

"Then why did you finally answer my call?" Faith asked.

"My phone went down earlier." Shawn sighed, feeling the tension from before dissipating. Still, she couldn't resist giving Faith a hard time. "How was your lap dance?"

"I didn't get a lap dance," Faith said. "Discussing business in a tittie bar was Dave's idea."

"Funny, whenever I meet him for business, it's in an office." Shawn was still feeling a little miffed. "I'm too tired to argue with you tonight, Faith." Shawn sighed again, not missing the way Carey bristled when she mentioned Faith.

She shook her head as it suddenly filled with the sound of a small girl crying.

"I have back-to-back shoots tomorrow. First, a boat ride out to Misery Island, then the Joshua Ward House."

"I thought you weren't going back there?" Faith asked. "Damn it, Shawn, the last time you went to the Ward House, you ended up with a migraine that lasted a week."

"It's Salem," Shawn said. "What's happening in Atchison? Did you go to Molly's Hollow?"

"Yes, and a fun-filled trip to the cemetery. Trudy kept screaming and scaring the locals. I swear I didn't see or hear a thing."

"You're working with Trudy." Shawn chuckled, knowing how Faith couldn't stand Trudy. It didn't matter that Shawn didn't enjoy working with the boisterous woman either; the fact that Faith was stuck in Kansas with Trudy pleased her. "I'm sure the sight of all those naked women made you feel better," she added in a bitter tone.

"For the last time, going to a nudie bar wasn't my idea."

"I didn't even know that they had strip clubs in Kansas," Shawn added, as she watched Carey fidgeting.

"Well, they do," Faith muttered. "Only you can't have alcohol if there's full nudity."

"And were we drinking this evening? Never mind, we can argue about this tomorrow, I'm ignoring my guest."

"Huh? Who's with you?"

"Excuse me?" Shawn shot back. "If you must know, I'm with Carey Jessup." Strangely, Carey seemed unconcerned that Shawn had revealed her name.

"Who's that?" Faith said.

I was hoping you'd tell me, Shawn thought.

"Never mind." Faith sighed. "Look, I'll call you tomorrow. Get some rest. I know how much these back-to-back shoots wear on you."

"I will, thanks." Shawn yawned. "I'm still mad at you."

"I know." Faith chuckled. "We'll talk soon, I'm almost done here. Good night."

"Good night." Shawn disconnected the call. "You look confused," she said to Carey.

"I am," Carey said. "Earlier, I would have sworn the call you got was from a boyfriend."

"Boyfriend?" Shawn laughed. "Some detective you are."

"Oh." Carey swallowed. "Faith is…"

"Yes."

"And the two of you are…"

"We were." Shawn sighed with disappointment. "Now, I don't know what's happening. I don't want to talk about it. I want to hear what you thought about tonight."

"I'm not sure what happened tonight," Carey said in a distant tone. "Whispering Pines isn't going to be what I thought it would be."

"Now *that* is an understatement," Shawn said.

Chapter 35

Stewart, Massachusetts
1923

Mary Dunhill was toiling in the kitchen of the grand manor. The young girl felt lucky when she was hired as the cook at the palatial home. She was new to the area, and with work being hard to find, she jumped at the opportunity. She didn't understand why the people in town gave her strange looks when she asked for directions to the manor. Many went so far as to caution her against accepting the position. Mr. Hughes, who was Captain Stratton's solicitor, had warned her that her new employer was a bit eccentric and demanding. She didn't care a lick if he liked to swing from the chandelier; she needed the work.

It was her first day at work, and the captain's dietary needs seemed to be quite simple, making her job that much easier. She had to admit, though, there was an ominous feel to the house. Perhaps it was the old man's gruff demeanor, or the way the rest of the staff seemed to skulk about, jumping at the slightest noise. Again, she didn't care. But she was curious as to why the kitchen woodwork was marred in the most unsightly manner.

She thanked the heavens that the captain was a simple meat-and-potatoes man, since she wasn't skilled enough to expand beyond the basics. Another thing that piqued the young woman's interest was the way the house seemed to be falling into a state of neglect, but the garden was pristine.

"Curious, but none of my business." She carried a large roast to the oven.

"You'd be wise to listen to the warnings," a soft voice whispered in her ear.

Mary jumped with a start, almost dropping the roast onto the floor. She shoved it quickly into the large oven as she looked about.

"What's this?" She looked around the empty room. "Go on, have a laugh at the new girl's expense," she taunted her unseen tormentor. "I don't scare easily," she said.

"You should," the same soft voice repeated, sending a shiver down her spine.

"I'll not give in to your tomfoolery." She convinced herself that it was just someone trying to give her a fright. Mary wiped her hands on a rag before ducking out the back door for a much-needed cigarette. Standing along the side of the house, she hid in the shadows so her new employer wouldn't catch her smoking. She glanced over towards the kitchen window. Mary's dark brown eyes widened with surprise as she spied the small woman looking down at her from the kitchen window. She blinked once, and the woman was gone.

"Who was that?" she muttered, looking about. She didn't recall seeing the woman before.

"Talking to yourself already?" A snicker came from behind her. Once again the young woman jumped with fright.

"For goodness sake, you scared the devil out of me," she exclaimed once she spotted Ned, the groundskeeper. The wispy older man seemed unsteady on his feet.

"No, the devil is hiding in his study, just like he always does," Ned slurred. The rancid smell of stale whisky assaulted Mary as he spoke.

"Ain't you a pretty picture." She took a drag on her cigarette. "I thought that old lady Miller and I were the only women who worked here."

"Ya." He shrugged, his eyelids dropping.

"But I just saw some lady standing in the kitchen window," she said.

"That would be one of the ladies of the house." Ned yawned and scratched his beard.

"I thought Captain Stratton was a widower?" she asked, truly confused by the events.

"Of his own making," Ned said gravely. "You get used to seeing them. Mrs. Miller says they keep her company while she's cleaning the big old house."

"What are you talking about, you drunken old fool?" Mary snubbed out her smoke.

"He killed them," Ned said. His eyes drifted to her small pouch of tobacco. "You wouldn't want to roll one of those for a poor old man would ya?"

"I might, if you tell me what you're talking about."

"His wife and his sister, killed them both," Ned said as Mary began rolling him a cigarette.

"Rubbish." She wet the edge of the paper with her tongue, smoothed it down, and thrust the neatly rolled smoke at him.

"I was here," he hissed at her. "I still hear Miranda screaming. She was the maid back then."

"Right. He murdered his wife and sister and is a free man." Mary scoffed at the notion.

"A rich and free man," Ned corrected her. "Never found the bodies, nothing the sheriff could do. Looked like a slaughterhouse," he said in a shaky voice.

"What did?"

"The kitchen." Ned snorted. "Why do ya think he has to hire a girl like you from out of state? No one in these parts will set foot in there." He pointed up towards the window. Mary felt another shiver.

"Believe what you wish, I saw it for myself. We work for the devil. You'll see soon enough. The ladies can be pranksters," he said, then sauntered off.

"Go on with you," she shouted after his retreating figure. He stopped and turned back to her, his eyes narrowed with a sad expression.

"As you wish," he said coldly. "It was Halloween morning, the kitchen was covered with blood, and my axe that was kept in the woodshed vanished after that day along with the ladies. But maybe they went off on holiday," he said with a cold sneer before wandering off.

"Crazy old bugger," Mary muttered before ducking back into the kitchen. She shrieked in horror as she stepped into the smoke-filled room. Mary was frantic. She rushed to the oven and yanked out the charred remains. She dumped the ruined roast into the sink, fearing that her first day of employment would be her last.

"I don't understand it," she gasped. She threw open the door in an effort to clear the smoke. Once the smoke trickled out, she checked the oven.

"What in the bloody hell?" She gaped at the oven. "I didn't set it this high. Oh, there are pranksters about, but they're quite amongst the living." She began to prepare a second meal. Mary refused to believe that what had happened was anything more than her co-workers having a lark at her expense.

A month later, after most of her meals were mysteriously ruined, Mary still refused to believe that the events were anything but someone's idea of a joke. Each time she tried to talk to the staff in an effort to unmask the culprit, she received blank stares and someone telling her that it was the ladies of the house having a bit of fun.

"Mrs. Miller," Mary bellowed, storming up the staircase. Once again, her work had been destroyed. If it weren't for the constant pranks, Mary's job would have been a walk in the park. She was paid very well and rarely saw her employer, who seemed content to lock himself up in the study all day alone. She heard the old man had a son, but the boy never came home from school.

"Mrs. Miller," she called out when she found the plump older woman toiling in the hall linen closet.

"Now what's all this fuss about?" Mrs. Miller calmly addressed the irate woman.

"I'll tell you what the fuss is about," Mary growled. "A perfect ham, that I spent all day preparing. I left it cooling on the counter, only to see it being tossed out the back door while I was getting a breath of fresh air. You and me are the only ones in the house, and I want to know why you did it."

"Oh, hush." Mrs. Miller chuckled as she closed the closet door. "It's just the ladies having a bit of sport."

"Don't hand me that rubbish," Mary snarled.

"I swear on my poor Johnny's grave, it's the truth," Mrs. Miller said with a broad smile. "They have to have some fun. The boy never comes home, and the old man hides in his study. The old devil only comes out for meals or to trample poor Mrs. Stratton's garden. Every time he steps out of that study, they're on him like flies on dung. Serves him right, if you ask me.

"Now, before you start calling me a foolish old woman, just listen to what I have to say. First, I wouldn't set foot in that kitchen. My brother was working up here when it happened. He was madder than a wet hen when I took a job up here. What choice did I have with Johnny gone and six children to support? My second day here, the old man was running about screaming at someone. 'Leave me be!' he kept shouting at the top of his lungs. I thought the old bugger was just loony until I saw her."

"Saw who?" Mary and Mrs. Miller strolled to the top of the landing.

"Catherine Stratton," Mrs. Miller said, pointing to the bottom of the staircase. "Standing in the foyer as clear as day, and then in the blink of an eye, she was gone. I was frightened at first, but then I remembered how she and Mrs. Stratton would stroll through town arm in arm, happy as the day was long, and if the boy was with them, they just strutted like peacocks. You wouldn't have known that they were the richest women in town by the way they would stop and chat with everyone. And they knew who you were. They were two of the sweetest souls to ever walk the earth. If you want my advice, if you're determined to stay on here, just get along with the ladies."

"You're crazier than that drunk Ned," Mary grumbled.

"Maybe. Then again, Ned never touched spirits until that day. Poor old fool hates himself for staying here."

Mary threw her hands up in disgust before storming back down the staircase. She felt an icy cold breeze wafting against her body as she stomped through the corridor that led to the kitchen.

"Awfully brisk for this time of year." She shivered as she swung open the kitchen door. She froze in her tracks when she discovered a petite woman standing in the middle of the room.

"Where is my son?" the woman asked sadly. Mary gaped at her.

"Your what?" Mary's gaze drifted down the woman's body, and she released a horrifying shriek when she realized that the woman was missing the lower half of her body, and seemed to be floating in midair. Mary's heart pounded against her chest, and her knees buckled. Then the woman faded into a mist and was gone. Mary's eyes rolled back as the room spun, and she collapsed onto the floor.

Mary had no idea just how long she was lying on the kitchen floor before she awoke.

"I'm sorry," someone whispered. *"No one will come in here to help you. They're afraid. Are you all right?"* Mary blinked open her eyes to discover a misty vision of a tall blonde kneeling beside her. Mary scrambled across the room. She snatched up her thin coat and purse before bolting out the door, never looking back as she tore down the driveway. She didn't stop running until she reached New York City.

Chapter 36

Stewart, Massachusetts
1957

Katy Ann Stratton stood on the porch of her ancestral home, fidgeting nervously.

"I can do this," she said. She tried to will herself to put the key in the lock and open the front door.

"Sweetheart, if it makes you that uncomfortable, then just forget I suggested it." Roland, her fiancé, caressed her shoulder.

"No." She tried to shake off the years of ghost and ghoulie stories from the townsfolk.

They were just starting out, and money would be tight. Sitting just a short distance from her childhood home was a great big house, falling into disrepair. They could live rent free, and with just a short walk into town catch the train to the city. They could save money while fixing up the old mansion that was more than big enough to start a family. Her father readily agreed, but cautioned her about the house. Her brother had tried to live there back when he was striking out on his own. He lasted ten minutes before he ran screaming from the house.

"Katy Ann, I'm serious. With our parents' help, we can get an apartment in the city," Roland said.

"Is that what you want?" she asked. "I want us to be able to stand on our own just as much as you do. It would be foolish to pass up on a free house, a mansion to boot." She laughed at her silliness.

"Come on." She slipped the key into the lock.

"Wow." She gasped as she drank in the craftsmanship.

"Why would anyone simply abandon this place?" Roland St. James said with appreciation. "When was it built?"

"1912," Katy Ann said. They began to explore the grand old home. "My grandfather had it built for himself and my grandmother."

"The cemetery is awfully full for it being just the two of them."

"Distant relatives, and some of the townsfolk mostly, and my grandfather, of course," Katy Ann said as they entered a large room with mahogany walls and a fireplace.

"Honey, this would be perfect for you," Roland said. "When you're drafting late at night, the fire can keep you warm, and I can build you a great big desk and drafting table."

"You don't want it?" She nudged him, knowing that he was already eyeing the old barn to use as his woodshop.

"No." He smiled. "I'll be out in the barn sawing wood while you create works of art. Wait." His brow furrowed. "Your grandmother isn't buried in the cemetery?"

"Um." Katy Ann hesitated, chewing on her bottom lip. "No, she isn't. My grandfather's buried in the large crypt in the center of the cemetery. My father had the one on the hill built for his family, which he hopes someday will include his mother and aunt."

"Your grandmother is alive?" Roland asked enthusiastically. Katy Ann took him gently by the hand.

"I doubt it," she said, patting his large, calloused hand. "Oh, Roland, sweetie, you know how you're always saying your family has a colorful past? Well, brace yourself," she said. The sound of a door slamming echoed through the house.

"What was that?" Roland asked.

"Let's hope it was the wind," Katy Ann muttered. "Roland, we don't know what happened to my grandmother, Anna, or my great aunt, Catherine."

"You don't know?" Another door slammed.

"Well, you see, Dad is convinced that my grandfather killed them," Katy Ann said reluctantly, "then hid their bodies somewhere on the property."

"Beg pardon?" Roland said with a hard swallow.

"I'll tell you what I know," Katy Ann said. The room temperature suddenly dropped. "On Halloween morning, 1916, while my father was away at boarding school, the staff arrived to discover the kitchen covered in blood, and both women missing. The sheriff investigated for years but never found anything that could explain their disappearance."

"My God, why would someone do something so horrible?" Roland blanched and the hair on the back of his neck prickled.

"The whores deserved it," an eerie voice hissed.

"Let's go," Roland said. He gripped Katy Ann's hand and dragged her out of the room. They stumbled, both trembling violently. Roland wrapped his arms around his soon-to-be bride. "I love you, but there's no way we're living here."

"Thank you." Katy Ann hugged him tighter. They jumped with surprise when the front door squeaked open.

"Tell my son that we love him. Now go," a soft, lilting voice said.

"I will," Katy Ann promised. A wave of sadness engulfed her. She was crying as Roland guided her out of the house. The tears didn't stop as they locked the door and walked away.

Katy Ann was still in a somber mood when they stepped up to the doorway of her parents' home. "Oh, Katy Ann." Richard sighed deeply as the young couple approached. "I was hoping—" his words were cut off when Katy Ann threw her arms around him and engulfed him in a warm hug.

"Your mother wanted you to know that they love you," she choked out before taking a step back.

Richard's eyes filled with tears. He slumped down onto the steps and buried his face in his hands.

"Did she say anything else?" he asked, wiping his eyes.

"To go, so we left."

"I keep hoping that they'll let someone stay. Then maybe I'll find out what happened," Richard said wearily.

"Sir, I love your daughter more than life itself, but there's no way we're living there." Roland was still shaking.

"I understand." Richard said. "Well then, Roland, you're just going to have to help me build an extension to this old place."

"Daddy—" Katy Ann said.

"No arguments. You kids are just starting graduate school and working," Richard cut her off. "We can discuss it over dinner."

Chapter 37

Katy Ann St. James stared out her kitchen window and smiled sadly at the cottage that she had designed, and that her husband and father had built together. They had lived there for many years, until her father passed on. She and Roland moved into the main house with their teenaged children so they could keep a better eye on her mother. Now her son Andrew lived in the cottage, enjoying his freedom while still being able to raid her refrigerator. She sighed deeply when she heard the kitchen door opening.

"Roland, you left your socks on the floor again," she said without turning around.

"Sorry, Mom, it's just me," she heard her daughter say.

Katy Ann smiled brightly, turning to find her firstborn peering into the refrigerator. "Your socks are probably on the floor, as well."

"Yes, they are, but since I no longer live at home, it's none of your business," Delia teased her mother.

"Then get your head out of my icebox." Katy Ann swatted her daughter playfully. "What brings my brilliant, overworked daughter home?"

"The film people have some papers for us to sign," Delia said as she pulled leftovers from the refrigerator. "They're on the table." She made a plate and put it in the microwave.

"Ever thinking of actually cooking for yourself?" Katy Ann asked, studying the papers.

"Why would I want to do that?" Delia snickered

"Just a thought." Katy Ann rolled her eyes. "This reads pretty much the same as the others. I hope they have better luck this time. Is Dr. Williams still refusing to go?"

"Yes, can't say that I blame her." Delia brought her food to the table. "It's just that she's gotten closer than anyone else."

"Tell me about the bracelet," Katy Anne requested.

"I'm almost positive that it was Anna's," Delia said. "I checked with the shop, and I couldn't find anything else that I could be definite about. There weren't any records, so it was another dead end."

"That reporter gave her the bracelet?" Katy Anne asked thoughtfully. "Interesting. Are they a couple?"

"I don't know." Delia recalled the bizarre interaction between the two women. "I think they were. Ms. Charles is certainly carrying a torch for Dr. Williams."

"Maybe that's the key," Katy Anne said. "It would be nice to finally put Anna and Catherine to rest."

"Don't get your hopes up. There might not be any bodies. He could have dumped them at sea. There's going to be this detective stopping by. It's some kind of new angle the television people are working. She's investigating the murders as if it were a current case."

"That should be interesting." Katy Anne smiled. "Now tell me, what are you working on, and how long will you be in town?"

Chapter 38

"I just want to go home," Faith whimpered. Every muscle in her body ached. She had endured another long day with Trudy and company. Since Dave's arrival, everyone's attitude had suddenly changed. Now that they knew she was working the upcoming Whispering Pines shoot, everyone wanted to be her best friend. Having Trudy sucking up to her was the worst part. She could tolerate the hefty woman when they openly hated one another, but her fake clinging to her was disgusting, and Faith was constantly searching for a sharp object.

"I want to go home," she wearily repeated as she flopped down onto the hotel bed. She frowned, realizing that she had no home. She had given up her tiny apartment in Boston when she went overseas. Most of her belongings were in storage, and she couldn't very well stay with Shawn.

"Okay, so I just want to get the hell out of Kansas," she said. She grinned wryly as *The Wizard of Oz* came to mind. "Just what in the hell was Dorothy thinking?"

She rubbed her throbbing temples and debated calling Shawn again. She grimaced at the thought. After the fiasco last evening, it might be best to wait until Shawn contacted her.

"Who the hell is Carey Jessup?" she snarled, recalling that Shawn was entertaining another woman when she finally made contact with her. The pounding in her head increased as she tried to will Shawn to call her.

"One more day, then I'm out of here. Then what? I have a shoot in Scotland, but that isn't for another two weeks."

She had nowhere to go.

"Not a problem, I can always visit my parents," she said grimly. The familiar stirrings of bitterness began to fill her. Growing up, she had been very close to her parents, until the day her father fell from the pedestal she had mistakenly believed he stood upon.

"Let it go, you're an adult now," she reminded herself. It was the same reminder she tried to reinforce each time she visited them. Somehow, she just couldn't let the betrayal go.

Faith sprang off the bed as her cell phone chirped.

"Hello?" she anxiously greeted the caller, whom she prayed was Shawn.

"What's wrong?" Shawn's voice came from the other end over a background din.

"What makes you think something's wrong?" Faith bristled until she recalled whom she was talking to. "Nothing, just worried about you. And Kansas sucks. I hate this shoot. Trudy's trying to be nice to me."

"And how is that a bad thing?" Shawn said with a throaty chuckle.

"You don't like her either, so don't even try to convince me to play nice." Faith snorted with disgust. "I told Dave she was all wrong for Whispering Pines, but I think they're going to sign her."

"What? Did I hear you correctly? They want Trudy for the shoot at Whispering Pines?"

"No." Faith sighed. "They want you. You keep saying no, so they're sticking me with Trudy. I think Dave's trying to punish me. For some reason, the brass seems to think I've become a problem child."

"You, a problem?" Shawn laughed heartily. "If they think you're being a pain in the ass, I could fill them in on some stories that would make your attitude in Kansas seem positively endearing."

"Such as?" Faith was suddenly feeling better. Her smile faded when Shawn failed to respond. "Shawn? Are you there?"

"I'm sorry," Shawn finally whispered. "I'm getting confused. Something about your family. I can't quite figure it out. Sorry, my mind is a mess right now. My head is pounding."

"You just finished at the Joshua Ward House." Faith wanted nothing more than to be there and comfort Shawn. "That place really messes with you."

"I know," Shawn said. "Carey was completely spooked. Althea is worried that she won't be able to go to Whispering Pines."

"Carey?" Faith's own headache returned. "And how is your new little friend? Let me guess, all that noise I'm hearing is because the two of you are in a bar."

"Everyone's here," Shawn snapped. "We just wrapped. Faith, Carey Jessup is straight, and you know her."

"No, I don't."

"Well, she knows you," Shawn said. "She was ready to pull out of her contract because she doesn't want to work with you. This woman really hates you."

"Okay, that would imply that she has met me before," Faith said. "Honestly, the name isn't ringing any bells. Is she on the crew?"

"No." Shawn's voice sounded weary. "She's a cop. She's investigating the murders as a sidepiece for the special."

"I still don't recognize the name," Faith said, her concern for Shawn's well-being growing. "Forget about it. I pissed off a lot of cops when I was a reporter. That's probably how she knows me. You don't sound well. I'm worried about you."

"I'm fine," Shawn lied. "Just a really long day. I'm heading back to New York for a little rest before Scotland. Why don't you stay with me, and we can fly over together, after you visit your parents."

"Wait, how did—" Faith almost laughed at the question she was about to ask. "Never mind. So, does this mean you're not mad at me anymore?"

"No, I'm still terribly upset with you."

"Liar." Faith sighed with relief. "I'll see you sometime next week. Promise me that you'll get some rest."

"I'm trying," Shawn said. "This town is so active, I just can't seem to shut the voices out."

"Baby," Faith said, feeling helpless that she wasn't there to help Shawn cope. "I'm flying out tonight."

"No, finish the job, and we'll see each other next week."

Faith didn't feel any better about things after she and Shawn said their good-byes. "Who the hell is Carey Jessup?" she repeated, thinking about the many times she had butted heads with the authorities in an effort to do her job.

Her next call was to her parents, who were overjoyed by the news that she was coming home for a short visit. Deep in her heart, she wished she could muster the same enthusiasm.

Chapter 39

Salem, Massachusetts
2005

Shawn had another headache. She walked back towards the booths where the crew was partying. After wrapping up the shoot, everyone retreated to the small Irish bar just down the street from the Ward house. She felt queasy as she reclaimed her seat next to Althea and the ever-mysterious Carey.

"Are you all right?" Carey asked.

"Headache." Shawn waved it off. "Places like that can be a bit much on me. What about you? After the last couple of days, you must be looking at things differently."

"You could say that." Carey took a sip of her drink. "Are you sure that trash can wasn't knocked over by a member of the crew?"

"It wasn't," Shawn said with a shake of her head. Once again, she tried to shut out the sound of a small girl crying and the voices that were calling to her. She turned to say something to Althea, who was studying Carey carefully. Turning her attention back towards Carey didn't help.

"Althea's worried about you," she whispered to Carey.

"I'll be fine," Carey said so that Althea could hear her. "I'm glad I got my feet wet over the past couple of days. I should be able to handle whatever the Pines has to offer."

"How's the investigation going?" Shawn asked.

"Very well," Carey said enthusiastically. "The case is really shaping up. After reviewing all of the witness statements, I can't understand why they didn't bring the husband in for questioning."

"From what I understand, Captain Stratton owned most of the town," Shawn said, the voices still trying to claim her. "Sheriff never let it go…" her voice trailed off as something popped into her head.

"You're divorced," she said.

"You know I am." Althea gave a toothy smile. She looked past Shawn, and her smile vanished. "Oh, you mean Carey?"

"Stop doing that," Carey said. "It isn't uncommon, given my profession."

"She can't help it," Althea said. "In fact, Shawn's the reason I'm divorced."

"I'm not the reason," Shawn protested. "Your husband's girlfriend is the reason."

"Anyone ever try taking you to the track?" Carey asked in a transparent attempt to ease the tension that had suddenly sprung up.

"Several times." Shawn shifted her body in an effort to get comfortable. "I can't pick horses, and I lost a lot of money in Atlantic City."

"That sucks." Carey laughed lightly.

The pain in Shawn's head drifted down to her neck.

"That's pretty much what my dad said the first time he took me to the track." Shawn tried to laugh it off as pain gripped her body. "Oh for the love of—" she muttered, hearing her cell ring before it actually did. She snatched the phone from her pocket and waited for it to ring.

"For the love of God, go to sleep," she barked, already knowing who was on the other end.

"I was calling to tell you the same thing," Faith whispered.

"I know." The throbbing in Shawn's body was increasing. "I'm not staying much longer."

She listened as Faith tried to comfort her. Out of the corner of her eye she spied Carey playing with her glass. The sound of it scraping against the wooden table was adding to her discomfort. She reached out and clasped Carey's wrist in an effort to cease the agitating noise.

Suddenly filled with sadness and pain, she released Carey's wrist and bolted to her feet. The cell phone dropped from her hand. Her chair crashed to the floor, and she raced out of the tiny barroom, crying.

Outside, in the brisk night air, the voices quieted and Shawn could finally breathe. She brushed the tears from her face and leaned against the brick building. She took deep, cleansing breaths, trying to understand what she had seen. A tiny girl stood shaking and whimpering, beside an indoor pool. Shawn could smell the chlorine and hear the sounds of water splashing and happy children giggling.

"Why?" the tiny little girl wailed at a tall, dark figure looming above her.

"Stay away from me!" the tall woman said with a snarl, breaking the little girl's heart.

Shawn felt sick as she recognized the cruel voice. It was younger, she was younger, but there was little doubt that the figure was Faith. The feelings began to ebb as the image slipped away.

"Jesus, Faith, I knew you could be brisk," Shawn mumbled into the night air. "But scaring small children?"

"Shawnie?" Mark, one of the techs, approached her.

"Hey, buddy." She felt the pain finally leaving her. "Did I manage to freak everyone out?"

"Yeah," he said with a warm smile as he rubbed her shoulder. "Are you all right?"

"Better. Tell everyone I don't have bad news," she teased, knowing that many of her colleagues were wondering if what she had seen was a bad omen pertaining to their lives.

"I just got one of those creepy Salem vibes," she said. "I'll be coming back in a minute, so tell the gang to stop changing the flight reservations."

Althea emerged from the large double doors that led to the tiny bar. "Good to know." Mark smiled and patted her shoulder again before returning to the party.

"Someone wants to talk to you," Althea said and handed Shawn the cell phone she had dropped. "I'd like to tell you that I managed to chill her out, but I'd be lying."

"I'm fine," Shawn calmly addressed Faith.

"Bullshit," Faith barked in response.

"I am," Shawn said. "I just had a funky vision. My senses are on overload. I really am feeling much better."

"Why don't I believe you?" Faith asked softly.

"I'll tell you all about it when I see you," Shawn said, body and mind finally relaxing. She listened carefully as Faith seemed to be grumbling about something. "Faith? Yo, oh tall one, I'm fine."

"Promise?"

"Yes." Shawn smiled, her heart warming at the way Faith was worrying about her. They talked for a little while longer until Shawn managed to convince Faith that everything was all right, and they both needed to get some sleep. Just as she was disconnecting the call, the crew stumbled out of the bar.

"Closing time already?"

"Are you sure that everything's okay?" Althea asked sternly.

"Yes." Shawn rolled her eyes. "Go on. I'm just going to walk back to my hotel. The fresh air will do me some good. Hey, before you take off, why is Trudy going to Whispering Pines?"

"She's on the short list," Althea said with a shrug. "Unless you've reconsidered?"

Shawn chewed on her bottom lip, wondering if she should just do the shoot.

"When do you have to know?"

"As soon as possible." Althea was beaming. "We're heading there right after Scotland. In fact, I'm doing some prelim work with Carey Jessup and the Stratton descendants this week."

"What about Faith?" she asked, her heart pounding for some unknown reason.

"She isn't going to be needed until we head up there," Althea said. "Shawn, are you really interested?"

"I don't want to go," Shawn muttered. "I just think that I can't avoid it."

"Get in touch with me before we leave for Scotland," Althea said. "I'll see you in two weeks."

They shared a quick hug just as Carey approached.

"How about I walk you back to your hotel, and you tell me what happened earlier?" Carey said.

"Oh, that was nothing." They began to stroll down the deserted streets.

"Not to me," Carey said with a sigh. "It isn't everyday a psychic touches my arm and freaks out. Should I be more careful the next time I go out on a call?"

"What I saw was the past."

"It couldn't have been my divorce," Carey said. "Brian and I parted on very good terms. Heck, we're still friends. What did you see?"

"I don't know," Shawn said as they approached the hotel. "A lot of the time, what I see or hear is just a quick flash or jumbled image. I like to explain it as trying to listen to a song that's caught between radio stations."

"That must be annoying." Carey scrunched her brow. They stepped into the lobby.

"Ready to call it a murder yet?" Shawn was eager to change the subject.

"Oh, yeah." Carey chuckled. "The bar's still open. Up for another round? I'll tell you all about the case."

"Cool." Shawn perked up.

"You know, it would be a lot easier if you could just tell me where the bodies are," Carey told her after they received their drinks and claimed a spot near the fireplace.

"So, now you believe me."

"Maybe," Carey said with a familiar cocky smirk. "Still, as so many defense attorneys like to say, no body no crime. Any idea where the bodies are hidden? Sheriff Mulder and Richard Stratton were convinced they were buried in the garden. They dug it up the day of Horatio Stratton's funeral and found nothing."

"They're in the house," Shawn said thoughtfully.

"Care to be more specific?"

"I wish I could." Shawn sighed with regret. "Why did they think it was the garden?"

"You're going to love this," Carey said eagerly. "Captain Stratton was constantly digging in it. By all accounts, he seemed to be obsessed with the garden. That is, if you can believe the witness statements. Most of them claimed that the garden would blossom overnight."

"She still tends her garden," Shawn said absently. "Sorry, just having one of those moments."

"Why the house?"

"Just a feeling." Shawn shrugged, her body relaxing from the heat emanating from the fire. "And what happened to the film crew after my visit there. They brought in a douser and the house went berserk."

"What's a douser?" Carey asked.

"They have a gift that allows them to find bodies," Shawn said, offering the short version. Carey furrowed her brow, clearly not believing what Shawn had told her.

"Have you found anything in the old records that might be helpful?" Shawn asked.

"No. On the morning Anna and Catherine disappeared, the kitchen was covered with blood. The sheriff requested to have a look after most of the staff showed up in his office, panicking about it. He drove up to the house, and the captain refused to show him the kitchen. The only statement he offered was that his wife and sister were out of town on a family matter. Apparently, it was quite a trip, since they never came home. They were never seen or heard from again. Unless you take into account the scattered statements of staff members who have claimed to have seen their ghosts."

"Which you don't." Shawn nodded with a smile.

"I can't," Carey said. "The only tangible evidence I have to work with is that their belongings were either burned or sold by the captain. I understand you have the only identifiable possession."

Shawn held up her wrist and allowed Carey to look at her bracelet. "You should check out the shop where it was purchased," she suggested. "A member of the family has already confirmed that it was Anna's."

"I did go to the antiques shop and couldn't find anything, as did Ms. St. James," Carey said. "I'm meeting with the rest of the family this week. Could I take this with me just to confirm that it was indeed Anna's?"

"No," Shawn politely declined. "Take a good look now and compare it to the photo. This doesn't leave my wrist."

"It must be very special to you."

"It was a gift from Faith." Shawn felt Carey's demeanor turning cold. "You really should stop doing that every time I mention her name."

"I don't know what you're talking about."

"Yes, you do." Shawn kept her tone soft. "I don't know what happened, but I will if you keep allowing your emotions to surge every time I mention Faith. You could just tell me. Why you changed your name, for starters. Maybe I could help."

"There's nothing to tell." Shawn didn't need her gift to know that Carey was fuming. "You already know why I have a different name. Jessup's my married name. There you have it, mystery solved."

"That's why you have a different last name," Shawn said. "I still don't know why you have a different first name."

Carey's jaw clenched before she blew out a heavy sigh. "You're pissing me off. You know that, don't you?" she grumbled. Shawn simply nodded in agreement.

"Does it ever get to you, knowing things that are meant to be private?"

"Constantly," Shawn said. "I don't want to invade your privacy. I just want you to know that it happens. If you don't want me to know, then try not getting so angry every time you hear Faith's name, and I promise to not mention her."

"Fair enough," Carey said. "So, let's talk about the case. I get to visit the actual crime scene in a couple of weeks."

"The kitchen?" Shawn swallowed hard, and she trembled.

"Yes. I understand it's never been remodeled," Carey said. "Are you all right? Is there a reason I shouldn't go into the kitchen?"

"You?" Shawn laughed. "No, you'll be just fine. I, on the other hand, would rather walk through fire than set foot in there again." Shawn was filled with a sudden sense of panic as she realized that, as the host of the special, Faith would have to accompany Carey into the kitchen while her investigation was being filmed.

"Oh, my God," she squeaked out in horror.

Chapter 40

Stewart, Massachusetts
1957

"This has to be the lamest task yet," Mitchell whispered to his best friend, Frank, as they stood on the porch of the dilapidated old house. Frank shrugged in agreement.

"No talking," one of upperclassmen scolded them. Mitchell glanced over his shoulder and spied his future fraternity brothers standing on the front lawn, drinking beer. Mitchell dutifully turned his attention back towards the manor. He couldn't understand what the big deal was. It was just an old house; spending the night should be the easiest task they would have to endure. Much better than when they were forced to run across the campus quad wearing nothing but their BVDs.

During the drive up to Stewart, the upperclassmen tried their level best to scare them with wild stories of a crazy old sea captain who went on a murderous rampage. He and Frank rolled their eyes at the ghost stories. A couple of the other pledges didn't seem as unaffected.

"It's time, if you dare," the pledge master challenged the small group of five freshmen. Mitchell was eager to get the task over with, since he had studying to do. He reached for the doorknob and wasn't worried when he discovered that the door was locked. He simply gripped his flashlight tightly and approached the window.

He raised his fist and smashed the flashlight against the glass. He yelped in pain when his hand recoiled and the glass remained unbroken.

"Whatever," he grumbled while the upperclassmen laughed at his plight. He nudged Harry, who was a member of the football team.

"Kick the door in," he told the large teenager, who smiled eagerly at the suggestion.

Harry lunged, shoving his large shoulder into the door.

"What the fuck?" Frank asked when Harry slammed into the door and nothing happened.

"There must be a way in. Let's scout around," Mitchell insisted as the snickering from the drunken frat boys continued. Just when he turned to step off the porch, the door slowly opened.

"Cool." He noticed his fellow pledges turning pale and staring at the open door. "Let's go in."

They switched their stares to him as if he'd lost his mind.

"What? Harry loosened the door." He stepped inside and turned on his flashlight. The others finally followed him into the abandoned house.

"I didn't," Harry whispered in his ear. Mitchell looked up, stunned to find Harry shaking like a leaf. "The door didn't budge when I slammed into it."

"Chill out, man." He shook his head. The others began to wander about. "I wonder why the locals didn't mess up the place?" he asked, thinking it would be the perfect spot for the local teens to throw a party.

"Man, you guys should see the kitchen," Frank exclaimed as he darted into the foyer. "The cabinets are all hacked up."

"I guess the locals did do a little partying." Mitchell followed the others towards the kitchen. He felt a cold wind blow past him but dismissed it as the night air. He stumbled backwards when Harry bolted past him with a look of sheer terror on his face.

"What the fuck?" he grumbled. "Stan, go get him, all of us have to stay the night," he said as he stepped into the freezing room. *"I know what you are,"* he heard a voice say. He felt hands on his throat as he dropped his flashlight. *"Sinner!"* an unseen person howled.

Mitchell bolted out of the room after Harry, this time not to stop him from leaving, but to join him in his escape. Belonging to Phi Delta wasn't worth the fear that was pounding through his body. He found Harry standing in the foyer, hugging his body. The others followed after them.

"How did it know?" Harry stammered, the tears streaming down his face.

Mitchell stared at Harry as the startling realization hit him. His secret. It knew his secret. How?

"What's with the two of you?" Stan demanded.

"I'm not staying," Harry squeaked out.

"We have to stay." Frank tried to reason with the whimpering linebacker.

Suddenly the sound of a woman wailing echoed through the house.

"It's just the guys goofing on us," Stan said. Then the doors and windows all shot open. Everyone stood in stunned silence as the doors and windows just as suddenly snapped shut.

"*Leave!*" a woman's voice screeched, sending the five young men rushing from the house.

Their feet didn't stop moving until they were face to face with their fraternity brothers.

"Something wrong, boys?" Tom, the pledge master taunted them.

"The lady didn't seem happy that we were in her house," Mitchell said; his entire body was shaking.

"You mean her?" Tom asked quietly, pointing to one of the upstairs windows.

Mitchell's heart clenched when he spied the glowing image of a woman watching them.

"That's it." He decided that his brothers had set them up. "They're yanking our chains. Let's go back inside."

"Are you shitting me?" Harry bellowed with a murderous gaze.

"You want to go back?" Tom seemed truly surprised by Mitchell's bravado.

"Yeah," Mitchell said, silently praying that the other pledges would talk him out of it. The front door swung open, and he jumped when he felt a hand on his shoulder.

"It's okay," Tom said. "You don't have to. We can head back to campus now."

"I don't get it," Frank muttered. "Who was in the window? Your sister?"

"I don't know," Tom said. "Guys, we aren't messing with you, and just so you know, none of us has lasted any longer in there than you did."

On the drive back to campus, everyone laughed at how frightened they had been, and no matter how much they coaxed the upperclassmen, they failed to get any of them to admit they had been behind the pranks.

A few months later, Mitchell and his frat brothers were hanging out in a local pub, trying to pick up girls. Mitchell did his best to pretend to be playing the game as well. He managed to sidestep a Vassar girl who eagerly accepted his advances. He spied Harry lurking alone in the corner. Something had been troubling him since the night they went to the old house, something that only he and Harry seemed to share.

"Hey," he greeted the football player and handed him a beer. "Can I talk to you about something? Outside?"

"Sure," Harry said, and they carried their beer outside. "What do you want to talk about?"

"That old house the guys dragged us up to," Mitchell carefully began to say. "What did you mean when you said it knew?"

Harry spun around and glared down at him. For some unknown reason, Mitchell stood his ground. "Tell me?" he asked as he felt his knees shake.

Harry's features softened as their eyes met.

"This," was all he said, cupping Mitchell's face in his hands and capturing him in a searing kiss. Mitchell melted into the kiss before reality struck him.

"I'm a sinner," he whimpered and jerked away.

"No, you're not," Harry said. "And neither am I. Whatever's trapped in that house is evil, not us."

Mitchell felt years of fear fading as Harry held him in a tender gaze.

"We should get back inside," he said softly.

"Or," Harry said brightly, "we could pretend we got lucky and just sneak off."

*　*　*

Houston Texas,
Halloween Night, 2002

"Mitch, get in here!" The shout came from the den of their home.

"What?" Mitchell grumbled, joining his lover. "Another special on football? We're going to be late for the party," he told the larger man as he scratched his graying beard and looked over at the television with disinterest.

"My God, are those boobs fake or what?" Mitchell snickered as he listened to the blonde prattling on. "Whispering Pines?" He was startled. "I can't believe it."

"We can be a little late for the party," Harry said, pulling him down onto his lap. They watched, trembling slightly as they remembered the past.

"Oh, no, honey, you and little blondie really shouldn't go in that kitchen," Mitchell squealed, covering his eyes. Harry snapped off the television.

"I can't watch," Harry said. "It feels like yesterday."

"As frightening as it was," Mitchell said, "it did bring us together."

Months later, Harry forced Mitchell to go with him when Dr. Williams was in Houston signing copies of her book, *Whispering Pines*. Harry was normally quiet and reserved, but once he met Shawn he wouldn't shut up until Mitchell pulled him away. "Jesus Mary, give the girl a break," Mitchell told his lover before dragging him from the bookstore.

Chapter 41

Arlington, Massachusetts
2005

Faith stood looking out the window of her parents' living room.

"Dinner will be ready soon," she heard her father say as he approached. She kept staring out the window, wondering if she would ever forgive him.

"It's nice to have you home," Stan Charles said. "Will Shawn be joining you soon?"

"No." She bristled, turning towards him. "I'm heading to New York in a couple of days."

"Good." He sighed with obvious relief. "I was afraid that something might have happened between the two of you."

"We broke up." She was surprised when his eyes dimmed.

"I'm sorry to hear that," he said. "Shawn was good for you. I was hoping that just maybe you were finally going to settle down. Of course, it couldn't have been easy on either of you after you went overseas."

"Strange, you giving me advice about relationships," she said harshly. She instantly regretted her words, seeing the hurt in his eyes.

"Faith, someday you really should take that chip off of your shoulder," he said. "It was a long time ago. Your mother forgave me. And frankly, based on the way you treat women, you really don't have any right to judge me."

"You're right," she said. "I keep telling myself that Dad just had a midlife crisis. No big deal, except you sneaked around and started a new family."

"All of which happened when you were just a child. And I'll forever regret what I did, and how you found out."

"I'm sorry," Faith said. "Being a teenager and discovering that I had a sister was a shock. Poor Jessica. I was so cruel to her. I really am sorry, Dad. I don't mean to dredge all of this up every time I come home. But you'll be happy to know that Shawn and I are trying to work things out."

"That's good," he said. "I really like her and the way she makes you smile. I'm also very happy that you're back in the United States."

"For now." She shrugged as her mother called them into the dining room. "I'm heading to Scotland soon."

"What's in Scotland?" her mother asked as they took their respective spots at the dining room table.

"City of the Dead." Faith chuckled as her mother's eyes widened. "Covenanters Prison, to be more precise. It's supposed to be very spooky."

"Sounds a lot safer than your last assignment," Myra Charles said.

"Kansas? Oh, you mean the war. Don't worry, I'm not going back into the hot spots. In fact, I mostly visit cold spots."

"You seem to have neglected telling us about Kansas," Myra said. "Why don't you tell us about Kansas, and then about your trip to Edinburgh?"

"How did you know I was going to Edinburgh?" Faith asked, busy loading her plate with mashed potatoes.

"Covenanters Prison, the Black Mausoleum?" Myra said. "I am a history professor. I don't know the ghost stories, but I can only imagine, given what happened there."

"So, is it haunted?" Stan asked. Faith smiled. Her father was as much of a skeptic as she once was.

"What happened at the prison?" Faith asked, eager to hear about her next assignment.

"Later. First tell us about Kansas," Myra said. "Was Shawn with you?"

"Kansas was boring, and Shawn was in Salem," Faith grumbled. "After Edinburgh, I'll be coming back to Massachusetts," she said in an effort to derail her mother from any further inquiries regarding Shawn.

"Lizzie Borden House?" Stan asked.

"Why don't you just drive down to Fall River?" Faith knew he was fascinated by the infamous murders. "I think I'm hitting Fall River later this year. If I do, why don't you take some time off and join me?" she offered, hoping to finally end the tension between them.

"Can I?"

"Of course." She rolled her eyes.

"Okay, so what are you working on here? It can't be Salem, you said Shawn was just there," Myra asked.

"Stewart," she mumbled. Stan dropped his fork.

"Faith? Are you going back to Whispering Pines? Are you sure you want to do that?"

"Want to? No," she said. "I feel like I have to go."

"But, Faith," Myra said.

"I'm going."

"At least Shawn will be with you."

Faith began to chew on the inside of her mouth but didn't answer.

"You didn't finish telling us about Kansas," Stan said, perhaps sensing that Faith didn't want to talk about Shawn.

Later that evening, Faith was relaxing on the front porch, enjoying the night air and a cup of coffee. "Shawn's not going with you, is she?" her father asked as he sat down beside her.

"No." She sighed. "I wish she was. I don't know how I'm going to handle that place without her. She just can't go back."

"Maybe you should follow her example?" he said. Faith gave him a curious glance. "I read your book and…"

"And?"

"When I was in college, my fraternity used to think it was funny to bring new pledges to Whispering Pines," he said. "I don't buy a lot of that hokey spooky stuff, but I can't forget how two of the pledges went running from the house."

"That wouldn't be Uncle Mitch and Uncle Harry would it?" Faith laughed. "Why didn't you tell me you'd been there?"

"I don't like talking about it. And I didn't know you were going there until your mother and I saw you on television. It isn't as if you're big on sharing your whereabouts."

"I'll try to be better," Faith said. "What happened when you were there?" she asked, feeling closer to her father than she had in years.

"Not much." He shivered slightly. "It was just a big dark house, then Mitch and Harry bolted out of the kitchen. The doors and windows opened and shut. Then a strange voice told us to get out."

"What did you do?"

"After I almost crapped my pants, I ran like the dickens," he said. "For the longest time, all of us convinced ourselves that the older guys had played a joke on us. I think I still believed that was the truth until you went there. I had seen a woman in the upstairs window," he added.

"Second or third floor?"

"Third, I think." He shuddered once again.

"Catherine." She nodded. "That was her room. How much of the house did you see?"

"Just the entryway and the kitchen. Really couldn't see much. It was at night, and all we had were flashlights."

"Want to go back?"

"No."

"Oh, come on, Dad, it's a great mystery," she teased him. "They even have a cop investigating the case."

"No, thank you," he repeated. "I'd rather go to my grave lying to myself that my fraternity brothers set the whole thing up."

"Wuss." She snickered.

"I'll go if you need me to," he said. "I don't want you going alone."

"I'll be fine."

"Want to talk about Shawn?" he asked gently.

"Well, you and Mom aren't the only ones I neglect telling where I'm going to be working. I failed to take her feelings into consideration when I took the assignment overseas."

"Bad call," he said. She bit her tongue to keep from snapping at him. They were finally getting along, and she didn't want to ruin the moment. "Sorry, like you said, I shouldn't be giving relationship advice."

"I almost said it again." She laughed and laced her fingers together. "I'm trying, Dad. I really am. I need to let the past go. And on that note, how's Jessica doing?"

"She hasn't talked to me for quite some time now," he said wearily. "You weren't the only one I hurt."

"No, that one falls in my lap," she said. "I was the one who hurt her. She was just a kid who didn't even know what was going on." She glanced over at her father. Her heart sank when she caught the look of sadness clearly written on his face.

"For a little over one month in my life," he said, "I acted like an ass. The end result was that I caused a great many people a lifetime of pain."

"I never realized that the affair was so short," she said.

"Frankly, it wasn't any of your business."

"True." Faith couldn't help wondering if he had simply come to his senses one day or had her mother found out? Then again, it really wasn't any of her business. It was, however, time to let it go.

"So what do you think about what Mom told us about the prison?"

"A mass grave and all those people locked up in deplorable conditions? No wonder it's haunted."

"Becoming a believer?"

"Who me? Nonsense."

"Yeah, that's just how I used to say it for the cameras." She snickered. "I remember I almost confessed once in Toronto. We were at this old farmhouse, walking from room to room. Shawn was going on about 'I feel this or that,' and I just ignored her. We get to the kid's bedroom, and I swear this rocking horse starts rocking. I just about jumped out of my skin."

"I would have peed my pants." Stan laughed.

"I almost did," Faith said. "I still went on camera denying that there was anything strange. I like not having to do that anymore."

"So, you like the aspect you're involved with now? You didn't seem to enjoy Kansas."

"I like it." She inhaled the brisk night air. "I get to interview people and research stuff. I just like it more when I get to do it with Shawn."

"I really hope the two of you are working things out." He wrapped his arm around her shoulders. For the first time in years, she allowed him to comfort her.

"So do I, Dad, so do I." She sighed happily.

Chapter 42

New York City
2005

Shawn stretched out her aching body. She had been working on the computer for days, trying to get things ready for her next book. She also busied herself researching her next project. She had hoped that by keeping busy, she wouldn't have to worry about what would happen when Faith arrived. Deep in her heart, she knew that she wanted things to work out between the two of them. She was just leery about jumping back into a relationship with the enigmatic reporter.

"Maybe that's where we went wrong the last time?" she pondered aloud. She stood and wandered off to her tiny kitchen so she could pour yet another cup of coffee. The constant wondering that maybe they had jumped from being adversaries to lovers much too quickly concerned her the most. What if Faith panicked again and left Shawn behind for a second time? Could she survive it?

"How am I going to keep things at a safe distance when she'll be staying with me?" she groused as she sipped her coffee.

Suddenly her skin prickled and her heart skipped a beat.

"And she's early." She placed her cup on the counter before making her way to the front door. Faith jumped with surprise when Shawn opened the door before she had the opportunity to knock.

"I hate it when you do that." Faith scowled as she tried to balance her traveling bags and the bouquet of flowers she was carrying.

"That's why I do it," Shawn said, noting Faith's uneasy manner. She stepped aside, allowing her to enter the apartment. "You're early."

"I'm not interrupting anything, am I?" Faith asked cautiously as she stepped into Shawn's home. Shawn was mildly amused by the way Faith was shifting nervously and averting her gaze.

"No, your timing is perfect," Shawn said. "I just sent the dancing girls home for the night."

"Sorry I missed that."

Shawn was perplexed as to why Faith was just standing there, strangling the flowers she had brought. She was frustrated that she couldn't get an idea of what was going through Faith's head. She gave Faith a curious glance before turning and closing the front door.

"Did those flowers do something heinous?"

"What?"

"The flowers. You're crushing them," Shawn said, pointing to the unfortunate roses that were crumbling in Faith's hand.

"Sorry," Faith exclaimed with a wide-eyed look. She thrust what was left of the roses at Shawn. "Here."

"Thank you," Shawn said, accepting what was left of the once-beautiful arrangement. She carefully examined the roses, all of which had been snapped at the stems. Faith glanced over at her with a forlorn expression. Shawn cradled the mess and carried it into the kitchen. She blew out a breath in exasperation as she cleared away the mangled stems and placed the buds in a bowl.

"They'll make a nice bowl of potpourri," she said before rejoining her moody guest. "The flowers are very nice, thank you."

"Sorry I smushed them." Faith shoved her hands in her pockets.

"Faith, what's going on? You're acting as though you've never given a woman flowers before."

"I haven't." Faith's face turned scarlet. "Well, except my mom."

"Really?" Shawn beamed as Faith took a sudden interest in her shoes. *God, she's so adorable when she gets all shy.*

"It was very sweet," she said in an effort to ease Faith's tension. "Why don't you take off your coat and sit? You were planning on staying, weren't you?"

"Thanks." Faith exhaled with obvious relief and finally shed her coat. "I'm sorry I got all goofy," she added as she plopped down onto the sofa. "I saw them at the airport and thought, 'I really want to give Shawn flowers.' I'm just nervous about staying with you. Weird, huh?"

"No," Shawn said softly. "I've been feeling somewhat anxious myself."

"Anxious? Anxious how?" Faith asked in a defensive manner. "I thought you wanted to work on things?"

"I do," Shawn said. "Relax. I've just been worried about rushing things. With you staying here, we'll be closer, not that we haven't dealt with that before. It's just that this is my home, and there isn't our work to buffer things."

"I should stay at a hotel," Faith said in a determined tone.

"Or my guest room?" Shawn suggested. She could feel her anger growing. "What the hell has gotten your knickers in a twist? Can't you just admit that you're afraid that if we sleep together now it might not be a good idea? Why is it so hard for you to just say what you mean? I swear you are the most infuriating, irrational, mmmf—" Shawn's words were cut off when Faith captured her in a fiery kiss. Shawn melted. She laced her fingers in Faith's long hair and drew her closer. Shawn was still tingling as the sultry kiss came to an end.

"Or you could just kiss me senseless." She rested her head on Faith's shoulder.

"I'm not good with expressing my feelings," Faith said softly. Shawn was content playing with the buttons on Faith's cotton blouse.

"Not with words." Shawn snickered as she continued to play with the buttons. "But you do have a unique way of breaking the ice with a girl. Feel better?"

"Hell, yeah." Faith laughed, her fingers gently massaging Shawn's scalp. "Am I still staying in the guest room?"

"Why don't we just enjoy our time off and not think about the sleeping arrangements?" Shawn suggested. "I'm going to put on a fresh pot of coffee, and then you can tell me how your visit home went."

"No work? No pressure? Just you and me hanging out, getting to know one another, I don't think we've ever done that before," Faith mused.

"We haven't." Shawn slipped from the warmth of Faith's body and padded off into the kitchen. "It could be fun," she said. She ground a fresh bunch of coffee beans and cleaned out her coffee maker.

"Fun?" Faith said from the other room. "Hey? Why is it that you aren't reading me?"

"I knew you were at the door." Shawn returned to the living room. "But you were so keyed up that you had the walls up. Now you're relaxed and comfortable, and when you're like that, I can't see what you're thinking. Then again, maybe there's nothing going on inside that pretty head of yours."

"If you only knew," Faith said in a husky tone. "You're right, though. Now that I'm here and I didn't find another woman with you, I feel much better."

"Wait. You thought I'd have a date here? Is that why you showed up early?" Shawn folded her arms across her chest.

"I thought it was possible," Faith admitted. "You only broke up with Deb a short time ago. I was worried that once you got back to New York, she'd be trying to get you back."

"She did." Shawn peered into the kitchen to check on how the coffee was progressing. "I'm not interested. Even when you and I didn't get along, I was attracted to you. And now that you've kissed me..."

"Yes?" Faith's eyes shone with hope.

"It was a nice way to break the tension." Shawn shook her head, knowing that Faith was up to her old tricks. "And I think leaving the sleeping arrangements ambiguous took the pressure off of us. So, did you have a good visit with your parents?"

"I did. It was nice for a change."

"That's good," Shawn called out as she ducked into the kitchen and poured the coffee. "I know many people can get edgy visiting their parents, but you've always seemed almost hostile." She rejoined Faith in the living room and handed her a cup of coffee.

"Hostile? I wouldn't say hostile. I love both of my parents," Faith said as Shawn sat down beside her. "Something happened when I was a teenager, and I've been bitter ever since. Which makes me nuts, because I know I should be an adult and get past it."

"Want to talk about it?" Shawn curled her legs under her body and eyed Faith carefully, looking for any sign that she had overstepped her bounds. Her heart dropped when Faith's smile morphed into a deep scowl.

"Yeah." Faith finally nodded. Shawn's eyes widened with surprise. "Shawn, I'm learning," Faith said with sincerity. "It's not easy for me to trust or open up, but I understand that it's all part of getting to know one another.

"When I was a teenager, I found out that my Dad had an affair years earlier. I never looked at him the same way again. I stopped trusting him, and even though I understood that what happened was none of my business, I've been mad at him ever since. I used to idolize my father, and discovering that he had cheated on my mother broke my heart."

"You were young. It's only natural you'd be angry," Shawn said.

"I know." Faith shrugged. "But carrying that anger into adulthood hasn't been healthy. I mean, my mother forgave him, and they saved their marriage. Not to mention that, because of the way

I've handled my own relationships, I really shouldn't be casting any stones. Not with you, anyway."

"I know that." Shawn smirked and wiggled her eyebrows.

Faith laughed. "Yes, another added bonus of dating a psychic. Dad and I really got along this week, probably because he finally called me on the carpet for my snotty attitude. He and Mom say hi. They were a little disappointed to hear that we split, but thrilled that I'm staying with you for a few days."

"Faith, that's amazing," Shawn said in appreciation. "Half the time, you hide your feelings from the people who care about you, and most of them don't even know where in the hell you are. I'm impressed that not only are you talking about your feelings, but that you also discussed our relationship with your parents. That's a huge step for you."

"Nothing like the cold, aloof reporter you used to fight with," Faith said.

"Oh, I'm still very fond of her." Shawn sighed happily.

"Speaking of my father," Faith continued, "he told me that when he was pledging his fraternity back in college, they made him go to Whispering Pines. How funky is that?"

"What happened?" Shawn asked as the ghost hunter in her emerged.

"Nothing like what happened to us. Just windows and doors slamming open and shut. A couple of his frat brothers didn't like the kitchen. He didn't need to tell me who, they're still a couple and are friends with Dad. He saw Catherine in the upstairs window. That's about it. I asked him if he wanted to join me on the shoot. He's worried about me going without you. But, much like everyone else who's been there, he doesn't want to go back."

"Well, the next time you talk to him, tell him not to worry," Shawn said.

"And why is that?"

"I signed the contract yesterday," Shawn said, grinning when Faith's eyes bugged out.

"You're going?"

"I'm going." Shawn caressed Faith's shoulder. "I don't want to, but I feel as though I'm supposed to be there."

"Hey, I'm not going to question why," Faith said excitedly. "I'm just happy that we'll be there together."

Chapter 43

"One more time, what is this supposed to do?" Faith asked.

Shawn rubbed her brow. "For the last time, it's an onyx. It helps keep negative energy at bay. The other one is an amethyst. It helps with inner strength and insight."

"Why isn't the amethyst as purple as it was at the shop?"

"Because you're sucking the energy from it," Shawn said bluntly. She began to wonder just why she had asked Faith to go with her to buy crystals. Faith was like a small child in the shop, touching everything, pestering her with questions, and being a nuisance.

Shawn wanted new crystals before the trip to Scotland, and Faith hated being alone in Shawn's apartment. Faith's discomfort stemmed from Willie, the impish ghost who resided with Shawn and took immeasurable pleasure in driving Faith up the wall. When she and Faith had first become a couple, Faith had refused to believe that Willie existed. After her first couple of sleepovers, she not only believed that Willie was real, but was bound and determined to send him to the other side. At times, Faith insisted that Shawn guide Willie into the light. Shawn explained that she tried, and Willie didn't want to go, but Faith still persisted.

"So, what are you saying, that even spiritually, I'm high maintenance?" Faith groused.

"Basically, yes." Shawn snickered as Faith glared down at her.

Shawn yelped when Faith snatched her up and tossed her over her shoulder. "Put me down!" she squawked as Faith carried her down the busy sidewalk like a sack of potatoes.

"Not until you apologize." Faith swatted Shawn on her backside while continuing down the street. Oddly enough, no one seemed to notice; then again, this was New York. Spending time with her old flame had been a blessing and a curse for Shawn. During the day they played, went for long walks, talked for hours on end, and really got to know each other. It was great until it was time to retire for the evening. Sleeping in separate bedrooms was becoming a trial for both women. Then there was Willie. Shawn said he was just a mischievous little boy, but Faith refused to enjoy his antics.

"I'm not going to apologize, so you can stop acting like a menace." Shawn squealed as Faith spun around making her dizzy. Her stomach started to churn. "Now!" she screeched.

"Spoilsport," Faith finally set Shawn on the stoop of an aging brownstone.

Shawn was laughing as Faith carefully set her down. She turned pale when her body touched the cold stone steps. Darkness loomed over her, and the smell of blood assaulted her. She saw a woman being forced down against the stone.

"No!" she screamed and jumped off the steps, trying to erase the image of the young woman's skull splitting open. She saw a dark figure flee in the darkness, climb the fire escape, and duck in the third-story window as every light in the building blinked on. She trembled, shaking her head in an effort to erase the image. Bile rose in her throat, even as the daylight and the present returned.

"Shawn?" Faith wrapped her arms around Shawn's trembling form. "What just happened?"

Shawn was unable to speak. She grabbed Faith by the hand, dragged her away from the building, and was almost halfway back to her apartment before she finally felt safe.

"A woman was murdered," Shawn finally managed to say. "'Just one kiss,' that's what he said as she tried to fight him off. He smelled like cheap bourbon. He was young. I couldn't see his face, because it was dark. I hate this." Faith hugged her.

"When did it happen?" Faith asked carefully as Shawn tried to calm down.

"Um, she was wearing a poodle skirt, so I'm thinking the fifties." She blew out a terse breath. "They never caught him."

"Are you sure?"

"I think so." Shawn sighed. She tried to feel what had happened. "Gone, it's gone. We could find out."

"Okay. Not my original thought of how to spend the day, but I'm game," Faith said. "You want to start with the Internet?"

"Or we could just call a cop." Shawn extracted her cell phone from her pocket.

"The mysterious Carey?" Faith grumbled as Shawn dialed Carey Jessup's number.

"Let me guess, she isn't on the Massachusetts police force."

"Years ago. Now she's a member of NYPD." Shawn motioned to Faith as she heard her new friend answer her call.

"Carey, it's Shawn Williams. I need a favor."

"Get a speeding ticket?" Carey asked.

"No." Shawn smiled. "Would it be possible to check out if a woman was murdered in the fifties on the front stoop of 26 Bleecker Street?"

"Let me jot this down. In the fifties, 26 Bleecker Street. Do I even want to ask why?"

"Can you check it out?" Shawn asked.

"Fine."

"And find out who was living in the third-floor apartment facing the alley."

"Anything else?" Carey asked. "You want me to deliver a pizza while I'm at it?"

"Only if you're going to deliver the information in person," Shawn said. "Just remember, I'm a vegetarian."

"Naturally." Carey disconnected the call.

* * *

"So, what is it with this Carey chick anyway?" Faith asked three hours later, after she had checked on the pot of coffee she had brewed.

"Turn it off," she shouted into the kitchen when the water faucets turned on full blast. Shawn snickered, knowing that Willie was at it again. Normally, he gave Shawn her space, but whenever Faith was around, the youngster did everything he could to get her to play with him.

"Thank you," Faith bellowed. "Tell me again why this Carey hates me?"

"You can ask her yourself, she's almost here," Shawn said. Faith ducked into the kitchen. Half a second later, there was a knock on the apartment door.

"I hate it when you do that," Faith called from the kitchen as though on cue. Shawn smiled, pleased with herself as she answered the door.

"Can you do card tricks, too?" Carey shoved two pizza boxes at her. "You just made my ex-husband very happy. He's the head of the cold case squad and wants to know everything. Although he thinks I should have my head examined for listening to you."

"I'll tell you what I saw if you tell me what you know," Shawn said, guiding Carey into her living room. Shawn smiled as she felt Faith enter the room. Her smile vanished when she was encompassed by a nervous energy.

"Ah, fuck," Carey growled. Shawn turned to find Faith staring at the younger woman.

"Jessica?" Faith gasped.

Shawn studied both women and suddenly felt the pieces locking into place. "You're sisters," she blurted. "Now it makes perfect sense. No wonder the two of you are so much alike."

"I'm nothing like her," Carey said.

Shawn placed the pizzas on the coffee table. "Yes, you are," she said quietly.

"Shawn, let it go. This one I deserve," Faith said with a hard swallow. "I'll go for a walk so the two of you can talk."

"Faith." Shawn tried to stop her as Faith headed towards the door.

"Jessica, I know this probably means nothing to you, but I am sorry," Faith said softly before making her exit.

"It doesn't," Carey mumbled as the door clicked shut.

"Jessica? Carey Jessup?" Shawn looked at her quizzically.

"Carey's my middle name."

Shawn sat on the sofa, hoping Carey would follow her lead. "Could have kept your maiden name."

"I wasn't overly attached to the name Charles." Carey began to pace. "Why should I be? It wasn't good enough for my mother."

"Faith was your swimming instructor," Shawn said slowly, the images playing out in her mind. "You were about five, and you idolized her. Until one day she told you to stay away from her. You never knew why until you were older, and your mother told you the truth. That explains that humongous chip you're still carrying on your shoulder."

"I was just a little girl!"

"And she was a hurt and confused teenager. Let it go," Shawn said, knowing that Carey wasn't going to let the past go easily.

Carey paced for a few more minutes before she retrieved a small notebook from her back pocket.

"Any more surprises for me?" she asked in a half-serious tone of voice. "Cute T-shirt, by the way."

Shawn looked down at the simple black tee that sported the words, "I see dead people."

"Well, I do," she said with a cocky grin.

"I'm beginning to believe you." Carey flipped open the notepad. "Hester Moscovich, murdered on September 13, 1955, on her front stoop. The police suspected she was raped, no witnesses, no suspects. She was murdered just shy of her eighteenth birthday."

"He didn't rape her," Shawn said. "He groped her, tried to kiss her, and he couldn't understand why she was refusing him. She wouldn't kiss him, so he forced her down on the steps. When he pushed her down, he had his hand wrapped around her throat, he was strangling her, and he didn't bang her head against the steps just once, it was several times. Her head split open. He loosened his grip just once, and she screamed. Her last thought was, 'Why?'"

"You saw her die?" Carey blinked. "Any ideas on who killed her?"

"He panicked when he saw the blood. He ran into the alley, climbed the fire escape, and ducked into an open window on the third floor," Shawn related as the scene played out in her mind. "It was a bedroom window. I'm assuming that he lived there. That was the last time anyone in the neighborhood left their windows or doors unlocked at night."

"The third-floor apartment off the alley was occupied by the Marshal family," Carey read from her notes. "They had two teenaged sons, Gilbert and Maynard. The police didn't question them right away, since their parents claimed the boys were both sound asleep when the murder happened. Maynard still lives there."

"Still?"

"Rent control," Carey said.

"So," Shawn said, "the only question is, which one of the Marshal boys did it?"

"They're both still alive," Carey continued. "Both are well into their late sixties. Gilbert moved to California. Think he wanted to get as far away as possible?"

"If he has a guilty conscience, maybe." Shawn tried to grasp the new images that were calling out to her. "And Maynard might have stayed because of the guilt and really cheap rent. I can't quite get a fix on it."

"Do you think it might help if you went back to the crime scene?" Carey asked. "I can't believe I just suggested that. Brian is going to love this."

"Call him and have him meet us there," Shawn said. She grabbed her keys and pulled a sweatshirt over her T-shirt. "If he gives you any flack about listening to a psychic, just use the fact that I'm dating your sister as a distraction."

"I don't think of her that way," Carey said.

"Yes, you do. That's why it hurts so much," Shawn said. "Let's go, and just so you know, that pepperoni pizza you brought is going to be history by the time we get back."

"Oh, is that a prediction?" Carey dialed her ex-husband's number.

"No, I just know Faith. She'll take one look at the vegetarian delight and think it's way too healthy to put in her body." They headed out of the apartment. "In fact, her exact words will be, 'Yuck! Green stuff.'"

Shawn was filled with a sense of apprehension as they approached the brick building on Bleecker Street. It came from many directions. The middle-aged man lurking in the shadows was one source, and another was an unseen person, pacing nervously in the building behind them. She had seen and felt everything Hester had experienced during her last few moments of life, and she wasn't eager to repeat the experience.

"Brian Jessup, this is Dr. Shawn Williams," Carey introduced the two.

"Hi," Shawn said and Brian nodded.

"You know, Jay," he said, "when I passed those television people off on you, I never suspected that you, of all people, would fall for this crap."

"Brian, I can't explain it, but I'm starting to believe it," Carey said, glaring at him.

Shawn studied the duo carefully. It was painfully obvious that Brian was still carrying a torch for his ex-wife.

"Detective Jessup," Shawn interrupted the standoff that the former spouses were starting. "You don't have to believe in what I do," she said slowly, weary of having to explain her gift to everyone she met. "Just let me tell you what I saw, and you can take it from there. Believe me, don't believe me, it doesn't really matter. Just do this for Hester. Fifty-some-odd years ago, someone got away with murdering her. Wouldn't you like to bring her some peace?"

"What the hell." He tapped an old file. "Go ahead, but if this is a waste of time, Jay, you owe me dinner."

"Why do I owe you dinner? Never mind. If you close this case, you're spending the night at the ballet," Carey said with a scowl. "Okay, Shawn, tell my pompous ex-husband what you saw."

"The two of you are really evenly matched aren't you?" Shawn laughed. "Fine. It was dark. Hester was walking from that direction," she said, the images returning. "She was wearing a poodle skirt, saddle shoes, bobby socks, a simple white blouse, and a light blue sweater."

Shawn watched with a small degree of amusement as Brian tore open the file and his eyes widened. "She was happy, for no reason in particular, just enjoying the night air and looking forward to a dance that weekend. Norman, Norbert, something like that, had asked her earlier that day to go with him. She saw someone stumbling as she approached the front steps. She knew him. For a brief moment, she wondered if he was sick, then she realized that he was drunk and felt sorry for him."

"Was this the guy who asked her out?" Carey said.

"No. This guy was someone she thought of as a kid, not someone she would date. I can't see his face. She's thinking that he's going to be in trouble if his parents find out he's been drinking. She doesn't want to talk to him because he's always following her around and doesn't understand that she doesn't think of him that way. She waves to him and tries to get in the building before he starts talking to her. He says hello, and she thinks he's silly, trying to act sober when he can barely stand. He staggers towards her. I can see his jacket. It's one of those letterman jackets, and it's red with white sleeves."

"Does it have a name on it?" Carey asked.

Shawn tried to focus. "Marsh," she said. "Which could have been either boy's nickname. He grabs her by the arm. He wants her to stay and talk with him. He stammers, begs her to stay. She doesn't take him seriously and tries to get away without hurting his feelings. She isn't afraid of him, even as his hold on her tightens. He asks her to the dance, she tells him she's going with someone else. She still isn't afraid, in fact she feels sorry for him.

"I can't understand what he's saying. He's very drunk. She's disgusted by the smell of cheap bourbon, definitely bourbon she notices. He asks her for just one kiss. She laughs and tries to push him away. He's holding on to both of her arms. Still she doesn't raise her voice, because she doesn't want him to get into trouble. She tries to push him away as he tries to kiss her. Even as he tightens his hold on her, she isn't afraid of him. 'Just one kiss,' he keeps repeating as he pushes her down. She laughs at him again, and one of his hands wraps around her throat. She's furious when she feels his other hand groping her. 'Just one kiss,' he keeps repeating. His hand tightens against her throat.

"Now she is afraid, she can't breathe, he slams her down against the steps. Her heart is pounding. She's in pain. He slams her against the stoop once again. His eyes are dark with anger. She gasps for air, his hand has slipped from her throat, and he tears open her blouse. She screams. He shoves her down harder, and her head splits open on that step. Her last thought is, 'Why?' as the blood spills from her body.

"The lights in the building turn on. He sees the blood and realizes what he's done. He races into the alley, climbs the fire escape, and ducks into that window.

"That's all I saw, except on his jacket there are a pair of what looks like shoes with wings embroidered on the letter."

"Track and field," Carey noted as she glanced over at Brian. "So, which one of the Marshal boys lettered in track?"

"Both," Brian said.

"Why did I think this would be easy?" Carey grumbled.

"I can't believe you're buying this," Brian said. "She could have looked the case up online and made up the rest."

"True," Shawn said, "but I didn't, and why would I?"

"Ms. Williams." Brian dropped her title and addressed her in a condescending tone. "The one thing I've learned from my job is that I will never understand why people do the things they do."

"Charming isn't he?" Carey snickered. "What about the witness statements?" she asked, wandering towards the alley. She looked up. "That's a hell of jump to reach the fire escape, unless you're a terrified teenaged boy who's on the track team."

Shawn could feel two people watching.

"No one saw or heard anything except Hester's scream," Brian said reluctantly as he and Shawn followed Carey into the alley.

"Even from this building?" Carey asked, pointing to the building adjacent to the crime scene. "If he climbed the fire escape, whoever was living there would have heard something."

"If it had happened last week," a gruff voice interrupted them. "Back then, this building wasn't overpriced condos for the upwardly mobile. It was a hardware store."

"Captain Mallory?" Carey was clearly surprised. "Sir, what brings you here?"

"It isn't captain anymore," the elderly gentleman said with a warm smile. "I heard that you were looking into the Moscovich homicide. You, I've seen you on television." He nodded at Shawn. *"The Discovery Channel,* I think. I hope you don't mind, but I was eavesdropping. I wanted to hear what you had to say."

"You covered her with a blanket," Shawn said, knowing this was one of the people she had felt watching them, the one who was filled with concern. "For her parents' sake, and because of her eyes."

"I felt like she was staring at me," he said sadly. "Jack Mallory, NYPD, retired." He offered Shawn his hand. "Hester was my first homicide. I still remember the look in her eyes. I never forgot, and I never stopped looking for the truth. She wasn't that much younger than me." His voice trailed off. "I always wondered why the lead detective never pushed the boys. I was just a rookie beat cop back then, so no one listened to me."

"Why is it that you thought they should talk to the Marshal boys, sir?" Brian asked.

"They were sound asleep at ten o'clock at night," Mallory said. "What fourteen- and sixteen-year-old boys are asleep at that hour? Now, I don't want to get in the way, but maybe I can help."

"Anything you can tell us would be helpful, captain," Carey said. "What can you tell us about the other tenants?"

"Some moved immediately after the murder, those that could find a new apartment. Back in those days, folks used to read the obituaries just to find an apartment," he said. "Three of the tenants from back then still live here. Most of the others are scattered, or have passed on. Frank Lanes owns the building. He lives on the first floor, and normally he would have been sitting by that window right there. That night, he and his wife were towards the back end of the apartment because the baby was colicky. Then there's Eileen Shavers. She's a retired schoolteacher. She's on the second floor towards the back. She heard the scream and called the police. And last, but not least, Maynard Marshal. You already know about him."

"Good, we'll talk to them one by one so it doesn't look like we're only focused on Maynard," Carey said.

"Um, Jay, a moment of your time?" Brian led her away from the others. Shawn followed closely behind, knowing that it was her contribution to the investigation that was troubling Brian.

"Look, Jay, this one means a lot to the captain. Maybe I should review the file before we go off half-cocked."

"Bri," Carey said. "The captain means the world to me, too. Sorry, Shawn, Mallory was a mentor to both of us. Hell, he gave me away at our wedding. Brian's worried that it'll turn into a wild-goose chase."

"And he still carries Hester's picture in his wallet," Shawn cut Carey off. "He calls her mother down in Boca Raton once a year to let her know that he hasn't forgotten."

"And despite his advanced years, he can hear you," Mallory shouted, waving for them to join him. The frantic motion of his arm informed all of them it wasn't a request. They hurried over to him.

"Kids, I want to be able to call Sophia and tell her that her daughter's killer has finally been locked away. If there's a snowball's chance in hell that this young lady has stumbled upon the key to answering that question, maybe I can go to sleep tonight and not see that girl staring up at me. Now let's start knocking on some doors."

"Yes, sir," Carey and Brian chimed in unison.

"That case in Arkansas, did you really see a workman running around that hotel?" Mallory asked, holding his arm out for Shawn. She smiled, accepted his gracious offer, and allowed him to lead her up to the building. Despite Jack Mallory's advancing years, the man was as sturdy as a rock. Shawn felt a strong sense of warmth and honor emanating from him.

"Michael was a carpenter when the hotel was being built," Shawn said as they entered the building. "He died during the construction. He was quite a prankster, loved lifting up the maid's skirts and such."

Mallory chuckled at the story. Brian knocked on the door of the first-floor apartment.

Brian and Carey showed their badges to a young brunette who appeared to be in her early twenties. "Good afternoon, miss," Brian said. "I'm Detective Jessup, and this, oddly enough, is Detective Jessup. We need to speak to Frank Lanes."

"Come in," she said, stepping aside. "I'm Candice Summers. What do you want with Gramps?"

"Thank you, Ms. Summers." Carey cut Brian off before he could take control. "We really hate bothering you and your grandfather, but we're looking into an old case from the fifties. If there's any chance either of your grandparents can remember something, it would really be helpful."

"Gram died three years ago," Candice said, guiding the group through the apartment to a back bedroom. Frank Lanes was propped up in a hospital bed, staring blankly.

"I don't know if Gramps can help you. Since the last stroke, he hasn't been very coherent. Every once in a while he seems to know what's going on, so you could try. When did you say this happened?"

"1955," Brian said.

"Wow, my mom wasn't even born yet," Candice said.

Jack Mallory approached Frank Lanes. "Mr. Lanes?" he said gently. "Sorry to bother you, sir. I'm Jack Mallory. I was one of the police officers who was here the night Hester Moscovich was murdered." Frank stared off into space. Mallory sighed deeply. "I'm sorry to hear about your wife, Mr. Lanes, she was a nice lady. I see your granddaughter has been keeping up the window boxes. They look beautiful." Frank blinked at the comment. His eyes turned to the window, and he smiled. "It was good seeing you again," Mallory added and patted the aging man on the shoulder.

"Thank you for saying that." Candice shook Mallory's hand. "Gram's window boxes were her little garden. I always asked her why she didn't just move and buy a nice little place with a yard. She said this was home. I've been trying to keep them up since she passed." Her eyes misted over. "So, um, this Hester, she died in the building? That's a little creepy."

"No, not in the building," Mallory said. "Her family lived here at the time, that's all."

* * *

"You saved that poor kid from nightmares," Carey noted as they climbed the stairs. "What a great old building," she added as they headed down the hallway towards Eileen Shavers's apartment. "Though an elevator might be a nice addition," she huffed.

"Eileen Shavers was thirty at the time, the first to call police. She heard the scream and some noise in the alleyway," Brian read from the old case file.

"She's a real pistol. Jay should handle this one," Mallory said.

"She heard noise in the alley," Carey said. "Did the detectives at the time check into that?"

"They assumed that the killer was a stranger, a vagrant who made his escape by running down the alley," Mallory said. "The alley used to run all the way to Mott Street. Mott Street wasn't one of the nicer neighborhoods back then. O'Shea and Ryan, the lead investigators at the time, were convinced the killer was from Mott Street."

"Because almost everyone who lived there at the time had names that ended with vowels," Shawn said accusingly.

"Yes," Mallory said reluctantly. "Mott Street was known for small-time numbers running, and a lot of wannabe thugs. I didn't buy the theory. The boys from Mott Street wanted to be wiseguys. They might hijack a truck and run illegal gambling, but assaulting a girl wasn't their style. If the killer did use the alley, I figured he jumped on the subway. There's a stop not far from where the alley let out."

"They ignored the people who were close to her because they didn't like the boys who lived on the next block?" Carey asked.

"That's the way things ran in those days," Mallory said.

"That would explain the men they brought in for questioning. They all lived on Mott Street and had an Italian last name," Brian said, knocking on Eileen Shavers's door. They waited a few moments before Brian knocked once again, only louder this time.

"Hold your water!" came a shout from inside and Mallory snickered. They continued to wait, listening to shuffling and the steady stream of curses being muttered before they heard the sounds of several locks clicking open.

"Jack Mallory, I knew you couldn't stay away," the elderly woman greeted the former policeman, moving her walker aside and allowing the group to enter her quaint apartment. "Finally come to your senses and decided to sweep me off my feet?" She wheezed as she shuffled across the room and took a seat.

Shawn cleared her throat as the dank aroma of stale cigarette smoke assaulted her. "Sit, you're making me nervous." Eileen lit a cigarette. "Unless we're going dancing?" she teased Mallory with a wry smirk. Shawn suppressed a laugh, knowing that the retired schoolteacher was gay.

"Anytime, Ms. Shavers," Jack replied with a smile. The group, with the exception of Shawn, took a seat. Eileen glanced at Shawn for a brief moment before snickering under her breath.

"What about you, young man?" she teased Brian. "Think you could keep up with me?"

"No, I-I honestly don't," Brian said with a slight stammer.

"Ms. Shavers," Carey cut in before Eileen could torment her ex-husband further. "As you've probably guessed, we're here because of Hester Moscovich."

"She loves playing with them," Shawn heard a voice echo. She smiled over at Eileen, spying the figure looming over her. *All the boys loved her, and she belonged to you,* Shawn silently responded to the misty apparition.

"Tell me you finally caught the sick bastard who hurt that girl," Eileen glared at Jack.

"We're looking into the case," Carey said carefully.

"No." Eileen sniffed. "One, two, three cops, and you." She pointed towards Shawn. "You're on to something."

"How did you know I'm not a cop?" Shawn asked Eileen, who took a drag on her cigarette.

"Because you don't look like you have a stick shoved up your ass like these three do." Eileen blew out a puff of smoke. Brian's jaw dropped while Carey and Mallory smiled at the commentary.

"I like her." Carey chuckled. "Yes, we do have some new information. What can you tell us about that night? Anything you can recall would be very helpful."

"Recall?" Eileen snorted with disgust. "I'll never forget the sound of that poor girl screaming. I still hear it sometimes at night."

"How did you hear her?" Carey pressed. "This apartment is way in back of the building."

"Back then, at that time of night, the streets were quiet. Not like today with all those damn boom boxes and everyone shouting into those freaking cell phones. Nope, back in those days, you could get a decent night's sleep, except when George and Mona got all hot and heavy. Those two humped like animals. You'd think that fat bastard was God's gift to women."

Shawn suppressed a laugh. Mallory smiled at Eileen, while Carey and Brian gaped at her.

"Um, getting back to the night of September 13, 1955," Carey said with a shake of her head. "What exactly did you hear, and when did you hear it?"

"I'll never forget that night," Eileen said sadly, extinguishing her cigarette, and instantly sparking another one. "I was asleep. It was just after ten. I remember looking at the clock when I woke up."

"What woke you up?" Carey asked. Brian reviewed Eileen's original statement.

"A blood-curdling scream," Eileen said. "I went white as a sheet when I heard it. I called the police immediately."

"You didn't check first to see what had happened?" Carey's brow furrowed.

"No. That sound wasn't kids kicking up their heels. Someone was in trouble. I called the cops, then I raced downstairs to see if I could help."

"When did you hear the footsteps in the alley?" Carey asked Eileen in a curious tone. It was more than obvious that something about the woman's story was off.

"When I called the cops," Eileen snapped. Shawn ran her fingers along a silver picture frame resting on the mantle.

"Ms. Shavers, I know it was a long time ago, but do you remember if you heard the footsteps for a long time, like someone went the length of the alley, or was it more of a short jaunt?" Carey doodled in her notepad.

"How the hell should I know?" Eileen's hand trembled. "It was footsteps, that's it."

"Well, I guess if there's nothing else you can remember, we should get going." Carey stood. Shawn folded her arms across her chest and gazed down at Eileen.

"What?" Carey asked, seeing the look in Shawn's eyes. "Something you want to add?"

"Just one question," Shawn softened her gaze, never wavering from the older woman. "What did Thelma see or hear that night?"

"Dr. Williams, you must be mistaken," Mallory said. "Ms. Shavers was alone that evening."

"No, she wasn't," Shawn said gently. "What did Thelma tell you?"

"Fuck." Eileen blew out a terse breath, releasing another stream of smoke.

"Eileen, this isn't 1955 anymore," Shawn said.

"I've noticed." Eileen extinguished her cigarette, this time failing to light another. "I never heard the footsteps. That was Thelma."

"What?" Mallory exclaimed.

"You weren't alone that night?" Carey asked. "Any reason why you chose to hide this information from the police?"

"Yeah, a damn good one," Eileen snarled. "How long do you think I would have kept my job if it got out?"

"I don't understand," Mallory said.

"No, you don't." Eileen glanced up at Shawn. "You do. She didn't move in until the following spring. Thank Christ this is a two-bedroom. The nosy parkers in this joint would have had a field day if they knew."

"Ms. Shavers, I still don't see," Jack said.

"Thelma was her girlfriend," Carey said.

"That's a pitiful label for what we shared," Eileen said. "We were together for forty-three years until she had the bad manners to die on me."

"Oh?" Jack gaped at her.

"When we heard the scream, I called the cops, just like I said," Eileen said. "When I hung up, Thelma told me she heard someone in the alley. I got dressed, told her to lock the bedroom window before I rushed downstairs. Poor Hester, seeing her like that broke my heart. She was such a sweet girl. I wish I could tell you more. I know Thelma looked out the window, but she said she didn't see anything. Not like you can ask her. Unless you've got a Ouija board or a psychic, you're shit out of luck."

"What?" Eileen asked as all eyes turned towards Shawn. Eileen quirked her eyebrows with disbelief while she studied Shawn, who smiled back at her with an amused grin. "Now, I know you're yanking my chain."

"Ms. Shavers, if it isn't too much of an inconvenience, could I look out your bedroom window?" Shawn politely requested.

"Knock yourself out. Best offer I've had in years."

"Thank you." Shawn spied a very amused Thelma watching over her lover. Carey followed closely behind Shawn as she headed directly towards the bedroom without asking which door led to the room.

"Anything I can do to help?" Carey asked, her gaze darting about the room.

"No." Shawn drank in the warm feelings that surrounded her. "There's so much warmth here," she said.

Carey looked around the room. "They must have loved one another very much."

"They still do," Shawn said with a soft smile. "Now, if I can just get Thelma to leave Eileen's side, I might be able to see what she saw that night." Shawn tried valiantly, but to no avail. "It won't work, she refuses to leave Eileen."

They returned to the living room. Shawn sighed as all eyes once again focused on her.

"So, what did you see besides the mountain of dust bunnies under my bed?" Eileen taunted her.

"Nothing," Shawn said glumly.

"Damn, I was hoping for the winning lottery number," Eileen said. Shawn released an exasperated sigh.

"May I?" Shawn asked, holding out her hand.

"You're not trying to get fresh with me?" Eileen laughed as she held out her gnarled hand for Shawn.

"No, ma'am." Shawn smiled. "Thelma watches over you, and I don't think she would take that very well."

"Tell me something I don't know." Eileen beamed when Shawn clasped her hand.

Shawn's body trembled as the night was shattered by an ungodly scream.

"What was that?" Thelma asked. She and her lover jerked up from the bed. She glanced over at Eileen, who was dialing the telephone. The sound of someone running, followed by a loud clunk of metal, echoed in the alley. Thelma thrust her head out the window.

"I heard someone running in the alleyway," she said when Eileen hung up the telephone and hastily began to dress.

"Get away from the window, woman," Eileen snapped. "You're naked. What in blue blazes are you thinking? I called the police. Stay here while I check out what's going on."

Thelma gasped. "Eileen, please be careful."

"I'll be right back," Eileen said, kissing Thelma lightly on the lips. Eileen paused only long enough to shut and lock the bedroom window before she raced out of her apartment.

"Sweet Jesus." Eileen sobbed when she opened the downstairs door. She felt sick as Hester's lifeless eyes stared up at her. "Poor child," she said. Other tenants filed out of the building and faltered at the grisly sight.

"No," Eileen gasped, grabbing Sophia and turning the poor woman away from the ugliness.

Shawn allowed Eileen's hand to slip from her grasp.

"You held her mother, trying to keep her from seeing Hester," Shawn said. "You didn't want her to remember her child that way. That was very kind of you."

"Well." Eileen cleared her throat. "This has been the most entertainment I've had in years. Did it help?"

"Yes," Shawn said softly. "Thelma did hear someone running, but not the length of the alley, and metal clanged, like the sound of someone climbing the fire escape."

"Are you saying that the maniac that killed Hester was hiding in the building?" Eileen squawked.

"I think so," Shawn said. "Thank you again, you've been very helpful," she added, motioning for the others to follow her.

"What, no lottery numbers?" Eileen stood and shuffled along behind them, wheeling her walker as quickly as she could manage.

"Sorry." Shawn smirked. "I do have a message for you. 'Cut back on the smokes. I'm with you, don't be in such a hurry to join me.'"

"Just like her to bitch me out from the great beyond." Eileen cackled. "Tell her I'll try."

"She can hear you," Shawn said before they made their departure.

"Told you she was a pistol," Mallory said as they headed towards the staircase. "I had no idea she was one of them."

"And if you did, she might have ended up a suspect," Shawn grunted as they climbed the stairs.

"Fine," Brian snapped. Carey glared at him. "I don't want to be rude, but so far all I've seen and heard are you making up things to back up the story you've been telling us. I'm sorry, but we're not any closer to finding out what really happened than the police were fifty years ago."

"Christ, Brian," Carey said. "What about Thelma?"

"Thelma?" Brian snorted. "Come on, Jay, how hard could it be to guess that a retired schoolteacher who never married is a lesbian?"

"I don't think I care for that generalization," Shawn said. "Although it's true that it was good-old-fashioned gaydar, not my gift, that clued me in to Eileen's orientation."

"Huh?" Brian said.

"Kids," Mallory said, "let's try to focus on the matter at hand, shall we? Brian, as Dr. Williams so aptly pointed out to you earlier, you don't have to believe her. Personally, I find it interesting that not only did she know Ms. Shavers wasn't alone that night, but she knew the name of her companion. My concern at the moment is Maynard Marshal. If you've read the reports, you might have noticed that not once in almost fifty years has his story varied."

"I did notice that," Brian said, looking as if a parent had just chastised him.

"Not once?" Carey asked.

"Word for word, every time," Brian said. They stopped at the end of the hallway.

"A well-spun lie." Carey sighed. "He might think it's the truth by now. Any suggestions on how we should proceed, sir?"

"I haven't a clue," Mallory said. "The Marshal family has been questioned over a dozen times. Each time the story was the same: the boys were sick, no one heard a thing except Hester's scream and the police sirens. But only the parents heard that, the boys were asleep. It is a plausible scenario, except the times I talked with the boys there was something in their eyes that told me they were lying. No one ever believed me, until now."

"Did either of them ever marry?" Carey asked.

"Maynard married and divorced quickly at least four times, and Gilbert is still married to his college sweetheart," Mallory said.

"Maynard is so moving up my list," Carey said. "Brian, why don't you take this one?"

"Why?"

"Maynard obviously has issues with women," Carey said. Brian glared at her. "Knock on the door."

He complied with her wishes only to receive no answer. He knocked again and again. "Guess he's out," he said.

"No, he's home. He just doesn't want to talk to us," Shawn said. "Pizza delivery!"

"Hey, you can't—"

"I just did." Shawn chuckled when the door swung open.

"I didn't order any goddamn..." Maynard Marshal bellowed before he realized he had been tricked. Carey and Brian flashed their badges quickly.

"What?" he asked, glancing over at Mallory.

"Sorry to disturb you, Mr. Marshal. I'm Detective Jessup. We have a few questions for you," Brian said tentatively. "May we come in?"

"No," Maynard said. The sounds of a television blared in the background.

"It will just take a moment," Brian said with a charming smile.

"I'm busy," Maynard growled.

"Fine, we'll do this in the hallway. We need to talk to you about what happened in 1955."

"The Brooklyn Dodgers won the world series." Maynard smirked. "Anything else?"

"Thanks for the trivia," Carey snapped before Brian could proceed. "Actually, we're here about your neighbor, the one who was murdered on the front steps of the building. Remember that?"

Wow, she is so much like her sister, Shawn noted.

"Oh, that." He shrugged with apparent indifference. "Long time ago, what was her name? Esther?"

"Hester," Carey said through clenched teeth. Mallory handed him the girl's picture. "Coming back to you now?"

"Don't know anything. My brother and I had the flu. We were asleep," Maynard said with indifference, shoving the picture into Brian's hands without even glancing at it. "We didn't see or hear anything and only found out what happened the following morning. Now, if there isn't anything else?"

"Just one more thing." Brian was still holding the picture in his hand. "Do you remember who her friends were, or who she was dating?"

"I didn't know her," Maynard said, glancing over his shoulder so he could see the television.

"Pretty girl like her?" Brian pressed. "You would have been about the same age. Certainly you must have noticed her."

"Back then, Catholic and Jewish kids didn't play together." Maynard dismissed Brian's observation.

He's lying. Shawn's heart was racing. She knew that Maynard was about to shut the door in their faces. She smiled when something occurred to her.

"Is that the game?" she squealed eagerly.

"Sure is," Maynard responded, still glancing over his shoulder.

"I'm sorry, but could you tell me what the score is?" she asked in an innocent tone.

"I lost track, thanks to you people," Maynard hissed.

"Oh, um, again, I'm sorry, but could you at least tell me what inning it is?" Shawn asked frantically. "I don't mean to be a pain in the ass, but the person I'm dating is a Red Sox fan."

"What is he, an idiot?" Maynard scoffed.

"Charley? Absolutely," she prattled on, standing on her toes in an effort to see inside his apartment. "I told him the only reason the series has lasted this long is because those bums from Boston got lucky."

"Tell me about it." Maynard snickered in agreement. Shawn pressed her advantage by pretending to sneak a peek at the game.

"Come on." Maynard stepped aside, allowing Shawn to enter the apartment.

She stood beside Maynard, who was lost in the game. "Knucklehead is still on the mound, what, are they stupid?" she shouted, all the while glancing around the apartment. She shot a wary look at the trio lingering in the doorway. She jerked her head, encouraging them to enter the apartment. They seemed puzzled, but followed her lead.

"Yes!" she and Maynard shouted when the Yankees scored.

"That's it," she shouted in encouragement as the Yankees scored again. She clasped Maynard on the shoulder, pretending to share his enjoyment of the game.

She gulped when the wave of nausea attacked her. She exhaled a terse breath and removed her hand from him.

"Yes." She clapped her hands, still fighting against the sickening feeling that was swelling inside of her.

"Now we can show them how to play the game," she said when the inning ended and a commercial began.

"Are those yours?" she asked in a flirtatious manner, pointing to some trophies stuffed in a corner of the room.

"Some of them," he said shyly. Shawn wandered over to the collection of pictures and trophies.

"Just crap my mother never threw out."

Shawn picked up a picture with a crumbling, gilded frame. It was a faded black-and-white photo of two teenaged boys in letterman jackets.

"Which one are you?" she gushed, already knowing the answer.

"That's m-me," Maynard said with a slight stammer. "And that's my brother, Gil."

"Oh, so you were the good-looking one," she prattled on, handing the photo to Carey.

"Yeah, um, like I said, I really should toss that stuff," Maynard said just as the game came back on.

"Don't you dare," Shawn scolded him playfully. "My dad lettered in baseball. He still has his jacket. Still have yours?"

"I… um…" he stammered, and his ears turned bright pink. "Probably," he said.

"Bet it still fits," Shawn cooed with a playful nudge.

"Hell, no." He laughed. "I-I…" he stammered once again before his face dimmed.

"We have to go," Carey called out.

"Rats." Shawn pouted. "Enjoy the game."

"You can't stay for the end?" he invited her. "You know, for a cop, you're not bad company."

"Oh, I'm not a cop," she told him, sensing that the information sent a wave of relief through him. "I'm just babysitting these idiots. Nice meeting you."

Once they had departed the Marshal apartment, Shawn pressed her fingers to her lips cautioning her companions not to speak. They strolled in silence until they were halfway down the block.

"Sorry, he was listening and watching," she explained. "He did it."

"Just like that," Brian said with obvious disbelief. "Why, because you said so? And what was so fascinating about that picture?"

"Two teenaged boys in letterman jackets," Carey said. "With their nicknames embroidered on the front. One said Marsh, the other said Gil. He's our guy."

"Jay," Brian said.

"What?" Carey threw her hands up in anger. "Ignore him, I always do," she told Shawn. "When you touched Maynard, what did you see? You looked like you were going to be sick."

"You were right, he has some serious issues with women," Shawn said. "He killed her because she laughed at him. You noticed the stammer? He had a speech impediment as a kid, made him an outcast, sports was the only thing he had going for himself. The stammer comes back when he's nervous or excited. And he didn't have the flu that day, his brother did. He only pretended to be sick as well, so he could skip school. He sneaked out later that night and got drunk. When he climbed in the window, Gil woke up. Maynard told him to go back to sleep. In the back of his mind, Gil is still wondering if Maynard was involved with the murder."

"Smart thing, using his love of sports to get us into the apartment," Carey said. "Still, you didn't have to call the Sox bums."

"Oops, forgot you're from Massachusetts." Shawn laughed. "But what I said is true. Sports are all that mean anything to him. And for the record, the Yankees are going to win tonight."

"No," Carey wailed and the two men cheered.

"Oh, now you believe I'm a psychic?" she asked Brian. "Chill, I don't do predictions. I'm from New York. They have to win or I'll never hear the end of it from my, for lack of a better term, girlfriend. Now what happens?"

"Now," Brian said, "I go back to work on the case, see what turns up."

"Thank you, Dr. Williams." Mallory clasped her hand. "Brian, would you mind if I join you?"

"Not at all, sir, I'd love your input," Brian said. "Dr. Williams, thank you," he said, hesitating in offering to shake her hand.

"Don't worry, you don't have to," Shawn said graciously. "Most people don't want to shake my hand."

"Can't imagine why," Brian said with an uneasy laugh. "Just out of curiosity, what should I look for?"

"His letterman jacket. He still has it. Her blood is on it. Or was. He hasn't looked at it since he hid it that night. He couldn't give it to his mother to clean, or take it to the dry cleaner because of the blood. He hid it in the back of his closet beneath a loose floorboard. He told his parents he lost it, and he never replaced it."

"Except now he's thinking about it," Carey said. "He might ditch it."

"Well, it looks as if we have some work to do, boy," Mallory said.

"Yes, sir." Brian nodded in agreement.

"Come on, I'll walk you home," Carey offered. "Headache?"

"Yes," Shawn groaned, her temple throbbing in agony.

"I don't know how you do it," Carey said sympathetically. "It's hard enough seeing the things I see at work, but I couldn't deal with the constant bombardment you live with on a day-to-day basis."

"It's what life handed me. What I choose to do with my gift is what makes a difference," Shawn said. "Besides, seeing someone's skull cracked open isn't an everyday event. Mostly I see jumbled images, just small glimpses into people's lives."

"In Salem, you were in agony," Carey noted.

"Salem has a tragic history, so many voices that need someone to hear that they were innocent," Shawn said. "I can hear them, and I can tell them that I know that they were wronged."

"You also hear the guilty," Carey annoyingly pointed out.

"Every job has its downside," Shawn quipped. "Coming up?" They stood on the steps to Shawn's building. Carey looked up with an unreadable expression on her face, and Shawn said, "Don't you think it's time?"

Chapter 44

Stewart, Massachusetts
1933

Horatio Stratton sat in his chair, staring out at nothing, his clothing soiled from his latest attempt to destroy the garden.

"Where is my son?" a lilting voice asked.

"Leave me be," he muttered, his eyes fixed on the door to the study. He was hiding again, praying that they would leave him alone.

"Where is my son?" she said again, unseen or heard by anyone but him.

"Leave me be," he repeated, lost in his own world.

"Never," a second voice taunted, laughing wildly.

"Then I'll join you. When my time comes, your trickery will come to an end. You belong to me. I'm going to make the two of you pay for your sins."

"Do it. End your miserable excuse of a life," the second voice challenged.

"All in good time." His insane laughter echoed through the manor, probably startling the meager staff who were toiling about the house. "All in good time."

Chapter 45

New York City
2005

"I said, don't you think it's time?" Shawn repeated. Carey was still staring up at the building.

"I should be going," Carey suddenly blurted out, shoving her hands in her pockets. "Hey, like you said, she ate the good pizza. I'm going to see if Brian and Captain Mallory need my help."

"Why am I not surprised?" Shawn sighed deeply, watching Carey disappear in the darkness. Her head pounded violently as she made her way up to her apartment. Her headache grew worse upon entering her home.

"I said stop it!" Faith shouted into thin air.

"What now?" Shawn asked, rubbing her aching temples.

"Fucking Willie keeps screwing with the television," Faith bellowed like an insane woman.

"Oh, for the love of God, he's just a little boy." Shawn was weary of everyone's nasty disposition.

"Send him into the light," Faith said.

"You know I can't do that. As I've explained to you time and time again, Willie's happy here and has no interest in crossing over. Besides, I happen to enjoy the company."

"Get a cat," Faith snapped, flinging the remote onto the sofa.

"Yeah, that would be a good idea." Shawn pulled off her sweatshirt. "Since I'm almost never home, a pet would be perfect. This isn't just about Willie. What's up?"

Shawn tilted her head, trying to understand Faith's muttering. "Come again?"

"I said, the Yankees won." Faith scowled as the sound of a child's laughter echoed in the air. "Knock it off, the Yankees weren't even a team when you were alive, you little shit. Were they?"

"I don't know," Shawn growled. Her headache was growing. "And stop telling him he's dead. He knows. He doesn't care. He likes it here with me. There isn't anyone waiting for him on the other side, and like I said, I enjoy his company. We play checkers together."

"Oh, now that's twisted," Faith said. Her jaw dropped. "Shawn? Oh, my God, what happened? Never mind. We need to get you into bed."

"Do I look that bad?" Shawn allowed Faith to usher her into her bedroom.

"Yes," Faith's soothing voice answered, her hands gently guiding Shawn down onto the bed. Shawn parted her lips, needing to say something. Her words were halted by Faith's fingers pressing against her lips.

"Shh, rest now." Faith undressed her. "You're spreading yourself too thin," she said, tucking Shawn under the blankets. "Maybe we can ditch Scotland, so you can take a break."

"I can't." Shawn rested her aching head against the pillows. "Wait. You'd stay behind just to take care of me?"

"Yes." Faith nestled beside her. "I'll even play nice with Willie."

"That's sweet of you, but we can't." Shawn sighed, praying for the pain to stop. "I'll be fine, it's just been a bit much. Salem, Whispering Pines... all of it's catching up to me. Maybe Scotland will be quieter."

"Maybe we could switch assignments." Faith massaged Shawn's throbbing scalp. "Hawaii might be nice."

Shawn chuckled. "Namaka's doing Hawaii."

"Lucky bastard." Faith pouted.

"Not luck, just location. It's the same reason we tend to get the East Coast and the same reason Connor's working Edinburgh. Why hire someone you have to fly a great distance and provide housing for, when you can hire local talent? It's just good business."

"Connor Alysia is working this gig with us?" Faith beamed.

"Oh, man, I keep forgetting how much trouble you guys can get into." Shawn felt the pain ebbing as Faith's talented fingers caressed the weariness away.

"Hey, Connor's a great guy," Faith said. "And he's one of the few who hasn't treated me like a redheaded stepchild since I jumped over the fence. I had no idea when I stopped debunking how many people it would piss off. Still, even though Connor knows the best pubs in the city, I think maybe we should just stay behind. The intensity of the back-to-back shoots isn't good for you. Or trade for some nice farmhouse, lighthouse, or outhouse even. My mother gave me a quick history lesson on what happened there. This is going to be another very intense shoot. Not to mention that after we wrap, we're supposed to go to Whispering Pines again. I don't want to risk your health over a job."

"I'll be fine." Shawn traced the bare flesh of Faith's forearm with her fingertips. "Thank you, though. I can't believe you were willing to take time off and play nice with Willie."

"Well, Willie isn't that bad. I'm thankful he stays out of your bedroom and doesn't play in the bathroom if anyone's using it. Still, I wish he'd stop messing with the remote. Speaking of Willie, I am curious about something."

"Why he keeps playing with the water in the kitchen? Flushing the toilet when no one's in there, flipping the lights on and off, or screwing with the television?" Shawn murmured, nestling closer to Faith's body. "These things weren't a part of his world when he was alive. He's just curious."

"That makes sense, but it wasn't what I was going to ask." Faith spooned Shawn's weary body. "What I was going to ask about was Deb. As much as I want to pretend that she never slept over, I know that at some point she visited your home. Didn't you say that she doesn't believe in your gift or ghosts?"

"She doesn't." Shawn tingled from the feel of being held in Faith's arms.

"How is that possible? Even if I had never set foot in Whispering Pines, I'm pretty certain that after one visit here, Willie's antics would have been very convincing that not only do you see dead people, but one of them is fascinated with flushing your toilet."

"He didn't like her." Shawn yawned, her eyelids growing heavy. "Because he didn't like her, he never wanted to play with her. Not once in all the times she stayed over did he make an appearance."

"All the times," Faith drew out slowly, her tone revealing how truly miffed she was.

"You could just go back to pretending that I never got naked with her," Shawn muttered.

"I think I will," Faith said. "Sleep."

* * *

Hours later, Faith hurried from the bedroom. The sound of the television blaring in the living room disrupted the quiet.

"Shh," she whispered, turning off the television. "We have to be quiet. Shawn isn't feeling good." She looked around for some sign that Willie understood and was going to behave.

"Man, I can't believe I just did that." She laughed, knowing that just a few short years ago she would have slapped herself for talking to a ghost. "Thank you," she said to the empty room. She turned to go back into the bedroom, but a knock on the door halted her. "Now what?"

Faith peered through the peephole. Her heart pounded when she saw the woman waiting in the hall. She opened the door, uncertain what she should say or do.

"Hi," she managed to say.

Carey's eyes narrowed. "I wanted to speak to Dr. Williams," she said coldly as Faith stepped aside, offering her sister a chance to enter the apartment. "I'll just wait here."

"Shawn's asleep," Faith said quietly, regretting the past and praying there was something, anything she could say that would erase the pain in Jessica's—now Carey's—eyes. "She had a rough go at it today. It happens with an intense vision."

"Yeah, I noticed that in Salem," Carey answered thoughtfully. "And today, she didn't look good when I left her."

"Come in?" Faith offered with a jerk of her head.

"Why?"

"Wow, we really are related." Faith snickered. "Um, well, we could just stand here with me feeling like the bitch of the universe and you agreeing, or you could come in and tell me what you need with Shawn. There's some pizza left," she said in a lame attempt to get Carey to enter the apartment. Much to her surprise, Carey did step in. Faith's heart was pounding as she closed the door.

"No pepperoni?" Carey asked, lifting the lid of the remaining pizza box. "You ate a whole pizza?"

"Yes, I did," Faith said. "What? Shawn won't touch anything with meat. I didn't want it to go to waste."

"I can't even pick all that healthy crap off," Carey muttered. Her head suddenly jerked. She looked down at the gun holstered to her hip.

"I could order a new one," Faith said in a hopeful tone. It was the first time in years that her sister had acknowledged her presence. Their paths had crossed on occasion, but all of Faith's attempts to mend fences were flatly rejected.

"No," Carey said. Her hands and eyes jerked to her hip once again. "What the fuck?"

"Something wrong?" Faith asked.

"Sorry." Carey shook her head. "I keep feeling like someone's tugging on my gun. God, I must be tired."

"No! Bad!" Faith bellowed into the air. "That isn't a toy."

"Who in the hell are you talking to?" Carey demanded, feeling yet another tug at her hip.

"Willie. He's Shawn's ghost." Faith shrugged. "So, how about that pizza?"

Carey laughed wildly, rubbing her brow. "I don't know what I find stranger at this moment," she said slowly. "Sharing breathing space with you, or that I really believe Shawn has a ghost. This entire month has been beyond funky. Um, no pizza. Just because I'm speaking to you doesn't mean we're going to get all warm and fuzzy."

"Warm and fuzzy?" Faith sneered. "You really don't know a thing about me, do you?"

"And I don't want to."

"Fine," Faith said, feeling a strange tugging at her heart. "So, sit, and instead of us trying to chat and wipe out a lifetime of pain, why don't you tell me about this case Shawn wangled you into?"

"No."

"Why not?" Faith noticed that Carey wasn't making any attempt to leave. "You're a cop. Certainly you've had to talk to people you hate. If I piss you off, you have a gun. You could just shoot me."

"Don't tempt me." Carey removed her jacket and sat on the sofa. "So, you ordering that pizza or what?"

* * *

"Excuse me." Carey stifled a belch and took another swig from her beer. "That's everything," she concluded after replaying the day's events. "Brian and Captain Mallory went back to the station to review the files. When I got there, we decided to set up a little stakeout. The three of us huddled together in the captain's Wrangler and watched the building."

"I spent more than a few nights like that when I was a reporter." Faith opened another bottle of Heineken. "So, did Maynard take his trash out? I just love trash. It's fair game. No subpoenas, no cops getting pissed, and no violating some scumbag's civil rights."

"Hey, I am the cops," Carey said. "But you're right. Discarded items are legally fair game. Maynard snuck down to the dumpster and buried a single trash bag at the bottom. Which is why I made Brian climb into the dumpster."

"Let me guess what was inside," Faith said eagerly. "An old letterman jacket, just like Shawn described, with a large, dark stain on it."

"Several medium-sized stains, but you get the idea. We bagged it, tagged it, and rushed it to the lab. Brian and the captain are going to contact Hester's mother in the morning, and we're going to try for a reverse DNA match. It isn't as strong as a DNA match, but if the samples are good enough, it will prove that the blood belongs to someone in Sophie's family."

"That's one approach," Faith said.

"What?"

"I was just thinking," Faith said slowly. "Moms never throw anything out. I'll bet your mother's refrigerator door is loaded with crap about you."

"What's your point?"

"Just I know my mom has boxes full of my crap. School papers, doodles, baby teeth, locks of hair, and stuff like that. I would imagine that these things mean a lot to a mother, more so if they survive their child."

"And chock full of DNA. The hair won't do any good. No follicles, so no DNA." Carey flipped open her cell phone. "Yo, Brian," she said. "It's your ever-loving ex-wife. When you talk to Hester's mother, ask if she saved any of Hester's baby teeth?" She paused for a moment.

Faith busied herself with cleaning up the mess from their impromptu meal. "Thanks for the suggestion," Carey said when Faith returned from the kitchen. "Tell me about Whispering Pines?"

Faith let out a sigh of relief that Carey wasn't bolting. She offered her another beer and sat down beside her.

"It was a freak show," Faith said in an unsteady tone. "Shawn wasn't the original psychic assigned to the case, Milo was. He's a major dufus, but he went screaming from the house. Everyone thought I had driven him out, but I didn't. It was the kitchen. Milo's gift is touching things and seeing the past. He made the mistake of touching the kitchen, and bolted like a fat, sweaty bunny rabbit. Chickenshit."

"What happened when Shawn arrived?" Carey peeled the label from her beer bottle.

"Oh, she loved the place. All that spooky energy." Faith snickered. "Until I got bitch-slapped in the kitchen. Then all hell broke loose. I can still hear that voice calling me a sinner. Freaking creepy," she added with a shiver.

"We were left alone in the house, which had already been wired with cameras and sound equipment. Neither of us wanted to go back into the kitchen. We decided we would bunk upstairs. Then it started, not just bumps in the night, it was a full show. I followed Shawn back into the kitchen. I could see them, kind of. Shawn saw it all, the murders, everything, and she just went into shock. I couldn't open the doors or windows. We were trapped. I managed to get her upstairs, and we just waited for the sunrise. The equipment had cut out long before that, but some of it was captured on film. That's it."

"That's it?" Carey pressed.

"Hey, buy the book." Faith laughed. "Well, there's more, but that's none of your business."

"Fair enough," Carey said, apparently realizing what Faith was discreetly omitting. "I should be going."

"How long were you married?" Faith asked in an attempt to delay Carey's departure.

"Look," Carey said. "I meant what I said. We're not going to get all warm and fuzzy. I appreciate Shawn's help, and it was nice to share a pizza and not dwell on how much I hate you, but it doesn't change anything."

"I don't do warm and fuzzy," Faith said dryly. "But it is nice to know that we'll be able to work together during Whispering Pines."

"I still might shoot you," Carey quipped as she stood.

"So long as you don't shove me into the kitchen," Faith replied earnestly. "I had to sell my soul to have Althea add an amendment in my contract stating that I didn't have to go in there."

"Because you got slapped?" Carey snickered.

"Not just slapped, it attacked us. Whatever's lurking in that house has a real hard-on for homos. Look what happened to Anna and Catherine."

"There were police reports that Captain Stratton beat Anna," Carey said. "A couple of staff members complained. Nothing was ever done since the old man owned most of the town."

"Some things never change," Faith said grimly. "Shawn's convinced the bodies are in the house, but where?"

"That's the million dollar question isn't it?" Carey slipped on her coat.

"Hey, were you two throwing a party without me?" Shawn staggered into the living room.

"Feeling better?" Faith asked, instantly rushing to Shawn's side.

"So-so," Shawn grumbled.

"I was just leaving," Carey said. "Faith can fill you in on what we found. I'll see you in a couple weeks."

"How did it go?" Shawn asked once Carey had departed and Faith guided her back into her bedroom.

"She didn't shoot me." Faith tucked Shawn back into bed before slipping beneath the covers and cradling the weary woman in her arms.

Chapter 46

Edinburgh, Scotland
2005

"This weather sucks," Faith grumbled as they trudged up to the quaint inn.

"Welcome to Scotland," Shawn said wearily.

"I still think we should have backed out. You don't look like you're feeling any better," Faith said as they stepped inside the cozy inn.

"I'm fine," Shawn snapped. "Sorry," she said, only to have Faith shrug in response. "We're with Sunny Hill," she informed the desk clerk. "Williams and Charles."

"Yes, Room Three. Do you need help with your bags?" the man asked with a heavy brogue.

"Oh, we're sharing again." Shawn sighed. "No, we're fine." She accepted the keys to the room.

"Just up the staircase, to the right," the clerk told them.

"It's not uncommon for us to share." Faith was disturbed by the way Shawn seemed disappointed with the room assignment. "We used to have to bunk together long before we got along. If it bothers you, I could see if there's another room available," she said. "Of course, I don't understand why it would bother you, since I just spent a week in your apartment. In the same bed, for the end of my visit."

"I just..." Shawn hesitated. "There's something."

"Fine, I'll ask for another room," Faith said, confused by Shawn's sudden interest in having space. When they stepped into the small room, she noted it was very cozy and had only one bed. "And that would be the problem you sensed?"

Shawn peered at the bed for a moment. Faith felt her ire growing as she tried to juggle the luggage. She narrowed her eyes, watching Shawn's gaze dart around the room. "Just a ghost," Shawn said. "Well, put the luggage down so we can unpack."

"Anything for you, princess," Faith snarled, tossing the bags on the bed. "Thank heavens you shipped your equipment so we could travel light. So that was it? A ghost, not the tiny bed we'll be sharing?"

"Yes," Shawn said. "Jilted lover, I'm sensing, late fourteenth century. She's displeased when couples share this room."

"We're not a couple," Faith noted grimly. "I am curious as to why Althea booked us in such a cozy room, not that I'm complaining. Just how displeased does our entity get? I'm not looking forward to being woken up at all hours of the night. Jet lag sucks enough without one of your little friends messing with me."

"Why are they my friends?" Shawn asked, pushing past Faith.

"Because you seem to attract them." Faith watched Shawn carefully unpacking their bags. "I can do my own."

"You're a slob. And for the record, I don't attract spirits, they're all around us. I'm just a better listener. Donald."

"Who?" Faith was itching to stop Shawn from touching her belongings.

"That was his name. The one who fled the night before the wedding," Shawn said calmly, as if she were reading an article in the Sunday paper and not peeking into the past. "I can't get a sense on her name. What time do we have to meet with Althea?"

"We have a couple of hours." Faith checked her watch, which she had reset after the airplane had landed. Shawn refolded the last of Faith's clothing. "I hate it when you do that."

"Fine, walk around with wrinkled clothing." Shawn stored the clothing in the antique dresser. "I'm going to try to catch a quick nap."

"Want company?" Faith suggested eagerly, already setting the alarm on her watch.

"Yeah." Shawn yawned, kicked off her shoes, and climbed onto the bed.

Faith curled up next to Shawn, cradling her in her arms and quickly drifting off to sleep. What seemed like only a few moments later, the persistent beeping from her watch awakened her. She cleared her throat, licking her lips as she glared at her watch. Her eyes widened with horror when she spied the petite redhead looming at the foot of the bed.

"Holy shit," she bellowed. She sprang from the bed, jostling Shawn's body in the process. She was shivering, the room felt cold, and then the mysterious redhead vanished. Shawn looked up at her with confusion.

"Sorry," Faith choked out. "We had company."

"Oh." Shawn yawned and combed her fingers through her hair in an effort to tame her unruly locks. "Did she do anything?"

"No. She was just looking at us."

"Okay." Shawn shrugged. "I'm going to take a shower. If you're afraid, you can join me."

"I'm not afraid," Faith said. Shawn snickered, gathered up her toiletries, and ducked into the bathroom.

"I'm not!" she repeated loudly, hearing Shawn laughing from behind the bathroom door. She paced back and forth, muttering under her breath that Shawn had dared accuse her of being frightened. After pacing for a few moments, reality dawned on her, and she halted her movements.

"Wait, did I just turn down a chance to take a shower with Shawn? Dumb ass," she muttered upon realizing that her bravado might have clouded her judgment. She quickly began to shed her clothing. She knocked timidly on the door. "Shawn, I take it back, I am afraid. Crap," she said when Shawn emerged from the bathroom wrapped in the towel.

"Too late." Shawn laughed, her hazel eyes slowly gazing up and down Faith's naked body.

"What did you do, just look at the water?" Faith planted her hands firmly on her hips.

"I took a very quick shower." Shawn's eyes darkened ever so slightly. "The water pressure sucks, and since I was alone, I didn't dally. Now, go freshen up, we have a meeting."

"You suck." Faith stomped into the tiny washroom.

* * *

The meeting took place in the dining room of the hotel. Faith always hated these pre-shoot meetings that could drag on for hours, since everyone had an opinion on how things should proceed. *What do we need to talk about? We go set up, shoot, and hopefully something entertaining will happen.* She scowled.

"Huh?" she said, realizing that Althea was addressing her. Faith had zoned out over an hour ago, becoming more focused with playing with the ice in her scotch than actually listening to what was going on around her.

"I said, is there anything you'd like to add?" Althea glared over at her.

"No," Faith said casually, praying that this meant that the tedious meeting was about to end. Thankfully, it did break up, most of the crew wandering off to get some sleep or hit the bar.

"Could you at least pretend to listen during these meetings?" Althea carried her drink around the table and sat down next to Faith.

"Why? It never changes."

"That's a bit presumptuous."

"Speaking of being presumptuous," Faith said tersely, "what's with my room assignment?"

"I thought the two of you were getting along," Althea said. "Don't tell me you're fighting again? Frankly, I don't have the strength to deal with it."

"No," Faith said. "We're fine, but a single? That's a little pushy."

"What?" Althea shook her head. "I specifically had my assistant request a double."

"Trust me, it's a single, very cozy space, not even enough room for a cot," Faith said, amused by Althea's look of shock.

"I'll have Esmeralda fix the problem right away." Althea snatched up her ever-present cell phone.

"Don't bother." Faith laughed.

"Really?"

"Not what you're thinking," she added. "We're getting along, but we're not getting along, if you get my drift. Bunking together won't be a problem. Heck, Shawn even found a ghost, so she's ecstatic, and no, we didn't take any pictures."

"A ghost?" Althea asked brightly.

"Yeah, some chick who got dumped back in the fourteenth century." Faith yawned. "Scared the bejesus out of me. I swear, hanging around with Shawn just attracts them. When I first started doing this crap, I didn't believe. Now I can't turn around without bumping into some bizarre specter. It can be a little nerve-racking at times."

"It's a part of what we work with," Althea said, taking a sip of her drink. "Speaking of business, the Whispering Pines shoot is going to include a police investigator from New York."

"I know." Faith snickered.

"Unbelievable as it may seem, she doesn't like you. Which tells me the two of you have met before. Promise me you'll play nice."

"Oh, I'll play nice."

"I mean it, Faith. Whatever you did to piss this woman off, forget about it," Althea said sternly. "She's done some very interesting work that will add a lot to the finished product. So no playing any of your pranks or trying to scare her."

"I wouldn't dream of annoying my sister," Faith said in a cocky manner.

Althea choked on her drink. "Your what? But she's so nice."

"Hey," Faith said. "So am I."

"Right." Althea laughed heartily.

"Fine, she's my half-sister, which is why she isn't so fond of me. Satisfied? We did talk in New York when I was visiting Shawn. I think things in Stewart will go smoothly."

"I hope so. I know how me and my sister get along. Sometimes we're glued at the hip, and other times we're ready to claw each other's eyes out."

"Maybe it's a good thing we grew up in separate households," Faith noted thoughtfully.

"So you spent time with Shawn in New York?" Althea asked.

"Yes," Faith said with a crooked smile. "And no, we're not back together. Oh, but she did solve a murder case from the fifties. Personally, I would have settled for shopping, but Shawn has a way of attracting these things."

"A murder?"

"Yeah. She got Jessica, I mean, Carey, involved, so you can ask her all about it. Knowing you, you'll get another special out of it."

"Do you have any idea how hot shows with psychic detectives are right now?" Althea said. "Never mind, one shoot at a time. I need to get some rest. Good night."

"Good night." Faith waved good-bye. "Connor," she greeted her old friend when he took the seat next to her.

"Charles." He smiled warmly. "Not hitting the bar? I was looking forward to a round or two before we have to start working. Or when you hopped the fence into spooky world, did you give up on hoisting a few?"

"I wrote the truth," she said. "Have you ever known me to lie?"

"Only to that barmaid in the shit hole back in Glasgow." He nudged her with his elbow.

"Oh, she was hot." Faith smiled at the memory of the beautiful redhead she had seduced a few years ago, after Connor had struck out with the lady. "I have time for a pint, but only one. Shawn isn't feeling well."

"I thought the two of you were on the outs," he said as they strolled into the bar. "Two pints," he ordered. "I don't understand you. First, all this nonsense about seeing ghosts, and now you're acting like a married lady. Whatever happened to the Charlie I once knew?"

"I grew up." She took a sip of her ale. "I know that on most of these little treks you and I have only seen and heard people who claim to see and hear things. What I experienced at Whispering Pines was the real deal. Not just a house settling, or the wind. I'm talking bitch-slapping, misty apparitions. As for Shawn and me, well, that all depends on what day you ask."

"Hey, don't get me wrong, love." He chuckled. "I've been happily married for over twenty-three years."

"And you and Sara haven't lived together for over what? Seventeen years?"

"And we couldn't be happier. Now Shawn, she's a special girl. What's the problem? Did you step out?"

"I left the country without consulting her," Faith said.

"So?" Connor shook his head, clearly not understanding.

"Okay." Faith laughed, still sipping her ale. "You're a scientist, let me try to explain it to you in terms you'll understand. You know how when you have two magnets, and if you face them in the right direction, they lock together so tightly you can't separate them? And if you face them in the wrong direction, they repel one another?"

"Yes."

"That's how Shawn and I are," she said with a shrug. "Sometimes we face the right way, and sometimes we don't."

"And today how are you facing?" He waved for another round.

"Somewhere in between." Faith pushed the fresh pint towards him. "I have an early shoot, and she's not feeling well. No pouting. I'm just trying to keep my magnets aligned."

"Carry on then, and I'll see you in the morning," Connor told her with a pat on the back.

* * *

Shawn was nestled comfortably in bed, happy that the voices seemed to be quiet, at least for the night. She sighed heavily, wondering if Faith was with Connor and stirring up trouble. She smiled, thinking about how the two of them were almost kicked out of London one year. The door creaked, and Faith stepped inside.

"Hey, I thought you'd be playing with Connor," she whispered, watching Faith move carefully into the room.

"Not tonight." Faith smiled, sending a warm current through Shawn's body. "Are we alone?" She began to disrobe.

"I think so." Shawn smiled in return. Faith turned so she could finish undressing in the washroom.

"You don't have to," Shawn blurted out a little too quickly. "I mean, the bathroom is very small, and it isn't as if I haven't seen you naked before."

"Well, not in a long time," Faith said shyly. Something about Faith's sudden shyness made Shawn blush.

"Just a few peeks here and there," Shawn said. She pulled back the comforter, making room for Faith to join her.

"Pervert." Faith laughed, the shyness still echoing in her tone.

"I wasn't the only one." Shawn smirked confidently. "And before you deny it, remember who you're talking to."

"Right, because you'd have to be a psychic to know I peeped at you while you were in the shower." Faith laughed heartily.

"Come to bed?"

Chapter 47

"I feel sick." Carey blanched, barely noticing Rishi, her friend and colleague, resting on the edge of her desk.

"Most people say hello," Rishi teased her.

"It's just this case," Carey said. "The ghost hunt from Massachusetts. Anna Stratton was sixteen when she married Horatio Stratton, who, at the time, was fifty-nine. She would have been twenty-four when she died."

"Speaking of ghost stories," Rishi said, "you've kept me busy in the lab." He handed her a folder. "Case closed, the DNA is a match. Brian has already arrested and gotten a confession from your suspect. Good job."

"I heard." Carey smiled, happy that at least one spirit could finally rest easy. "It wasn't me. Believe it or not, the case was solved by a psychic."

"Dr. Williams," he said. "I heard. I read her book about Whispering Pines. I'm interested in the case."

"You CSI geeks." She laughed. "What, don't we have enough fresh bodies to keep you busy?"

"Have you ever heard about the East India Companies?" Rishi asked in an odd tone. "Silk, spices, all part of the trade routes that forced my ancestors into servitude. Horatio Stratton is a name I've heard before, from my grandmother. She called him the devil. If the rumors are true, he was her father."

"The more I learn about the great Horatio Stratton, the more I wish he hadn't died peacefully in his sleep," Carey said, feeling the pangs of her own lineage gnawing at her. "Did he acknowledge your grandmother? Or do anything for your family?"

"No," Rishi said. "He denied he fathered any of the children. That didn't stop him from calling upon my great grandmother every time his ship docked. One day, he sailed off and never came back. My great grandmother was shamed, leaving my grandmother and her brothers and sisters to work as slaves until they left the country. So you see, my interest runs much deeper than just seeing an old crime scene. I'm actually related to the bastard, and I would love to shame his name as he has mine."

"I'll talk to the producer. Having a CSI tech on board might be something that interests her," Carey said.

"Thanks."

* * *

Edinburgh, Scotland
2005

"Would you mind repeating that?" Faith asked, clearly nervous about the unexpected invitation.

"I said, come to bed." Shawn smiled, amused by Faith's antics.

"I don't know," Faith hedged.

"I'm not yanking your chain, I promise," Shawn said, patting the bed. "No more come here, go away, or distrusting you because of one mistake. I'm sorry for putting you through all of that just because I was scared. Last week, spending time together, just the two of us, reminded me why I fell for you in the first place. I mean, solving murders and long-lost siblings aside, it was good to get to know one another again."

"It was," Faith said, climbing into bed. "You weren't the only one who didn't want to rush things by jumping back into bed together. Neither of us wanted that. I mean, I wanted it, I really wanted it, but it might have confused things. I really liked spending last week with you. The only thing I need to know is, how do you feel about me?"

"I'm still in love with you," Shawn said. "And I know that the past couple of years might have been a lot different if I had told you that I loved you instead of waiting to hear you say it."

"News flash, I love you, too." Faith smiled, clasping Shawn's wrist and tracing the bracelet slowly. "I tried to tell you with this, because I'm not so good with words. I want to start over." She wrapped her arms around Shawn's waist and drew her closer. "I want to do it right this time. No ghosts pushing us into bed, which is ironic, since first thing in the morning we're off on a ghost hunt. No drunken fumbling, no other women barging in, just us dating and acting like a normal couple, or as normal as either of us can be. I foresee this as long-term, so if you don't, tell me now."

"This is it," Shawn promised. "Before we were together and after we split up, I couldn't get you out of my thoughts, and considering how wild my thoughts are, that's amazing. I love you, Faith, and I promise to put you and us first."

"Good. Now shut up and kiss me, woman," Faith said with a wry chuckle.

"I love it when you take charge." Shawn wrapped her fingers in Faith's long, dark hair, drawing her closer and capturing her in a searing kiss. Shawn's senses reeled as she explored the warmth of Faith's mouth, and Faith's body covered her own. She moaned deeply, and her hands wandered along Faith's supple curves.

Shawn felt alive. She made her living out of exploring the past, and now, for the first time in her life, she was eager to let the past go. They had both made mistakes; now she looked forward to the future, which was beginning by making love to the only woman who had ever held her heart. She gasped as Faith's long, dark tresses tickled her face, and Faith's kisses drifted down her neck.

Faith tugged on the hem of Shawn's nightshirt "You're wearing far too many clothes," she whispered against her skin. Shawn smiled and leaned back, allowing Faith to take control and slowly undress her.

She quivered now, lying completely naked beneath her lover. Faith's eyes were glazed over with desire as she drank in Shawn's body. Shawn licked her lips, her excitement growing from Faith's intense gaze. Faith straddled her, still not touching her, but simply raking her eyes up and down Shawn's body. But Shawn could feel Faith's desire caressing her. *My God, she hasn't even touched me yet.* Shawn shuddered, unable to resist touching Faith's lean body.

She brushed the swell of Faith's breasts with the back of her fingers, feeling pleased when Faith released a soft moan.

"Why do I feel like this is the first time?" Faith asked in wonder, dragging her blunt nails down along Shawn's body. Shawn was unable to answer, her body giving in to Faith's touch.

Faith purred softly as she kissed her way down Shawn's body, like a jungle animal stalking its prey. The sound was one that Shawn was more than familiar with, and one she hadn't heard in a very long time.

Shawn released a tense breath, knowing by the sensual sound that Faith was planning on taking things very slowly. She gasped when Faith's tongue slowly traced the curve of her breasts. She ran her fingers through Faith's tresses, encouraging her to explore every inch of her body.

She wrapped one leg around Faith's lean body, tickling her lover with her foot, her body reeling from Faith's tender caresses. All sights, sounds, and outside intrusions vanished, and all Shawn could feel and sense was Faith's tongue flicking against her nipple, coaxing the bud to harden.

A small part of her wanted to take control and flip Faith over, to ravish her. The rest of her was basking in the sensation of Faith's hands gliding along her body while she suckled her nipple. Shawn's body swayed, matching Faith's slow rhythm, their bodies moving in unison as their passion mingled. Shawn caressed Faith's shoulders and surrendered to the pure pleasure of Faith worshipping her breasts.

The bed creaked beneath them as their bodies became one. Shawn fought against the tide, her wetness overflowing as her desire threatened to consume her. *I'll never let you go again,* she vowed silently. Her skin quivered from the moist kisses Faith was bestowing upon her breasts. Her nipples ached while her lower anatomy pulsated in a demanding rhythm. Her eyes narrowed with desire, and she ground her clit against Faith's throbbing nub. She was certain that their hearts were beating in unison as she clung tightly to her lover.

Shawn whimpered with disappointment when Faith's mouth abandoned her breasts and drifted lower. She released a tiny yelp at the feel of Faith's lips and teeth teasing her flesh.

"Soon," Faith said quietly against Shawn's taut stomach.

"Faith," Shawn pleaded, unable to stop from arching and grinding her wetness against Faith's body. Faith seemed determined to explore every inch of Shawn before granting Shawn's wish.

Shawn could smell her own arousal filling the room, her body thrusting harder as she begged her lover for release. Faith's sultry purr echoed in the darkness. Her tongue dipped playfully into Shawn's navel before tracing her hips. Shawn cried out as Faith's warm breath teased the glistening curls near her center. Her cries grew louder as Faith nestled between her thighs and cupped her backside. Faith's tongue tormented the inside of Shawn's thighs as she drew her closer. Shawn fought to keep her eyes open. Faith's hands caressed her bottom and her warm breath bathed Shawn's sex.

Shawn almost passed out when Faith parted her and dipped her tongue inside of her wetness.

Faith's tongue glided slowly along Shawn's slick folds while her hands caressed Shawn's body. Shawn's breathing became ragged as she fought against the tidal wave that threatened to send her over the edge. A guttural moan escaped her when Faith's lips captured her throbbing clit.

Shawn rocked her hips, pressing her wetness harder against her lover's face while Faith slowly teased the engorged nub. *Not yet,* she silently pleaded, fighting against the storm brewing inside of her. She bit down on her bottom lip as Faith's fingers slipped inside of her. Shawn's screams echoed loudly, her body riding against Faith's fingers and mouth.

"Faith!" she cried out, her body thrusting wildly as Faith pleasured her. Shawn's ears were ringing, her body convulsing, and each time she reached the crest, her lover's touch withdrew.

The sweet torture lasted for what seemed like hours. Shawn's throat was raw from begging. Finally, Faith gave in to Shawn's frantic pleas, her hand and mouth devouring Shawn until her body exploded. Shawn's lungs seized; her body flushed with pleasure as Faith took her higher, forcing her to thrash wildly, climaxing again and again.

Shawn ignored the soreness of her muscles as her focus returned and she captured Faith in her arms. She straddled Faith's body, and unable to calm her desires, she plunged her fingers deep inside Faith's warm, wet center. She could feel Faith's body tightening against her touch. She kissed Faith deeply, all the while plunging in and out of her. She trembled as she felt Faith climaxing, and she smiled down at Faith's writhing form, slowing her touch.

Their eyes were locked in a smoldering gaze as Shawn slowly made love to Faith, tenderly guiding both of them over the edge. Cradled in one another's arms, they knew that sleep would not be coming that night as they kissed and touched, determined to drive each other insane.

* * *

New York City
2005

"Oh, for the love of heaven." Carey was still searching for her other shoe. Her ex-husband sighed dramatically. "I get it, Brian. No talking to the television people about the case until everyone's certain that Maynard's locked up for good. What am I, a rookie? Just help me find my other shoe before we miss the ballet."

"I don't think you get it, Jay." Brian got on his hands and knees, searching for the errant shoe. "The brass is less than pleased about the call from that television producer. Frankly, they don't want it advertised that a psychic solved this case."

"I get it," she repeated. "At last!" She emerged from her closet with the missing shoe. "I bet you thought you'd get out of going," she taunted him as he groaned and climbed to his feet. She studied him for a moment, sensing that there was something else bothering him.

She loved Brian dearly. When she first met him, it was magical, or at least Carey had thought so at the time. He had come to Boston working on a case, and the duo hit it off immediately. After he returned to New York, they kept in touch. It didn't take Brian very long to convince her to relocate. She truly cared for Brian, and to this day, the two of them remained close friends. But it didn't take a genius to figure out that Carey's initial attraction to the older cop had more to do with needing a father figure in her life than a husband. When Carey finally realized her mistake, the two parted as friends.

"What is it?" she asked him.

"Why didn't you tell me that Dr. Williams is Faith Charles's girlfriend?"

"What does my sister have to do with any of this? You of all people know that Faith and I aren't close."

"Faith Charles doesn't have a lot of friends on the force," Brian said tentatively. "Three good cops will never rise in ranks because of that story she did five years ago. One of those cops is your CO. It could hurt you, if people found out that you're related to her."

"Good cops? I seem to recall that when she broke that story, you said they got what they deserved for crossing the line. As for Faith, have you ever heard me say anything nice about her?"

"Not until just now, when you referred to her as your sister. Is she involved in the Marshal case?"

"No." Carey dragged him out of her bedroom. "She just happens to be dating Shawn, and she's working on the Whispering Pines case. I did talk to her last week."

"And?" Brian asked as they made their way downstairs.

Carey was silent as they hailed a taxi, her emotions still confused by the chat she had shared with Faith.

"Well? Are you going to tell me what happened when you talked to Faith?" Brian asked when they had climbed into the taxi.

"She isn't the ogre I had assumed she was," Carey said. "Actually, she's nice. Well, a little edgy, like me. You know?"

"Sadly, I do." He laughed. "As your friend and someone who cares about you, I think it's great that you and your sister are finally speaking. As a fellow cop, I feel I should warn you that she's a reporter."

"Hey, these days all she does is chase after ghosts and, apparently, Dr. Williams," Carey said. "Strange, all these years seeing her on television, hating her, and I didn't even know she was gay. We're here." The cab pulled up in front of the theatre. "Growing up, I thought my parents were divorced. But my Dad was always there for the special events, until I found out the truth and told him to go to hell. I was convinced that he and Faith were evil, and now I don't know what to think. But then again, she could be evil, and she did say I could shoot her."

"Well, there you go." Brian laughed as he picked up the tickets at the box office. "Let me know if you need help hiding the body."

"I will." Carey linked her arm in his. "Oh, brother, my life just gets more and more complicated, and all because I said sure, I'll work with those pesky television people. How hard can it be?"

Chapter 48

Edinburgh, Scotland
2005

Faith felt content as she sat in Althea's hotel room and sipped a cup of coffee. She watched Althea pace about the room, yammering into her cell phone. All was right with the world, even if Faith's body ached and she hadn't slept since the short nap she had the day before. She grinned wickedly, recalling the previous night's passion, which had lasted until she and Shawn were forced to climb out of bed. They made love in the shower, or tried to, until the specter that lurked about their room decided to shut off the water and start wailing.

Curious looks had greeted them when they arrived late to the early-morning staff meeting. Now, Shawn and Connor were off shooting various spots around town, and Faith was waiting for Althea to get off the phone so they could have their meeting to prepare for the main shoot scheduled for that evening.

"Save me some coffee," Althea said as Faith helped herself to another cup.

"Hang up the phone and I will." Faith smirked, feeling positively giddy.

Althea scowled and snapped her cell phone shut. "Wait until the company gets the bill on all of these calls." She poured a cup of coffee and shuffled through her notes.

"Okay, the crew is off shooting various points of interests," she said in a cold, professional manner. Faith simply grinned back at her. "You will do the narration in postproduction. Tonight's the big one, The City of the Dead. The only way to get inside the Black Mausoleum is by tour. The tours run at 8:30, 9:15, and 10 p.m. every night. Each one lasts about an hour and a half. It starts at the St. Giles Cathedral, near the Mercat Cross on the Royal Mile. It winds through Old Town and into Greyfriars Graveyard. Then we enter the permanently-locked Covenanters Prison, which contains the Black

Mausoleum. I didn't want to deal with tourists, so we're booked for a private tour at midnight. Here's a list of questions and comments I want you to use." She handed Faith a slip of paper.

"Yes, no, very good, and not a chance," Faith said, marking the sheet with her own notes.

"Tell me what you know about the prison, and then tell me why you look so freaking happy."

"I have no idea what you're referring to." Faith feigned innocence while making more notes. "What, would you rather have Lanie back?"

"Lanie?" Althea scoffed. "At least she was easy to deal with. I just had her show up at hair and makeup, told her what to say and where to stand, told her how pretty she was, and she did whatever I said. You, on the other hand, challenge everything and add your own material, which frankly makes the shoot better. So no, I'd rather work with you and your reporter's instincts. Now, tell me why you're glowing, you slut."

"Slut?" Faith laughed. "I should sue! Come on, do I really have to tell you?" she said with a knowing smile.

"It's about time," Althea said.

"I know." Faith nodded. "But sadly, relationships don't come with an owner's manual. Enough about my love life. Let's get down to business. My mother's a history professor, and she gave me a quick rundown on the place. In 1679, the Covenanters engaged in a battle with Charles II, the battle of Bothwell Bridge on the river Clyde. They got the snot beat out of them, and those that survived were taken prisoner and returned to Edinburgh. There really wasn't any place prepared for the thousands of Covenanters, so they were crammed into an enclosure at the north end of Greyfriars to await their fate. There was no real shelter, and little food, during that winter. Many of them died, and many were executed. Those that survived were shipped off to the West Indies as slaves. They didn't make it, because the ship wrecked en route.

"The present site of the prison isn't the real site. What we're seeing tonight was erected around 1703. In recent years, a lot of spooky things have happened, many of which have been blamed on the MacKenzie poltergeist. George MacKenzie was the prison judge, and he's buried in a mausoleum near the prison grounds. Have I missed anything?"

"No, that about sums it up," Althea said. "Should be an interesting shoot tonight."

"And cold." Faith glanced out the window at the gloomy weather outside. "Any chance wardrobe's going to be kind to me, or do I have to dress like Barbie again?"

"You'll have a warm coat. The graveyard and the walk to the prison aren't suitable for the usual on-camera look. The tour guide you'll be working with will be Mary Summers. She knows the place up and down. One more thing, about that amendment you insisted on for the Whispering Pines shoot—"

"No," Faith cut Althea off. "I will not, repeat will not, go into that kitchen ever again."

"Faith," Althea said carefully, "Carey's bringing a CSI guy along, and it would be good to have you on camera asking questions when they go through the kitchen."

"No fucking way." Faith drew the refusal out slowly so there would be no room for an argument. "The only thing I'll do on camera regarding the kitchen is explain that I'll never go in there again. If it makes you happy, I'll go into great detail as to why I won't go. I'm serious, the bitch-slapping isn't going to happen again. I don't care how good it looks on camera, got it?"

"Got it," Althea said. "I'll have them go in this week, before we arrive with the second unit. I guess I don't have a shot at convincing Shawn to go back in there?"

"You guess correctly," Faith said. "You saw what happened. You were there when that thing tried to choke Shawn. Why on earth would you even consider sending us back in there? Never mind, I know. It would be good footage. Forget it. Send some other homo in to start the freak show. This little dyke will be more than happy to hide up in Anna's bedroom, thank you very much."

* * *

"This weather sucks," Faith repeated with a scowl later that evening as the group plodded down the road towards the graveyard.

"What?" Connor laughed, seemingly content in his surroundings.

"Try being out in it all day long." Shawn shivered and tilted her head slightly.

"I hear that you and Connor have been going at it all day," Faith commented as Althea waved for them to hurry up.

"He's worse than you were," Shawn said. "Oh, man." She trembled, stumbling slightly. "I think we need a camera set up."

"What is it?" Faith asked, waving for the crew.

"Death," Shawn said. The crew was hurrying to catch on film whatever was happening. "That mound is filled with bodies, isn't it?" She addressed the tour guide while pointing to the large mound.

"Yes," Mary said. "It's a mass grave."

"The cries of the innocent," Shawn said, before Mary could relate the history.

"Anyone could have looked that up." Connor shrugged for the benefit of the camera. "It was a dark page in history."

"Did you see that?" Ronnie, the cameraman, exclaimed.

"What did you see?" Faith looked around, seeing nothing but the landscape.

"A flash of light." Ronnie pointed his camera at the spot in question.

"I don't see anything," Connor said. "Could have been a reflection, or someone wandering about."

Mary explained the history as the group entered the graveyard and headed towards the prison. At this point, Faith and Mary were a good distance ahead of Shawn and Connor. Each pair had their own crew members recording them.

"Okay, before we open the gates, I need Charles on camera. Keep Dr. Williams and the others behind," Althea instructed.

"Yeah, you just love that element of surprise," Faith said. "Where do you want me?"

"In front of the gate, and move it along, it's getting late," Althea said. "Speaking of surprises, are you sticking to the script?"

"We'll see." Faith stood on her mark.

"On three," Althea said.

Faith recited the history of the graveyard and the prison, as she had done earlier that day for Althea's benefit. Then, she went into some of the strange occurrences that included people feeling scratched, being pushed, and suffering physical injuries.

"Many say it starts with a tingling sensation in their feet. Is this just the work of overactive imaginations, or is there really something lingering in this desolate prison? We're about to find out."

"Cut," Althea called out, motioning for Connor and Shawn. "You stuck to the script, mostly. Hot sex must agree with you."

"Shut up," Faith whispered, spying Shawn's approach.

"Doesn't it with everyone?" Shawn said. She nudged Faith in a playful manner. "Blabbermouth."

"She guessed." Faith felt herself blush.

"Wasn't that hard," Althea said. "Ronnie and Justine, you go in first and film the prison, then I need you to shoot Shawn and Connor entering. Faith and Mary will be last. Keep the cameras on Shawn and Connor, and on anything Shawn points out, got it? Good, now let's go, I'd like to finish before the sun comes up."

Faith was filled with apprehension when she entered the tiny space that had once held thousands of people captive. She wasn't certain if it was the coldness of the night, the eerie surroundings, or the way Shawn seemed ill at ease that was the source of her nervousness. She was miffed, too, by the way Connor was strutting about, dismissing everything Shawn pointed out.

Suddenly, Connor jerked and looked behind him. She almost laughed at how he played it off. *Then again, that's what I used to do.* She sighed, keeping a watchful eye on Shawn. She knew Shawn's body language; something was happening.

"Cold, hungry," Shawn said, shifting her feet nervously.

Faith spun around, feeling something yank her hair. She quickly returned her focus to Shawn, recalling that many of the physical encounters began with a tingling sensation in the feet.

"Nice try," Shawn taunted whatever was toying with her. "Over there," she instructed Ronnie calmly. All eyes turned to the corner, and jaws hung open when a shadow passed in a space that held no light.

"Reflection," Connor said, denying what they had just witnessed.

"Evil," Shawn said. The area grew chillier with each passing moment.

"Evil?" Connor said with a sneer.

"Fine, why don't you stroll on over and check it out?" Shawn said with a confident smile.

Connor pursed his lips, clearly knowing he couldn't back down. He strutted to the area in question, smiling when nothing happened. Suddenly he fell forward. When he climbed to his feet, his eyes were filled with fear.

"I must have tripped over something." He scurried quickly from the spot.

Faith would have burst out laughing if she hadn't been so focused on Shawn. Her lover's breathing was growing ragged.

"Dr. Williams?" she asked. The cameras turned to the shivering Shawn.

"'Execute me,'" Shawn whispered. "'Spare me from this slow, torturous death,'" she recited.

"It isn't just one voice pleading, it's many. There's something else lurking here," she tried to explain as one of the camera lights blinked off.

"Justine, keep filming," Althea said. "Forget it Ronnie, we'll get what we can and call it a night," she calmly told the young cameraman who was about to run off to get a new battery.

Faith blew out a sigh of relief. She knew that changing the batteries would be futile. The only thing she cared about was finishing and getting Shawn away from the bad energy that was obviously wearing on her. Faith watched for another agonizing hour as shadows lurked about and noises erupted from what should have been a quiet space.

"Cut," Althea wearily called out just as the second camera died. "Okay, people, it's after four. Time to call it a night. The talent has the day off. I need to go over the editing. We can do the post shots on Wednesday. I'll call with the times. Pack it up. Mary, thank you."

"I need a drink," Connor grunted as he brushed past the weary group.

"Ditto," Shawn groaned.

Faith wrapped her arms around her tired lover. "The bar it is."

* * *

"A round of scotch and pints, please," Shawn begged, slapping a wad of money down on the bar.

"We can sleep in," Faith said. The group grabbed the drinks and headed for a spot by the fireplace.

"Shawnie, you're not looking quite right," Connor said. He downed his scotch and waved for another.

"Back-to-back shoots," Shawn said in tired voice. "How's your knee?"

"Fine, nothing happened," Connor lied. "So, just overworked, or is it a lack of sleep that has you wrung out?"

"Bite me," Shawn said.

"I believe that post has been taken," he teased. Faith glared at him. "Got your magnets aligned, did you, Charlie?"

"Do I want to know what he's referring to?" Shawn asked Faith, who was still glaring at Connor.

"Nope," Faith said dryly. "So, Connor, getting clumsy all of a sudden, or did something happen back there?"

"I tripped," he muttered.

"Yeah, or you were pushed." Faith snickered.

"Bloody hell. I will never go on camera admitting that, but yes, something pushed me. What happened to you, Charlie? You seemed a might skittish."

"Something yanked on my hair." Faith shrugged. "I'm glad Althea pulled the plug. I wasn't looking forward to going back tomorrow. Maybe we can get some rest before going home."

"I hope so." Shawn yawned and finished off her drink. "I think I need to be up to par for the Pines shoot. I'm not looking forward to it."

"Neither am I," Faith said, brushing aside Connor's offer for another round. "Althea's already trying to get me to go into the kitchen."

"Fat chance." Shawn laughed and released another yawn.

"Bed?" Faith asked tenderly, rubbing the nape of Shawn's neck.

"Bed." Shawn nodded. She took Faith by the hand and helped her to feet. "Night, Connor."

"Have fun," he called out as the couple exited the bar.

"I'm exhausted." Faith opened the door to their room. "I can only imagine how you feel."

"I'm wiped," Shawn said, looking about the room for their unwanted roommate. "Good, we're alone. Forgive me if I fall asleep on you."

"No worries." Faith shrugged out of her coat. "I may just steal this from wardrobe. The sun's almost up, and I'm planning on sleeping the day away."

"I like the way you think," Shawn murmured, nestling her face against Faith's chest.

"Just wait to see what I have planned for you when our batteries are charged," Faith said in a husky tone.

"Hmm, I can't wait."

"Is it just me, or is Connor being a bit of an asshole this trip?" Faith asked as they climbed into bed.

"No, he's being a jerk," Shawn said. She cuddled against Faith's warm, inviting flesh. "He misses having you as a playmate. I think he blames me."

"Why would he blame you?" Faith busied herself rubbing Shawn's back in a soothing manner.

"Because he's always had a bit of a crush on you."

"Get out," Faith said. "He knows that I only play with parts that match, not fit."

"True, but before this trip he could at least cling to the hope that he still had a shot. And in the meantime, the two of you could kick up your heels and chase girls together."

"Idiot," Faith murmured.

"Can't say that I blame him." Shawn kissed Faith's shoulder. "You can't help it if you're drop-dead gorgeous."

"Are you getting fresh with me?" Faith gasped as Shawn's kisses began to drift lower.

"Perhaps," Shawn whispered. Her body warmed from the feel of Faith's hands wrapping around her.

"Sleep," Faith said wearily. "I really don't want to start something neither of us is going to be able to finish." She kissed Shawn tenderly.

"Sleep," Shawn agreed after they exchanged a few more kisses.

Chapter 49

Stewart, Massachusetts
October 2005

"Somehow, I thought it would be bigger," Carey said wryly while she and Rishi unloaded his equipment from the rented Chevy. "You know, after all the hype," she added. They studied the aging manor. Whispering Pines might not have been as foreboding as she had feared it would, but the old homestead still filled her with an uneasy feeling.

"Wait until we go inside," Kyle said, checking his camera.

"Kyle," Freddie, the dark-skinned young woman directing the second unit, said in a dismissive tone, "we don't know if anything's going to happen."

"You haven't been here before." Kyle grabbed an extra battery pack.

"You've been here before?" Carey asked.

"Yeah, I was on the team the last time," Kyle said with a hard swallow. "I saw the whole freak show up close and personal. I thought, when I signed on for the second unit, that I wouldn't have to go back in there."

"What exactly is a second unit?" Carey asked, intrigued by the young cameraman's agitation.

"You know when you watch a movie or a television program, and the lead is riding through the woods or something like that, and you can't quite see the actor clearly?" Freddie said. "That stuff is usually filmed by the second unit. We're the smaller crew that films the extra bits so the main crew can work on more important aspects."

"We're filler," Carey told Rishi, who snorted in response. "That would explain why there are only four of us."

"Five," Freddie said as a late model SUV pulled up the lengthy driveway. "Ms. St. James, I'm Freddie Stillman," she greeted the brunette who climbed out of the vehicle.

"A pleasure." Delia shook Freddie's hand. "Detective Jessup," she greeted Carey warmly.

"Ms. St. James, it's nice to see you again," Carey replied politely. "This is my colleague, Dr. Kapoor. He's with the CSI division."

"Doctor," Delia said. "I hope the two of you can find something that will finally help."

"We'll do our best," Rishi said. He unrolled a copy of the original plans for the large home.

Carey studied Delia and Rishi, looking for some clue that the two might be distant relatives. There were small similarities in their features and mannerisms that might be a link, but she could just be imagining it.

"I've gone over all of the old case files, and I'd like to start by retracing the steps the original witnesses went through on the morning in question," Carey said.

"This is wrong," Rishi noted, studying the old blueprints carefully.

"What do you mean?" Carey peered over his shoulder, looking from the old blueprints up to the house. "It looks the same."

"It isn't," Delia said. "Whoever drew up those plans didn't build this house."

"How can you tell?" Carey asked, completely confused, her untrained eye missing what the others could clearly see.

"Little things," Delia said. "For starters, the house is bigger, the front porch is different, and there isn't a widow's walk. See?" She pointed to the plans. "Though I could understand skipping that. I doubt Anna would have been pacing the walk waiting for the captain's return. If I had to guess, I'd bet the real designer was Benjamin Willis. He was a shipbuilder and had connections to the family. The design's similar to other houses he built. My only guess is that he was fired during construction and a new designer was brought in."

"Fascinating," Freddie said. "We need to get started before we lose the light. We should get some shots of the garden, since the sheriff thought the bodies were buried there."

"They weren't," Carey said. "Why don't we retrace what happened? The staff arrived on the morning of October 31, 1916.

They wouldn't have entered through the front door. They went this way," she said. Kyle lifted his camera and started filming her. The others followed as she led the group around to the side of the house.

"Ned Brown and Terrance Landry, the only men on the staff, headed along here. Terrance went straight to the barn."

"It was torn down before I was born," Delia said. "From what I understand, it was ready to collapse."

"Ned went to the woodshed to collect the tools he would need for the day," Carey continued as they passed the rickety shed. "It was locked as always. When Ned unlocked the shed, he noticed his axe was missing.

"The other members of the staff were all maids. Miranda Wilkins, Sara Hawk, Raquel Summers, Freda Martin, and Stacy Connors continued towards the back of the house. They passed by a doorway that led to the kitchen."

Suddenly, the side door opened and then slammed shut. The group stood paralyzed, staring at the door.

"What the hell was that?" Rishi asked.

"Did you get it?" Freddie asked eagerly.

"Yes, I got it," Kyle responded, his body trembling.

"Well, that was fun," Carey finally said after a long silence. "Moving along," she said, urging the group to continue, "the women went to the back of the house, passing the garden." They looked over the barren area. "Wow," she whispered.

"What?" Delia asked.

"You can see the graveyard from here," she noted. "On the morning that Horatio Stratton was buried, his son stood here while they dug up the garden. He would have seen his father's funeral. So much pain," she said. They turned towards the house. "The women used the servants' entrance."

"Down here." Delia guided them towards a doorway. She unlocked the door and allowed the group to shuffle past her, down a staircase and into a small room. "This was the mudroom. The staff would hang their coats on these pegs and leave their personal belongings down here."

"Beautiful woodwork," Freddie noted as they looked around.

"This way." Delia led the entourage through another doorway and into the large basement. Rishi and Carey studied the hard cement floor, looking for some sign it had been disturbed.

"Might be a good place," Carey said. They followed Delia up a small staircase, where she unlocked another door, and they proceeded into the main house.

"That was the captain's study." She nodded towards it as the others gaped at the magnificent workmanship.

"Down here." She led them past the study, through a hallway that opened up into the main room and foyer.

"The dining room is over there, and that hall leads to the kitchen."

Carey began narrating. "The staff said they entered here and found Captain Stratton sitting by the fire right over there, smoking his pipe, looking completely calm. Then Miranda left the others, who went about their duties. No one knew anything was amiss until they heard Miranda screaming. The entire staff, even the men who had been outside, rushed into the kitchen. All the witnesses claimed that the room was covered in blood. Miranda made a statement to the effect that it looked like the walls were bleeding. The captain never joined them or reacted. Most of the staff, with the exception of Ned and Stacy, fled. So, who wants to see the kitchen?"

"I'd rather not." Kyle gulped.

"You have to," Freddie said.

"Um, before I take you in there, is anyone here gay?" Delia asked.

"I beg your pardon?" Freddie asked.

"Hold on," Kyle cut in. "She's asking for a reason. Whatever that thing is, it was really focused on Shawn and Faith."

"Most of the more violent events have happened in the kitchen, and if you're gay, it will attack you," Delia said. "So, again, if anyone here is gay, I suggest you stay behind."

"Anyone?" Carey asked. "No? Okay then, let's see the scene of the crime."

Everyone was tense as they stepped into the infamous kitchen. Delia looked around nervously.

"An eighty-year-old crime scene," Rishi noted as he set his kit down. "Lots of dust. Why didn't they fix the woodwork?" He examined the multitude of cuts in the cabinets and flooring.

"Bastard was probably proud," Delia said. "Dr. Kapoor, do you think you'll be able to find anything?"

"A lot of years of dust and cleanings, hard to say." Rishi began measuring the deep marks.

"Film him for a bit," Freddie instructed. "Delia, why don't you show us the rest of the house? We can come back to film more of Doctor Kapoor after we get the whole tour."

"What else did the police report say?" Delia asked Carey.

"Nothing much," Carey said. "The sheriff was denied access to the house for weeks. When he finally got a warrant, there was nothing to see except marks made by a sharp object. Most of the staff quit on the spot, and Anna and Catherine Stratton were never seen or heard from again. The day after their disappearance, Captain Stratton burned or sold their belongings, including the furniture from the bedrooms. The only other reports were of strange happenings."

Rishi went about his work; the others watched him briefly before heading off to see the rest of the house. Delia explained each room as they ventured farther, wandering about, until they were in Catherine's room.

"No dust," Carey noted. "Just like Anna's bedroom."

"I know." Delia checked her watch. "I think this is the longest I've ever spent in this house. Normally, by now, something totally freaky would happen."

"What do you consider freaky?" Carey asked. "Doors slamming all by themselves and two rooms that have sat empty for over eighty years with not one sign of time passing don't qualify?"

"Not in this house." Delia shivered.

"Carey!" Rishi screamed from below.

"What the hell?" she whispered as Rishi screamed her name over and over again, until he burst into the room. "Rishi?"

"Now that's more like it." Delia snickered.

"What happened?" she asked Rishi, who was pale and trembling.

"Kitchen." Rishi wiped the beads of sweat from his brow. "I was on the floor, trying to see if I could get a sample, when I heard a voice. I thought it was one of you. When I looked up, there she was. Her body didn't go all the way down."

"A woman, that's good," Delia said.

"Good?" Rishi asked in a hysterical tone. "She was misty, and her body didn't go all the way to the floor. How is that a good thing?"

"Trust me, it could have been Horatio Stratton," Delia said. "He isn't very nice. What did she say? Where is my son, or get out?"

"Neither," Rishi said.

"Hold on." Carey opened the file she had been toting around. She pulled out the copy of the picture of Anna and Catherine she had made from the family photo. "Was it one of these women?"

"Oh, this is great." Freddie nudged Kyle closer so he could film the encounter.

"Her." Rishi pointed to one of the women in the old photograph.

"Catherine," Delia said. "What did she say?"

"'He's afraid of you.'" Rishi quivered.

"That's a new one," Delia said thoughtfully.

"How can you be so cavalier about this?"

"Years of practice," Delia said. "The first time I came here, doors opened and closed, voices told me to get out, and I saw the captain, who said I was worthless, just like my grandfather. I was fifteen and I peed my pants. If, for some reason, that sick bastard is afraid of you, then I'm happy you're here."

"I think we need more film of the kitchen," Freddie whispered.

"What?" Rishi asked with a hard swallow.

"We'll go together," Carey said, wrapping her arm around his shoulder. "I've never seen you like this, not even when we found that severed body in a dumpster."

"Seeing dead people doesn't bother me." He trembled as they made their way back down the main staircase. "Having them speak to me is completely different. Oh, my God," he yelled.

"What?" Carey asked as they entered the foyer.

"My kit." He pointed to the large metal case that was sitting by the open front door. "I left it in the kitchen."

"Are you sure?" Freddie asked in a nervous tone of voice.

"Yes! Look, I'm very careful about my equipment. I bolted out of the kitchen as soon as I saw whatever it was that I saw. I was working, my kit was open, and I left it there because I was scared. I saw her, started screaming, and ran out of there looking for Carey. I don't know if I can do this."

"If you don't, then he wins," Carey whispered softly, guiding him towards his kit. "I want to run, too, but we can't. No matter the reasons why we're here, I can't let a murderer just walk. But if you leave, I'll understand."

"No." Rishi gulped. "I can do it," he said with conviction.

* * *

"Nice digs." Rishi approached Carey, who was lounging on the balcony of the inexpensive motel they were staying at.

"No kidding, huh?" Carey laughed. "I thought show business would be more glamorous. How did it go at the crime lab? I can't believe that the St. James family was so eager to offer up their DNA."

"They're nice people," Rishi said. "I have to admit, visiting their house was a lot easier than spending time at the ancestral home. That place was beyond creepy."

"How many samples of DNA are you processing?" Carey asked, curious to see if her friend had included his own sample. "There was the mother, Delia, Andrew, and, of course, the stuff you found at the manor."

"And mine," he said. "I have to know. As for the small specks I found at Whispering Pines, after all this time, I doubt there will be any readable DNA. The gashes in the wood are consistent with an axe, no doubt about it."

"And the axe has been missing for over eighty years." Carey sighed.

"Why would he do that?" Rishi asked. "I mean, I had heard he was a son of a bitch, but why hack up his wife and sister?"

"From what I've heard, they were romantically involved," Carey said.

"No kidding. That might set a man off, especially one who was already unbalanced. How did you know about that?"

"Dr. Williams's book," Carey said. "I read parts of it last week. According to her and Faith, the women were lovers and Horatio found out and killed them."

"We'd be in a better position if we could find the bodies," Rishi said. "Match the gashes to the wounds on the bodies. The basement, maybe? Or he could have just dumped them at sea."

"He wasn't sailing that much by that time," Carey said. "I checked. He was getting on in years and had been reduced to short cargo trips years before that. Most of his so-called trips had been a ruse for him to sneak off and spend time in Rhode Island, drinking and patronizing prostitutes. I'm surprised though. I mean, in modern terms, he really wasn't that old."

"Then again," Rishi said, "he probably began his life at sea at a very young age. Back then, it wasn't uncommon for boys as young as six or seven to be signed on as members of a crew."

"Okay. So, he was sailing as a child, and by the time he hit puberty, he picked up all of the bad habits, drinking, cavorting, and being a general jackass. When he was getting up in age, he decided he needed an heir and married a teenager. I so don't like this guy."

"Me neither, but I'm biased," Rishi said with a rakish grin.

"When I was going through the old police records, there had to be at least a dozen reports that he beat his wife, and no one ever did anything about it," Carey said bitterly.

"Different times," Rishi said.

"Bullshit," Carey sneered. "It all comes down to the fact that he owned half the town."

"What happened today?" Rishi asked in a hushed voice. "I've never seen or experienced anything like it before."

"I went through the same thing in Salem," Carey said in an effort to comfort him. "I thought I was losing my mind, and I didn't see or experience half of what happened today."

"I have to be honest. I thought the whole haunting stories were a load of crap," Rishi said. "That woman, I mean she was there, but she wasn't. What do you think she meant, he's afraid of me?"

"Could be because of your skills as a scientist, or perhaps he knows that you're one of his descendants. This is going to be a very strange experience. Speaking of which, I think there's something you should know. Faith Charles is my sister."

Chapter 50

New York City
2005

"What?" Shawn asked in an amused tone as she brewed a pot of coffee, very aware of the impish child watching her every move. "You know I want to talk to you."

"Don't want to go," Willie sheepishly said. *"I want to stay with you."*

"Okay." Shawn knew it was futile to try to convince Willie to cross over. He was happy where he was. "Was there something you wanted to ask me?"

"Faith will stay?" Willie asked quietly.

"Yes, Faith is staying." Shawn smiled, feeling truly happy for the first time in years.

"Good." Willie giggled. *"Do you think she will play checkers with me?"*

"Maybe someday."

"Someday?" Faith padded her way into the kitchen and wrapped her arms around Shawn's body.

"Willie wants to know if you'll play checkers with him," Shawn said.

Faith nuzzled her neck. "You do know that's weird, don't you?" she muttered, snuggling closer to Shawn.

"Depends on your point of view," Shawn murmured, enjoying the feel of Faith's hands caressing her body. She yawned loudly, surprising them both. "I hate jet lag."

"Hmm," Faith moaned softly. "Why don't we take our coffee in the bedroom and try to catch up with the time change?"

"Is that all you have in mind?" Shawn asked playfully.

"No," Faith said slyly. "We don't have that much time together before Halloween. You know what that means."

"Back to Whispering Pines." Shawn shivered at the thought of returning to the old manor. "Don't let them talk you into going back into the kitchen."

"No problem. I'd rather walk through fire."

Chapter 51

Stewart, Massachusetts
October 30, 2005

"I said no." Faith glared at Althea. They were back in Stewart, standing outside the one place on earth she had hoped to never see again. The exterior of Whispering Pines was a flurry of activity. Althea had the cameramen rushing about shooting Shawn, Carey, and the St. James family. Faith was very clear when it came to her duties; she was the host, and she had a rider in her contract that clearly stated she would not set foot in the kitchen. Thus far, no one had entered the house. Faith was dreading the moment she would need to go back in there. Now Althea was trying to charm her into doing a setup in the kitchen.

"I don't give a damn how good it will look on film, no way, no how. It's in my contract, so don't even go there. This time, I'm the host. All I do is chat for the camera."

"Excuse me, ladies," Carey said. "I don't mean to intrude, but I'm cold, I'm tired, and after the gallon of coffee I drank, I need to hit the ladies' room. Now, I understand there's a lot of hurry up and wait with these things, but are we going to get started anytime soon?"

"Seriously, we've been here for hours," Rishi added.

"My apologies," Faith said. "I'm being difficult."

"Fancy that," Carey said. "How are you?" she asked in a conciliatory tone.

"Good, except our boss here is hell-bent on doing the forensic shoot at the scene of the crime." Faith smiled shyly at sister.

"The kitchen?" Rishi gulped.

"Ah, been in there, have you?" Faith beamed. "Wait, you should have been fine. Never mind. Althea, it's in my contract. I'm not going in there. You can shoot these two in there, but I'll do the interview right here on the porch, or in the main room by the fire. I'm assuming you already sent the boys in to light a fire, so it will look pretty."

"What happened to you?" Rishi asked. "I didn't think anything fazed you."

"Jasper?" Faith called out. "I know you have the clip from the last shoot prepped, would you mind running it for our friends?"

"No problem," Jasper said.

"Wait." Althea was growing visibly angrier with each passing moment.

"Althea," Faith said slowly, while Jasper set up a small monitor and replayed the scene for the others, "I know the kitchen is a hot spot that will look fabulous on camera, but you seem to be forgetting that every time I went in there, I was attacked."

"This sucks," Althea said.

"What was it saying?" Carey asked as they rejoined them.

"Sinner," Faith said.

"Someone has to go into the kitchen," Althea said.

"I'll go," Carey said. "I'll explain our findings, and then Rishi and I can go over everything with Faith in another room. We have pictures and lots of documents. It will be fine."

"Althea, I know you want the same freak show you got the last time," Faith said, "but either you accept the terms of my contract or I'm out of here."

"And if she goes, I'm certain Dr. Williams will follow," Carey added.

"Absolutely," Shawn said as she joined the agitated group.

"Fine." Althea finally conceded. "Jasper, Detective Jessup, we need to set up. Now!" she barked. "Freddie, I want you to do a second setup in the main room with Faith and Dr. Kapoor, to have them discuss the DNA and everything else."

"He's afraid of you," Shawn whispered to Rishi. "I'm sorry. I'm Dr. Shawn Williams," she said.

"Dr. Rishi Kapoor," he replied. "I'm the forensics geek."

"Yes." Shawn nodded. Faith watched the man shifting nervously.

"What did she mean?" Shawn finally asked. "When she said that he's afraid of you?"

"How did you know about that?" Rishi asked.

"That's what she said," Shawn said. "In the kitchen, the first time you were here. He's afraid, because you hold a secret that could disgrace him."

"I beg your pardon?" Rishi asked.

"The answer is in the envelope," Shawn said vaguely. "I'm sorry. I didn't mean to pry. It just happens."

"You really are a psychic," Rishi said. Faith smiled slyly, knowing that, despite his attitude, Rishi believed in what Shawn was saying.

"We should go inside and get this over with," Faith said, offering Rishi an escape from the conversation. "Why don't you go over your findings with me, and we can work on how to do this for the camera?"

"I'd appreciate the help," Rishi said. "I'm not good with people. Having a camera in my face isn't something I'm looking forward to."

"After a couple of seconds, you forget it's there." Faith hesitated by the front door. She exhaled a terse breath and glanced over her shoulder. She calmed as she spied Shawn following closely behind. "So, Rishi, what's in the envelope?"

"Oh, um, just the DNA results," he muttered. They finally stepped into the manor.

Faith held her breath for a moment, waiting for something to happen. She sighed with relief when the only activity that greeted her was the film crew trying to get ready. "Whenever you're ready, Ms. Charles," Freddie said, guiding Faith to her mark in front of the main fireplace. "I'll hold up the cue cards."

"Don't bother." Faith smirked. "Just start filming."

"But—"

"Trust me, Althea will love it." Faith smiled brightly, intercepting a curious look from Shawn. She was lingering behind Kyle, who was balancing a heavy camera on his shoulder. "Anytime you're ready."

"Fine," Freddie said. "Action."

"Good evening, I'm Faith Charles," she said confidently. "Three years ago today, I was invited to film a Halloween special here at Whispering Pines, the former home of Captain Horatio Stratton, and his young wife, Anna. That night, my job was to prove that nothing out of the ordinary was happening in this quaint New England manor. Instead, I encountered something I had never experienced before. It was a terrifying ordeal, one that I will never forget.

"Tonight we are, once again, seeking answers to what happened in this house over eighty years ago. Joining me are Dr. Shawn Williams, a professional ghost hunter who was with me the last time I set foot in this house, Detective Carey Jessup of the New York Police Department, Dr. Rishi Kapoor, who is a member of the NYPD CSI

Unit, James Simmons, a professional naysayer, as I once was, and our original film crew. Well, those of the crew who were brave enough to return. Even now, I'm not certain I want to be here, and I refuse to enter the kitchen of this once stately home. Why, you ask?

"Eighty years ago, the staff that had worked for the Stratton family for years entered the manor. They found Captain Stratton sitting by this fireplace, relaxed and smoking his pipe. Nothing seemed amiss until Miranda Wilkins, the maid, entered the kitchen and discovered it covered with blood. Most of the staff fled the house, never to return. Mrs. Anna Stratton and her sister-in-law, Catherine Stratton, were never seen or heard from again. Or were they? Three years ago, I entered that kitchen and was attacked by something I couldn't see. What happened in this house eighty years ago? That's what we're here to find out. Dr. Kapoor?"

"Cut!" Freddie called out. "Wow, that was perfect."

"Not quite." Althea had entered during the filming. "Hold on, Faith, I like it. But I need to change a couple things. Add the part about the murders last. I want you to interview Detective Jessup first, then Dr. Kapoor. Also, I want you to add that a second film crew tried to investigate last spring, and was driven out of the house. You can't go into detail. Then we're going to edit in what happened to you and Shawn the first time you were here."

Faith rolled her shoulders while Althea scribbled some notes. She waited patiently while Althea went over them again and again.

"We'll cut after you say 'that's what we're here to find out.' Bobby, I'll need a couple of chairs set up in front of the fire," she instructed her PA.

"Okay, that will work," Faith said, once again taking her place in front of the fire. "So, I do the spiel, and then interview Carey, Dr. Kapoor, James Simmons, and Shawn last?"

"On five." Althea nodded, seemingly pleased by the way things were going.

Faith repeated her introduction with the changes Althea had made. It was easy, since it was almost exactly what she had just said. The only things troubling her were the way James Simmons, this year's naysayer, was glaring at her from a far corner of the room, and that the house seemed almost too quiet. After her first visit, she had been on edge, waiting for all hell to break loose; so far nothing had happened.

Once she had completed the introduction, Althea bellowed, "Cut!" Then she demanded that the set of chairs be put in place. Faith glanced around nervously, feeling uncomfortable.

"How are you holding up?" Shawn whispered as they waited for the chairs to be set up and everything double-checked with light meters.

"I hate dressing up," Faith said, her gaze still darting around nervously. "Before, I could be comfortable."

"You're doing fine." Shawn gently stroked her arm.

"I don't know," Faith whispered. "It's just like last time, only with more people. Everything's quiet, and I know it isn't going to stay that way. Last time, when I first arrived, I thought, what's the big deal? Then Milo went screaming into the night, and I was slapped. The serene setting isn't fooling me this time. It's scaring the bejesus out of me."

"Everything isn't quiet," Shawn said softly. "They're here, and he isn't happy. Something's keeping him at bay. It won't last. Once we start searching, he's going to freak out."

"You still think they're in the house?" Faith asked tersely. Althea waved for her to take her place.

"Yes," Shawn replied. "I just don't have a clue as to where in the house. If I did, we could get the hell out of here."

"That would be nice," Faith murmured, her pulse quickening as the memory of the morning after their first ordeal invaded her senses. She and Shawn had wrapped up the shoot and spent the entire weekend in bed getting to know one another.

"Charles!" Althea barked.

"Coming," Faith snapped.

Faith and Carey took their places in the chairs that had been placed in front of the fire.

"What do I do? I'm not accustomed to doing interviews for the camera." Carey fidgeted.

"Relax." Faith smiled, pleased that Carey was more concerned with having to speak in front of the camera than with dwelling on the past. "I ask questions and you answer. It's that simple."

"Oh, easy for you to say, you do this all the time," Carey said, trying to balance her notes and files.

"You'll be fine. I've reviewed your notes so I can sound like I know what I'm talking about, and remember, you can always shoot me if I annoy you."

"I'm feeling better already." Carey grinned. "Damn, I never thought I'd be sitting here, talking with you. After this is over, are you heading back to New York?"

"As a matter of fact, I am."

"I take it that you and Dr. Williams have ironed out your differences."

"Yeah, and I promised not to skip the country without telling her."

"She'd probably appreciate that. So, how do we start?"

"I'll introduce you, go over your credentials, and start asking about the investigation," Faith explained. "We really should include the early reports of spousal abuse, and then you can explain what you did and what you've discovered."

"That sounds easy enough. Um, just one thing. We can't mention the case that Shawn worked on in New York. My department is very leery about it getting out that the case was solved by a psychic."

"Fancy that." Faith snorted, knowing that Althea must be pissed. "No problem. Now sit up straight, and when in doubt, we can stop filming. Ready?"

"Thanks," Carey said warmly.

"Are we ready, ladies?" Althea asked.

"Feel free to shoot her, too," Faith muttered before flashing Althea a bright smile. "Yes, we're ready, oh great one."

"You're such a pain in the ass," Althea said. "On five."

Faith introduced Carey and told of her years as a homicide detective for NYPD. She turned towards Carey and asked how she got involved with the case. Gently, Faith eased her into discussing her findings. Carey proceeded slowly, finally warming up to the situation. She covered everything and had just begun discussing the fateful morning when the staff fled the manor. Suddenly, the power shut down.

"Hate it when that happens," Faith snarled. The crew grumbled. "Something I've gotten used to. Seems the little buggers just love draining batteries."

"I don't think that's what happened," Shawn said tersely. "The fire is out as well."

Faith's gaze darted around nervously as she suddenly realized that the temperature in the room had dropped dramatically.

"Oh crap," she whispered, her body tensing as she spied her breath leaving puffs in the air. Suddenly, the front door flew open, the windows rattled, and a loud boom filled the room. She braced herself, preparing for the worst. She saw Carey clinging to her chair.

"Welcome to Whispering Pines," she said, placing a comforting hand on Carey's arm in an effort to keep her from fleeing.

The crew scurried about, searching for the problem that had caused the power to shut down. Shawn shrugged on her coat in an effort to fend off the sudden chill that had filled the room. She was amazed that, despite the numerous times the crew had experienced a sudden power loss, they were still checking the generator in the van. Shawn scowled at the way Freddie kept Faith busy. Normally, Shawn was fine on her own, but being here filled her with an overwhelming need to stay close to Faith.

"So, got a deck of cards?" Carey asked, shoving her hands in her leather jacket.

"I'm sure if you ask the crew you'll find one. One of them usually carries a deck." Shawn laughed, noticing the similar gestures Carey shared with Faith.

"Yeah, picked up on the whole 'hurry up and wait' thing back in Salem," Carey tried to joke, but the troubled look in her eyes revealed her true feelings. "Faith seems to be on top of things."

"Not really." Shawn watched Faith. "This place..." her voice trailed off.

"I couldn't help notice that you're trying to stay very close to her," Carey said. "In Salem and New York, you seemed fine to venture off."

"I don't like this place," Shawn said grimly. "There's trouble brewing. This little power failure is just the beginning. Of course, I just bet you're going to disagree, aren't you, Jimmy?" she asked the older man who approached them.

"Yes," he said in a bored tone. "Don't you think it's possible that the power went down because of all the lights and cameras the crew is running off of one generator? It might have been easier if the family had the power turned back on for this. James Simmons," he said to Carey, who frowned at his tone of voice.

"Carey Jessup," she said politely. Shawn snickered, knowing that Carey had picked up on Jimmy's try at acting suave in a lame attempt to impress her. Then again, he was always hitting on her and Faith, ignoring that they had made it perfectly clear they weren't interested in him.

"If I can be of any assistance," he continued, apparently oblivious to the way Carey was rolling her eyes.

"Dr. Williams has been more than helpful, thank you." Carey stepped back slightly, creating a little space between her and the older man. Jimmy closed the gap between them, forcing Carey to move away. She bumped into Shawn, who laughed when Carey brushed against her.

"What's so funny?" Carey asked.

Shawn bit down on her lip. "Nothing," she said with a smirk.

"As I was saying," Jimmy prattled on. "If you need help learning the ropes, I'm available."

"I'm fine," Carey growled.

"Back off," Faith said, approaching the group.

"Faith, my favorite brunette." Jimmy smiled at her. "It's so nice working with you again, although I am disappointed that you sold out."

"I haven't, you lowly jackass," Faith growled in the identical manner her younger sibling had just done. "Now, shoo," she added, waving at him. "Go on!"

"Okay, now that he's gone," Carey said. "What was so funny?"

"What you were thinking," Shawn said. "'At times like this, I'm so glad I carry a gun.'"

"Can I borrow it?" Faith asked merrily.

"No." Carey smiled slightly. "Is he always so charming?"

"Yes," Faith said. "Even after I threatened to castrate him. He took it as a come-on. The power's back up. Are you ready to give it another try?"

Shawn watched as the siblings went back to the chairs in front of the fire. The hair on the back of her neck prickled, and she felt suddenly uneasy. Carey seemed calm as she explained her findings. She ran through the list of spousal abuse reports, the witness statements, and the sheriff's findings.

"They searched the basement," she whispered, her stomach churning as strange images assaulted her. She was only vaguely aware of Carey explaining that a team from the Massachusetts State Crime Lab had indeed searched the basement earlier that week.

"Not there, not the garden," she whispered, stepping away from the others so her voice wouldn't be heard during filming.

She stumbled out onto the porch and buried her face in her hands. The images were coming quickly, much too quickly for her to decipher. She could see a backhoe digging up a garden, then the police crawling around the basement, searching for some small clue that all was not what it appeared to be. There was another image, a drawing. Each time, it slipped away just as quickly as it appeared.

"A sketch, a diagram, what are you?" Her eyes drifted towards the back of the house. Beads of sweat formed on her brow as she watched Horatio pour kerosene over the shards that had once been beautiful furniture. Shawn fought against the bile rising in her throat as he grabbed another canister, doused the remains of Anna's and Catherine's clothing and furniture, and trailed the kerosene off towards the garden.

She watched in horror as a man pestered the captain with questions while he set everything ablaze.

"'Why are you burning their belongings if they're coming back?'" Shawn whispered the words that were echoing through her mind.

* * *

"At the time, everyone was under the impression that Captain Stratton was sailing to far-off places," Carey continued, having finally relaxed in front of the camera.

"The truth was, he mostly sailed from Hayden Wharf, located in town and owned in part by the Stratton family, up to Cape Ann, and down to Newport. His career at this point was less than stellar. Many times, when he left his family, he didn't have a voyage scheduled at all. He spent a great deal of time in Rhode Island, patronizing houses of ill repute. This would explain why he could return often to surprise his wife, whom he was convinced was unfaithful."

"And was she?" Faith prompted.

"There's no evidence that there was another man in Mrs. Stratton's life," Carey said. "There's also no evidence he could have disposed of his wife's or sister's body at sea, given the limited area he was allowed to travel."

"You brought in a CSI expert from New York and worked with the Massachusetts crime lab. Have you found anything to suggest that there was a murder?" Faith asked with a slight smile, amazed by her younger sister's capability.

"The kitchen, the witness statements, and of course, the fact that neither woman was ever seen or heard from again, lead me to believe that their disappearances were suspicious," Carey said. "Plus, by all accounts, Mrs. Stratton was completely devoted to her son and would never have abandoned him."

"Have you, or the team of experts, found anything to support your conclusion?" Faith asked, hoping that they had found something, anything, that might help bring Anna and Catherine peace.

"No," Carey said. "The garden was excavated after the captain's death, the grounds searched just last week, and the basement and house checked up and down, and still we have no evidence, other than the damage in the kitchen, that a crime had occurred. If this crime happened yesterday, and not eighty years ago, with the available evidence, no charges could be brought."

Faith continued with the interview, knowing that she had to ask certain things so Althea could tie in the film that had already been shot the previous week. She also had to get Carey to talk about the strange occurrences she had witnessed while investigating the house. Next, she interviewed Rishi, who explained that the DNA discovered in the kitchen was unreadable, but the tool markings of the gashes were consistent with an axe that would have been manufactured around the time of the women's disappearances.

Interviewing Rishi was an arduous task, as the man was nervous in front of the camera. Faith peppered him with scientific queries, sensing if she could get him to talk about the scientific aspects, he would be much calmer. Getting him to talk about what happened in the kitchen proved to be an unnerving experience for her.

Finally, she let Rishi climb out of his chair and proceeded to interview Jimmy. He proved to be a much easier, albeit annoying, subject. He prattled on and on about the history, and yes, he was certain that based on the evidence, a heinous crime had occurred. But no, the house wasn't haunted, since such things do not exist. He refused to budge from his convictions, despite Faith presenting him with her own experiences and the experiences of others.

"Cut!" Althea cried out when it looked as if Faith and Jimmy were about to come to blows.

"Fine, you pompous ass," Faith snarled, tearing the small microphone from her body. "I know what I saw."

"And I know what I haven't seen," Jimmy countered snidely.

"Where's Shawn?" she asked, suddenly filled with a sense of panic. She bolted from her chair and began searching for her missing lover. The bile rose in her throat when she discovered Shawn standing in the middle of the yard shaking and gasping for air.

* * *

"Shawn?" Faith's voice dispelled the smell of burning flowers that was choking Shawn.

She gasped sharply, her eyes finally focusing on the vision of Faith standing in front of her, caressing her shoulders.

"Put the fucking camera down," Faith ordered.

"I'm good," Shawn choked out, trying to catch her bearings. "It's okay," she said, trying to calm Faith. She blinked with surprise when she discovered everyone standing around her. She glanced up at the sky, noticing that the sun had dropped dramatically.

"What time is it?"

"Six thirty-five," Althea said. "We've been filming for a couple of hours. Do you think you could go on camera and tell us what happened?"

"Althea," Faith snarled.

"Down, girl." Shawn almost laughed. "Yes, I can go on camera. Whenever you're ready." She brushed back her hair and plastered a smile on her face, trying to calm her coworkers. She blew out a terse breath as the camera started rolling.

"I saw a series of jumbled images," she said in a professional tone. "The garden being dug up, a team of policemen searching the basement, and then it changed. The captain was smashing furniture right here, while another man, his lawyer, Russell something, questioned him."

"What was he questioning him about?" Faith asked.

"Why the captain was destroying their belongings if they were away on a trip," Shawn said. "All the while he was shredding their clothing, the captain repeated that his wife was away on a family matter. Then he doused everything with kerosene."

"Detective Jessup explained that in her interview," Jimmy said. "It was in the police report that he sold off or destroyed their belongings."

"He didn't just destroy their belongings," Shawn said. "He used every drop of kerosene he had available and lit a huge bonfire, torching not only their beds but the garden as well."

"Convenient that you can't prove that," Jimmy said.

"Was I as annoying as he is?" Faith whispered.

"At times," Shawn teased, hoping to ease the tension. She sensed Faith was fighting against the urge to grab her and get the hell out of there.

"Maybe—" Faith began to say, and Shawn held up her hand.

"We have to try." She looked down at her wrist and rubbed the bracelet, which was warm. "You know..." she muttered. "There was something else. I keep seeing a diagram or picture. I can't get a read on it. I just know that it's important."

"A photograph?" Delia asked.

"No." Shawn shook her head, the faint image still plaguing her. "It's a drawing, technical in style, very faint. All I know is, it's wrong."

"Wrong?" Delia asked. "What do you mean?"

"I don't know," Shawn said. "Just wrong. That's all I know."

She looked past the crowd and spied Anna standing by the kitchen door.

"Help us," Anna pleaded, her eyes filling with tears. Then she vanished.

Shawn rubbed her throbbing brow. Voices from the cemetery were mixing together, and suddenly, nothing was clear.

"I need a break," she said, her body swaying.

"That's it," Faith announced. "We're out of here."

"Faith," Althea said.

"No, it's too much," Faith said. "You've been pushing her on back-to-back shoots for over a year, and I didn't help by dragging her back here. We're done."

"Faith," Shawn whimpered. "I can do this. I just need a little breather."

* * *

"Wow, this is certainly a major step up from last time," Shawn said as she glanced around the new and improved van. "I saw the old one out front. No wonder she hid this one out of sight. It's like a small television studio."

"It is," Faith said. "Althea scored some major perks for this special. They can probably edit and put the entire project in the can right from here." She led Shawn towards the back of the large vehicle. Shawn gasped as she opened the door to reveal the small, but comfortable bedroom nestled in the back of the converted RV.

"No wonder she isn't bunking down at that cheap hotel with us," Shawn groused.

"In Althea's defense, she did put together the impossible project," Faith said, guiding Shawn down onto the bed. "You said you needed a breather. Take a nap, and if you still aren't feeling good, I meant what I said, we're out of here."

"Stay with me?" Shawn asked.

"Gladly." Faith kicked off her shoes and curled up beside Shawn.

She held Shawn in her arms, pleased that she quickly drifted off to sleep. Faith had known this trip was going to be stressful. She feared returning to the manor. Still, in her heart, she felt it was something she needed to do. When she discovered that Shawn would be by her side, she was elated. Now, she wished that Shawn had stuck to her original plan to stay as far away from Whispering Pines as possible.

Then again, there was the nagging feeling she had experienced since her first visit. For some unknown reason, she wanted to give Anna and Catherine peace. She often wondered if it was because she felt their pain. She was blessed to be alive at a time when homophobia wasn't the extreme hardship for her that it had been for women like Anna and Catherine.

Shawn snuggled closer as she slept. Faith absently stroked her hair as she pondered the question everyone was asking. *Just where do you hide your wife's and sister's bodies after you hack them up?* The question plagued her, since she initially assumed that the good old captain would have buried them in the garden or somewhere on the property. Police and family searched those areas for over eight decades and found nothing. And Shawn was convinced that the bodies were in the house. If she had learned anything from knowing Shawn, it was to trust Shawn's instincts.

* * *

Shawn was still sound asleep when Faith slipped from her grasp. She made a trip out to the rental car and then changed into more comfortable clothing.

"Althea can bite me," she said as she finished dressing in the large RV. She stepped out into the darkness to find the crew mingling about the porch area.

"Give me a drag," she beckoned to Carey, who was lingering on the porch, smoking with Rishi and Delia.

"Sure," Carey said, handing Faith her cigarette. "I didn't know you smoked."

"I don't." Faith spied the blueprints spread out on the floorboards of the porch. "I used to."

"Me, too." Carey sighed. "I had to bum that one off of one of the grips." Her brow furrowed as she stared at the blueprints. "I thought this was it, but I don't see it."

"Okay, I'll bite," Faith said as everyone else seemed to abandon interest in the blueprints. "What are we looking at?" She took a long drag, her head spinning slightly from the effects of not smoking for many years.

"I thought this was what Shawn was talking about," Carey said. "That first drag is a bitch, isn't it?"

"No kidding." Faith coughed and handed the cigarette back to her sister. "Now I remember why I quit. So what are these blueprints for?"

"This house," Delia said.

"This house?" Faith asked in disbelief "I haven't seen a lot of blueprints in my day, especially a set this old, but no way is this Whispering Pines. There isn't a structure on the roof, the porch is smaller, and what's that?"

"The closet in Anna's bedroom," Delia said. "And you're right, these plans aren't accurate, and no, we don't know why."

"What closet?" Shawn inquired as she climbed the porch steps.

"Hey, how are you feeling?" Faith asked with concern.

"Much better." Shawn smiled slightly and took her place by Faith's side. "You were right, I've been pushing myself too hard. I feel completely recharged."

"Good." Faith sighed in relief, resting her hand on Shawn's shoulder. "Well, now I have to ask the same question, what closet? Shawn and I never saw a closet in that room."

"The door was closed," Delia said with a shrug. "You must have noticed that the house, despite the years of neglect, is still in very good condition. Whoever built the house was a master craftsman. The interior is pristine."

"Except for the hatchet marks in the kitchen," Shawn said, finally glancing down at the plans. "This is what I saw. This is the drawing I saw in my vision."

"Come off it," Jimmy said as he approached the group. "Who cares if there's a closet?"

"Bite me," Faith snapped. Shawn snickered at her lover's antics.

"Careful, babe, he might just take you up on that," Shawn said. "Delia, I never saw a closet door."

"As I was trying to explain," Delia said, "the door is flush with the wall. You can't see it. You have to push on it to open it. The workmanship is amazing. The only reason I knew there was a closet in that room was because of the blueprints."

"I've seen it," Carey said. "There are built-in shelves and drawers. It's really creepy."

"As opposed to the rest of this place?" Faith asked wryly.

"All of the drawers had been pulled out, and it looked like it was ransacked," Carey said. "Like a house that has been burglarized, only the thief didn't leave anything behind."

* * *

"Why leave so much space?" Rishi interrupted Shawn's thoughts. "For only one closet, it doesn't make sense."

"It wasn't meant to be," Shawn absently whispered, beads of sweat forming on her brow. The images were bombarding her, none lasting long enough for her to gain a clear picture.

"'I won't work for a man who beats his wife,'" she said.

"Admirable, but what has that got to do with anything?" Jimmy asked.

"Yo, Jimbo, focus here," Faith said curtly. "She isn't speaking for herself. Shawn, are you okay?"

"We need to go inside," Shawn said. The hair on the back of her neck prickled.

"Better tell Althea."

"Are you sure that you're okay?" Faith repeated. Shawn fought against the wave of anxiety that was threatening to consume her. Jim raced off to find the producer. Shawn could sense that, despite his bravado, he was eager to finish up and get as far away from Whispering Pines as possible.

"This is not going to be fun," she mumbled. "I'm so close I can feel it."

"Okay." Faith caressed Shawn's back.

"He can feel it, too," she added in an ominous tone.

"Peachy," Faith whispered, her hand never leaving the small of Shawn's back.

Shawn failed to respond; her mind was filled with disturbing images. She tried to shut out the din from the real world and focus on the past. She was only dimly aware that the crew had set up and the cameras were about to roll.

"Anytime you're ready," Althea said.

"Go ahead," Shawn replied absently. "This drawing is what I saw in my earlier vision." She bent over and picked up the old blueprint. "Ms. St. James, I need a quick lesson in early twentieth-century architecture."

"I'll tell you what I can," Delia said.

"First, why would someone leave this much space between the rooms and the wall of a structure?" Shawn asked, fighting the hostile energy that was surrounding her.

"They wouldn't," Delia said. Shawn approached the front door. "Not then, and certainly not now."

"Do you think whoever drew this plan built this house?" Shawn asked. She reached for the doorknob. She jerked her hand back when an eerily cold gust of wind assaulted her.

"No," Delia said. All eyes watched Shawn reach again to grasp the doorknob.

Shawn was filled with anger when the door refused to open. "Come on, you bastard, you can't keep us out forever," she hissed, pressing harder against the door.

"Well, this is getting us nowhere fast," Faith said after almost everyone took turns trying to break into the house. She glanced over at Delia St. James, who was sporting a mildly amused look. "What?"

"If he doesn't want you to get in, you won't," she said.

"Fine," Faith said. "Any suggestions? It's cold, dark, and by the way, someone's watching us." She pointed beyond the porch roof to an upstairs window.

All heads jerked up, and people gasped as they spied the shadowy image looming there.

"It isn't reading on film," Jasper said, tapping his camera.

"Of course not," Jimmy said. "It's just a trick of the light."

"What light?" Faith taunted him. "We have the only lights. There's no power in the house except for the cables the film crew ran through. Tell me you don't see her?"

They were standing toe to toe, their faces turning red.

"A pissing contest. Goodie," Shawn intervened, slipping between the two of them. "Not going to help. Unless we can get inside, this project is over."

"Don't even say that," Althea said.

"Dr. Kapoor?" Shawn felt slightly queasy. "I noticed you didn't try to help us. He's afraid of you. Care to tell us why?"

"No," Rishi said. All eyes studied him. "Fine. There was a rumor in my family that we might be his descendants."

"I've heard that he had fathered children overseas," Delia said. "No one ever proved it. You matched the DNA, didn't you?"

"Yes." Rishi nodded. "Yours, your brother's, your mother's, and my own."

"And we're related?" Delia said with a warm smile.

"No question about it," Rishi said, blowing out a heavy sigh. "I'm a living, breathing reminder of the captain's dirty little secret."

"Not his only one," Shawn said. "The captain had many secrets that would have led to his fall from grace. True, in this day and age, it isn't a big deal," she added, noting the hurt look on Carey's face. "Still, he isn't living in this century. Would you do me a favor and try to open the door?"

"I don't know what good it would do," he muttered, moving closer to the front door. Everyone was stunned when he turned the knob and the door easily swung open.

"I don't understand," he gasped, looking down at his own hand, clearly surprised at how easily the door opened after so many people had tried to force it open.

"He's afraid of you," Shawn said again. "Less and less with each passing moment, but for now, we can get inside."

"Okay, who's ready to go back into the funhouse?" Faith asked. Her words were met with silence. "Fine, none of us wants to go inside, but we have to. Shawn, where to?"

"Roll cameras," Althea instructed as the group huddled together and slowly entered the manor.

"Anna's bedroom," Shawn said. "It's the safest room in the house, and I want to see this closet."

Suddenly, the lights blinked on and everyone froze. "I thought the power was off?" Jimmy scoffed.

"It is," Delia said. "If we ever get out of here, you can check with the power company."

Shawn smirked at Jimmy as she finally began to ascend the staircase. Kyle followed closely behind her with his camera, while Jasper followed with the rest of the entourage. The front door slammed shut, the temperature dropped, and once again feet stopped moving forward as nervous gazes darted around the empty house.

Shawn pinched the bridge of her nose as doors opened and closed. Still nothing made sense. Jumbled images invaded her thoughts. She continued climbing the staircase. In her mind, she saw the captain's return, and Catherine grabbing the gun. She had seen this before, but nothing led to the violent events of the following morning.

Shawn coughed out a small laugh upon entering Anna's bedroom and seeing the fire burning in the fireplace.

"It's like they're waiting for us again," Faith said. "Hey, Jimbo, got an explanation for this?"

Delia snickered along with the others as she walked into the room and ran her hand along the wall. She pressed down, opened the closet, and then stepped away, allowing Shawn and the others to look inside. Shawn ignored the closet; her focus was on the wall.

"'I have something to show you,'" she repeated the words invading her thoughts. "'Hurry, he's returned.'" Shawn tried to grasp the words and images. "'What trickery is this?'" she continued, running her hands along the wall. Her breathing grew labored as she felt the very small indentation that had gone unnoticed for almost a century.

"This is the only room we could have found it," she said, knowing that the captain, for whatever reason, was unable to enter the bedroom. She pressed. Nothing happened. She pressed harder, and her body trembled as the latch finally gave way.

"What the hell is that?" Delia said when the heavy door swung open, revealing a brick wall.

"A brick wall," Faith quipped, bringing a small smile to Shawn's lips.

"A poorly built one at that," Delia said. "A back staircase had been built for a home that would house servants. Only the great Captain Stratton didn't want his help living in his house. I often wondered if the room Catherine lived in was built for a maid. This explains the gap in the wall. It probably runs the height of the manor and was designed and constructed before the captain saw the plans, if he ever even bothered to look at them. The second architect probably tried to hide it, hoping that the captain wouldn't find it until after he had been paid."

"The captain didn't look at the plans," Shawn said. "He commissioned the construction before he married. Upon learning that the captain was opposed to servants roaming freely in his home, the builder hid the stairwell as best he could. He had done such a good job creating the hidden doorways it was easy. Imagine being alone night after night, your husband away at sea. Anna explored her home and found this quite by accident."

"So the second builder bricked up the wall," Jimmy said. "And this means what?"

"No, this brick wall wasn't constructed by a craftsman," Delia said. "The work is sloppy. The person who slapped this together had no skills whatsoever. They probably never built anything before this."

"Built by a madman, late at night, in an effort to hide his sins," Shawn said. She brushed back the tears. "'What trickery is this?' That's what he said when he was spying on his sister that night. The room was empty. He had stepped out the door to her room when he saw her slipping into her room from the hidden doorway. That's why he was spying on them in the kitchen the following morning. He saw the caresses, and he knew. With complete calm, he ducked out to the woodshed, got the axe, and murdered both of them. You need to call the police. Tell them to ignore the door in Catherine's room and the one in the corridor just outside of this room."

"Oh, my God," Delia gasped. "There's one in the kitchen?"

"Behind the pantry," Shawn whispered, hearing the pained voices begging for her help. "Don't bother with your cell phone," she told Carey. "Won't work. Try calling from the van."

"In the meantime," Faith said, "until the cops arrive, anyone got a sledgehammer?"

"We can get one," Delia said.

* * *

"Are you sure about this?" Althea asked half an hour later. "The police are on their way."

"Let them start with the kitchen." Faith held the large sledgehammer Andrew St. James had handed her. Delia had called her brother to bring tools, while Carey called the local authorities. Althea went about, quickly setting up cameras in both rooms.

"That's where I'd start if I weren't such a chickenshit about that room," Faith admitted.

"Not to mention, it's a crime scene," Carey said. "Wait for them."

"Anna and Catherine have waited long enough," Faith said. "This is the only room where he can't stop us."

"Rishi and I will be downstairs with the troopers," Carey said. "See you at the other end." She paused when the entire house seemed to shudder. "I hope," she added under her breath.

"Me, too," Faith said. "Ready?" she asked the St. James siblings, who each held a large sledgehammer.

"All my life," Andrew said. "Let's do it."

"Shawn?" Faith asked her lover, who was looking on from the fireplace.

"You're safe," Shawn said. "I don't know what will happen when you break through, but for now Anna and Catherine are right here, watching. They want you to do this."

"Tell them it's my pleasure," Faith said as Delia delivered the first blow, forcing the wall to start crumbling.

"Yeah, crappy workmanship," Delia said. The three of them began tearing into the wall.

Shawn held her breath, watching. Anna and Catherine lingered in the corner, silently urging the trio on. From below, she could hear the sounds of the police hammering away. She spied another figure lurking outside of the room, a dark, angry force, hissing as the wall fell. She rubbed the bracelet on her wrist, and the cool silver warmed.

"That's it," Delia announced. The trio brushed dust and debris from their bodies while Jasper filmed the scene.

"Unbelievable," Jimmy said. "How did you know?"

Shawn stepped closer and grabbed a flashlight. "They told me."

"Who wants to go first?" Andrew asked, his face turning ashen as he glanced into the dark void.

"As eager as I am to find the truth," Delia said slowly, "I'm not thrilled at the thought of stepping in there."

"I'll go," Faith said.

"I'm right beside you," Shawn said.

They stepped into the darkness. An icy wind assaulted them as they fumbled inside the long-forgotten stairwell.

"Up is Catherine's room," Shawn said, trying to adjust her senses to the dim lighting. "That way is the corridor, and down is..." her voice trailed off. Her stomach became queasy, and images of blood dripping from the kitchen walls bombarded her.

"God, I can smell their blood," she choked out. She relaxed slightly when she felt Faith's hand resting against the small of her back.

"You don't have to—" Faith tenderly began to say.

"Yes, I do." Shawn's voice quivered. She pushed forward. "From the sounds of it, they haven't broken through the downstairs yet. It was so easy for him. The only person who knew about the door was dead."

She could see it happening: the axe swinging, their limp remains being tucked into the wall, and Horatio bricking it up later that night. She pushed past the cobwebs as they began their descent. Guided only by the light from their flashlights and Jasper's camera, they stumbled downward, clinging to the wall and each another. Suddenly, on the last flight of steps, they saw the stairwell just below them flood with light; the police were finally breaking through the kitchen wall.

Shawn choked back her tears at the horrific sight of shattered bones covered by decaying cloth.

"Bastard," she whispered, unable to look away.

"All this time," Delia said sadly from behind Jasper.

"Hold up," Carey called up from the entrance in the kitchen. "We need to process the scene."

"Knock yourself out," Faith said. "I've seen enough."

"Jasper?" Shawn looked over her shoulder at the shaking man. "Can you finish filming?"

"I got it," he said.

The rest of them squeezed back up through the stairwell. Covered with dust and cobwebs, they stepped back into the bedroom and brushed themselves off.

"The fire is out," Faith noted, wrapping her hands around Shawn's shoulders. "Are they gone?"

Shawn smiled at the sounds of laughter that only she could hear. "No." Her smile grew wider. "Come with me?" She took Faith by the hand, and the others followed. They stood at the top of the staircase, Shawn's gaze fixed on the foyer.

"What is it?" Delia asked.

"Your grandfather," Shawn said, looking down at the man standing by the front door. "He's waiting for them."

Anna and Catherine lingered on the staircase. "Go to him," she quietly urged the women.

The others blinked for a moment, catching a glimpse of something they couldn't explain. The image passed so quickly, all but Faith dismissed it as nothing. Shawn was the only one who saw them glide down and greet Richard.

The others jumped back when the door opened, then slowly closed. Shawn was the only one who smiled. "Now they're gone," she sighed happily.

"Are they at peace?" Delia asked later, as they huddled in the foyer.

"Not yet," Shawn said. "Soon. After the police finish, and your family can give them a proper burial, they will finally rest in peace."

"And him?" Andrew asked, his lip curling.

"They tormented him before he died," Shawn said slowly. "Once he joined them in death, he eagerly returned the favor. He isn't as strong as he was. Revealing his crimes has taken some of the wind out of his sails. He'll never leave, but perhaps Whispering Pines can finally be utilized. I can't guarantee that."

"Really?" Faith beamed. "Wait here."

"Faith, I wouldn't," Shawn called after her, but she was already sprinting towards the kitchen.

"Fine." She sighed, waiting for Faith's hasty return, which occurred a few short moments later.

"Fuck that," Faith snarled as she bolted back into the foyer.

Shawn laughed. "I know you wanted to tell him off for slapping you. He's still evil, and that doesn't change, not in death and not by outing him as a murderer. He might be weaker, but he's still an evil son of a bitch, and always will be."

Epilogue

New York City
December 2005

"I swear, I'll never get used to that," Carey said, watching the ornaments move on the Christmas tree.

"Willie just likes to play." Shawn laughed. She finished typing away on her computer. "I think that's it."

"Do I get a copy of this book?" Carey asked.

"But of course, since we'll be working together more often."

"Is Althea still pissed you signed that deal with Court TV?"

"Yes," Shawn said. "Not much choice, as your department has a better relationship with them than with Sunny Hill. I've agreed to still work with Althea, just not as much. I prefer staying closer to home these days."

"Fancy that." Carey smiled. "How is my sister? I haven't seen her since the St. James family invited us to the funeral for Anna and Catherine."

"Busy," Shawn said. "But also enjoying not traveling as much. She should be back soon. She's trying to find a Christmas gift for me. Bless her heart, she's trying to surprise me with something."

"That must be a little futile with you," Carey noted.

Shawn grinned. "A definite downside to my gift."

"So you know what she's getting you?"

"Yes. She hasn't bought it yet, but I know. She's almost here. I'm glad the two of you are getting along."

"Me, too," Carey said. "A lot of wasted years. We still aren't there, though."

"You're sisters. You'll always have your squabbles." Shawn shut down her computer. "Speak of the devil."

"It's as cold as a well digger's arse out there," Faith announced as she stormed into the apartment. "Shopping for you is a bitch."

"My parents would agree," Shawn said. "Coffee?"

"Absolutely." Faith slipped off her coat. "Hey, Jess, um... Carey."

"Hi, Faith." Carey smiled.

"Did you kids finish your homework?" Faith asked.

"Yes," Carey said. "I just finished going over all of the crime lab findings and the final police report. Surprise, the bodies we discovered were those of Anna and Catherine Stratton and yes, they met with foul play. The case is officially closed. It just sucks that Horatio never stood trial."

"No kidding." Shawn handed her a cup of hot coffee.

"He's in his own hell," Shawn said. "Trapped at Whispering Pines, his name always preceded by the word 'murderer.' His victims are at peace, but he remains a tortured soul."

"Not enough," Faith snarled.

"He got off easy," Carey said. "Hate to do this, but I have to get going," she said reluctantly. "I have to work tonight."

"I see Willie has been decorating again," Faith said after Carey made her departure. "Carey isn't really working tonight, is she?"

"No." Shawn curled up next to Faith. "She has a date. Rishi. They've been together since Whispering Pines."

"And I thought it was us who made all that noise." Faith snickered.

"It was," Shawn felt the blush suffusing her cheeks. "They switched rooms because of it. Frankly, it grossed Carey out."

"Understandable," Faith said.

Shawn glanced over at her with a knowing smile. "What?" Faith asked.

"I think it's a good idea," Shawn said.

"Not fair." Faith laughed. "Okay, so what's a good idea?"

"Leaving Willie out here to play with the tree while we slip into the bedroom," Shawn repeated her lover's thoughts.

"Hmm." Faith stood, taking Shawn by the hand. "I'm glad you like the way I think. How about an early Christmas present?"

"For you or for me?"

Faith laughed. "You figure it out. You're good at that."

About the Author

Mavis Applewater was born and raised just outside of Boston. After earning her degree in Theatre from Salem State College, she began a successful career as a bartender. Still itching for a creative outlet she began writing. Her first novel, *The Brass Ring*, was published in 2003. This was followed by her second novel, *My Sister's Keeper*. Her third novel, *Tempus Fugit*, was just published. In addition to her full-length novels, Mavis has published four collections of short stories, including the 2007 Goldie Finalist *Home for the Holidays*. *Whispering Pines* is her fourth full-length novel. Mavis still lives in the Boston area, and in 2006 legally married her longtime partner Heather.

Other Mavis titles:

Mavis Bites

But only if you ask her nicely. Vampires, ghosts, and… sorority sisters? Well, that's Mavis for you.

Join the Queen of Scream for five supernatural stories of sex, horror, sex, and more sex. (Did we mention the sex?) They'll set you shivering and send you running for your bed. If not to sleep!

Home for the Holidays

Tressa and Lindsey grew up living next door to each other, and were high school sweethearts until a terrible fight broke them apart.

Now, ten years later—thanks to Tressa's scheming mother—the two meet again to head home for the Thanksgiving holiday.

Follow Tressa's and Lindsey's romantic misadventures through a year full of holidays, misunderstandings, maternal scheming, steamy sex, and love.

Tempus Fugit

Buchanan High School senior Ellen Druette has a secure spot on the Varsity cheerleading squad, a first-string football player boyfriend, and a solid plan for her life.

Then the Swenson twins sweep into town in their matching Chevy Bel Air convertibles. Tall, blonde, and gorgeous, the twins are quickly accepted into the cheerleading squad, and Ellen's plan begins to unravel. Though Laurie Swenson makes the first move on her, it's Ginny who captures her heart.

But malicious forces are at work in the Swenson family, and Ginny, their scapegoat, is convicted of crimes she didn't commit and sent to prison. Determined to prove her lover's innocence, Ellen investigates the case even as she completes her pre-law studies and enters law school.

By the time Ginny is released from prison, she and Ellen have grown apart. They're still attracted to one another, but neither is confident of the other's feelings. Are they really in love, or are they just very good friends? Against the turbulent, psychedelic backdrop of the Sixties, Ellen and Ginny drift in and out of each other's lives as they strive for the courage to reveal their hearts.

My Sister's Keeper

Nothing is ever easy for policewoman Jenny Jacobs. She just wants to be in love. Sound simple? Well, there's a catch. She wants to be deeply in love with someone who is also deeply in love with her.

Jenny must face the past and the present when she discovers her lover's infidelity and her first love walks back into her life. Her life becomes even more complicated when old feelings surface for her first love—the woman who broke her heart as a teenager, then entered the church and became "Sister Rachel".

In her third published book, Mavis Applewater brings to the printed page a perfect combination of heat and romance, with just the right amount of adventure.

Available now, only from

Other exciting Blue Feather Books titles

Tempus Fugit	Mavis Applewater	978-0-9794120-0-4
Yesterday Once More	Karen Badger	978-0-9794120-3-5
Addison Black and the Eye of Bastet	M.J. Walker	978-0-9794120-2-8
The Thirty-Ninth Victim	Arleen Williams	978-0-9794120-4-2
Merker's Outpost	I. Christie	978-0-9794120-1-1
The Fifth Stage	Margaret Helms	0-9770318-7-X
Celtic Shadows	West and Welsh	0-97703186-1

www.bluefeatherbooks.com

Printed in the United States
131809LV00002B/95/P